Book One
Firebird

FLOXX

Kathleen King

Chickaloon Press

To Dwayne, for believing in me.

To my family, for sticking with me through it all.

To my friends who've encouraged me.

My deepest thanks.

Acknowledgements

Many have helped with this book, with ideas, suggestions, critiques, edits, and encouragement. Thanks to Christine Rogers for the book's beautiful cover and willingness to critique several drafts over the years; to Lee Rogers for endless hours of formatting and typesetting; to Tiffany Gerwig and Rhea Linus for insights into Alaska native culture in the context of this story; to Christine Kindberg, Tam Ketcher, Talitha Daniels, Terah Lites, and Lisa Jenkins who each provided thoughtful editorial input.

I can't forget the students and professors at Queens University of Charlotte who read many chapters in their initial stages and provided critiques and encouragement in equal measure. Special thanks to Pinckney Benedict, writer and inspiring professor, who cheered me on with both the story and the craft of writing. It meant so much.

And to my husband, Dwayne King, my biggest encourager, who provided me an office with a mountain view and the time I needed to write.

Thank you all so very much.

Table of Contents

Prologue

Gamloden. Sixteen years prior

The surrogate whelp thrashed in its sack, loosened the tie and nearly slipped out. Tazit shoved it back inside and yanked the rope firmly, closing the filthy bag tight, but not before the whelp wailed and bit Tazit's emaciated arm. He curled his four clawed fingers around the bundle and shook.

"Shhh," his companion Neztar hissed. "There's wolves about. Amaroks. They'd eat two Trows like us for dinner and that whelp for dessert." They skulked along the edge of the Tennindrow River—two skinny, hairless, weasel-like creatures, intent on following orders. They kept to the darkest part of the woods, walking upright, yet ready to drop to all fours and run at the first sound of danger. The waxing crescent moon gave just enough light to keep from tripping on rocks.

Tazit's eyes gleamed yellow. "I'd like to stay to hear the mother's scream when she uncovers this ugly thing in the morning." He snorted, and slime flew from his nose. "Seems a shame to waste all of this skinny whelp on the Royals, when we could just nibble at it. What difference would it make if it had no fingers?"

Neztar shook his head. "Keep to the job. No time to stop and eat. The King's army will be after us at first light. We have to hurry, so we're back in the tunnel well before daybreak."

So, the Trows crept on, coming to the bridge over the Caladrius River. It was too dark to see the agitated water below, but they could hear the roar as the two great rivers—the Caladrius flowing south and the Tennindrow flowing east roiled together a short way downstream before plummeting over the cliff's edge into the lake below. The creatures hunched down and raced on all fours across the bridge, its wooden planks swaying above the churning water. The bundle hung from Tazit's teeth, its contents swinging madly as he leapt into the shadows on the east side of the bridge. Not too much farther now.

Byerman was home to most of the human population of Gamloden, along with a few Tomtees who favored city life. The night was filled with noises familiar to the Trows, owls hooting, small predators scuffling for smaller food, larger animals prowling. They hurried toward the castle, a few miles away. They spoke no more, careful to avoid detection, listening intently. The sliver of moon vanished from the sky; they would arrive in the darkest part of night. They approached the capital city of Masirika and crept toward the castle. Nothing stirred. If there were guards—and, no doubt, there were—they slept somewhere in the shadows of the high walls. The Trows found the window to the royal bedroom, just where they'd been told it would be. They looked at each other, blinking their yellow eyes in agreement and began their four-legged ascent of the castle wall. Quickly, they crawled spider-like straight up the stones, their gray color blending flawlessly with the rock, their skinny fingers finding grips in the tiny crevices of the wall. Noiselessly, they approached the open bedroom window.

With a glance at Tazit, Nezter slid first into the room. It was large. Whiffling snores came from the curtained bed on the far side of the room. In a corner close to the window, sat a polished oak rocking chair, with a small colorful quilt hung over its arm, and next to it, a matching oak cradle carved with intricate pictures of elves and winged creatures and dogs. Its corners were inlaid with jewels. The newborn child slept soundly within it, wrapped in a lavender blanket. Nezter deftly tied the ends of the baby's blanket around the head and feet of the sleeping infant. Then, he lifted it carefully from the cradle; he didn't want to jostle her awake. Soundlessly, he stepped to the window, and held the baby out. Tazit, then, crept through the window and laid his grimy bundle in the still-warm cradle. The whelp was deep in sleep as he reached for the quilt on the arm of the rocker and covered it completely up.

Tazit tiptoed over to the curtained bed and parted the panels for a peek. The edges of his teeth glistened, and a thin strand of drool hung from his jaw as he gazed at the sleeping King and Queen cozy in their royal bed, but he knew he could do no further mischief there. Sleep tight, it's the last night you will, he thought. He glanced at the window. Nezter had already left with the baby, so he turned to follow him down the wall and through the sleeping city.

They raced against daylight toward the bridge, not risking a word until they were close enough to the river to hear its roar. Nezter dropped the babe, who immediately began to wail, and wiped his slobbery mouth.

Tazit grabbed the bundle. "Lemme 'ave a taste of it. Just a bite." He had her nearly unwrapped, when they were startled by a growl, fierce and low, just behind them. An enormous black-haired creature leapt toward them, baring its teeth. A strange, blue orb glowed over its head and reflected in its angry eyes.

Nezter yelled, "Wolf! Amarok wolf!" He snatched the baby from Tazit, scraping her face with his claws. Catching her arm between his teeth, he fell to all fours racing ahead, dragging the baby, her blanket trailing. The wolf sprung and ripped a large piece of blanket loose. The Trows leapt away, their stringy bodies sprinting for the bridge, bashing the baby in their haste. The wolf lunged, his snapping jaw just missing them.

As Nezter leapt up on the bridge, he lost his grip on the child and she fell wailing onto the bank, bouncing and rolling into the turbulent water below. By the time the Trows had reached the other side of the bridge, they saw a scrap of lavender blanket swirl downstream and over the falls. They didn't linger. Into the familiar dark woods, they ran, racing for the tunnel leading to Murthrid, the underground labyrinth of Trow caves. The sky was brightening as the kidnappers tore past a small grove of black-trunked eucalyptus trees, marking the nearby tunnel entrance, and scurried beneath the earth, seconds before first light would have turned them into stone.

As dawn broke, the wolf-like creature strained toward the bank, its powerful legs fighting the current with all of its strength. In its mouth, it gently held the child above the water. It struggled to shore, laid the wet, unconscious infant on the piece of blanket it had torn from the Trows, shook its thick coat in an immense spray of water, then dried the baby with the side of its head. It licked the child's mangled arm and bruised body until it stopped bleeding, then tucked the ragged cloth around her with the tip of its nose.

The huge animal, which daylight revealed to be no more than a dog, laid down close to the baby, curling around her shivering body to warm her. They rested for hours, but in late afternoon, the dog tenderly lifted the babe, blanket and all in its mouth, carried her over the bridge, and walked all night through the tangled autumn woods to the edge of Tomitarn, where the Dryad River rippled through an ancient apple orchard.

While the sunrise painted the horizon, the blue orb over the dog's head brightened as a large, long-necked bird—each outstretched wing easily as long as a man—swooped low, its feathers glistening with the golds, and pinks, and purples of the dawn; so low, it touched the dog and in that shimmering moment they all vanished: the bird, the dog, and the infant. The astounding event went completely unnoticed, except for a dwarf child, who happened to be up early playing in the orchard.

Chapter 1: Rory

Geese honked as they flew over the house, waking Rory up. She smiled before she opened her eyes; her sixteenth birthday had finally arrived! She hugged herself against the thrill in her stomach. Today, she soloed! Dad had returned home two days ago—had taken a whole week off from his airline job—and they'd spent much of yesterday flying, getting ready for today, practicing takeoffs and landings on their snow-packed runway. He'd been teaching her to fly for years, but today was the day they'd had to wait for; the day when she could legally fly solo. One of her landings yesterday had been rough, but she'd nailed the others, setting the Cessna down smoothly right at the aiming point.

"Again," Dad had said over and over until finally he laughed. "Ok, Rory, that was great. Let's wrap it up. We can debrief as we wipe 'er down; we want our plane to shine for pictures tomorrow." She'd never forget how he'd looked when he'd said that, sitting shoulder to shoulder with her in the small airplane; his smile creasing the familiar wrinkles by his blue eyes, his salt and pepper hair sticking up a little around his headset. A two-day stubble darkened his face because he'd not taken the time to shave. He sighed a big satisfied sigh and shook his head, still grinning at her.

"You're good, Rory. You're real good. The solo should be no problem." She'd shut the plane down and he'd climbed out first, stretching his six-foot self out before reaching for the tie-down rope.

She snuggled under the comforter; the January sun wouldn't be up till 10, and then only for four or five hours. She studied the knots on her A-framed ceiling, remembering the stories she'd made up about them when she was small. Like the legends about constellations, her tales covered the ceiling of her little universe. Her dog was the biggest knot, conveniently located where the ceiling touched the loft floor. Cue always laid right in front of it; he seemed to know it was his special spot. He saw her looking, raised his huge head and thumped his tail. Near the roofline, Dad and Mom stood together watching her, multi-shaped knots vaguely resembling people; Gram stood nearby, under a cluster of markings that looked like spruce trees, her face also turned in her direction. And there she was, way over on the opposite side of the room, flying away, just under the Northern Lights, a curtain of textured wood grain that swirled from wall to wall.

And today she really would fly away. By herself. All alone. She was born to fly; she'd always known it. She'd be safe. Nothing would go wrong. It couldn't; she was destined for this. And yet, she couldn't explain the dread that curled in her stomach.

She took a deep breath, threw back the covers and reached for her jeans, dressing fast against the cold, pulled on her sneakers and scrambled down the ladder to the great room below. Cue followed soon after, leaving the loft in a graceful leap and skidding to a halt inches from the wood stove.

"Don't understand how he nails it every time." Dad whispered from the side of the stove. He'd been so

7

quiet, she hadn't even noticed him. "Happy birthday, Rory!" He gave her a hug. "Excited?"

"That doesn't begin to cover it! Mom up?"

"Not yet. She had a rough night. We should let her sleep a little longer."

She tiptoed to her parents' bedroom and peeked in; Mom was curled like a shrimp, her nose buried under the quilt, her short brown hair sticking out. She'd lost so much weight in the past year, Rory could barely see the bump she made under the covers. The chemo had been hard on her, but the doctors were hopeful. Rory pulled the door all the way shut.

"You want to fly early?" Dad asked.

"Soon as the sun's up."

They talked through the procedures for her takeoffs and landings. "If you're doing well, Rory, I'll motion to you after you land to keep going, so just take off, again. As long as you land on your aiming spot, you don't have to stop and taxi back and start all over. Remember, three takeoffs and three landings. You good with that?

She swallowed hard. "Got it." She hoped he didn't hear the tremor in her voice.

As he signed her logbook for the solo flight, she reached for one of Gram's blueberry muffins. Its flavor exploded in her mouth, both sweet and tart. "I'm sure you'll be up before me," Gram had said late last night, pulling the muffins from the oven, "and you'll need a little happy birthday first thing." Rory washed it down with ice cold milk, wanting another. But her stomach was clenching. Better not.

Before she knew it, the sky was getting light. She grabbed her jacket, and headed for the door, Cue bounding behind her.

"I'll go preflight."

"Right behind you," Dad assured her raising his coffee cup, his eyes sparkling.

The morning sky was a deep blue; clear enough to see all three of the snow-covered mountain ranges on the horizon. It had been an unusually mild winter and Rory guessed it was maybe 20 degrees out. Perfect! Cold dense air was awesome for flying. She zipped her jacket, pulled on her gloves, and headed down the short path to the runway. In summer, the trees along the path were full of birds, but this time of year, the woods were quiet. Really quiet. The loudest sound was the crunching of her boots on the crusty couple of inches of snow. Even in winter, icy and stark, she loved her home. How did she get so lucky?

Gram and Pap had homesteaded the land decades ago when you could do that in Alaska. Their 50 acres were partially wooded, bordered by a shallow creek on one side and ringed with foothills on the other three. They'd slowly cleared about half the land, living first in the tiny, sod-roofed cabin they now used as a shed. A few years later, they'd started on the log house, with its big porch and large great room, eventually adding a storage room, which served as a food freezer all winter.

Pap had been a pilot and had taught Dad to fly. Together they'd carved their 3000-foot runway out of the bush. Dad still groaned every time he recalled pulling the stumps out of the ground and filling the huge holes they'd left. The 30-foot-wide grass strip had been Pap's proudest accomplishment.

"We may be way up here in the bush," he'd told her once, "With no roads, or phones, or neighbors, but we're not trapped, nope not us. We got our own highway to the sky to come and go whenever and wherever we want."

She'd probably gotten her flying dream from Pap. To come and go as she pleased. She'd hate to be trapped. No way could she live like that. She glanced at the shed up ahead. It was seriously tiny. How did the two of them ever manage to live in there? A few bare, frozen stalks of fireweed still stuck up from its snow-covered sod roof, which had bloomed all summer in tall magenta blossoms; they'd swayed for weeks in brilliant celebration of the midnight sun. Fireweed. It grew everywhere! From June to August, as far as you could see, the mountains were painted with its rosy color.

Dad's high-winged, red and white Cessna Skyhawk sat on the side of the runway. She opened the door, set her headset on the pilot's seat and tossed her pack in the back. Cue jumped in, tracking snow all over her seat before settling down on the other one. He thumped his tail, hopeful he'd be allowed to come. She climbed on the wing strut to check the fuel. The plane had two fuel tanks—one inside each of its high wings. She unscrewed the fuel cap, dipped the measuring stick into the tank and found it was half full, about 10 gallons. A gust of wind blew her hair across her face. Cold. She looked up to see a few clouds building from the north. Smelled like snow. She closed the fuel cap, climbed down, and repeated the task on the other wing. The fuel tank showed the same amount. Plenty.

Dad walked over as she was finishing the preflight. "Ok, we're all here, cheering for ya."

She saw Gram standing by a big spruce tree, smiling at her from the side of the runway. Gram was still a big, strong woman, healthy and active at 75 with a love for food that showed in her round middle. Tough and capable, she ran a tight house, and Rory'd learned not to challenge her very often. Mom was next to her, her down coat half-buttoned over her pajamas, boots pulled on in such haste, one pajama leg was tucked in and the other wasn't. She'd promised Rory she would watch her solo, and she was as good as her word, already snapping pictures while Gram was trying to wrap a blanket around her shoulders.

"Okay if Cue comes?"

Dad started to shake his head but relented. "I suppose. But in the back seat."

The propeller blurred through the windshield, and Rory's legs trembled as she held the brakes, keeping the quivering Cessna still as she pushed the throttle all the way in. *Okay, now. Release the brakes, keep it lined up in the center, here we go.* She raced past Gram and Dad and Mom, blurs on the side of the runway. *Pull the yoke back. That's right, just like he taught me. Point the nose up, not too much, yes, there. Hold it there.* The sky filled her windshield as the ground dropped away. She was flying alone! Her first solo. Yes! Cue barked, as excited as she was. Focus, she scolded herself. *That's high enough, level off now, bring the power back and turn crosswind, downwind, base and final. Less power, flaps down. That's right, like I've done a hundred times. Easy now. Nice and stable. Head for the aiming point. Don't let it wander. Good, good, another notch of flaps, hand on the throttle. Flare, just a little, now a little more, keep it straight, let it settle, there just like that, gentle on the snow.* Dad was waving her on. Go, again. Twice more, she took off and landed. On the third landing, she let the airplane come to a complete stop, shut it down and jumped out.

Dad picked her up and spun her around like he'd done when she was little; Mom and Gram went for gentler hugs.

"Hungry?" Gram asked. "How's waffles, bacon, and eggs sound?"

"Yes, I'm starving! Oh my gosh, it was so exciting!" She told them all about it as they tromped back to the warm cabin.

Mom needed to rest in the afternoon, so they planned to have dinner, birthday cake, and presents when she woke up. No problem. Rory figured there'd be more pictures later, so she decided to shower and fix her hair. Maybe clip it so it covered her right cheek. She shook her head as she studied her reflection in the mirror. We're not sure what happened, Mom had said, just that she'd been badly injured as an infant. The authorities had never found her birth parents, so the investigation had reached a dead end. If you caught her left profile, she wasn't too bad. Pretty, even, if you liked curly brown hair and brown eyes. But when she turned her head, people gasped. Then, whispered. The real jerks even pointed. Seriously, she'd been trying to ignore them all her life. She stood in the hot shower remembering one incident in particular.

At Fairbanks airport when she was 10, she'd seen a man in a wheelchair, who'd lost his legs in a war and part of his face had been burned bad. She'd walked right up to him and shaken his hand; she wanted him to know she thought he was okay. He'd smiled and seemed kind of surprised that she'd do that. He was sitting on her good side; she'd learned to always position herself like that. They'd talked for a while and when she'd found out he'd been injured in the army, she thanked him for his service to our country, then asked him if he was arriving or departing Alaska. Arriving, he said, so she told him the best parts of the state to see. The train across the Kenai Peninsula, definitely. And Denali. And fireweed. It was blooming now, and it was her favorite flower, so he shouldn't miss it. She told him she lived deep in the bush where there were no roads and they traveled in and out by snow machine or airplane.

Mom eventually missed her and rushed over, greeting the man briefly before hurrying Rory away. She'd felt such camaraderie with him because of their mutual marred appearances. She had a scarred friend; she wasn't alone. But when she turned her head, he'd gasped. That had gotten to her, his gasp; she had shocked even him. She'd held her hand over her cheek for days after. Said her eye hurt when the light hit it. How could someone that tough, who'd been through hell and back, who knew all about sacrifice and suffering, be shocked with her scars? At least, he could've swallowed his gasp. Rory reached for the shampoo and scrubbed the memory away.

It started snowing at 3:00. Rory stood on the porch with Cue, wearing jeans and her favorite soft sweater, watching the fat flakes fall, slowly painting new white edges on the trees. No wind. Silence. It was so still, she could hear the flakes touch. A birthday snow. Beautiful. And now she was sixteen. Able to fly. Able to take off on her own. But where would she fly to? What would she do? She didn't want to be an airline pilot like Dad; it seemed too much like a bus driver. She wanted to do something unusual. Different. Challenging. Something big maybe. Or something small. It didn't matter as long as she made a difference. But when? And how?

When she'd confided to Mom one day, her mother had put her hand on Rory's cheek. "You've already made a huge difference to me, dear." She hadn't understood what Rory'd meant. Neither had Dad; he'd suggested joining the Air Force or maybe the Peace Corps. Sure, those are high and noble callings, but neither fit the hole inside her. Gram didn't say much when they'd touched on the subject. She'd looked at Rory kinda weird, actually. "Let's wait and see what happens," she'd said, and started to say something else, but didn't. What did Gram think might happen? Wasn't there anyone who could help her figure out what she should do? Flying away. What kind of a destiny was that?

They sat down to eat around 5:00. Gram had cooked all day and had Rory's favorites: moose roast, mashed potatoes and gravy, corn, homemade rolls—it was amazing—and a red velvet cake with her signature cream cheese icing. Mom and Dad gave her a dark blue ski jacket and ski pants.

Then they dropped the bomb. She couldn't believe they hadn't told her sooner. Years sooner. They'd always been terrible secret-keepers. She'd overheard them whispering about gifts and surprises so many times it was ridiculous—she knew about the hidden dolls, the skis, the rifle way before the special day. That trip to Florida for a Caribbean cruise? Not a surprise. But this secret had been locked up tight for sixteen years.

Mom looked particularly pale that night; maybe the early morning trek to the runway had been too much for her. She had tied a pretty green and yellow scarf around her head, partly for looks and partly to keep her balding head warm. But the bright colors made her face look sallow. Her sweater hung loose, the outline of her shoulder bones visible beneath. But it was her eyes that troubled Rory the most. Sad. So very sad. Deep pools of grief. It didn't seem right on her birthday. Not at all.

Mom began to talk, and her voice wavered. "Rory, we are so glad we've had you for sixteen years. You are so special to us."

This was a little morose, though Mom tended to be emotional and her illness made her even more so. But, still, it seemed off somehow after such a fun celebration.

"We have something to share with you. About you. About when you came to us."

Rory sat up straighter, dread prickling the skin on the back of her neck. Uh oh. She knew she'd been abandoned, mauled by a bear, and adopted, but she'd made peace with that. She was happy with the way things had turned out and didn't want there to be more.

Mom frowned, a troubled look in her eyes. "We've waited all these years, not knowing if we should tell you. And now, we think we should. But, it won't be easy for you and well, can you just bear with me while I get it out?"

Rory set her fork down, noticing Dad looked terrible, too, eyebrows furrowed, the edges of his mouth turned down. Gram had one hand covering the side of her face; the other hugging her middle.

Her stomach sunk. What the heck? What horrible news was this? Had they found her birth parents who wanted her back now? No way was she leaving.

"It had been a warm winter the year you were born. Hardly dropped below zero. The northern lights had been spectacular for a week and the night you arrived, Dad and I had gone outside to watch them, just a short distance from the house; you know, where it's clear of most of the trees. We were startled by an enormous bird swooping over us, sparkling with color as the northern lights danced above it. We ducked, it dove so low, then laughed about it. One of its feathers floated down and I caught it. It shimmered with iridescence.

15

We'd never seen anything like it." She smiled a little as the scene replayed in her mind and I let out the breath I'd been holding. "Dad kissed me and called it our lucky feather and after a while we got cold and walked back to the house. That's when we saw Cue and, eventually, you on the top step."

What? Rory wasn't sure she'd heard them right. She sat up straighter. "I was left on the porch in the middle of winter?"

Dad took over. "At first, we thought Cue was a bear and were scared to death when he ambled down the steps. But he just sat down and looked at you. We followed his gaze and when we saw you, we went crazy. Mom screamed, and we rushed to get you inside."

Mom had tears in her eyes as Dad talked; Rory just looked back and forth between them, trying to make sense of what they were saying. Her birthday cake stuck in her throat.

"You were barely breathing," Mom remembered. "And your wounds were terrible, the ones on your face, and especially the ones on your arm, oozing a dark pus. What we've told you all these years was true, Rory; we really don't know what happened. So, when we had to give you a reason for your scars, we blamed it on a bear."

What are they talking about? It wasn't a bear? Do they know what it was? But before she could ask, Dad picked up, again.

"As far as we were concerned, you were ours—a gift from heaven, left on our doorstep. We loved you at first sight and were so sure you'd be our daughter, we named you Aurora, after the Aurora Borealis. It seemed perfect. We'd called for help immediately and while we waited for the medivac to fly in, Mom tucked our lucky feather into the scarf we'd wrapped you in, the best we could do in lieu of a baby blanket, and prayed you'd live."

Rory held up her hand. "Wait. I just showed up on your porch one night, bleeding so bad I was nearly dead. Cue was with me. And you wrapped me in a scarf and called 911. You're seriously freaking me out."

Mom looked down, twisting her fingers. Dad's mouth was stuck in a frown. He abruptly left the table and returned with his navy cashmere scarf, the one he wore on special occasions. He had tears in his eyes as he laid it on Rory's lap.

"This is the scarf?" Rory teared up, too, and Dad handed her a tissue. She bunched the scarf up and held it under her chin, feeling its softness, breathing the faint scent of his aftershave. Okay, so, she'd showed up out of nowhere on the porch. This was news, but she guessed she could live with it. "So, is that it? You didn't get me from the hospital like you said." *Please don't let there be more.*

Mom was a weepy mess, so Dad kept talking. "Well, we did get you from the hospital, ultimately; that wasn't a lie, but it wasn't the whole truth, either. The emergency medical team flew us to the Fairbanks hospital where the police met us. You were there for two weeks getting antibiotics and special care while the authorities did a criminal investigation. We stayed with you in the hospital; we never left your side. The forensics team examined both you and the blood-stained rag of a blanket you came wrapped in, looking for evidence. There were no human prints found and no one else's blood was on the blanket besides your own, so they ruled out attempted murder."

Attempted murder! Dad paused, waiting for her to say something, but she had no idea what to say. They'd ruled it out, anyway; they'd always said it was an animal that had mauled her.

He sighed and ran his hand over his face. "The thing is, Rory, while there were no human fingerprints on the blanket, there were other prints." He set both hands on the table and held her gaze. "The other prints couldn't be identified. They were neither human nor animal. No scientists had ever seen them before. We don't know what or who held you in that blanket."

This was ridiculous. She'd had about enough. "What do they think it was, some kind of alien? Some space monster tried to eat me?"

Dad didn't respond.

"You didn't believe them, I hope. There has to be some explanation."

"No, we did not believe them. Not at first anyway. We told them we were going to get a second opinion— it was just too bizarre—but when I asked for the blanket back, the detective said it had been destroyed. They'd cut it up to run dozens of lab tests. Since the first results had been inconclusive, they'd ordered a second set from a competing investigative firm; then finally took it to the top for a third round from a highly respected U.S. intelligence group. After six months, they met with us to discuss the results. Rory, there was no match to those prints. Anywhere in the world."

She thought she was going to throw up. *What horrible thing tried to kill me? Where did I even come from? Could I really be some kind of alien? No doctor ever said I wasn't human. Just injured.*

Mom hiccupped. "The night you arrived, while we were waiting for the plane, I snipped a little piece of your blanket off and I saved it, Rory. I don't really know why I did that; I just felt I should, so I went with my hunch, figuring they'd never miss it. After we decided not to pursue further investigation and after we'd legally adopted you, I put it away, figuring one day we'd tell you about it. And, well, I've made something with it. For you. For your birthday."

Rory definitely did not want to see a bloody scrap of blanket that'd been framed or something. But Mom was already out of her chair.

While she was gone, Dad kept talking. "Gram was in Fairbanks the night you arrived, so she met us at the hospital."

"Oh, my Lord, my Lord," Gram finally joined the conversation, waving her hands the way she did when she was excited. "I couldn't believe it. I was so horrified; so afraid for you. I was rocking you, snuggling you, telling you what a precious miracle you were. And then I saw the feather."

Rory had forgotten about the feather. "What does the feather have to do with anything?"

"Well, ah …."

Just then Mom returned with something lavender dangling from her hand and gave it to Rory. It was a braided cloth lanyard about six inches long with several small pearl buttons caught at intervals. A metal ring was attached to one end and held the keys to the airplane; a white feather, about as long as the lanyard, itself, hung from the other end, its barbs dancing with soft color in the dim winter light. Mom ran her fingers over the feather, causing color to ripple through it.

"Beautiful!" Rory muttered half-heartedly, touching the feather, then the buttons, wondering about their significance.

"From the dress you wore at your baby dedication," Mom said, putting her hand over her daughter's and squeezing. "We thanked God for you, our very own miracle! We love you so much, dear."

Something broke inside Rory and she shook with gut-wrenching sobs. *This can't be real. Who am I?*

What terrors have I survived? Where did I come from? She couldn't catch her breath.

"Oh, sweetheart," Mom said reaching for her and pulling her close.

"You mean the world to us," Dad said, joining them.

Rory felt suffocated, and suddenly angry. Betrayed. *Why didn't they tell me this way sooner? Why ruin my birthday?* She pulled away and bolted for her room.

Chapter 2: Rosie

It snowed for two days, and Rory and her dad spent the next day digging out.

"How will you get back to Fairbanks with the runway snowed under?"

"We'll clear a path to the shed tomorrow and I'll get the tractor out and plow the runway. Next day, I'll clean the airplane off. Hopefully, I'll be able to fly out in time."

Shoveling was the highlight of those days. Time crawled. Rory carried her lanyard in her pocket with the feather hanging out, careful not to damage it, her imagination constantly conjuring up dark images that lurked at the edges of her thoughts. Her dreams were nightmarish; she ran from something she couldn't see, dreading its pounce, its bite. She woke up screaming one night when she felt teeth, but it was only Cue licking her hand.

Her family was concerned about her. Of course, they'd be worried. She couldn't eat, not even Gram's goodies. She sat and stared, absently rubbing the tiny buttons on her lanyard. At night, she pondered the knots on her ceiling. *Where am I flying to? Why are they watching me go? Did they even try to stop me?*

Dad gave her space. He kept the fire going and spent a lot of time with her mother, who needed to rest; he was inclined to curl up with her for a nap on the cold, dark afternoons. Sometimes Rory would walk by their bedroom and see them snuggling and close the door, figuring they'd be warm enough with the heat shut out. She was glad they had each other, but that was a little awkward.

That left Gram. She chattered away, telling Rory stories about her and Pap. Rory just let her talk, half listening, while they baked bread and made soup. They talked about everything except what they were both thinking the most about. Where had she come from? What was the thing that had tried to kill her?

Gram surprised her toward the end of the week. Rory was sitting at the table fiddling with the lanyard, twisting the feather around in the light to see it change color. Gram picked up the conversation as if no time had passed since Rory's birthday.

"So, I saw that feather tucked into your father's scarf. And I wondered, could it be?"

"Could what be?"

"Well, I didn't get to tell you the rest of the story. It wasn't the right time with your mom giving you that lanyard and all. But, maybe now?"

Rory shrugged. "Sure. I can't see what difference another crazy story will make."

"Come with me," Gram said, heading for her room. Rory followed, sitting on the bed as Gram rummaged through her cluttered closet. She shoved some clothes aside and pulled two or three boxes from a side shelf.

"Need any help?" Rory asked.

"Nope, it's in this one, right here." Gram carried a small wooden box to the bed and lifted the top. "Look at this." She held up a feather.

"I got one, too!"

"Whoa," Rory said, holding hers next to Grams. They matched! She couldn't believe it. The two of them waved the feathers around, smiling a little, then bursting into hilarity, as they watched prisms of light dance on the walls, knick-knacks, family pictures. It felt so good to laugh; so good not to be alone.

"How did you get yours?"

"It's a crazy story," Gram said, "maybe not as dramatic as yours, but I'd never told a soul for fear they'd think I was off my rocker. But when you arrived along with that feather sixteen years ago, I showed mine to your mom and dad. Coincidence, they'd said, even after hearing my story."

"Tell me."

"When I was a girl, 10 years old, I was skating alone on a lake one afternoon and I fell through the ice. I tried to pull myself out, but it was so slippery I couldn't get a grip, and I was getting numb fast. Then this gigantic bird landed right next to me, glistening with all the colors of the rainbow. I figured I was seeing things, having near-death hallucinations, maybe. But the bird didn't go away; it just stood right there on the edge of the hole. I could hardly feel my body I was so cold, but in desperation I reached up and grabbed hold of one of its skinny legs. It felt real. I couldn't believe it. I mustered enough strength to lift my other arm out of the water and grabbed its other leg. Then, that bird—that huge blessed bird—started walking backwards, one step at a time. I held on for all I was worth, and it walked me clear out of the water. Saved my life. Then, it flew off, leaving me this feather."

Rory turned the feathers around, studying them. They were identical and astoundingly beautiful. "What do you make of it? You think it's the same bird?"

23

"Course I don't know for sure, Rory, but I'd say yes. The same bird seems to have saved both our lives."

The next day, the weather cleared. Dad was stoking the fire and Rory was reading. He glanced at the book cover. "<u>The Fellowship of the Ring</u>?" he asked.

"Yep. I needed a vacation."

"Well, I wouldn't go to Middle Earth," he grinned. "Don't you know there's a war brewing?"

She threw a couch pillow at him and he tossed it back, laughing. He was just always so happy; she loved that about him. Always wanting to make things better for her. As he fussed with the fire, her mind drifted. "You're the lift that keeps me up," he'd once said when she was down in the dumps. He was referring to the force of lift that holds an airplane in the air. Then, he'd stretched his arms out sideways like they were airplane wings, yelled "clear prop," and started the engine, zooming around the room like he was flying. She laughed out loud at the memory.

"That's a good sound," he said smiling. "You gonna be okay?"

Rory shrugged. She needed to talk with her best friend. "I wanna go see Rosie."

"All right, let's check the weather, then we'll go."

"Maybe I could stay the weekend?"

"Fine with me. We'll firm it up when we get there."

But another storm moved in that afternoon, and they scratched their plans.

It was two months, the middle of March, before she and Dad flew to Rosie's village. Rory had texted her from the air telling her she was on the way with clothes enough to stay awhile. Find some snowshoes, she told her; we need to get away and talk. Super crazy stuff—you won't believe it! It was just a 30-minute flight, but it seriously felt like hours. She felt her lanyard in her pocket, thinking about what she'd say when she told Rosie. She was kind of distracted, not paying as much attention to flying as she should have, and she set the Cessna down a little rough on its skis.

"Oops, sorry, Dad." She cringed as they bounced.

"Just a little rusty, that's all," he encouraged. "Came in a little fast."

Rosie was waiting on a four-wheeler, the fur ruff on the hood of her pale blue jacket framing her round face. Her almond eyes glistened with mischief, as she jumped from the seat, racing over to give Rory a big hug.

"Lights!" she said, laughing, her breath puffing white in the cold. "Missed you!" She reached over to rub Cue's head. Rory was so glad to see her. She and she alone could call her "Lights," code for Aurora, which she hated. Rosie was code, too; her real name was Rosabelle and everyone in the village called her that. Some kids, though, had dubbed her Belly in first grade before she outgrew her baby fat, and she'd never forgotten. The same kids had called Rory, Scar. So, the two of them had become inseparable. Besties forever.

Rosie was gorgeous now, slim and curvy; with her smooth brown skin and long black hair, she looked a lot like her Athabascan mother. Most people had forgotten Rosie's hair was really auburn, which she had gotten from her Irish father. She kept it dyed black, her way of denying any relationship with him. She was the one friend Rory had who'd been loyal to her forever. In eighth grade, watching her try to cover her scars with make-up one morning, Rosie'd decided to paint her face to match Rory's, totally crazy, but the thing is, it caught on. Kind of like Harry Potter's scar gone trendy. The rest of that year, the kids at school tried to outdo each other with face paint, designing the prettiest, ugliest, weirdest, scariest scar designs on their faces. Rory was actually voted eighth grade princess, because she had the real deal. She and Rosie decided to leave public school on that happy note and signed up for the online high school program.

"Mom says you can stay as long as you want," Rosie said.

"Yay!" Rory looked at Dad. "How long can I stay?"

"Mmm, I have a trip next week. How about I pick you up on my way home. So, probably Saturday?"

A week! She'd never been able to stay a week!

"You brought your laptop, right?" He said as if he might change his mind if she hadn't.

She tapped her backpack.

"We'll keep up with school, don't worry," Rosie assured him.

"Okay, then, have fun girls."

They'd snowshoed a couple miles; it was overcast, maybe 25 degrees and damp, like it was going to snow, again. But, Rory was flushed from the workout and way too hot, so she pulled Dad's scarf off her neck and unzipped her new jacket. They were near the river, where it started its curve around the village. They'd never seen anyone out here; it was their secret spot. They cleared off the overturned rowboat that had been their seat for years. The river was narrow and deep there, widening downriver as it straightened, and they could see it moving beneath several inches of ice. They'd talked about just walking there on the frozen river—it was way shorter—but the ice was thin where the water ran fast. Must have been like that for Gram when she fell through. A stand of skinny spruce blocked most of the homes from sight, but they could see smoke from the village chimneys drifting downriver. The quiet was disrupted by the echo of someone chopping wood far away. Cue was unusually still; his head lifted, listening to sounds they could not hear.

"So?" Rosie asked, adjusting her position to look at her friend. "You gonna keep me in suspense all day?"

Rory pulled the lanyard from an inside jacket pocket and held it up. The feather glistened in the gray daylight.

"Whoa! What a cool lanyard! And that feather, where'd you get it?"

She told her the story. Rosie had a million questions and Rory had no answers. They imagined all the scenarios, though. Maybe it was a big animal that had kidnapped her, one who walked on his hind legs. Or maybe something small, like a fox with vampire teeth. Or a werewolf.

"You weren't very big," Rosie said, "only five or six pounds." As if Rory needed reminding. "Could'a been one of the little people."

Rory snorted. "Or maybe Sasquatch's other world cousin."

"No seriously, little people make sense. They're just the right size. And mean."

"What? That's super rude. Remember Janis, the kid in school who was a little person. He was really nice."

Rosie laughed and tossed a snowball at Rory. "Not like him. He still is nice; I saw him in Fairbanks last fall. I'm talking about a legend. You know, little people."

Rory stared at her. "Nope, no idea."

"Aw, c'mon, you've never heard the stories?"

She shook her head.

"Everyone's heard them. I'll have Mom tell you; she's the best storyteller. Kind of creepy, really. Growing up, she'd warn me, 'Don't wander; the little people will catch you and take you away,' and I think she still half believes it."

"Seriously?"

"Yup. All my childhood. She might be upset if she knew we were out here."

"So, they're mean? Tell me about them."

Rosie looked off at the river, frowning. "They hide and wait for a child to wander away from the village. Then, they grab her, and she's never seen, again."

Rory shuddered. Little people did fit perfectly with her story. "So, do you suppose these little people can live in other places, like maybe other worlds? What if they could go back and forth between them?"

Fear flashed on Rosie's face and she glanced over her shoulder, then into the shadowy woods, then back at Rory. "You're freaking me out, Lights. Let's head back."

That night as they were cleaning up the dinner dishes, Rosie's mother gave them highlights of what she knew about the legendary little people. Sneaky. Rarely seen, but there had been some sightings. Not all of them were little; some were tall. Skinny. Sharp teeth. They kidnap and eat small children. Rory was glad she got the Cliff Notes version and not all the horrible details.

It snowed, again, that night and most of the next day. It took till the end of the week and a lot of convincing to get Rosie to snowshoe back to their secret place.

"It's my last day, Rosie. Come on! Please! We have Cue; we'll be fine."

Rosie jumped at every little noise along the way and when a clump of snow thumped from a tree branch, she screamed, cutting it short when she realized what had happened, and giving Rory an apologetic grin.

"You're a mess!" She laughed at Rosie. "Stop worrying." Cue ran ahead. "Scare 'em away, boy!" Rory teased.

Rosie didn't have a comeback and when Rory turned to look at her, she was staring, wide-eyed into the woods. Rory spun around, suddenly terrified, but didn't see anything.

"Got'cha!" Rosie yelled, pushing her friend into the snow, and took off laughing.

They made their peace after a serious snow ball fight and eventually settled down on the boat. Rosie pulled off her wet gloves and absently rubbed her wrist. She'd done that a lot over the past few days.

"Your wrist sore?"

"It's nothing."

"What?"

"Nothing, really." But Rosie's eyes teared up.

"C'mon. Please. Tell me."

Rosie sighed. "My father. He was in the village a month ago, so drunk he nearly froze to death. While Mom and I were at church, some of the guys found him and brought him to our house."

"Oh. That couldn't have been good. How long was he there?"

"Just one night. He stumbled into my room while I was sleeping, though, and I had to fight him off and that's when he hurt my wrist."

"Oh my gosh, Rosie! He didn't …."

"No. Mom heard me scream and came running. While he was fighting with me, she kicked his feet out and he went down, hard. Hit his face on the brick bookshelves in my room. Got a black eye; nearly broke his nose." She kicked at the snow. "I hate him."

"I hate him, too. So, he's gone?"

"I heard he caught a ride on the mail plane the next day."

Rory wondered if Rosie's mom was thinking of him when she'd said some little people are tall. Rosie's mother had been 15 when she'd met him. He'd been hiking around the state, fishing, hunting, drinking, doing whatever he wanted. She'd been intrigued with him and his freedom to come and go as he pleased. The two of them had flirted briefly, then he'd coerced her into the woods where he'd raped her. Rosie had been conceived. He'd gone to jail for the crime, but the child he'd conceived bore a stigma; it had taken a dozen years for the village to learn to love his daughter.

So, Rosie had gone to school in Fairbanks, rather than attend the village school. Her aunt had an apartment in the city, so Rosie'd lived there during the school year. Rory's family also had a place in Fairbanks where her Dad still stayed between airline flights when he was on a tight schedule. She and her mother had lived there during the school year till she finished eighth grade. Rosie stayed with Rory a lot.

Cue came tearing toward them from the scraggly spruce woods, dashing around and around, kicking up snow, sending them shrieking and triggering another snow ball fight, this time with him.

"My fingers are totally numb!" Rosie said. She'd neglected to put her gloves back on.

"Here, wrap your hands in this." Rory handed her Dad's scarf and it hit her that she'd never realized what a great dad she had.

She watched Cue, covered now in clumps of snow. The orb above his head seemed bluer than usual against his frosty head. "Did I ever tell you about the time we took Cue to the vet?"

"Nope, didn't hear that one."

"It's so funny. I was six. He weighed in at more than 200 pounds. The only way the vet could get him on the scale was for me to climb on his back and ride him onto it."

"No way!"

"Yep. Then, I had to stand on the scale and be weighed so the vet could subtract my weight from Cue's. I barked, but the dumb vet was so freaked out by Cue's size, he didn't even laugh. He examined him as if he was a lion, scared to get close. When he was done, he stepped back a safe distance and pronounced him healthy as a horse. Both of you, he'd winked, finally looking at me. What's this blue thing floating over his head, he'd wanted to know, trying to touch it, but seeing his fingers pass right through. No idea, Mom assured him, he's always had that. The vet looked at me. I shrugged my shoulders. He looked from Mom to me and asked no more questions. 'That was awkward,' Mom said when we left, and we never went back."

Rosie laughed. "I can't believe you never told me that."

"I guess back then, we weren't best friends yet."

They heard an airplane overhead and looked up to see a red and white Cessna circling the village. "Oh, no," Rory groaned. "Dad's here!"

Chapter 3: Fireweed

Seven months later, Rory walked the path from the house to the top of the hill; the golden leaves that had fallen a few weeks ago were dead, crunching underfoot. She couldn't believe Mom was gone. The doctor had told them she was doing so well; she'll probably beat this, he'd said. She felt the buttons on the lanyard in her pocket. Mom must have suspected it would be the last birthday they'd have together. She'd wanted her daughter to know the truth and to give her the lanyard and the feather. Rory was so glad she had. She crossed her arms against the cold and tucked Dad's scarf over her nose, feeling it soft against her face.

A flash of color caught her eye, a stem of late blooming fireweed. A rare gift! How had it managed to survive the cold? The thin October light painted it a paler pink than its magenta summer cousins; just one stalk, reedy and half their height, its delicate blossoms reached as high as her knee, swaying in silent greeting. Mom. Every petal held her memory. Rory picked it, remembering when her mother had woven several stems into a wreath; it must have been two summers ago. Its rosy blossoms had lit their cabin door ablaze with hope. Hope that she'd live. But slowly, the wreath had withered, along with Mom's health.

Rory thought of when she was little, and they would wander through fields of fireweed taller than she was, and she'd catch glimpses of the sky through its lacey-leafed patterns. Mom would pick a stalk, like the one she was holding, and twist it into a small circle, her slender fingers working it just so, carefully shaping it. The half-moons on her nails were still white then, not yet yellowed from the cancer. Rory'd watch, enthralled, until Mom held it up, a crown of pink sapphire fit for a princess. For my Aurora, brown-eyed beauty of the North, she'd said with much aplomb, setting it on her dark curls, then scooping her up to kiss her flushed cheeks under its petals. Light of my life, she'd murmured.

Cue bounded from the woods, startling Rory out of her reverie. "Hey, boy. Where you been?" She rubbed his head. "You coming with me?" They reached the top of the hill and there was the grave, the headstone set between two of the largest evergreens on the property. Cue walked soundlessly at her side; for all his size, he could pad like a cat when he wanted. He nuzzled her arm, sensing her emotions even when she thought she'd hidden them well. They stood in front of the stone marker, listening to the wind whisper through the trees.

Rory cleared her throat and spoke in a soft voice. "Hey, Mom, it's me. And Cue. It's nice here right now even though the leaves are down. You'd like it, so peaceful and beautiful. Wherever you are, I hope it's as awesome there." She held up her lucky feather, swallowing the lump in her throat. "It's been almost ten months, Mom, since you gave this to me and I know you'd be amazed I haven't lost it. Seriously, it's a treasure. It makes me think of you. I'll keep it safe always."

She stood, listening to the birds and wondered if her mother could hear them. She dug her hand into the thick fur on Cue's neck, scuffing her shoe in the dirt, then stopped scuffing when she realized what Mom would have said about it.

"So, I'm almost done with my flight training. Dad thinks I can take my check ride before winter sets in. I'm working on my cross-country solos right now; gonna fly to town and pick up some food and stuff this week, just in case we get an early snowstorm. You should see the size of the list Gram's making—I might have to make two trips as long as it is." She tried to chuckle, but her jaw was clenching, and tears were making wet dots on her shoes.

"Whelp, I guess I'll go now. I miss you so much, Mom. Don't worry about us; we're doing okay. Here, look, I made something for you. Can you believe I found some fireweed still blooming!"

She kissed the small wreath she'd woven while she'd been standing there and propped it against the headstone.

"Light of my life," she whispered, touching the letters of her mother's name.

Later that afternoon, Rory sat at the kitchen table studying the grocery list.

"Add 40 pounds of butter," Gram called to her from the cold room. "And you got the flour and sugar on the list already, right?" The cold room was mostly empty now; it was time to load in supplies for winter. Dad would go hunting soon, and hopefully get a moose. He always traded some meat for salmon—he had a fisherman friend in Fairbanks—and they kept it all frozen in the cold room till April. Gram already had the freezer full of blueberries, raspberries, and cranberries. They'd add store-bought vegetables, butter, cream, milk, eggs and keep it all frozen until they needed it. White and wheat flours, oats, and sugar would fill the bins along the opposite wall. She'd probably need to make another flight to Fairbanks before they were really set.

Gram came into the kitchen and Rory frowned at her. "Forty pounds? Seriously? No way we need that much."

"We'll use every bit of it. We go through a couple pounds a week, easy, with baking and all."

"Ok, fine. But that's it for this trip. The groceries will weigh about 200 pounds and I want to fuel the plane in Fairbanks. Any more and I'll have to leave Cue there."

Gram was about to question Rory's math, but they heard an airplane in the distance. A minute later, Dad roared over the roof and Rory bolted from the kitchen to meet him.

Dad signed her off for her grocery flight early the next morning. She'd already flown one of the three cross-country flights required for her pilot certificate and though she had a few more months to get everything done, she wanted to complete all the requirements before winter settled in. She was planning to take her check ride when she turned 17, maybe on her January birthday if the weather allowed. She hadn't expected to leave for Fairbanks quite so early in the morning, but snow was forecast to start around 5:00 in the afternoon. She'd planned to get the groceries and be home by 2:00. No later, Dad had said firmly; we want to be sure you're way ahead of the weather and we'll need time to unload the airplane before dark.

Dad walked with her to the runway and followed her around the airplane as she went through the preflight checklist. She opened the passenger door for Cue and he jumped in, tail thumping.

"Be safe, Rory," Dad said as he hugged her. "And have fun!"

"I will! See you this afternoon!"

He waved and walked away as if he was leaving. But, she knew him; he'd watch until they were out of sight.

She climbed into the pilot's seat and reached over to pull Cue's seatbelt across his massive chest. He licked her face and she pushed him away laughing. "I know, I know. I'm excited, too. We might even look for some wildlife." Cue was an expert at animal sighting. His eyesight was phenomenal and when he barked in a certain direction, she'd follow his gaze and, sure enough, the animals were exactly where he was looking. Moose, sheep, goats, bears, nothing escaped his notice.

She glanced out the window and yelled "Clear prop!" just before she started the engine, then back-taxied to the end of the runway, pushed in the throttle and started rolling. At 65 knots, she climbed out, and Cue immediately started barking. Seriously, she couldn't believe he saw wildlife already. But, there, just ahead and slightly to the right were three bears scrambling away from the noisy airplane. One of them turned and looked up at them just before it disappeared into a thick wooded area. Cue strained against his seatbelt and slobbered all over the window.

"Well, they were easy to find. Too easy. Let's see if there's any sheep up here." They climbed to 7,000 feet, then 8,000. The mountains were bare rock; no trees grew past 6,000 feet. Cue bristled and whined, and she turned where he was looking and spotted a white speck on the rock. As they got closer, sure enough, there was a ram, curved horns and all, standing proud atop a rock, staring at them. "Nerves of steel, that one," she told Cue. "No running away for him." She turned the airplane away from the ridge to get back on course for Fairbanks.

Suddenly, Cue freaked out, barking like crazy. She looked at him to see where he was looking, but he was focused straight ahead, at the clear blue sky. She strained to see, but there was nothing there. Or so she thought. Abruptly, from out of nowhere, a large bird appeared in the sky, heading straight for the airplane.

She veered away trying to avoid a collision but felt a hard bump. She'd hit it! Stay calm, she told herself. Keep the nose down. Fly the airplane. Don't let it stall. Do whatever it takes. Her hands were shaking as she struggled to level the wings, pulling the power back to buy some time. She managed to get the airplane flying straight, but not without a lot of control input. This wasn't good; there was no way she'd make it to Fairbanks. She was descending at about 300 feet per minute, which gave her about four miles, or four minutes, of flying. She realized she would have to do an emergency landing.

She had to find a spot, now! She looked around for a clear, flat place to land and nearly panicked when she saw mountains on one side, tree tops on the other. This was terrible! She was supposed to always have a landing spot in sight. She thought about what Dad had taught her and remembered her emergency landing lessons: Look behind you, he'd said! She did and was relieved to see a small clearing in the woods behind her left shoulder.

She headed for it and as she descended through 1,500 feet, realized it was an even better landing spot than she'd hoped. The woods seemed to open up as she got closer. She let herself breathe a little and, deciding she was too high, circled to lose some altitude. When the landing spot was in front of her, she lined up to land as perfectly as possible. She tightened her seatbelt, then unlatched her door and pushed against it enough to shove her jacket into the open space, so it couldn't close. She'd read that doors can get jammed in a crash making it impossible to get out. "I hope this works," she said, wiping her sweaty palms on her jeans. "Here we go, boy. Let's hope we walk away from this one."

Chapter 4: Gamloden

The landing spot was actually a wide path through the woods. Trees overhung some of it, but Rory thought she could clear them. She almost did, but not quite. Leaves swatted the windshield for a few seconds, then the ground loomed in front of her. She pulled the nose up and landed hard. Really hard. One of the wheels caught on something and before she could react, the airplane flipped over.

She managed to shut the airplane off, relieved she was alive. Everything was very still. What was causing the pressure on her chest? She was so disoriented, it took her a few seconds to realize she was hanging upside down. The moon was shining through the window below. The moon? Why was the moon out? She had left in the morning. What in the world had happened? Had she been unconscious all day? In a panic, she remembered the forecast snow storm. Was it snowing out? She couldn't see much, but it didn't feel cold. She unlatched her seatbelt and fell onto the roof of the airplane. As she rubbed her head, her heart sunk with the knowledge that she'd flipped Dad's airplane. He'd be so disappointed.

"Cue, you okay?" She craned her neck at him and, in spite of the mess they were in, laughed. His jowls were hanging upside down, exposing white canines and red gums. A long string of drool dangled from his mouth. She unhooked his seatbelt then dodged, barely avoiding him crashing on top of her. He hit hard with a whimper.

The door opened without a problem, so she crawled out, Cue scrabbling behind her. No snow. In fact, it felt warm; she for sure didn't need a jacket. Rory was trying to make sense of it when she heard the birds chirping and noticed the sky was brightening. Dawn. She must have been knocked out for a long time. She was going to be in so much trouble. But at least she wasn't dead; not even hurt as far as she could tell. She looked for damage. The propeller blades were curled, but the windshield wasn't cracked, and the body of the airplane looked okay; not even a dent on the wing tip where the bird had hit. She didn't understand why there wasn't more damage.

She stood and studied the woods, looking for the landing path she'd aimed for. It wasn't there. Just forest all around. This was getting weird. How could she have missed all these trees? It was like the forest had opened its mouth and swallowed her. Wait a minute. She studied the trees. This was a fully-leafed forest, not like the woods in Alaska. There were no scraggly spruce trees and no dead leaves anywhere. Where was she?

The bird Rory'd hit lay on the ground not far away, flapping its good wing like crazy, its other wing twisted at an odd angle. It was enormous for a bird, nearly as big as she was. Cue ran over, jumping up and down, wagging his tail like he was greeting an old friend.

"Cue, what're you doing? Be gentle." She knelt down beside it and tried to sooth it. "You poor thing, you're hurt bad; I'm so sorry. I never saw you coming." The light from the rising sun touched the feathers and she was startled to see them shimmering with color—reds, purples, greens, yellows—changing with each small movement. Those feathers looked familiar. She looked down to see her lucky feather glistening just like them. No way! This was the bird! The one who'd saved Gram's life and maybe hers. And she'd nearly killed it.

She heard someone or something running toward her and frightening images of Rosie's little people flashed through her mind. She had the urge to run but had no time to react before a tall man burst into view. Lean and lithe, his brown-skinned arms swung effortlessly in graceful rhythm to his long strides. A lumpy sack bounced on one shoulder; a bow and quiver hung on his back. A bow and a quiver? She was surprised she even knew what they were. And embarrassed to find herself blushing. Cue ran up to him, sniffing.

If the man was put off by the dog's size, he didn't show it. "Well, hello there, fella," he said, scratching him behind the ears. "Did you see it, too, that huge flying thing in the sky?" When he noticed the blue orb over Cue's head, he pulled his hand back.

Rory shifted her weight and drew the man's attention. Their eyes met. No one said anything. He looked from her to Cue and back, again, averting his eyes when he saw her legs. It was awkward. Hadn't he ever seen a girl in jeans before? Then he looked at her, her face, taking in the scars. She crossed her arms and let him look; she wasn't going to flinch. What did she care what this stranger thought? She expected him to gasp or grimace or at least look away, but he didn't. His frank perusal was unnerving. Wasn't he going to even speak to her? She hoped he couldn't see she was blushing. Her heart hammered. She tried to smile but couldn't. Self-conscious, she reached up and pulled her hair over her marred cheek.

And then, he bowed. He bowed! Who does that?

"I beg your pardon, miss," he said. "I've completely forgotten my manners. I so seldom meet anyone on this path and, well, you really startled me. Are you lost? Can I help ...?" Then, he saw the upside-down airplane and hurried over to look. "Merciful Tennins, this is it! This gigantic thing was flying." He ran his long-fingered hands over the smooth metal, the rubber tires, the Plexiglas windows, stooping to see inside.

He'd never seen an airplane? He seemed to have no idea what it was. Where was she? She walked to the plane, cautious, confused, and upset. What was going on? It was like she'd flown through a time warp.

"I was just flying it and ...."

"*You* were flying it?"

"Yes."

"Ah, so you arrived with it."

"In it, actually. Me and my dog."

"You can control where it goes?"

"Uh, yes, that's the idea."

"I see," the young man said, though the confused expression on his face told her he didn't see at all.

"I had some trouble, though. I hit that bird," she said, pointing. "It's hurt. Broken wing, I think."

"Let's have a look," he said, walking to it slowly so as not to scare it. "What a magnificent creature!" He bent down and touched it, admiring how the color on its feathers seemed to dance. He sat back on his heels and scratched his head. "Could it be?" he muttered.

That's exactly what Gram had said about her feather. What was it about this bird?

He absently ran his fingers through his shoulder-length brown hair, pushing it behind his ear. His ear!

It was long and pointy like the elves in <u>The Fellowship of the Ring</u>. And, much to her shame, Rory gasped. He must have heard her, since he immediately covered it with his hair, again. She liked him instantly.

But he wasn't paying her much attention; he was focused on the bird. "All right now," he whispered. "Let me see if I can help you. I won't hurt you, not at all, so don't you worry." The bird opened its eyes and Rory was pretty sure she saw them soften when it met his gaze.

"Why look at you!" he said. "Prettiest green eyes I've ever seen. The color of new spring leaves. There now, it will be okay." He gently probed for less obvious injuries, avoiding the injured wing, talking quietly to the creature. Rory looked on, shifting her weight from one leg to the other, not sure whether to kneel down near him or keep her distance. Cue apparently trusted him, so she decided to squat and have a look, leaving plenty of space between them.

"Is it hurt anywhere else?" she asked.

He shook his head. "Just a broken wing. And I think I can help." He leaned over and laid his hand on the bird's large head. Its neck was slender and at least a foot long.

He spoke to it. "I'll tend to your wing if you'll let me. I've set a few wings in my time, though on smaller birds; but I think I could do a good job."

The bird looked at him and replied in a soft, feminine voice. "I'm sure you will do a fine job. Thank you."

Rory was so startled, she fell back, landing hard on her bottom. "It talks?"

The man looked back at her, amused.

"I --- I've never heard an animal speak before." She stood and brushed herself off. It really wasn't funny.

"I'm not sure where I am. But I'm definitely not where I came from."

"You're in the birch forest, a short walk from Tomitarn," he said absently, focusing on the bird.

"Do they all talk?"

"The birds?" He glanced at her.

She was scanning the trees for other birds and when she looked back at him, saw him grinning.

"No, not all," he said.

Her cheeks flushed, and her knees felt weak. What was happening to her? She'd crashed Dad's airplane in a bizarre world and already had a crush on an elf? Maybe she had died after all. Or maybe she was in some coma and this was all a very strange dream.

She reached for Cue, wanting to touch his face, feel his wet nose, smell his gross dog breath. If he was real, this couldn't be a dream. He slobbered all over her arm in a very wet, very real way. Oh no.

The man was gently positioning the bird's wing, binding it snugly to her body. "I'll carry you back to my uncle's house and set it properly there."

"Alright, thank you," the bird answered, and Rory pinched herself. It hurt; she clearly wasn't dreaming.

Something flickered on the bird's neck. The man leaned closer for a look. He moved aside some feathers to see a blue gemstone, the size of a chestnut, round on top and flat on the bottom as if the nut had been cut in half. It was set in a simple silver pendant. He lifted it to have a closer look, and a six-rayed white star floated across its surface. "Will you look at that," he said.

Rory couldn't believe the bird was wearing a necklace! It spoke, and it wore jewelry. She pinched herself, again, to be sure. Ouch. She leaned closer. "That's a star sapphire. A really big one."

The man looked at it for a long moment, tilting it this way and that to see the star move. "I wonder," he murmured to himself. Rory watched him catch the bird's eye, and they held each other's gaze for what seemed an uncomfortably long time. What were they doing? Were they telepathic, too?

Eventually he broke the stare and spoke to the bird. "Well, I guess it's time to get going. You can rest and recover once we get to Uncle's house and I'll stay till you're mended."

The bird did not reply.

The man looked at Rory. "You're welcome to come, too, and perhaps we could be of some help to you with your, ah, flying thing."

"Airplane."

"Airplane. Aptly named."

"And no," she replied firmly, standing. No way was she going home with this guy, nice as he was. Seeing a flicker of disappointment, she added, "Thank you, though, for offering."

He turned to pick the bird up, and her face heated as his muscles flexed. She liked him. She definitely liked him, and it was completely unnerving.

But before he could get a good grip on the bird, it spoke. "There's no need to carry me, dear. I can manage." And just like that, in front of them both, the bird transformed into a woman.

Rory took a few fast steps back and tripped over Cue, finding herself on the ground behind the dog. She scrambled to her knees and crouched behind him. *What just happened? What's going on? Am I hallucinating? Why isn't Cue growling? And come to think of it, why isn't the man terrified like I am?* She watched them warily.

But, the smiling, silver-haired lady didn't seem like a threat. Her hair hung about her shoulders in luminous soft waves, muted colors flickering through it when she moved her head. Her eyes were warm and seemed to be lit from within, like green glass globes alight with candles. She had high cheekbones and deep curving hollows in her cheeks, a straight narrow nose—perhaps a tad long, and a wide mouth, turned up at its edges. The sapphire sat in the hollow of her slender neck, its star gliding back and forth as she gracefully shifted her weight from one long leg to the other. She was very slender, and several inches taller than Rory, making her about five-feet-nine or ten. Her ankles, laced snugly in a pair of black boots, peeked from the bottom of a soft gray dress.

"Oh my," her emerald eyes sparkled, "I had no idea our meeting would be like this! But, I didn't think you needed to carry me when I could walk perfectly fine. And look," she held up her arm. "Healed already. It happens sometimes like that."

The man bowed to her. "Firebird," he said. "I thought it might be you. I hoped it was—I've often dreamed of meeting you and now, well, I'm so honored."

"Call me Floxx," she said, holding out her hand. "I'm pleased to meet you, ah…."

"Finn," he said, grasping her hand politely.

Cue padded over to Floxx, leaving Rory awkwardly exposed on her knees. She stood as the dog nudged Floxx's hand with his big head. "It's good to see you again, too," Floxx said to him, running one hand through the blue orb and scratching his neck with the other. The blue orb over Cue's head glowed brighter than usual.

They both turned to her and she realized she was totally gawking. She cleared her throat and stepped forward, extending her hand to each in turn. "I'm Rory. Well, Aurora, really, but I go by Rory. And my dog, Cue."

"Cue?" Floxx raised her eyebrows.

"Rescue, actually. But I shortened it when I was little."

"A perfect name! And he's kept you safe all these years," Floxx said, smiling, her kind eyes as clear as an Alaskan stream.

Rory stared at her, adrenaline pumping. She knows Cue? Floxx caught her expression and smiled.

"I'll explain later, dear. Meanwhile, no harm done, thank Eldurrin. I am so sorry I had to crash into your airplane. I'd hoped it would be easier, but I always suspected it would be a challenge to bring you back."

"Excuse me?" Rory moved a couple of steps closer, her temper flaring. "You crashed into me on purpose?"

Floxx absently rubbed her arm.

"We could have all been killed!" She glared at her. "Not to mention I wrecked Dad's plane and ruined my cross-country flight."

Floxx's warm eyes appraised her. "I was the only one hurt, Rory. Not a scratch on you or Cue."

"And what are you talking about, bringing me back? Back where?"

"Why, here, of course. To Gamloden. At exactly the right time."

Okay, it was time to wake up. This had gone far enough. She tried to think of something to say, but Floxx had walked away.

"I promise I'll explain," she called to them. "But, first I need to check that I didn't lose any feathers in that fall." She walked slowly toward the airplane, studying the ground. "They are exceedingly rare, my feathers." She turned and eyed Rory's lucky feather. "And valuable. Best you keep it out of sight."

A chill ran up Rory's spine as she tucked it in her pocket. So, it really was a Firebird feather. She couldn't believe she was meeting the bird. Her. That it—she—could talk and change shapes. Floxx and Cue were old friends. Wait till she told Dad and Gram. At the thought of her dad, her heart sunk. He was going to be so upset with her about the airplane.

Floxx returned a few minutes later and Rory was already starting to feel less jumpy. She couldn't explain it, but she wasn't terrified any more. Both Floxx and Finn seemed nice, really nice, actually. She felt maybe she could trust them enough to ask for their help. But just then, a raven the size of an eagle burst from a branch directly over her head, hackles spiked, shredding green leaves in its haste. She screamed, and it screeched; its piercing cry lingering well after it was out of sight.

Chapter 5: Marinna

Far in the north of Gamloden, under the icy peaks of the Caladrius Mountains the Queen paced in her throne room, waiting for her father. "He said he had killed that bird," she fumed to herself. "That we were free to build our army and sweep the world."

Her throne sat toward the back of an immense rectangular room, in which all decisions regarding the rule of Droome were made. This central room had been carved deep in the heart of the northernmost Caladrius Mountains. The stone walls had been polished until they shone, then studded with gems, mined and transported by the dwarves who lived in Orizin, a week's journey east through the underground tunnels. The political alliance forged with the dwarves after the war had proven quite lucrative.

The room glistened, washed in the light of the gold sconces set into the walls at six-foot intervals. The throne, itself was carved from white alabaster, which grew in stalagmitic formation from the floor and walls of the great limestone caverns, a fortnight's journey south.

Marinna stood for a moment and studied the throne. Her father, himself, had overseen its elaborate construction—no doubt a drudgery for his wild nature.

She allowed herself a smile, remembering his words one night just before he transformed and left for his hunt, "I love you deeply, my daughter. You will one day rule the world and not be limited to governing from this palace. But for now, you must stay here, and I want this throne room to be beautiful for you." He had, he told her, begun conscribing workers and artisans when she was just an infant.

She considered the back of the throne, sea-themed, a tribute to her mother's heritage. What had she been like? Angry and cunning as Sirens were reputed to be? Or would she have had a gentle side for her daughter? Marinna would never know, as her mother had died during childbirth. Inset across its arched back were shells of all kinds: mollusks, including beaded periwinkles, King's crown, banded tulip, horse conch and lion's paw, as well as starfish and seahorses. In the center of the arch was an enormous chambered nautilus shell, fully three feet in diameter, its lustrous nacre pink, purple, ivory, and gold. Pearls of all sizes, shapes, and colors were inset among the shells, along with large aquamarine gems. Her father had told her with pride that none of the aquamarines weighed less than 25 carats.

While the arched back of the throne was a tribute to her water-loving mother, its arms reflected her father's heritage. A dragon lay on each, mirror images of the other, wings folded, heads facing into the throne room, jaws agape, tongues extended. Their scaled bodies stretched the length of the arms; spiny tails framed the sides of the throne with a spikey edge, their sharp tips pointing inward, gems glistening. The emerald spade at the tips of the two tails embraced the nautilus and touched at the apex of the throne's arch. The dragons, themselves, were covered with gold and inlaid with gems; their scales set with green beryl, emerald, and multicolored opal. That was a good way to duplicate father's dragon scales, as his could be any color he chose; his camouflage scales blended with the background, giving him tremendous tactical advantage. Each of their eyes was an enormous black star sapphire; the star moved in the sconce light, giving the illusion that the dragons were actually watching. The dragons' teeth were white moonstone, their open jaws and protruding tongues overlaid with red ruby.

The golden horns, however, were similar to his. They angled backward from the dragons' heads, encrusted with dark red rubies set around enormous diamonds, fully the size of the aquamarines. He'd confided that he could retract his own dragon horns at will, hiding them under scales on his head. At night, when hunting, he'd raise them, allowing light from the gems to scatter in the darkness, attracting his victims. They come to me, he'd said, the rumbling of his glee exploding into hoarse, harsh laughter so intense it shook the room, dislodging some gems from the throne and extinguishing the sconce lights. She'd been careful to hide her terror and quickly relit the lamps; it was good he didn't laugh often.

She stood back, admiring the whole gem-encrusted throne. He loved his jewels, perhaps more than anything. Perhaps more than her. But, at least he was generous with them; clearly her throne was a gift of immeasurable worth, given with the hope of a sovereign and eternal reign, from the great Thaumaturge, Draegin, the last of the lizard-skinned wizards of old, to Marinna, his only beloved child.

She sat, elbows resting on the curve of the dragons' backs, absently stroking the feathers of Dread, her Caladrius bird, who'd flown to her lap as soon as she'd settled. Dread's white feathers contrasted sharply with the Queen's ebony hair. Her red fingernails slid back and forth across the bird's right wing, belying the tension she felt. Dread made no noise, his glazed eyes staring straight ahead. She mused as she stroked his wing, appreciating how rare he was. Though thousands of Caladrius birds had once lived high in the mountains above, Draegin had hunted them nearly into extinction over the millennium, his appetite for their flesh never quite satiated.

He had, however, spared some of them for what he called modifications, and had given one to her 16 years ago in celebration of the murder of a royal baby who had threatened her claim to sovereign reign. While Dread's feathered ancestors had had the extraordinary ability to heal the sick with a look, this bird had been surreptitiously altered. Dread now had the ability to inflict illness with a stare. It's the Caladrius Curse, Marinna remembered him saying with a sly smile as he handed this new protector to her. "Of course," he added, "you and I are shielded from its harm."

Her reverie abruptly ended at the sound of Draegin's footsteps. Dread snapped to attention, rose on her long legs, and flew out of the room. Marinna watched her graceful exit, understanding why she avoided contact with her father whenever possible. He strode past the uniformed guards, straight to the throne, whipped his effulgent cape back and bowed deeply to her. "Your Majesssty," he said, his voice deep and smooth. "You are looking exquisite today." She saw his admiration and knew he was pleased she had sent for him.

Marinna appraised her father. He was a striking figure, commanding awe and respect in his sorcerer form, and fear, as well, though not as much as in his dragon form. He was fully seven feet tall, and exceedingly thin. His skin had a subtle glow to it, but that was because it was not skin at all, rather, tiny scales that covered him from head to foot. They changed color, from gray to green to tan depending on the light. The changes were subtle, though, and by now so familiar to her, she paid them no attention. Even others rarely noticed; it seemed so natural and was, of course, not expected. One might just think he looked different today, as one might say of an acquaintance who had trimmed his hair or combed it differently.

He always wore a head covering—she was one of the few who had ever seen him without it—a draped head scarf with a band to hold it in place, covering the nubs of his horns. The scarf matched his cape, which was iridescent, changing colors as the fabric flowed with his graceful movements, diminishing the likelihood of his own color changes being noticed. His head was hairless, as creatures with scales have no hair follicles at all. The scarf hid the place where his ears should have been; his were mere slits in the scales on the sides of his head. His hearing, however, was very keen. As far as she knew, it was superior to any other creature alive. It seemed he could hear even her thoughts. Her father's eyes, soft with love at the moment, were yellow with large black irises and no lashes, nor eyebrows.

And she knew another secret about him. Cleverly hidden on his forehead, centered slightly above and between his eyes was a parietal eye—a third eye—which had been a common dragon trait in ancient times. His scales covered it completely, although one night when he was very angry at an elusive owl he was hunting, the scales over the eye had opened of their own accord, providing him with exceptional night vision. He had bruised it in the hunt, though, and called on her to tend to it. His nose was small in the center of his narrow face, and the two thin colorless lines of his lips hid a ballistic tongue, trident-tipped, though much smaller than his dragon-sized tongue. It flicked in and out of his mouth when he was anxious or angry.

As a child, she had secretly crept out one night to spy on him. She liked to watch him fly. She had caught him crouching that night, stalking local prey and had seen that tongue shoot out of his mouth to snare a bird ten feet away. She still remembered her terror as she'd raced back to bed. He'd seen her run and scolded her the next day, not for sneaking out, but for her fear. He'd told her that power belonged to the strongest; conquest to the bravest. The weak ones were eaten. She was tougher now.

"Thank you," she said, acknowledging his compliment. "I'm glad you came. Sit down, Draegin. We have much to discuss."

He eyed her clenched fists. "What'sss happened?"

She relayed the raven's news that the Firebird had been spotted—injured somehow and rescued by a man in the birch woods.

"The Firebird!" Draegin boomed. The sconce light flickered.

"You said it was dead." Marinna cut him with a glare.

"Did I?" He smoothly regained his composure and smiled, his hairline lips stretching across his thin face.

"Asss I recall, I said I'd taken care of her. That she was gone and no longer a threat to usss."

Marinna narrowed her eyes at him, uneasy with his answer.

Chapter 6: Friends

Floxx didn't find any more of her feathers. Rory had the only one, and she had an uneasy feeling about who, exactly, would think her feather was valuable? But, Finn had a lot of questions as they stood by the airplane, and she didn't have a chance to ask about the feather.

Rory had to admit she liked being the one with the answers, at least the airplane answers. She told Finn how it flew, explained the forces of flight: lift, weight, thrust, and drag. He was intrigued. He couldn't get over the notion that something that heavy could carry people through the air. Floxx didn't say a whole lot, but she flew without an airplane, which was way cooler. She seemed a little distracted, actually, and Rory tried not to be bitter about the bird lady ruining her day and her airplane. Whatever Floxx's reasons were for bringing her here, well, she'd done it, but she wasn't staying long. She'd be gone as soon as the plane was flyable, again. They were really helpful trying to help her flip it right side up, but even the three of them together didn't have the strength. As they were kicking around ideas about how they might do it, someone else popped through the forest. Rory's heart rate did pick up, but only for a minute. Finn knew him.

"Uncle Werner!" Finn waved him over. "Perfect timing!"

"You saw it, too?" Werner said, gesturing to the airplane.

"I did. And this is the young lady who flew it."

"Rory," Finn said, "This is my uncle, Werner Tizawink."

"A pleasure to meet you, Miss," Werner extended his hand and she took it. He bowed, like his nephew had. "I saw this fly over the farm and then heard it scraping the trees as it dove through them. I came as quickly as I could, but I'm not so good at running anymore."

"And, Uncle, this is Floxx," Finn gestured.

"A pleasure to meet you, as well." Werner bowed, again. "Were you also flying?"

"Well, yes," she said, an amused smile on her lips.

Rory snorted and shook her head at Floxx, but had to admit, it was pretty funny.

Werner's attention turned to the airplane. "May I look?" he asked politely, already studying the aircraft.

"Of course," Rory said. "We were just trying to figure out how to flip it right-side-up."

Finn talked with his uncle about the airplane and the two of them inspected every inch of it, discussing the qualities of the strange materials—aluminum, plexiglass, rubber. They were deep into it and their enthusiasm made Rory smile. She stood back and took a moment to study Werner. He was short, maybe five feet tall, round through the middle, and thickly bearded. His brown skin was darker than his nephew's, and his curly russet hair, cut short, was laced with white around his face. And he had a tail! She couldn't believe it! Short and perfectly round, like a rabbit's tail, it protruded from his trousers like a ball of Gram's brown and white speckled yarn, wiggling as he moved.

She must have been staring at the tail cause Floxx walked over to her. "He's a Tomtee," she whispered, her eyes sparkling. "Wonderful folks."

"We have an idea that just might work," Werner said, walking toward them. "I need to go back to the farm to get some tools and rope. You're both welcome to come; it's a couple miles or so. You could meet, Ardith, my wife; she'd be so thrilled." He looked at the sun. "And, you're probably hungry. Our food's not fancy, but we've plenty of it." He saw Rory's hesitation. "Don't you worry. We'll all come back this afternoon to work on your airplane." He patted Cue. "You, too, fella."

She was very hungry. And truly felt at ease. So, ignoring a lifetime of warnings not to go with strangers, Rory agreed.

Finn walked next to her, and Floxx walked ahead with Werner, who took two steps for every one of hers, his short legs nearly jogging. Rory kept staring at his cute little tail until she realized how inappropriate that was. Finn talked to her about the woods; he knew the names of the trees like they were friends. Oaks and Ash, Elders, Hawthorns and Hazels. Wild Boxwoods and Blackthornes, Cherry Plums, and Black Dogwoods. He'd lived in these woods his whole life, though not with his Uncle. He had a place of his own a few miles in the opposite direction. But there was an apple tree by his uncle's farm that he liked to pick and that's what was in his sack. He gave her one and it was the best apple she'd ever eaten, hands down. Eye-popping flavor, juicy and crisp.

"I know!" he said, watching her reaction when she took her first bite. "Best apples anywhere in Gamloden!"

They walked in silence. Well, except for Rory crunching as she ate. But her thoughts were loud. How did she get here? What did Floxx mean about it being exactly the right time? She had to go home. If they could flip the airplane over and somehow get it to a field with room for takeoff, she could be home tonight. Oh. Wait. The prop was busted. And there'd be no airplane mechanics around here. Dad and Gram will be out of their minds worrying.

Finn broke the silence. "I remember playing in these woods as a child, pretending I lived in the stories my father had told me. Mostly the ones about elves."

Rory glanced at his ears, but his hair covered them.

"So," she asked carefully, "Are there elves here? Or just in stories?"

"Just in stories, nowadays. They all left after the war."

Oh really. How is it that you have elf ears, then? But, she answered nonchalantly, "There are no elves where I live, either." This was a ridiculous conversation, she realized, as she tried not to stare at his ears. "No Tomtees, either. Just humans."

She glanced at them, though, and he noticed. He tried but couldn't hold back a laugh, and tucked his hair behind his ears, allowing her a good look. "My parents were concerned about me always playing elf games and couldn't wait for me to grow out of it. Which I did. But when my already large ears got their points, they told me I had an ancestor way, way back on my father's side who had been a full-blooded elf. And that must be where my ears came from, though no one in several generations had had ears like mine."

He wiggled them, and Rory burst out laughing. "But, aside from the ears, I'm half human, my mother, and half Tomtee, Da."

A movement on a branch caught Finn's eye. Ravens, many of them silently hidden in the leaves, were tracking them with their beady eyes.

"Floxx—ravens!" Finn called to her.

Rory frowned, remembering the huge one that had scared her to death. "Should we be concerned about ravens?"

"Many of them work for the Queen. Her spies. They watch us."

They picked up the pace, but Rory glanced up every few minutes, wary of the birds. A half-hour later, they crossed a stone footbridge over a river. The wide canopy of an old apple tree loaded with fruit spanned both sides of the shallow river.

"The wondrous tree," Finn pointed up. "And the Tiziwink farm," he gestured in a wide circular motion. "Everything you can see on this side of the bridge."

The fields were flat and went on forever. Rory could take off from here, no problem. A cow watched them through the open doors of a barn, and a donkey, tied loosely to a nearby tree, munched hay. Several horses grazed in a far pasture and beyond them, were a couple of outbuildings, one of which looked big. Chickens ran free, scattering at their approach. The house, itself, was a small stone cottage with a wooden porch that extended across its front. Two people were sitting on the porch steps. It seemed perfectly normal. Picture perfect, actually, like one of Gram's Thomas Kinkade paintings. Until the people on the porch stood up.

Finn sprung up the front steps in an effortless leap. His ears were not the only thing elven about him. "I can't believe you're here!" he said. "What perfect timing! Wait till you meet our guests."

He introduced them to Rory as Zad and Jakin, two friends he'd known his whole life. They'd actually been heading to Finn's house, but had decided to stop here on the off chance he might be visiting.

Ardith Tizawink threw open the front door and hurried down the steps. She looked a lot like Werner, just slightly shorter, her hair long and caught up on her head with an ornate comb. Curly white wisps escaped around her plump face.

"Werner!" she exclaimed. "Now this is a surprise—you ran off alone and have brought back a house full." She eyed Floxx and Rory, trying not to stare and smiled graciously as Finn made the introductions. At the mention of a meal, she ushered them inside. Her tail, fluffed and tied with a blue ribbon, bobbed from an opening in the back of her pale, yellow dress. "What a pleasure to have your company! Here, sit and make yourselves comfortable. I'll put on some tea to tide us over till the meal."

She was a lot like Gram, fussing around when Dad brought home unexpected company. Rory couldn't wait to tell her about all of this; she would savor every detail. Rory didn't say much, didn't have to with all the chatter going on, just sipped her surprisingly delicious tea, and observed.

Zad was very short, shorter than Werner; Rory guessing about four-and-a-half feet tall and built like a black bear. Dark shrewd eyes and a lumpy nose were all that showed on his face; frizzy brown hair hung in damp strands around a beard that hid his mouth completely. His demeanor was gruff; his voice husky. He kept staring at Cue, then he'd glance at her, then back to Cue. It was unnerving. *Note to self: Don't get on his bad side.*

Jakin was as tall as Finn, lean and lithe, but blonde. He looked like the surfer guys Rory had seen on the beach when she'd visited California a few summers ago. No pointy ears, no tail; he looked totally human. She was pretty sure Finn had introduced Jakin as Zad's brother, but, well, that was a big stretch. She must have misunderstood. That Jakin, though, what a flirt; he kept trying to catch her eye! She wondered if girls were kind of scarce in this weird place. He was hot, she admitted to herself, but something about him put her off, made her wary. Not her type. She turned her attention to the others.

"My father told us about ye." Zad was talking to Floxx. "About the last battle, when the Queen nearly killed you. We were afraid ye'd left for good."

It was clear to Rory that Floxx didn't want to discuss it, but Zad persisted.

"Why is it ye've come back? Is there another war brewin'? Have y'come to finally defeat Draegin?"

"Something like that," Floxx replied. When no one said anything, she set her cup down and smiled. "It's simple, really. Eldurrin sent me."

At the name of Eldurrin, a hush fell over the room.

"Eldurrin?" Finn asked quietly. "The One who made—everything?"

"Yes. Exactly. Him," she replied.

Zad cleared his throat. His face reddened, and he mumbled into his beard. "Well, I can't say as I know much about all that."

Floxx looked at him thoughtfully but didn't say anything.

Zad leaned forward. "Well then, if Eldurrin sent ye, surely you are going to kill them once and for all. Draegin and his foul Queen, I mean."

"I am leaving all that to Eldurrin. He's in charge. I do what he tells me to do." She lifted her cup, a two-handled sturdy piece of pottery, and took a thoughtful sip. "As we all should," she added, gazing evenly at Zad.

Zad's shoulders stiffened, but he said nothing more.

Jakin glanced at Rory and she thought she saw him wink at her before turning to Floxx. "I'm intrigued that you change shapes, Floxx. I don't mean to be rude, but can you tell us what it's like? How do you do it? Which one is really you?"

Floxx laughed a musical laugh. "Well, that's a lot of questions. And far too difficult to explain. But the truth is, I don't have one appearance that's more me, as you say, than another. When I am a bird, I am me, and when I'm a woman, I am me. Different forms, same me."

That was totally weird. No one knew what to say. Werner and Ardith shifted on the couch. Finn cleared his throat. Rory grabbed her chunky cup for a sip and found it empty. The awkward moment passed, thankfully, when Werner broke the silence.

"Well now, Floxx, the things you're talking about are mostly a mystery to us. Don't even know what kinda questions to ask. One thing's for sure, though, we are very honored to have you sitting in our home, plain and simple as it is."

"Can I get you more tea?" Ardith asked, standing.

"No, no, many thanks, but I'm fine," Floxx answered.

Ardith looked at Rory.

"So delicious," she said raising her cup a little. "But, no more for me, either. Thank you, though."

Ardith disappeared into the kitchen.

Finn looked around the room. "So, I met Rory in the woods this morning. Her airplane was damaged when she and Floxx collided."

"Excuse me?" Jakin turned toward Rory, curious. "What, exactly, is an airplane?"

They all looked at her. So much for staying out of the spotlight. "It's a flying machine that's used for transportation," she tried to explain. "There are a lot of them where I came from—Alaska—and people, um, pilots, are trained to fly them, to travel quickly to and from distant places."

"Huh. Never heard of Alaska. Anyone know where that is?" Jakin looked at the others.

"Just me," Floxx spoke for them all.

He leaned toward Rory, his eyes twinkling. "Can we go see this airplane?"

"Yes, that's actually what I was hoping. It's sitting upside down in the woods right now and I need help flipping it over. The three of us tried, but it's too heavy. So, Werner invited us back here to eat while he got some rope and tools. He has an idea he thinks will work."

"Well, why didn't you say so. What're we waiting for?" Zad scrambled to his feet, just as Ardith called them to the table.

"First, we eat!" Werner said, grabbing Zad's shoulder. "Ardith's dished up a feast."

Rory was surprised their food was pretty normal. And glad, too, since she was starving. Cheese, cold chicken, a couple of loaves of home-made bread, and a jug of apple cider. Gram would have whipped up a blueberry pie, too, but she wasn't complaining. It was mid-afternoon by the time they returned to the airplane. Zad and Jakin rushed ahead.

"Will ye look at this, Jakin." Zad ran his hands over the metal fuselage. "Never seen anything like it. So light." He pressed on the belly of the airplane and it flexed slightly, then popped back into place. "What is it?" he asked Rory.

"Aluminum," she said. "It's perfect for airplanes because it's light and strong both." She walked with him around the airplane; he was totally fascinated, touching the rivets, running his finger through the grease on its belly, shaking his head. She saw that Jakin had crawled into the aircraft and was curled upside down eyeing the instrument panel.

He hollered to Zad, "Wait till you see the inside of this contraption."

"C'mon out, Jakin," Zad told him. "Werner wants t'talk about flippin' it."

While they were talking, Rory studied the trees and could see the gashes the propeller had made on the way down; several branches had been severed and lay on the ground amid a wreckage of shorn leaves. She couldn't believe she hadn't been hurt. And to think that Floxx had done this on purpose. Why would anyone do something like this? It was crazy and so high risk. Who was she? What did she want with her? She turned her attention to Werner. He wanted to lift the airplane straight up, so it was several feet off the ground, then pivot it through the air on its nose. That way the wings wouldn't need much additional space to turn.

With Zad's help, they engineered an ingenious series of pulleys, sending Jakin and Finn up a few trees to run lengths of rope from the high branches. Ardith, Floxx, and Rory pitched in to hoist the aircraft up; the pulley systems made it relatively easy to maneuver, and when the ropes were tied securely around the tree trunks, it held. Dad would never believe this. Rory reached in her pocket for her cell phone and snapped a few pictures of her new friends and the Cessna suspended upside down in the woods. She saw that her battery was still nearly full but there was no way to recharge it here. She'd better save it to call for help.

The sun was low on the horizon. Dad and Gram must be so worried.

Slowly and carefully, she directed Jakin and Finn to hold the propeller and pull the nose down, as if the airplane was doing a backward flip. Zad and Werner monitored the ropes, adjusting them as needed. Ardith watched for branches in the way, calling for them to stop a few times while she cleared space. The tail swung up and around, barely clearing the high branches, then they carefully lowered the Cessna to rest on its wheels.

Rory was thrilled! "Brilliant! Oh, thank you so much." She walked around it, inspecting the damage, explaining to the others as they went. "Looks like the propeller took the worst of it; it's bent probably beyond repair. And a broken strobe light on the wing tip. Other than that, lots of scratches, but nothing major."

She opened the pilot's door and got in. Zad went around to the other side and climbed in next to her. Finn and Jakin squeezed into the back, jostling for room to see up front. She left her door open so Werner and Ardith could stand next to her; they didn't want to miss a word. She showed them how the control surfaces worked, pulling the yoke close to her chest. "Look behind you. See how the tail has come up? Now watch it go down. The part of the tail that moves is called the elevator. When you're flying, you move the elevator by pushing the yoke in and out and control the airplane's climb and descent."

Zad was mesmerized, smitten with the idea of flying, and Rory tried to hide a smile. "Now, Zad, turn the yoke toward me and watch the wing on my side." He did, and he saw a hinged part of the wing move down. "Now look out your window. See, that side has moved up. They're rigged to move in opposite directions. Those are the ailerons and moving them in flight turns the airplane." Zad was intent, nodding, listening, not saying much, but Finn and Jakin voiced plenty of amazement from the back.

Then she pointed to places on the airplane's panel. "Here's where the key goes; this is the master switch; here's the fuel selector. These buttons control the lights and the electrical system." She pointed to a row of switches along the bottom. "And these round instruments tell me about the flight: how high off the ground I am, whether I'm going up or down or turning, which direction I'm heading, how fast I'm going, and how much fuel I have left. And these are radios. I can listen and talk to others using this button."

Finn poked his head up front. "You can talk to others with that?"

"Yes." She suddenly realized she should do that— try to raise air traffic control, or another pilot flying over and tell them where she was.

"Like this." She switched on the master switch and turned a few knobs, entering four numbers into the transponder—7700—the code for emergencies. Then she put on her headset and entered the numbers 121.5. "Cessna Skyhawk November Seven Four Five Alpha Kilo. Mayday. Mayday. Come in please. November Seven Four Five Alpha Kilo. Mayday." She waited. No one responded. She tried two more times with no better results, so she shut the switches off. "I'll save the battery and try, again, in the morning." Her heart sunk. Dad and Gram would be frantic. She barely managed to control her emotions. "My family will be looking for me when they realize I'm missing, worried that I'm hurt somewhere."

Finn reached up from the back seat and patted her shoulder. "It will be all right, Rory."

Zad was touching everything he could on the front panel, pushing buttons, pulling knobs. She had to ask him to stop and helped him reset them all. His eyes were glazed with wonder. "Here," Rory said, reaching into the door pocket. "This is the owner's manual. It says this is a 1969 Cessna, Model 172. A Skyhawk." She handed it to him. "Not sure how much of it you can understand, but there are some good diagrams." And she climbed out, the others following.

Werner eyed the sun touching the horizon. "It's getting late. Let's go back to my house where we can all rest. We'll come back tomorrow."

Chapter 7: Thief

Rory licked her spoon thinking she'd never eaten a better stew and passed her bowl for seconds. Tender pieces of meat and carrots, onions, and potatoes floated in a rich gravy. Ardith handed her the basket of butter squash bread and a crock of Tenninberry jam, an old family recipe. It was an odd color for jam, turquoise, but so scrumptious!

Later, they sat under a cherry tree heavy with blossoms watching the stars come out. As they ate Ardith's apple pie, Finn talked about baking in his dwarf-made oven and how Zad's family had transported the iron stove in pieces to his home when he'd been born.

"I remember it some," Zad boomed. "Though I was a just a mite of a lad myself. T'was a baby gift t'be proud of; one of our finest craftsmen built it." He rubbed his beard as he remembered. "I rode on it some o' the time, small as I was. Why it wasn't long after our visit here, d'ye remember, Werner?"

"Course I do," Werner said.

"That was the time I saw the strangest thing right there by the river," Zad continued, his voice growing softer. "I been meanin' to bring it up but didn't quite know how." To Rory's astonishment, he stood and pointed to Cue. "It's when I first saw him!" Cue's ears flattened, and she put her hand on his neck. "With 'is strange blue light. Right over there all those years ago with a bleeding baby hangin' from 'is mouth.'"

Rory gasped. This fit perfectly with her birth story. Could she have been the bleeding baby? Zad had seen her and Cue here? She studied the spot by the river. This was bizarre. Totally insane. What was she doing here? Here, where she'd almost died before she'd ever lived. She crossed her arms over her stomach, feeling queasy. Floxx moved closer and put her arm around Rory's shoulder.

Zad continued. "I thought the wolf was eating the child and I grabbed some rocks to throw at it, hoping it'd drop the babe and run. But before I could throw even one, a bird flew over, biggest bird I'd ever seen." He pointed to Floxx. "It was you, wasn't it? You swept in and took 'em. Vanished. All o' you, gone in a flash."

Floxx hesitated and Zad took it as a yes. "And all these years, I wondered if I'd imagined it!"

"Oh my, Zad."

Rory bit the tears back. She wanted Mom more than she'd ever wanted her before. Knowing she'd never be able to tell her tore at her heart.

Zad was upset that Rory was upset. "Oh, I'm sorry, miss. I didn't mean t'upset ye." He looked at Floxx. "She didn't know, then, did she?"

Floxx glanced at the lanyard peeking from Rory's pocket. "No, but she knows much of what happened."

Rory hiccupped. "That night. You dropped one of your feathers on Mom's lap?"

"Yes, dear, I did," Floxx took her hand. "I wanted you to be well cared for, loved and cherished."

"I was. My family is the best." Floxx rubbed her back and pulled her close.

"So," Rory sniffed hard and tried to compose herself. "You said earlier that you'd brought me back.

I didn't get it then, but I do now. You brought me back here where I was born."

"That's right, dear."

"Do I have birth parents here? What happened to me?"

Floxx explained she was the only child of the King and Queen of Byerman, and she'd been kidnapped at just a few weeks old. She described Cue's rescue, speaking gently and slowly, and answering every question until there were no more.

Rory ran her fingers over the scars on her face. "Well, that explains these. But this business about me being a princess? Um, no. That's really a stretch for me. Seriously, do I look like princess material? And even if it was true, the King and Queen have thought me dead for a long time; they'd never believe it."

"Well," Werner said, "You should meet them and tell them your story. Let them decide for themselves."

Meet them? She could actually meet them? "They live around here?"

"Not exactly around here," Floxx laughed. "But you could travel there in a week or so."

Everyone agreed she should go. "I'll be glad to accompany you to the castle," Finn offered. "I've been to Masirika many times."

"I'll come, as well," Jakin said quickly.

"Aye." Zad looked around and spoke for them all. "I think we'd all be honored t' take ye home, Rory."

She wiped her nose, really wishing they had tissues. She wanted to go home, for sure. To Alaska. Back to Dad and Gram and Rosie. But she was curious now. If she couldn't fly home, maybe she should do this crazy thing. She couldn't believe she was even considering it.

"We'd need to get a move on, though," Zad continued, "King Merek and his hunters leave for the mountains at summer solstice every year for their big game hunt. Course he don't really need t'go with 'em but he usually does. Fine marksman 'e is."

"When is summer solstice?" Rory asked.

Why soon." He glanced at her surprised. "'Tis the longest day o' the year, o' course, not more 'n two weeks from now."

Though the day had been warm, the air chilled as evening approached. Werner and Finn built up the fire and they all moved a little closer to it. Cue lay down near Rory and she absently scratched his head. Jakin walked over and spread a blanket on the ground. "Nothing like a fire to cheer you up," he said, motioning for her to sit with him.

Finn joined them as soon as the fire was blazing and sat on the other side of Rory. She was pretty sure she saw Jakin glare at him. Finn ignored him, and smiling at her, mumbled something about Cue needing more room and moved closer, his shoulder brushing hers as he settled. Though she'd thought she wanted to be alone, to curl up and process everything that had happened, something about Finn comforted her. She felt safe with him, protected. She relaxed when he was near, glad for his company.

Jakin looked over at them and scowled—this time there was no mistaking it—stood and said he'd forgotten something inside and disappeared into the house. Ardith brought her flute and played a soothing piece; the music sweet and calming. Then Werner and Ardith sang a few Tomtee folk songs—one about growing big cabbages had Rory laughing hysterically. The music, the leaping flames, the stirring of the branches in the breeze, Finn's closeness, and under it all, the ripple of the Dryad River. Gamloden. Her birthplace. Mysterious. Magical. She felt an unexpected kinship; as if somehow, she fit, though she shivered at the bizarre possibility. Finn noticed and thinking she was cold, moved closer, his shoulder pressed firmly against hers. She didn't mind at all. The music was captivating, and she gradually became aware of a pulse in the air, a quickening, a peace, an invisible, palpable presence.

Floxx, seated on the other side of the fire, began to sing. Softly at first, then louder and stronger. Rory shivered. What a beautiful voice! Though she couldn't make out the words, it was clearly a song of joy. Of love. Of longing. She watched Floxx, just able to see her silhouette. Her head was raised to the sky as if she was singing to someone above. The air seemed charged. The music was so personal. A love song. Who was she singing to? And what was she saying?

They sat in silence for some time after Floxx finished, lingering in the sweetness of the moment. Rory wiped the edges of her eyes. Then, a branch cracked, and Cue rushed toward the trees, and they heard the scuffle of creatures running away. Reality came rushing back. Gamloden. She was going to spend the night here under the stars. And she was suddenly exhausted.

Ardith made sure each of them had a cloak or a covering of some kind, and one by one, they curled up by the fire for the night. Rory tucked her feather in her pack, wrapped Dad's wool scarf around her, and fell asleep. She dreamt she was chasing Mom through a field of fireweed. But it was so thick, it hid her from view and slapped against her cheeks, cutting her face as she ran. She'd catch a glimpse of her, then Mom darted to the left, wait, there she was, footprints, follow her footprints, but they led the wrong way. Her fragrance, so close, fresh like laundry that's dried outside, smelling faintly of soap and strongly of sun and wind. Fireweed tangled above her head, choking the sky, blocking the light, snaking over her like a poisonous vine.

Rory's eyes flew open; a scream caught in her throat. Where was she? Why was she outside? Oh. Her stomach sank as she remembered. Gamloden. Mom wasn't here; wasn't anywhere she could reach her. Dad and Gram, they were as good as gone, too. Fear twisted in her. She had to hold it together. What would Dad do? Keep your head, he'd say. You're a pilot. Don't panic. Stay in control and think. She would not crumble; she'd rest and figure it out in the morning.

She rolled over, but Rory couldn't sleep. She heard some scuffling by her backpack. It persisted long enough that she tiptoed over. The fabric of her pack was moving, as if something had crawled inside. An animal? She touched it, trying to feel what it was, careful to disturb it as little as possible. Finn was suddenly at her side. She jumped, unnerved at his silent approach, yet glad for his company.

"Is everything okay?" he whispered, his breath warm on her cheek.

Her face flushed.

"I got it!" she whispered back, inches from him, and nodded toward her hands. He placed his hands over hers, helping her hold whatever was squirming inside. His touch! She couldn't think; her brain was nearly paralyzed. Thankfully the others stirred and sat up, wondering what was going on, distracting her enough to function, again.

A raspy, muffled voice hollered, "What'r y' doin? Lemme out!"

"Hold it tight," Finn said, tightening one of his hands over hers, and reaching inside with the other. "Ow," he yelled, yanking his hand out. "It bit me! Here, allow me, please." He swept the pack onto his lap, holding the wiggling fabric with one hand and reaching inside with the other. He deftly pulled out a very angry, very tiny person, who was shaking one fist at them and clutching Rory's feather firmly in the other. Somehow, this little person had managed to pull it off the lanyard.

"Just lemme go and I won't hurt ye," he shouted, way louder than Rory had ever imagined such a small person could shout.

Zad leaned in for a close look and a tiny fist thumped his nose. "Back off, ye hairy dwarf. Don't git near me."

Zad lurched back as if he'd been stung. "What is it?" he roared. They all burst out laughing and crouched to see.

"Why, it's a ghillie," Floxx said. "A few of them still live in these birch trees, but it's very rare to actually see one."

He looked like a miniature troll or maybe a really homely pixie. About eight inches tall, a large bulbous nose dominated his long face; his small furious eyes slanted upwards at a sharp angle. Green hair wisped about his head, long and fine, like the silk on an ear of corn. A few green strands hung ragged from the tip of his chin. His skin mimicked the look of birch bark, silvery with thin black markings, as if tattooed with Morse code. Rory thought of Rosie's little people. But, mean as he was, he was too small to be much of a threat to anyone. He caught a glimpse of Floxx and immediately quieted. He glanced from her to the feather he held. Rory's feather.

"Firebird," he said trembling. "I seen all 'at's happened. And when you said about yer feathers bringin' good luck an' all, I 'ad to 'ave it. It's me only hope."

"Your only hope?" Floxx said gently. "For what?"

"To find Catkin. M'sweetheart!"

"I see. Tell me. Start with your name please."

"Name's Dew."

Floxx waited.

Dew took a deep breath, then began. "It's like this. Well," he stopped, then started again. "Luck. I need some luck, y'see. Some time ago, me and Catkin were enjoyin' a night together high up in one o'the birch trees, pointing out star pictures and telling stories about 'em. She climbed too high, Cat did, out of the cover of leaves, trying t'see a star better. I called t'her to come down—knowin' there could be creatures about, owls or worse. But it was too late. A Roc came out'a nowhere, snatched 'er in its vulture claws and flew off. I searched for her till winter, all the way up the slopes of the Caladrius Mountains to the peaks where Rocs build their nests. But, I couldn't find 'er. She's out there, somewhere, though, I'm sure of it. And this lucky feather'll help me find 'er, I jus' know it." His hands were trembling, as he pleaded with Floxx.

Rory didn't like him and wasn't buying it. He wasn't getting her lucky feather, even with his sad story. "Um, no. That's mine." She leaned in to take it from him; he had messed up some of its pinfeathers already. "My mother gave it to me." He was holding on tight. Really tight. She pulled harder. "It's very special to me. Let me have it back."

A raven cawed from a nearby tree, answered by the raucous squawks of dozens more.

"The feather!" Floxx urged. "Grab it, Rory."

She tried, really, she did, but the birds attacked. Dozens of them dove at her and Finn, pecking their heads, faces, and arms. Finn dropped the ghillie, and as they were fighting off ravens, Rory glimpsed the tiny man running for the closest tree, still clutching her feather. But before Dew could hide, a great gray bird shrieked and swooped, its wing span nearly as wide as the Firebird's. It plucked Dew in its talons and flew off into the night. Finn grabbed his bow to shoot, but the Roc was already out of range. Rory raced after them yelling, "Wait! My feather! My lucky feather! Give it back." Dew's screams faded into the distance along with her glimmering feather. She couldn't believe it. Long after they'd disappeared, she seethed. No way was she going to let him keep it!

Chapter 8: Feather

Marinna and Draegin heard the Roc shriek as it flew past the hidden entrance to the palace. Shortly after, four Inozak guards, six-fingered creatures of extraordinary strength, stood at the doorway of the throne room. One carried a cage, in which Dew, still clutching the feather, trembled.

"Enter," the Queen said.

The Inozak approached, holding the cage up. Marinna peered into it. "Well look at this! Another ghillie! Now I have a set."

Draegin glanced into the cage, then leaned over to scrutinize, a smile slowly spreading across his face.

"Take it out, Marinna."

She reached in and retrieved Dew, raising him to eye level to study.

Her father reached over and pried the feather from Dew's grasp.

"No, lemme 'av that. Give it back."

Draegin snapped his finger across Dew's face, nearly knocking him out of Marinna's grasp.

"Draegin, be careful!" She turned away from him, readjusting the ghillie in her hand.

"Thisss feather," Draegin said nonchalantly to Dew. "Where did you get it?"

"Found it, fair and square."

Draegin raised his finger for another snap, his tongue flicking out of his mouth.

"Don't you dare," Marinna scolded. "It's a feather. What are you so worked up about?"

Draegin smiled, his thin lips stretching lopsided, the right side higher than the left.

"You don't know, do you?"

She looked at him blankly, one hand protecting Dew.

"It's not jussst any feather, Marinna. It's a Firebird feather. See how color rides its barbsss." He stroked it gently from shaft to tip, holding it under the sconce light.

She raised an eyebrow, skeptically.

"Don't you remember the old storiesss, my dear? The ancient lore about the Firebird's feathersss? They are said to be magical, powerful, utterly rare. The Firebird is said to bestow them to a select few for very special reasonsss. The storiesss say each one brings favor and unusual power to itsss possessor." Draegin erupted in a loud laugh that rippled the feather and caused the ghillie to crouch.

"And you actually believe it?" Marinna shook her head. "Have you gone mad?"

"You doubt." Draegin said amused. "We shall sssee. The wild tales may be true, and if ssso, think of the power we would have at our disposal!" He waved the feather above his head and burst into booming hilarity, again. She had never seen him so excited. And over a feather! The room shook with each wave of his laughter, like the rumblings of an earthquake, deep and powerful. The sconce lights flickered dangerously.

"Well then," Marinna said, thinking his glee ridiculous, but attempting to calm him down lest he do more damage. "Let's find a safe place for it, shall we?" She looked at her throne. "The large conch shell; it would be safe there. And I would be able to retrieve it easily should we fall under attack, when I'd certainly need its feathery power." She smiled wickedly.

"Oh no, no, not here! You are not in danger here. Not with our Inozaks close at hand and this impenetrable throne room. This treasure must be preserved, perhaps, for a long, long time. It's a gift not likely to be seen, again. Somewhere unusual, distant, unreachable, where the elements of nature cannot touch it." His eyes gleamed brighter than usual, as they did when he thought of his treasures. "I know just the place."

She shook her head in disgust. "If you hide it in your lair, I will not be able to retrieve it under any circumstances."

He stiffened at her reaction. "No, you would not. But, neither will you need to. It will be safe there. Now and through the ages. Sheltered from attack, from destruction, from thieves. Waiting for the moment it can be used to our best advantage."

Marinna turned her back on him, picked up the cage the guard had bought for the ghillie and locked Dew in it. Sometimes his love for treasures bordered on insanity. Yet, why did he talk of attack, destruction, thieves? Was it more than paranoia? Was there something he wasn't saying? Were they in danger? Surely, he wouldn't keep anything that important from her, would he?

She hung the cage from a hook on the throne room wall, and stepped back, looking from one cage to the other across the room. Her new pets! She took some consolidation in having a pair, rare as they were. To her surprise, one ghillie called to the other.

"Cat, me sweet love. I've come for ye."

Now it was Marinna's turn to laugh. "You came to rescue her?" She shook the cage. "That didn't go very well, now, did it." She saw the ghillie across the room reach through the bars of the cage, sobbing. "Well, isn't this touching."

Draegin shook his head, amused. "A happy reunion. You could breed them, you know. Would you like that little fellow?" He teased Dew, sticking his skinny finger through the cage and tickling him. Dew bit it. Draegin yanked his hand back, hissing. "Never mind. I'll just eat the wretched creaturesss." Then he stalked out of the room.

"You will not touch my ghillies!" she called after him.

Later that day, Draegin returned as though nothing had happened, though Marinna's earlier irritation with him still rankled her. "Good newsss, Your Majesty. Our army is growing. We have just bred our 10,000th Inozak whelp." She remained seated, coolly appraising him. "Don't sulk, Marinna. It's unbecoming."

She stood. "I may be your daughter, but I am also the Queen. You will treat me with more respect. And you most certainly will not threaten to eat my new pets. You kept the feather; I keep the ghillies and I will do with them whatever I please."

"All right," he said, uncharacteristically amiable.

That was far too easy. She narrowed her eyes. "And what of your concerns about attack, destruction, thieves?"

He gestured to a side table and they sat together. "Ah, yesss. You sense some unease. You are young, Marinna, however, I have watched the ages passs." His eyes took on a thoughtful look and he lowered his voice. "Yet, perhaps you are old enough." He looked at her. "Yesss, I think it's time."

Draegin looked behind to be sure they were alone. Marinna leaned closer.

"Your world reign isss not so far away as you might think. There is a prophecy about an ancient three-stoned crown that will be reconstructed for the world ruler to wear—your crown, my dear. The gemsss were lost eonsss ago, and I have searched for them as I've roamed over the land. Centuriesss ago, long before you were born, I found one of them. The King Stone."

She frowned at him.

"It was when I found that gem that I knew I would have an heir someday. You. Why else would it have come to me? I hadn't even met your mother, but I was sure I would. And when she came to be with child, it was no surprise. Boy or girl, it didn't matter; my heir would rule the world."

She struggled to piece his rambling thoughts together. "This crown, that gem, the King Stone. This is what you are afraid will be stolen?"

"Yesss. Just two more gemsss to find. Then with the feather we can restore the crown. It'sss key to your reign."

She crossed her arms over her chest. This lore. He puts so much weight on it. Still, she humored him.

"Tell me about this gem."

"It must have belonged to an ancient ruler, one who lived ages passst, before even my father's time. He had the red gem set in a ring. He must have had large hands as it slipped over one of my talonsss, making it possible for me to carry it to my lair. I've kept it safe these long eons. For you. I can see it in my mind, Marinna. The Eldur Crown of old placed upon your head with great celebration. And now, with the luck of this enchanted feather, I am certain that you will rule the world with unchallenged power!"

Regardless of his words, she caught the hint of uncertainty. "You speak of unchallenged power. You mean the Firebird. We must remove her once and for all. We must destroy her."

"Yesss. It will be no small task. Her power is formidable, yesss, but not nearly as great as oursss."

"And that is why our 10,000th Inozak is cause for celebration."

"Ah, now you begin to see. With that number, we can overcome any enemy, especially one like her who has no troopsss of her own."

Marinna sighed. "I thought we were rid of her; I thought we were rid of all threats to our claim to power. That none could stand in our way. Since King Merek's infant, whom we kidnapped and killed, there hasn't been another heir born!"

To her utter surprise, the ghillie stood and gripped the bars of his cage, yelling as loud as he could. "That child, the King's daughter, is not dead. She lives! I have seen 'er. And I'll tell ye where she is, if ye set me and my Catkin free."

The two ghillies gripped each other's hands, trembling on Draegin's palm, as Dew relayed the story he'd heard Zad tell his friends.

Marinna scoffed. "The King and Queen were completely bereft. They showed us the torn blanket that had been recovered from the lake. The child couldn't possibly have lived."

Draegin's eyes narrowed as he considered the remote possibility. "We shall have to sssee. At once."

He looked at Dew. "On the bank of the Dryad River, across from the Birch Forest?"

"Right. An apple tree marks the spot. Old and very large."

Draegin turned to put Dew back in his cage, saying to Marinna, "I'll send the wolvesss. If the girl is there, they'll make quick work of it."

"Wait, no!" Dew screamed, clutching Cat's hand. "Ye promised to let us go. Me and my Catkin. Ye promised t' set us free if I told ye about the girl."

"Is that ssso?" Draegin's long fingers tightened around them. He lifted them close to his face, which was longer than they were tall.

Dew was furious and erupted in a volatile string of insults. "Why, ye lizard-skinned, oily bag of lies! Look at ye, strong and mighty king of all that's vile and detestable, scared of a little girl, sendin' wolves to do yer dirty work. Can't face 'er yourself, is that it? 'Fraid she might get the crown first, steal yer miserable filthy pow'r...."

"Enough!" Draegin thundered, his face trembling. Then, suddenly, the scales on his forehead opened to expose his hidden eye just inches from Dew. Without thinking, Dew jabbed it with his fist, packing the full force of his strength behind his punch. Draegin flinched. So unexpected was an attack from the tiny ghillie that his grip momentarily loosened. Dew saw his chance and they slid from Draegin's grip and leapt to the floor, racing for escape.

Marinna screamed for the guards to catch them and they turned to give chase. But Inozak are strong and large, not quick or agile, and the ghillies outmaneuvered them.

Marinna was furious. "They've gotten away!"

"Don't worry, Marinna," Draegin hissed. "There's no way out in that direction. They could run for weeks in the labyrinth of tunnels under these mountains. But they won't live that long. Not with the creatures they will meet."

Chapter 9: Wolves

Rory was in the kitchen with Floxx and Ardith, preparing food for their week-long trip to Masirika, the capital of Byerman, where most humans in this world lived. She would have been happy, very happy, to have just stayed there and worked on her airplane. But, there was a lot of fuss about meeting her so-called parents. Seriously, this was becoming much too much. First of all, there was no way she could believe she was a princess. Surely Floxx would have hinted about that to her parents. And even if she was deluded enough to believe it, any King and Queen in their right minds would be highly skeptical. Showing up after sixteen years? *Hello, there, I'm your daughter, the missing princess, returning from another world, which by the way, I want to go back to.* If they didn't kill her, which was definitely a possibility, they could lock her up in some dank dungeon. But, maybe, just maybe, he'd be a nice King and listen; maybe he'd tell her how to get home like Glinda did for Dorothy in Oz.

Her mind raced with impossible ideas as three loaves of bread baked in the oven. Three more were rising on the table. She realized Ardith was telling her to keep the bread cool and dry in the saddlebags, so it'd last till they got there. They'd made a loaf for each day. Several wheels of cheese were already wrapped in cloth and stacked next to the bread. This was a whole lot more work than flying to Fairbanks for supplies. They were busy bagging apples when Werner pulled up to the door with two horses hitched to a long wagon. Finn, Zad, and Jakin were sitting in it.

"I think I can take the airplane apart and haul it back here," he told her. "When I have some time, I'll take a look at the damage. That bent—what did you call it?"

"Propeller."

"Are they ever made from wood?"

"Yes. I was actually just thinking about that."

"Well, I'll study on it. It's a challenge, for sure, with its curve and all. I have some birch in the barn and who knows? Maybe I can make a new one using the bent one as a pattern."

She smiled her best smile at him. "That would be so wonderful, Werner."

"Meantime, we'll take the airplane apart today. I got my tools and I'll make detailed notes and sketches, and we'll haul it back to the barn in pieces, if that's okay with you?"

Rory knew there was a miniscule chance Werner would succeed but realized that even if the airplane had been in perfect condition, she couldn't take off from the middle of the woods.

"Want to come?"

"Definitely." She smiled at Ardith and Floxx and tossed her apron on the chair.

It took all that day and half of the next to get the airplane disassembled, hauled, and stowed in the barn. Werner had made copious notes in the margins of the airplane's handbook and sketches in a spiral notebook Rory'd found in her flight bag. He and Zad were almost as enthralled with the notebook and her ballpoint pen as they were with the airplane, itself. Rory was counting the days. A week and a half till summer solstice.

The sky was just beginning to lighten the morning of the third day when Rory heard Werner open the door, milk bucket in hand, and head toward the barn. He left the door ajar, probably planning to slip back in quietly. The weather had turned cool, so they'd made a bed for her on the kitchen floor near the stove. Finn, Zad, and Jakin were sleeping in the barn. Werner hadn't gone more than a few steps when she heard him scream. She jumped up to see two wolves tearing at him. One knocked him over, ripping at his side. She yelled for help, but before she could close her mouth, Finn had shot the wolf. The other one saw Rory and leapt through the open door. In that split second, she dove behind the iron stove, crouching in that tight space, barely evading its snapping jaw. It lunged, its breath hot on her face, its engorged tongue flicking slobber all over her, an enraged monster, seconds from killing her when Finn's arrow pierced its neck. The beast yelped and twisted in fury, sending a spray of blood against the wall; its eyes finding Finn just before the life left them.

"He will live," Finn said with certainty after Werner's wounds had been cleansed and bandaged. They had carried him to his bed and made him as comfortable as they could. The wolf had ripped flesh from Werner's right arm, side, and thigh. His face was torn above the eye, and his head heavily wrapped in bandages, but the eye, itself, was untouched. He watched his stricken wife with his left eye, as she hovered over him. The rest of them tried to keep out of her way.

"I don't understand," Ardith struggled to keep her voice composed. "Why would they attack us?" She'd asked the question a few times, but no one had an answer.

Finally, Werner spoke with great effort from the bed. "I think they were after Rory. Somehow, we are not the only ones who know the Princess lives."

What? No! This can't be my fault! A wolf attack because of me? And both of us nearly killed? This is crazy! She left the room and Finn followed her to the kitchen where she stood in shock staring at the blood on the wall. Her thoughts raced. This was sick. Terrifying. Werner had almost died, and, if not for Finn, she would have been next. Up till then, Gamloden had been weird, but nice enough. Pleasant. Well, except for losing her feather. She turned to Finn. "Werner thinks the wolves were after me. I don't understand what's happening."

Floxx overheard her and joined them, brushing a stray curl from Rory's cheek. "It's not your fault at all. You've done nothing wrong. Absolutely nothing. But I think Werner may be right. If Draegin has somehow heard that you have survived all these years, he would be furious."

"Who is Draegin?"

Floxx and Finn exchanged glances but neither answered.

Later in the day, Ardith joined them at the kitchen table. "Werner's resting, and seems comfortable, more or less. No fever. But, it's impossible for him to make the trip now and I won't leave him. We think you should go without us." She looked at her nephew. "You understand?"

"Of course," Finn said quietly. His eyes found Rory while he answered Ardith. "We'll take her to the King. We will leave as soon as possi...."

Ardith interrupted him. "But the wolves. There may be more of them."

"There are four of us to protect her. We'll be back before you know it and tell you all about it."

Ardith sighed raggedly. "We have the food ready and the supplies are packed. Each of you are to take a horse."

When Finn started to object, she stopped him. "I insist," she said firmly. "You saved Werner's life, and the wolves would likely have killed not just him and Rory but all of us had you not killed them first. Horses and supplies are the least we can do."

"Ardith," Werner called from his bed, having heard most of the discussion. "Give Rory your bow." Ardith retrieved it immediately and although it was a little short for Rory, she did pretty well on the quick lesson Finn gave her.

"Your aim is surprisingly good," he commented.

"I've shot before."

He looked at her curiously.

"But not with a bow. A rifle."

He raised an eyebrow. "I'd like to hear more about that. But no time now."

Ardith suggested Rory borrow some of her clothes, so she didn't draw attention. She liked her jeans well enough—so practical, she'd said. She picked them up while Rory was changing and ran the zipper up and down, shaking her head in fascination. Rory borrowed a brown dress, green wool cape, and boots, as well as a thin undergarment that looked like an old-fashioned cotton nightgown.

Werner insisted the men try on his dress clothes—
they were meeting the King, he reminded them. Zad
was able to squeeze into Werner's doublet, though he
grumbled about the fit, and Finn found a heavy woven
shirt. Ardith handed Jakin her husband's heavy black
cloak. Can get cold at night, even in summer, she said,
as he took it with thanks. Ardith gave Rory her lovely
hair comb and showed her how to catch her hair up
with it the way women there did. Some rebellious curls
escaped, but the overall effect was pretty.

The afternoon grew late and Werner seemed stable.
Ardith suggested they stay another night, but Finn was
concerned about a second attack and felt certain they
should leave before dark. They ate an early supper, and
shortly after stood by the horses, their saddle bags
crammed full. A small saddle that Werner had made
for a pony several years ago fit Zad's donkey perfectly,
but Zad complained he would rather walk than be
stuck in a saddle.

"We don't have time for you to walk," Finn told
him in no uncertain terms. "Summer solstice gets
closer every day."

Zad glared at him, then at Rory, muttered
something indistinguishable into his beard, and
climbed on.

Finn hugged his aunt, assuring her they would be
fine—back before she knew it, then climbed on Redd,
the tallest and most spirited of the horses. Rory hugged
Ardith, thanking her for everything, and climbed on a
gentle mare named Willow. Cue trotted beside her, as
they rode out single file: Finn, Floxx, Rory, Jakin, and
Zad, bouncing behind them on Beast.

They followed the Dryad River east. The canopy of
leaves laced the late afternoon sky in delicate patterns
as they rode beneath. The river rippled pleasantly, its
rocky bottom clear in the late light. But Rory's mind

was fixated on the horrors of the morning. Werner's words replayed over and over. *I think they were after Rory. Somehow, we are not the only ones who know the Princess lives.* This seeming aircraft accident had spiraled out of control. Just a few days ago, she'd left home in Alaska on a grocery flight, and now she was the object of a deadly search. It was clear that even if she thought it was bizarre she could really be that kidnapped princess, the enemy, whoever that was, was eager to obliterate the remote possibility of it being true.

They rode in silence till they made camp at dusk, watching and listening for wolves, but encountering nothing but squirrels and rabbits. Rory slept curled next to Floxx, and twice jolted and cried out, shielding her face, the nightmare so real the wolf's slobber felt wet on her face. No one slept much; all of them were on edge about another attack. The next day they plodded on, tired and a little grumpy. This was utter foolishness. And dangerous. Completely irresponsible. She should have insisted they stay with Werner. What if he got worse? What if he died because of her?

Rory shuddered. She didn't like these woods; she sensed something sinister in them, watching. Yet, every noise they investigated proved to be small creatures with no ill intent; no wolves, no ravens, no threats that they could determine.

Chapter 10: Pool of Tennindrow

Rory was surprised that Floxx suggested they stop at a place she wanted them to see. They had a deadline to beat.

"It's not far out of the way," Floxx had assured them. "We'll still reach Masirika before summer solstice."

The sun was low in the horizon and the air had chilled when they heard water ahead. They emerged from the cover of forest to see waterfalls spouting from the westernmost peaks of the Caladrius Mountains. There were dozens of falls, small and large, some pouring over high peaks, others spouting from crags that could be easily climbed. The bluffs were painted pink and red with the setting sun, and the water spray reflected dancing prisms of color against them. The falls careened to a narrow, fast moving river, which hurried around some very large rocks in its center, churning the surface of the upstream water into frothing rapids.

But near them, the water quieted. Not far from where they stood, the large river met the smaller one in a wide, deep pool, where they settled before continuing quietly on their separate courses some distance away. The pool held the prettiest water Rory'd ever seen, as blue as the berries that grew wild in Alaska, and clear to the bottom. It was bordered by great oaks and willows, their branches heavy with leaf. Flowers brought a riotous shot of color along the south bank, close to where they stood, and other patches of blooms grew wild on the north bank.

Cue ran ahead, barking and racing around like he'd been here before. Oh no. She wondered what was next. But the beauty of the place won over her apprehension and she couldn't help but relax and soak in its splendor. This was a new experience for Finn and the others as well, so at least they had that in common.

"Floxx," Finn said, gawking at the waterfalls. "Where exactly are we?"

"This is the Pool of Tennindrow. That's the Tennindrow River," she said pointing. "It runs from the north, cascading off the mountains in those spectacular falls, and meets the Dryad River right here in this beautiful pool. Here is where we'll make camp."

They found a clear spot off the trail at the edge of the forest, where they'd be sheltered by high branches, but could still see the glistening pool just off to their left. They unloaded the animals, piling saddles and packs at the base of a towering oak. The horses and the donkey were tied to the trees on long leads, allowing them plenty of room to graze. Zad and Jakin had a large pile of wood gathered in no time and a fire was blazing as darkness set in. Floxx and Rory searched the packs and passed out food; there was still plenty to eat without having to cook anything. Finn carried the bedrolls to the fire and as the sky darkened from gray to black, they settled down in awe of their surroundings. The peace in that place was palpable, such a relief from the fear that had stalked them.

Floxx hummed a haunting melody as Jakin spread his blanket not far from Rory and stretched out to look at the night sky.

"So many stars." he observed. "So thick in places they look like clouds. Some nights up in the mountains where I was raised, the stars were so intense, it seemed I could reach up and touch them. I remember staring into the sky for so long it felt like I was looking down into it, a bottomless black bowl of starlight."

"Me, too, Jakin. They are like this in Alaska, where I come from, though the constellations are different. Sometimes on a clear night like this, if it wasn't too cold, Cue and I would sit outside like you did. I once tried to count the stars but didn't get through more than a fist's worth of sky before I lost my place." She laughed. "It makes me feel very small."

Jakin's smile came through in his voice, "Yes. I know what you mean, Rory."

A figure blotted out the stars. "Mind if I join you?" Finn asked, dropping his bedroll between them before either could reply.

"Smoke's blowing in my eyes over there," he said as he quickly sat, though Rory noticed there was no wind. Jakin started to object, but Floxx spoke from the other side of the fire and Finn shushed him.

She was leaning back on her elbows, gazing up at the pinpoints of light, her elegant profile outlined by the firelight. "Eldurrin made them—each of the stars, and the space that holds them."

"You sound like you know him. Eldurrin." Finn called to her. "You speak of him as if he was familiar."

"Yes. Well, I do know him, Finn. And, he is more than familiar, we have been close friends for a long, long time. I watched him set each of these stars in its place and give each one a name. He made some brighter than others, some in different colors, and even gave a few of them stories."

Rory sat up straighter. *What? Did Floxx just say she'd seen Eldurrin make the stars? They were millions of years old, if they were anything like the ones in Alaska. How could that possibly be true?* Rory must have misunderstood her. Finn raised his eyebrows but didn't question Floxx. Rory followed his lead. But there was something else she was intrigued about.

"Stories?" Rory asked her. "The ghillie mentioned star stories. Is there a story about the stars we're looking at tonight?"

"There is." Floxx studied the sky. "See those three bright stars nearly straight overhead?" She pointed. "The one in the center—the yellow one—is the brightest star in the sky. Do you see it?" They all did.

"Well, those three stars represent three gemstones in a crown. The yellow star, the Eldur Stone. The blue star on the left, the Stone of Valor, or some call it the Star of Power. The red star on the right, the King Stone. The three stars sit in the middle of a crown, the Eldur Crown. It was an actual ancient crown, made by the elves, the first beings Eldurrin created. It was forged for a future ruler who would bring peace and establish unity among many discordant nations.

"So, who was this king?" Jakin asked. Rory noticed his tone was a little sour. Was he still miffed at Finn's intrusion? "Was it one of the great mythical kings?"

"Oh, no," Floxx said quietly. "This is not a mythical king. This is a star story of a real king. But he hasn't come to power yet."

"Oh," Rory murmured, disappointed, hoping the story might be about her possible father, the king she was going to meet.

"The crown was never worn by its rightful owner and, being highly coveted, sparked a tragic ancient war. There has been oppression and strife between rulers and peoples ever since. There's a very old ballad that tells the story." And Floxx began to sing, her voice captivating, the rhythm slow and even; the tune laced with tones of deepest grief.

By the edge of the Tennin Sea
Eldurrin's hand did mold
The Eldur Crown, and in it, three
Jewels in a band of gold.

T'was delicate as Tennifel
Grown there beside the Sea.
And cast in light, too great to tell,
Magnificent to see.

The ruler will find her, and gently will bind her
When that which was stolen is found.

The stones it held in its circlet
Foretold of its great pow'r.
The stars affirm; we shan't forget
The coming of its hour.

The Eldur Stone sits at its core,
Gem of eternity.
Bright as the sun, the purest ore
That one shall ever see.

The ruler will find her, and gently will bind her
When that which was stolen is found.

The red King Stone, bright as hot flame
For from a line of kings

Floxx

This monarch comes, though no one names
The family that brings.

Blue Stone of Valor shining strong
Brings pow'r to the fair throne.
Its might will overcome the wrong
Its force protects its own.

The ruler will find her, and gently will bind her
When that which was stolen is found.

But greed and lust o'ertook the minds
Of those who saw its glory,
Waging war on their own kinds
Brutal, bleak, and gory.

The Elven Wars destroyed the crown
And with it hope of peace.
Great crown, the highest glory known
Lay in pieces, pow'r ceased.

The ruler will find her, and gently will bind her
When that which was stolen is found.

No one could mend, no forge reshape
The Eldur Crown—for two
Gemstones were stolen, snatched away
And hidden from all view.

The Eldur Stone alone endured
The ravage of that hour
Eldurrin sent the Firebird
To save eternal pow'r.

The ruler will find her, and gently will bind her
When that which was stolen is found.

Both Stone and Bird were kept hidden
Lest used for woe and pain.
In time are sent to one bidden
To claim the promised reign.

The ruler will find her, and gently will bind her
When that which was stolen is found.

Rory was deeply moved as the last refrain ended. "What a beautiful song, Floxx. Haunting, really."

"Beautiful—yes," Zad rumbled, "but terrible what the song tells. That crown—where was it destroyed? We dwarves could repair it, if ye knew where to look!"

"I wish I did, Zad."

Just then, Cue bolted from his place by Rory and raced into the woods snarling. Finn grabbed his bow and followed with Zad and Jakin. For several minutes, Cue barked and growled, racing back and forth in the shadows of the woods. But the men found nothing.

"Not wolves—they would've attacked." Zad said with relief as he plopped by the fire. "Probably just some animal sniffin' round for food."

Chapter 11: Kalvara

At dawn the next morning, Rory noticed a loaf of bread and a sack of apples were missing. "I'll catch 'em, whatever critter it is," Zad promised.

"Odd that it took a sack of apples. Animals wouldn't eat fruit," Finn said.

Jakin agreed. "Most animals would have gone for the dried meat."

"A person, then?" Rory asked. "Floxx, what do you think?" She looked around but didn't see her.

"Floxx left an hour ago," Finn told her. "Said not to worry, she had something to do and wouldn't be long."

"Okay. In the meantime, I'd like to check out this place."

They set out to explore soon after breakfast. Zad, hauling a coil of rope, decided he wanted to explore the mountains. "Come with me, Jakin."

But his brother shook his head and glanced at Rory. "I'm staying with the group." So Zad went off by himself and the rest of them headed toward the falls along the south side of the pool.

They'd walked about a mile when Cue abruptly stopped. He stood very still, his ears straight up. "What is it, boy?" Rory whispered, scanning the area. Finn moved closer to her, fitting an arrow to his bow. Cue turned and charged into the forest. They ran after him, following the sound of his bark.

About a quarter of a mile into the woods, Cue stopped at the base of a very old, immense Maidenhair tree. Its low thick branches, covered in new green leaves, spread nearly as wide as it was tall. Cue was focused on a spot about halfway up the tree.

Finn, with his keen eyesight, saw him first. "Merciful Tennins! It's a child!" He pointed to a small boy wearing filthy, torn clothes. His hair was disheveled and snow white; his skin pale as a foggy morning. He clung trembling to a branch.

Rory gasped. "Finn! Don't move." She was looking a short distance away, where a tall thin woman, white hair hanging in tangles, had an arrow trained on him. Her copper-colored eyes, narrowed and loathing, were fixed on Finn.

"Elf!" she hissed and let the arrow fly. Rory screamed and in that breath of a moment, Finn moved just enough that the arrow pierced his shoulder, not his chest. Rory caught him as he fell, sort of. He actually knocked her over, but at least she'd broken his fall. Jakin and Cue raced for the shooter, who'd hesitated a moment too long. In that second of indecision, something burst from behind the trees, knocking her flat. There was a brief tussle, and though she tried, she couldn't get away.

"Got 'er," Zad said, breathless. "Help me tie 'er up, Jakin." Zad pulled an apple from her ragged cloak. "She's a no good, sneakin' thief—and a bloody murderer!"

He bound the woman with his rope, bending her arms behind her in a painful position that lessened her desire to continue thrashing. Her curses and threats were silenced with a gag.

Who was she? Why had she shot Finn? What a horrible, hateful woman. And totally filthy. Rory was seething; thinking how narrowly Finn had escaped death. He was bleeding bad and clearly in pain. She studied the arrow; it had to come out. She'd removed a jagged piece of barbed wire from Cue's neck once and guessed the same technique would apply. Pull slowly, firmly, and carefully. Get it out as quickly as possible with the least amount of tearing. She shouted for Jakin and while he stabilized Finn, she struggled with the arrow. Finn yelled once at the beginning, so she lightened her touch and warned him when the tip was about to come out. It was terrible for both of them when she finally had to yank, but at least she got it all. Cue was there to lick the wound and she hoped that was as good as alcohol, which she didn't have. She wrapped Finn's shoulder with a sort-of-clean strip of fabric from his ruined shirt, hoping he would heal without infection.

"Let me see that arrow," Finn groaned, and she handed it to him. "I can't believe it. Shot me with my own arrow. Must have stolen it, too!" He stood and steadied himself. "Let's get the child."

They walked to the base of the huge tree. The boy had climbed higher and was sobbing, curled in a ball in the crook of a branch about 40 feet up.

"I'll go after him," Rory whispered. "Maybe he won't be so frightened of me since I wasn't involved in the fighting. And, besides, I'm a good climber."

Jakin objected. "He's way up there—you sure?"

"I'll be fine. I've climbed a lot of trees before." She tied up Ardith's skirt, wishing for her jeans, and started up. She took her time, not wanting to scare the child into jumping or falling, talking to him quietly as she approached, and it wasn't long before she made eye contact. She noticed his eyes looked red, really red and seriously hoped this kid and his guardian were not vampires. Then she remembered vampires don't eat apples. Good. She was careful not to reach for him, but just kept talking to him softly, telling him her name and assuring him she would not hurt him, nor would the others. After a while, she coaxed him down, branch by branch, all the way to the bottom, holding his eyes with hers as she told him stories of the trees she'd climbed when she was a child. After she'd jumped to the ground, she held her arms up for him. He took a shuddering breath, then with a resigned sigh, slid into them and let her lower him to the ground. She grasped his hand firmly and squatted to his level.

"I've told you my name, but what is yours?"

"Aric," he whispered, glancing around uneasily. He caught a glimpse of Finn's bandaged shoulder, and quickly looked away.

Then he spotted her. "Kalvara!" he sobbed and tearing his hand away, ran to her. But not before Rory noticed he had six fingers.

The fire blazed against the evening sky, marking 24 hours since they'd arrived at the Pool of Tennindrow. They had cooked a dozen fish that Jakin had caught that afternoon, pink like Alaska red salmon and almost as good. Aric was sitting by Kalvara, who was still bound, though in a more comfortable position. She was tied to the trunk of a tree not too far from the fire. Her gag had been removed to allow her to eat and Aric had fed her an entire fish, as long as his arm, piece by piece with his small fingers. And then, he had devoured one of his own.

Rory brought over half a loaf of Ardith's bread, now several days old, but not too bad, and handed it to

Aric, who tore into it immediately, shoving a large piece into Kalvara's mouth, and another into his. She watched their guarded expressions and could see their surprise at its delicious taste. When they'd finished, Aric leaned against her, silently staring at the fire. Cue took a liking to the child and lay close to him, occasionally nudging him with his huge muzzle for a pat. Aric would try to hide a smile as he obliged.

Zad sat guard near Kalvara, watching her suspiciously, but saying nothing. The woman stared straight ahead, her expression hard. She was seriously scary. Rory didn't trust her for a minute, suspecting she'd try to shoot Finn, again, given a chance. For Aric's sake, though, she tried to reach out to her. She sat down in front of them, noticing the guarded look on Aric's face. Kalvara twisted her head to avoid eye contact.

"Hello. I'm Rory. Um, I've met Aric, but not you, yet."

Kalvara turned to face her, her hair still caked with blood from the morning fight. Her reddish eyes glared at Rory with undisguised scorn and she spat in her face. Rory nearly fell over, she was so shocked. How dare she! Zad was immediately next to her, wielding his ax; he made no attempt to hide his animosity for Kalvara. Rory scrambled to her feet and wiped the disgusting spittle off, shook her head at Zad, then turned and stalked back to the fire, hoping good company would calm the fury pounding in her veins.

Later, Floxx and Rory walked Finn away from the camp, over to the edge of the deep pool of water, where they picked some Tennifel blossoms, a purple flowering plant that grew proliferous on the bank. Floxx soaked the blossoms in the water while Rory cleansed Finn's wound, then they placed the wet blooms on it as a poultice before wrapping it in a clean bandage.

"Wondrous plant, Tennifel. Blossoms, leaves, stem, root, even its seeds can heal most any wound," Floxx said. "We've come full circle, my friend," she teased Finn as she bandaged, "First you tended my wound; now I tend yours."

Finn grimaced. "Thanks, I think."

"Floxx," Rory asked while they worked. "Who are they?" She gestured to Kalvera and Aric. "Why would she want to kill Finn?"

"I don't know anything about those two, specifically," Floxx answered, careful to keep her voice low, "but they are Eldrows. They are rarely seen above ground. That's what is so strange. They live as captives in the caves of those mountains," she glanced at the nearby cliffs.

"Captives of who?"

"Draegin. He's held them there for ages past, ever since the ancient Elvin Wars."

"The wars your song spoke of?"

"Yes." Floxx gently tied Finn's bandage. "There were many elves, then, all different kinds. The high elves, led by Trummarius, were inventors and gifted craftsmen, coveting knowledge of all kinds. Their cousins, the woodland elves, were adventurers, discoverers, a high-spirited folk who explored the world. There were also pixies—a kind of tree elf, many ghillies, like Dew, water sprites who lived by rivers and many others. As time passed, the high elves and the woodland elves argued over everything: land, rule, mineral and water rights, and their disagreements erupted into war after war."

"The woodland elves were led by the Thaumaturge, Ryszard, of ancient lore—a malicious wizard, who devised spells to curse and corrupt, maim and destroy all living creatures. Ryszard craved power above all else and was merciless and cruel in crushing his enemies. His grim tactics are the stuff of nightmares, his torturous strategies designed to break the will of even the strongest opponent. He had one weakness, though. Ryszard loved the dragon, Forsilvra, a shimmering silver creature. Ancient lore tells of Forsilvra changing into a beautiful woman at night. Draegin, himself, is said to be the son of Ryszard and Forsilvra. It was in protecting their son from death that both Ryszard and Forsilvra perished at the end of the Elven Wars."

Finn sucked in a painful breath. "I didn't know that."

"Yes, it's some story," Floxx continued. "And in killing them, the high elves ended the war, though at bitter cost. Nearly two thirds of the elves who had fought had been killed; entire clans destroyed, their wondrous civilizations nearly annihilated. Even so, when the high elves met with the woodland elves to negotiate a final peace settlement, the Eldrow leaders refused to negotiate. Finally, the high elves wielded their remaining strength and power and banished all surviving woodland elves to the Caladrius Mountains to live underground. They were forbidden to have contact with anyone living above ground and those who did venture out were killed on sight." She adjusted the bandage on Finn's wound.

He scowled at the mountains, tentatively rotating his shoulder. "Underground? All these years? That's absolutely terrible for elves."

"Yes. It's done much damage. As ages passed, these underground elves changed in appearance. Their skin and hair paled to white; their eyes lost much of their color, lightening to a pale clay red. These elves still call themselves Eldrows."

Finn looked at her startled. "What? Those two are actually elves? Why, that's the one word she uttered so venomously just before she shot me!"

"Yes. They have forsaken their elven heritage and hate elves with a deep-rooted animosity that's been fed for generations. To Kalvara, you are the enemy. Your people banished her people underground."

Finn shook his head. "No, not my people, Floxx. I may have gotten my ears from a trace of elf blood, but there's little else in me that's elven. My father was Tomtee and my mother was human."

"Finn, that ancient elf leader, Trummarius, the one I mentioned, was your direct ancestor."

Finn looked at her in disbelief. "Impossible."

"Trummarius lived for thousands of years, as all elves did before the war. Eventually, he took a human wife and they had a son, Thatcher, who also lived for several millennia."

"Thatcher! Da's grandfather's name was Thatcher!"

"Exactly! I was very fond of Thatcher, half elf and half human. It seemed he got the best of both races. He married a Tomtee woman and they had a son, Tillary. And Tillary's son was Frederick, who was your father. So, you, Finn, are a fifth-generation elf."

Finn was shocked. "I can't believe it! I've actually always hoped it was so, but that was a child's dream." He laughed. "Fifth generation, you said. Is that somehow important?"

"Very important. In the fifth generation, the elf blood resurges! You are far more elven than you realize, my dear. Kalvara saw it right away." She saw Rory's face redden and winked at her. "And so did Rory!"

Chapter 12: Night of the Tennins

The sky darkened, and Rory carried an extra blanket to Aric, keeping her distance from Kalvara, then returned to her place by the fire. She got comfortable leaning against Cue, and gazed at the sky, watching for the Eldur Stars to come out.

Finn built up the fire against the night chill and sat down next to her, guarding his shoulder, and giving her a tender smile when she adjusted a bedroll for him to lean against. Her heart raced at his nearness and it must have shown on her face. She glanced up and caught Jakin frowning at them, then he quickly looked away, poking angrily at the fire. He was so jealous. She liked Jakin, but as a friend, nothing more.

She'd never thought any guys would be interested in her because of her scars. But now two of them were! Then, the truth hit her. She couldn't believe she hadn't seen it before. It's because she might be the King's daughter. That's what they're attracted to. Not her, not really. She looked at Finn and their eyes met. Was that true? Did Finn like her only because she might be royalty? She tried to look away but couldn't. He held her gaze with such a caring look, she couldn't help but smile at him. For now, she'd just enjoy it. When she turned back to the fire, Jakin got up and stalked to the trees where the packs were. She heard him banging things around. He was very angry.

Finn seemed oblivious to Jakin's petulance and leaned against his pack at an angle that gave him a view of Kalvara without seeming to stare at her. Rory could see he wasn't in too much pain. Floxx's poultice seemed to have helped. She also studied Kalvara and Aric covertly. Was she Aric's mother? But then, why did he call her Kalvara? She touched her face where Kalvara had spit on her. Why was she so hateful? And why were they alone out here, stealing food to survive?

Floxx sat down nearby and Rory smiled at her. "I loved your star story last night. Are there any more?"

"Yes, there are actually quite a few."

After everyone had settled by the fire, Floxx pointed to a spot in the sky. "Rory wants another star story, so, see the bright star about a hand's width above the horizon? That's the tip of the Sword of the King. As the sky darkens, you will see three dimmer stars that form the raised sword, itself. After that will come the King, holding its hilt. Now, look up, over the top of the cliffs across the pool. The sky is a bit too light, still, but in an hour or so you will be able to see the dragon emerge from a spot over the farthest waterfall. Tonight, we have a new moon, and the sky will be especially black, so even his scales will be visible."

Rory glanced over to see Aric staring at the sky. She caught his eye and motioned for him to join them, but he looked away and snuggled in with Kalvara, covering them both with his blanket.

Floxx continued. "This star story tells of a battle between a king and a dragon. Some say it has already happened, and there is at least one ancient story about it. Others say the battle has yet to be fought."

"What do you think, Floxx?" Finn asked.

"I think Eldurrin knows, but we can only guess."

Finn slid closer to Rory. A thrill exploded in the pit of her stomach. Whoa. Was this some kind of elven enchantment? She felt dizzy. Get a grip, she scolded herself. Remember what he's probably really after—a leg in with the King of Byerman. Well, no worries; slim chances that will ever happen.

She watched Jakin turn and look at them from the shadows, then stomp off into the woods. She felt so sorry for him. What a shame to miss this beautiful evening and Floxx's story. Couldn't he just calm down and be her friend?

"It's another ballad, but very different from the Ballad of the Eldur Crown. That one was slow and had a sadness to it. And it was historic, looking back. This one is upbeat, more of a battle march, and it is prophetic, looking forward."

Then Floxx stood up and began to sing a quick tune, clapping lightly to its rhythm.

From days of old, Eldurrin loved
The elven race and others.
He gave them bounty from above
Even his greatest treasures.

He made their home a winsome place
Where Tennins lived among them,
And humans, too, a blessed race
With all he could imagine.

The king will reign, Fa lei, Fa la.
No one can stand against him.
The battle rages through the ages,
Tis the plan of Eldurrin.

From far away the dire threat

Grew strong from dark desire.
Envy, greed, and anger fed
The enemy of fire.

First a shadow, then a dread
Crept over all the land.
The dragon wanting all elves dead
Attacked Eldurrin's band.

The king will reign, Fa lei, Fa la.
No one can stand against him.
The battle rages through the ages,
Tis the plan of Eldurrin.

A mighty King, an elven son
Then rose to give him fight.
With pow'r from Eldurrin's throne
Tore down the beast with might.

Upon his head, the Eldur crown,
His sword a fearsome blade
Forged by elves with skill renowned
From the fire Eldurrin made.

The king will reign, Fa lei, Fa la.
No one can stand against him.
The battle rages through the ages,
Tis the plan of Eldurrin.

Everyone was moving to the rhythm of the song, clapping and singing the refrain over and over. Even Zad had joined in, a rare smile on his face. Aric was sitting up, tapping his small hands on his knees.

Finn heard the noise before Rory did. She could feel his senses quicken as he shifted closer to her. It sounded like distant thunder, and the rumbling grew from aural to tactile, vibrating around them, or maybe they were vibrating in it, she couldn't tell. The air throbbed; the fire bloomed, then dimmed. Her heart constricted, thumping hard and irregular. What was this? She drew her knees up to her chest and curled over them, putting her hands over her head, and peeking out to see what she could. Nothing. She saw nothing. Yet, something was there, and its presence was weighty. She had difficulty sitting upright and felt powerless under its heaviness.

Finn wrapped an arm around her and pulled her close. If he knew what this was, he wasn't saying. She doubted he could have spoken anyway. Neither of them could move. Like being caught in a strong downdraft in an airplane, or on a centrifugal spinning ride at an amusement park that pressed you back in your seat and held you there, they were its captive; they had no choice but to sink with it, no power to overcome it. And yet, she wasn't afraid. She didn't understand why, thinking she should be terrified. Maybe she was dying. She let her arms slide to her sides and raised her head. It was like moving underwater.

She saw Finn's face was also turned upward. Whatever it was, whoever it was, it was peaceful. And something else: An ache, a yearning, welling from a place deep in her core; then it mushroomed, a thrilling, ecstatic ache, squeezing her stomach, tightening her throat, and erupting from her mouth in huge gulping sobs. Love. This presence, whatever, whoever, loved her. Like a mother loves her newborn child; like a widower loves his departed wife; like a soldier loves his fallen friend. She felt it, deep and overpowering in its cycle. Love. Grief. Peace. And under it all, joy. Not happiness, exactly. Not like making a perfect landing and hearing Dad applaud, not like hanging with her family on her birthday; more like sitting by the fire late at night when everyone was sleeping, wrapped in the warmth and silence; or camping under the stars, contemplating the enormity of the galaxies.

Rory watched as Floxx turned to face the Pool of Tennindrow, raised her hands to the sky, and transformed into the Firebird, lifting gracefully into the air, her wings beating in rhythm to the deep pulsations. She began to sing, lifting her head skyward as she'd done before. Rory began to distinguish other voices, deep basses, tenors and altos harmonizing with higher voices, all blending into a melodious chorus. Soon, hundreds of voices, rising and falling together, singing in a language she could not understand, and yet understood. They were worshipping. They were adoring this presence. She remembered what Floxx had said about the powerful one she called Eldurrin. The One who made everything. Her friend. Someone maybe she could know, too.

Finn, able somehow to move, stood and walked away from her, joining his voice to the great choir, reaching out both hands to Eldurrin. She had no ability to follow. She watched him walk a short distance toward the Pool and kneel in a patch of Tennifel. He lifted his face to the sky; he was weeping. Zad lay prostrate on the other side of the fire pit. Kalvara and Aric had pulled their blanket over their heads. *Who are you? What do you want with us? With Finn? With Zad? With me? Floxx said she brought me here to Gamloden at just the right time? The right time for what? Is what she told us true? Am I really here for a reason? The accident wasn't an accident?* And in response to her questions came another wave of love so profound, it tore her heart. How could love hurt so much?

The music gradually gave way to a voice, clearer and deeper than any voice she'd ever heard, resonating power and authority. The voice of Eldurrin! Finn fell under the weight of the invisible power. She struggled to keep her eyes on him. She didn't know if he'd need her, but wanted to be ready to run to him, help him, protect him. The tie that ran between them, that made her weak in his presence made her strong in his absence. She didn't understand, but she couldn't deny it.

"Finian." The voice spoke to him! "You and the others here tonight have felt my power and the depths of my love for you. I've come with my mighty army to talk with you in the presence of my Firebird, who is Floxx; she has been with me since the beginning. It is time for the ancient prophecies to be fulfilled. I have sent her to help you accomplish what was planned long before the ages began. She hears my voice and will tell you what to do. Listen to her. Trust her. Follow her."

The heaviness lifted. Rory looked up to see blue orbs—hundreds upon hundreds—hovering over the Pool of Tennindrow. And the Firebird was resplendent, wings spread above the middle of the pool, shimmering in vibrant colors, her reflection brilliant on the water below.

Finn stood, unsteady, visibly shaken.

"Don't be afraid," the Firebird assured him. "You are among friends. These are Tennins."

And before her eyes, each of the blue orbs transformed into a warrior-like being. They were huge, all of them twice the size of a human, and many greater still. Some had wings, some did not. Some had human features, others had heads like various beasts—a lion, an ox, a bear. Some were covered with shining scales, others with fur. All of them had weapons. Great bows were slung over many shoulders, others held immense maces; many wore swords at their sides. They filled the sky, fearsome in strength, formidable in power.

The Firebird spoke. "Finian, son of Frederick, son of Tillary, son of Thatcher, son of Trummarius, the High Elf, tonight I speak for Eldurrin. He has confirmed that the time has come to restore the Eldur Crown. The events of the ages have led to this very moment. You, Finian, have been called to be that chosen King of whom the legends speak. You, Finian, can find and restore the Eldur Crown. You, Finian, are the one who can bring peace to Gamloden for all the ages to come. Finian, these are feats far beyond your own capability, impossible to accomplish in just your strength, and yet Eldurrin has called you to do this. Therefore, he, himself, will go with you; he will supply the strength you need; the wisdom, the power, the direction. Though without him you would fail; with him, you can accomplish all that he has asked. And he has sent me, this mighty army of Tennins, and those who are with you tonight to help you. He will not, however, force you. He puts before you a choice. You can take up the challenge and fulfill your destiny, or you can say no. The fate of Gamloden is in your hands."

Rory's eyes widened. *What a calling! What an honor! I hope he does it. He has so much help with the Tennins and the Firebird and those with him. Wait, I am one of those with him! Am I included in helping him fulfill this tremendous calling? Whoa. This is a lot more important than maybe being a long-lost princess. There is something really big happening here.*

Finn stared at the Firebird. He licked his lips and looked stricken, uncertain; fear flickered across his face. He bowed his head and for a few moments, teetered on the edge of his decision.

Trust him, Finn. Trust Eldurrin. Say yes. I will help you.

Then, he straightened, his legs growing steady, his shoulders squared, and held his head high. "I accept Eldurrin's call," he shouted. "I will do all I can, and trust Eldurrin to do what I cannot. May his purpose be fulfilled, and may he be pleased with my service."

At the Firebird's command, the Tennins came to Finn. One by one, they gave their names, vowed protection and aid, then bowed before him. He met Ingall, a human-like giant with wings, fitted with a sword as tall as Finn; Navid, a bear who could walk on two legs or four, with dagger-like claws on each of his paws. Erela, a two-legged creature with the head of a fox, one of the smallest and lithest of the throng, wielded a slender, but deadly, dagger. Melangell had two large curved horns on his oxen head; his muscular shoulders were the size of small boulders. He stood on two hoofed feet and grasped an enormous spiked club in one hand. Tenshi appeared nearly human though covered in a glistening, armor-like skin, with four wings that moved him swiftly in any direction. On and on they came, until all of them had sworn allegiance.

Then the Firebird said, "There is one more, Finn. Look to your side."

Cue was lying next to him, thumping his tail and gazing up at the Tennin who had been with Rory all of her life. She couldn't believe it! His blue orb was a warrior who towered above Finn, nine or ten feet tall. He was covered with coarse black fur and bulging with muscles. Folded behind his back were enormous silver wings. His countenance was fierce; keen understanding shone in his dark eyes, which sat deeply recessed in the gigantic head of a wolf. "I am Uriel," he bowed, his words edged in a growl.

Uriel! I had the mightiest of Tennins guarding me my whole life? Eldurrin, how do you know me? Why have you have been so good to me, caring for me since the day I was born?

Uriel turned to the throng of Tennins. "Hail, Finian!" he boomed, and the entire assembly of Tennins took up the chant, the clamor so intense it shook rocks loose from the surrounding cliffs. They careened from great heights, crashing into the Tennindrow river, piling one on top of the other, creating a stone tribute to the wondrous night. Finn fell face down into the Tennifel. Rory fell, too, and remembered nothing more until morning.

Chapter 13: Specter

Jakin pushed his way through the forest fuming out loud. He couldn't believe Rory liked Finn and not him. Why couldn't she see that he was the one who really cared about her? He'd give her anything she wanted. From the moment he'd seen her, before he'd had any idea she was a princess, he'd known she was the one for him. But she was all eyes for Finn. It made him sick. He stormed for some time, oblivious to his surroundings, gripped by his anger. Night fell fully and with it the realization he had no idea where he was, or which path would lead him out. What did it matter? He stood dejected in the dark. They probably didn't even notice he was gone. He might as well be invisible.

He sat slumped against a tree trunk, arms tight across his chest, staring into the dark. A raven cawed nearby, and the night sounds seemed suddenly loud; a rustle in the tree top as a bird settled, a scuffle in the leaves as some small creature scurried past. A trikle, maybe. He'd never seen one of the tiny leathery animals, but he knew they liked blood, puncturing prey with their sole needlelike tooth and sucking their fill. Or, worse, a snink—sleek, fanged lizards that ate trikles. He pulled his legs up to his chest.

Craning his neck, he could see stars through the gaps in the branches. They seemed especially bright. He thought about Floxx and the star story she'd sung last night. Who was she? What was she? Had she really been there when Eldurrin placed the stars? How was that even possible? And what about Eldurrin? So many held him in awe, but who was he, really? Was he watching? Did he care about him at all? Did he know how hurt he felt? He pulled Werner's cloak around him, covering his head with the hood, thankful for its warmth and closed his eyes. He'd just rest a few minutes, then try to find his way back.

He woke to find himself curled on the ground beneath the tree. His left hip was sore from laying on a protruding rock. He wiped sleepy seeds out of his eyes, yawned and pushed the hood off his head. The sky was light gray, and dawn wasn't far off. He sat up, heart racing. He couldn't believe he'd slept all night! What if they didn't even realize he was missing and left without him? He had to get back.

He stood and brushed debris from his cloak. Just as he turned to leave, a branch snapped behind him. He spun around and peered into the surrounding forest. Nothing but trees. He stood very still and listened. His skin prickled.

"Who's there?"

Out of the corner of his eye he saw a tall thin shape. He froze.

"Don't be afraid." Its voice was deep and smooth. "I've been here all night, watching you. If I'd meant to harm you, I would have."

Jakin could see no one. "Show yourself," he said, annoyed at his own quavering voice.

The form moved but he could see no more than a shimmer at its edges.

"Who are you? What do you want? What are you doing here?"

"Ssso many questions," the voice held a hint of amusement. "May I come closer?"

Before Jakin could answer, it approached, its movement smooth and soundless, stopping a few feet away. It smelled vaguely of smoke. And metal. Like hot iron smells when it's pulled from the fire in a blacksmith's shop. The figure stood at least a foot taller than Jakin and very thin, its face obscured by a hooded cape; the growing light catching on its iridescent cloth. While it looked manlike, Jakin doubted it was human.

"Sssee now. There'sss nothing to fear." A rhythmic voice, soothing, hypnotic.

"What do you want?" Jakin repeated, pulling himself up to his full height and squaring his shoulders. He would not be intimated by it.

"I've been wondering the sssame thing about you."

"I don't want a thing. I was just leaving."

"Leaving? To go back to your camp? They don't even know you're gone."

"How do you …."

"They had quite a time last night. I could hear sssome of it. Celebrating that girl, no doubt."

Jakin caught his breath.

"You know, the pretty one you like ssso much."

"Rory." Jakin immediately regretted blurting her name.

"Yesss, Rory. The lost princesss."

Dread curled in Jakin's stomach. How did this creeper know about Rory?

"She should be yoursss, you know. Because of how deeply you care for her."

Jakin took a step back. How could this specter possibly know how he felt?

"I could make her love you. Yesss, I certainly could do that."

Jakin glared at it. "Stay away from her. From both of us." Then, he turned to leave.

"There isss much that can harm you in these woods. Had I not been here to protect you...." The figure looked to its left. Jakin followed its gaze and saw several wolves, their eyes gleaming in the shadows. He struggled to control his panic. How would he get out alive?

"It'sss that way," the creature lifted its arm, pointing a long skinny finger. "Keep the sssun behind you." Its voice was entrancing.

Jakin tried to walk but his feet were stuck like in a nightmare where he struggled to run from attack but couldn't.

"Here." The figure moved close to him. The air chilled.

Jakin recoiled, turning his face away.

"Now, now, I won't hurt you," it said. "I want to help you. With Rory. Give thisss to her. Make sure you fasten it on her wrist, yourself." The specter held something out but Jakin leaned away. No way was he taking that. But the thin arm reached around him and dropped it into a pocket of his pack.

"Now, go."

In that instant, Jakin's feet were freed from whatever had held them and he strode away, terrified the wolves would follow him.

"I'll sssee you, again, Jakin."

The horrifying creature knew his name! Without a glance back, he tore into a run, sprinting for all he was worth.

Chapter 14: Cue

Rory woke well before dawn with an uneasy feeling. As she sat up, Floxx came over to her. "Something doesn't feel right," she whispered.

"I feel it, too," Floxx said. "Let's wake the others and pack up."

The group needed no second warning and hurried. As Finn strapped down his gear, he glanced around for Jakin and not seeing him, asked if anyone knew where he was. His blanket was still rolled up by the embers.

As if in answer, Jakin burst through the trees, startling the horses, and scaring them half to death. "Wolves," he gasped. "A whole pack of them. Not far behind."

They bolted for the horses, Finn leading the group and setting a brisk pace. Aric rode with Rory after Kalvara shushed his crying, and she rode ahead with Floxx.

When the trail widened, Zad urged his donkey next to Finn. "You can count on me, Finn. I'm with you."

"Thanks," Finn said, and looked away, blushing. Rory wondered what he was thinking. She had hoped to talk with him this morning. It had been such a huge night for him, the revealing of his incredible calling;

the memories of winged Tennins very fresh in their minds. And yet, here they were at dawn running from wolves. She didn't know what to think. Did he struggle with the irony, too? Aric pointed, jostling her out of her reverie.

To the east, they could see the pool mirroring the cliffs, now frosted with pink clouds. The river dove from its great height, crashing boldly, its droplets like scattered jewels. The first ray of light touched the pillar of rocks sculpted from the night's celebration, unmoved by the swift current rushing around it. It stood solid and sure, a fitting reminder of Eldurrin's promise. After the daunting display of power and fealty last night, Rory figured Eldurrin and Floxx would do their parts. But what about Finn? Could he be as strong as that monument or would he be washed away? And what about her?

An hour later, they reached the Tennindrow River. It ran through a shallow rocky gorge about twenty feet wide, then disappeared around a bend into the forested foothills of the Caladruis Mountains. One by one the horses crossed with their riders, with Zad crossing last on Beast, whose short legs were completely submerged in the deepest places. Finally, Cue plunged in and swam across. Finn, standing next to Rory pointed out the orb floating above the dog's head. Uriel was with them! They were both suddenly encouraged; they were not alone. The Tennins had vowed protection and were staying with them! Finn squeezed her hand and they laughed as Zad reached their side of the river, complaining loudly about his soggy boots.

They moved north all morning, wary of wolves, but seeing none. Their pace slowed as the path disappeared and they picked their way up the foothills. The trees grew closer together, forcing them to ride single file, weaving their way through the shadows. Cue took the lead, Finn trusting the dog's instinct to know the way and Uriel to protect. They turned east in search of the bridge that spanned the Caladrius River—the same bridge, Floxx said, over which Cue had carried Rory sixteen years ago. She shuddered at the thought.

The trees gradually thinned, and they emerged into a small glade, ringed with shrubs and trees. On its far side was a grove of black-trunked eucalyptus trees. Finn saw the hair on the back of Cue's neck bristle and raising his hand for silence, slid off his horse. It was utterly silent. No birds, not even insects. Finn took his bow, fitted an arrow to it and walked slowly into the clearing.

Just as he approached its center, a wolf sprang at him from behind the barrier of foliage. Cue flew from the edge and barreled into the wolf, knocking it over. They snapped and snarled, twisting and lunging, each seeking the other's soft flesh. A second wolf leapt from behind Finn and knocked him over just as Cue yelped and crumbled in a bloody heap. The center of the grove exploded in blue light and Uriel loomed, huge and terrifying, his wolf head contorted in a vicious snarl as he grabbed the slathering beasts off Finn and Cue breaking their thick necks as if they were kindling.

Six more wolves attacked all at once from different directions. Rory wrapped her arms around Aric, terrified to move and terrified not to. Zad swung at the closest wolf, his ax wielding a deadly gash. Jakin crouched with his bow and slayed one as it sprung for Rory. Her horse spooked and reared, throwing them to the ground. Jakin stood in front of them, defending them with his bow, but was attacked from behind, the wolf's jaw missing his neck, but raking his shoulder.

Zad ran shouting at it, swinging his ax and driving it off.

Floxx stood blocking Kalvara, whose hands were tied behind her, and Rory grabbed a bow as Aric ran to her. The wolf that had bitten Jakin turned to her, blood on its face. She shot, but her shaking hands missed their mark, hitting its shoulder, not its neck, enraging it further. Uriel was there in an instant, caught it by its tail and smashed it against a tree.

Three wolves remained, wary now of the power of their opponents. They crouched together for a second then sprang, two for Rory, the third for Aric. Kalvara threw herself on the child as a human shield. But the wolf fell dead at her side, pierced by Finn's arrow.

Rory screamed as pain shot through her leg; one of the wolves was tearing at her ankle. Jakin's arrow lodged in its hip and it released its grip, howling and limping away. The last wolf leapt for her neck; she was sure she was going to die. But Finn shot from behind her, piercing its eye, the arrow's tip protruding out the back of its skull as it fell lifeless on top of her. Jakin shoved the beast off her and helped her sit up. Finn knelt by her feet, gently manipulating her ankle. It hurt, but she couldn't focus on it.

She was watching Cue, still laying where he'd fallen. Why hadn't he moved? She hobbled over and knelt by him, stroking his head and saying his name over and over. He did not respond. She shook him, gently at first, then harder; he had to wake up. He'd been hurt before, but he'd always survived. But, this time, no rough tongue licked her, no gross dog breath blew in her face. She gripped the thick ruff of his neck and sobbed. Looking up, she pleaded with Uriel. "Can't you save him?"

The Tennin shook his head. "Eldurrin has him now. His time in Gamloden is over."

"But I need him now, more than ever!" Sobs racked her; she couldn't get her breath.

Uriel knelt by them and stroked Cue's head. "He was a faithful dog and a fearless protector. He guarded you until the time came for you to return here, which set the prophecy into motion. Apparently, he has completed his part in Eldurrin's unfolding story. I will miss him greatly."

As upset as she was, Rory wondered what Uriel was talking about. Her return set the prophecy in motion? She must have misunderstood. Last night set the prophecy in motion. They all witnessed it. She took a shuddering breath and laid her head on Cue. The others had the decency to leave her alone with him for a few minutes.

"We should bury him," she said brokenly. "Will you help me find a good spot?"

"Of course," Floxx said, walking over with the others. "But first, let's have a look at your leg."

It was late afternoon by the time they finished tending each other's injuries. They carried Cue from the bloody grove, strewn with wolf carcasses and already starting to smell, and buried him in a deep grave to hide his scent from predators. Then they sat near it, passing around water and food. No one had much of an appetite, but they ate, not knowing when they'd have their next chance.

Kalvara, now unbound, sat with Aric sleeping against her. Mean as she was, Aric brought out a gentle side.

Floxx passed her the sack of apples, smiling at the child. "May I ask you a question?"

Kalvara actually nodded. Not even a hiss.

"How are you two related?"

Kalvara's eyes hardened. She glanced at them, clearly struggling with whether to answer. "He is my brother's son. Both his father and mother are dead."

"I'm so sorry," Floxx said and clearly meant it. She passed the water and Kalvara drank, then poured some in a small skin she carried.

"You know it was Finn's arrow that saved you from the wolf," Floxx said. "It should be clear we mean you no harm."

Kalvara held her head high. "I did not intend to harm anyone, either. Only to take what food we needed to live."

"No harm, eh?" Zad countered. "What, then, do you call an arrow aimed at Finn's heart?"

Kalvara glanced at Finn, then back at Zad, uncertainly flickering in her copper eyes. "I was taught to kill his kind." She stood, grasping Aric.

Floxx stood, too, and looked her in the eye. "The past cannot be changed, Kalvara. You have no power to undo the deeds of Finn's ancestors, or your own, but neither are you bound to perpetuate them. You know the evil that thrives underground."

Fear brushed Kalvara's face.

"You also witnessed the night of the Tennins. You know what is at stake here. Choose the side on which you will fight."

Kalvara held herself rigid, every sinew of her body tense. She hesitated as she made up her mind. She looked past Floxx and spoke directly to Finn, her words terse. "I have chosen to let you live, elf. Your life for mine."

"Wait just a minute, now!" Zad strode over to stand in front of her, bringing himself to his full height as he looked up at her haughty face. "The elf saved two lives—the boy's and yours. 'Tis two great favors you owe him, and I can't agree that letting 'im live should count as one 'o them."

The edges of Kalvara's mouth tipped up for a moment as she regarded Zad. "Well, then, Master Dwarf," she looked down at him with one eyebrow raised. "Here's another favor. The entrance to the underground Trow caves is just the other side of that grove of Eucalyptus trees. They emerge at night—detestable creatures, bent on dark deeds. If I were you, I'd put as much distance between you and them as you can before dusk." And in one fluid motion, Kalvara swung Aric to her hip, turned gracefully and ran back in the direction from which they'd come.

"Well, if that don't beat all!" Zad huffed as Kalvara disappeared.

Finn stood and brushed himself off. "That second favor is worth listening to. We'd best be moving on." He eyed the sun just a few hand-widths above the horizon. "We've got an hour or two before sunset. Let's put some miles behind us."

The path widened not far from the grove, making it possible for two to ride abreast. The sun, low at their backs, cast long shadows ahead. They traveled in silence, tired and engrossed in their own thoughts. Rory couldn't believe Cue was gone. He'd been with her all of her life. Her heart was broken; she'd loved him so much. She felt so vulnerable without him; never realizing how much she'd depended on him for protection. As the sun sank below the horizon, noisy birds jostled for places in the trees, hurrying to get settled before nightfall. The smell of damp earth rose. Finn led the way off the trail to a fairly level place between a stand of gray-knotted birch trees.

"With any luck," Finn said smiling, "we'll be in Masirika in a day or two." That didn't cheer Rory up at all. Even if they did meet the King, she'd be there without Cue. This wasn't what she'd planned. Neither were Tennins, prophecies, hostile Eldrows, and wolf attacks. What had she gotten herself into? Too tired to bother with a fire, they ate a cold dinner, wrapped in their blankets and slept.

Chapter 15: Kidnapped

Sometime in the night, Floxx shook each of them awake. Rory sat up in a flash, and Floxx covered her mouth, warning her not to speak. She saw that Kalvara was waking the others. What was Kalvara doing here? She should be miles away by now.

"Dragon," Floxx whispered pointing up. Rory's heart nearly stopped. Dragon! Wolves weren't enough? The dragon was hunting her, too? Wait, why was she the target? It should be Finn, not her. She was just here temporarily and not by choice, either. Finn's the guy, the chosen ruler. She was just a princess. Perhaps.

Kalvara motioned for them to follow her and they moved as quickly as possible, leading the horses through the dark. Thankfully, the moon was out, about three-quarters full; otherwise, there was no way they could have stayed on the path. Rory scanned the sky looking for signs of a dragon, not really knowing what that might be, sparks, maybe. But she saw nothing but tree tops and stars. The air felt weird, though, she could feel it in her ears, a kind of pressure change every couple of seconds, like a giant bellows was moving air. What was that from?

They wound through the woods to a cave about a half mile from where they'd camped. Bushes hid its entrance, which stood about five feet high, and opened to twice that height inside. It was a huge inky black cavern; Rory could barely see her hand in front of her face. They moved the animals deep into the cave, no easy task in the blackness. Then they waited, huddled together, barely daring to breathe. It wasn't long before the bushes began scraping against the cave. Those swooshing pressure changes grew stronger. Rory looked at Kalvara and pointed to her ears, eyebrows raised in question. Kalvara held out her arms, made flying motions, and pointed up.

The dragon. It must be huge to move that much air. And it was after her. She hoped no one else got hurt because of her. It made no sense, but trouble seemed to chase her. Deadly trouble. Why had Floxx brought her back here? The dragon was nearly overhead; branches beat against the cave, allowing her to glimpse snatches of the night outside. Her ears hurt, she covered them with her hands and squeezed her eyes shut. The horses nickered and skittered about; the seconds passed slowly, each one a nightmare. She braced for a blast of fire to scorch the bushes and rip through the cave. She dared a peek and caught a glimpse of an immense shadow gliding away, like a large cloud driven by the wind. The painful pulsing of the air gradually lessened. The dragon had flown past them; it was leaving!

If Kalvara hadn't come back for them, they might all be dead. Rory studied her, Aric wrapped tight in her arms, protecting him until she was sure it was safe. She'd risked a lot to come warn them. Kalvara met her eyes and Rory nodded in silent thanks. And ever so slightly, in a tiny gesture Rory almost missed, Kalvara nodded back.

"How's your foot?" Finn whispered, touching Rory's arm as dawn lightened the cave.

"So much better. Walking should be easier today." She smiled at him. "Your shoulder?"

"Near good as new. Amazing plant, that Tennifel."

They waited until the sun was fully above the horizon before leaving the cave, wanting to be completely sure there would be no Trows prowling about. Finn led the way on foot, one hand on his horse's reins, the other lifting low-hanging branches as they wove their way through the woods looking for the trail. Rory walked close to him, alert for another attack. Finn held himself taller; even his stride was more confident. She admired him. Trusted him. Eldurrin had picked a good man. The others followed in silence. She glanced behind. Even Aric, young as he was, knew well the importance of stealth and clung to Kalvara, making no noise.

Once they reached the trail, they climbed on the animals. Kalvara handed Aric to Zad. Her finger on her lips reminded the child to stay silent, but caution couldn't quench the boy's wide grin at the prospect of a donkey ride with a dwarf. Finn took the lead, waiting for Kalvara to join him. She was familiar with the area and had agreed to lay her animosity aside long enough to guide them across the bridge, through the thinning woods on the other side of the Caladrius River until they had the city of Masirika in sight. Kalvara stared straight ahead, her head high and chin up. Finn thanked her for helping them hide from the dragon and for guiding them to the city. Kalvara, her long strides matching the gait of his horse, frowned and said nothing. That was big of Finn. He seemed to have forgiven her for trying to kill him. Rory really hoped they could trust her, but she'd be watching her every move.

They heard the rumble of the river as they neared the bridge; around a curve, past a stand of trees, and there it was, wide and gray, running fast under the morning overcast. Kalvara raised her arm and they stopped. They could hear the thunder of the falls some distance to the south, where the river careened into Changeling Lake, hundreds of feet below. The air smelled wet; the leaden sky pressed low. This was not the kind of day Rory'd pictured for visiting a castle. A haunted house, maybe. It was creepy here. Zad shifted in his saddle and whispered, "There, now" to Aric, his words breaking the silence. Floxx ran from her rear position to talk with Kalvara.

"Something's not right."

"No. I sense it, too."

A raven screeched in the distance.

Floxx raised her arms above her head, pressing her hands together. Rory watched as her fingers shimmered first, then the light raced down her body like fire on a dry leaf, growing so bright she couldn't make out her features. Then, as quickly as it had bloomed, the cloak of light faded, and the Firebird emerged, feathers sparkling like the sun on fresh snow. Rory's heart leapt to her throat and she reached out and touched the Firebird, so magnificent, yet fearsome. Taller than Kalvara, the Firebird tipped her head at them, spread her great wings and lifted gracefully to the steely sky, disappearing almost immediately into the overcast.

An instant later, an enormous Roc streaked across the sky, its shrill shriek piercing the air. Rory held her breath as the Firebird answered the challenge, her call fierce and strong. She searched the sky a few moments longer, hoping for a glimpse, but their cries faded into the distance.

Finn signaled them to move off the trail, and as they did, a dozen broad-shouldered brutes attacked from behind the cover of the surrounding trees. One wielded a double-bladed ax, its edges still coated with dried blood and bits of fur from its last unfortunate victim. It shrieked unnervingly with each thundering step.

Another grinned wildly, its sharp teeth snapping as it flung knife after knife at them. They scattered and dove for cover. A particularly tall thug snarled behind two fangs a foot long that curved like tusks. His six-fingered hand grasped a huge wooden lance, eight feet tall at least, and five or six inches thick, notched along its length for grip, and chiseled at its end to a sharp, sturdy point, shiny and foul with stench from the bowels it had recently pierced.

Finn leapt off his horse, his arrows flying before his feet hit the ground. As he diverted the attackers, Rory whisked Aric from Zad, then on impulse tossed her bow and quiver of arrows to Kalvara before she galloped away. Kalvara was a dead shot—way better than she was—and she didn't want anyone else dying on her account, most certainly not a child.

When they'd gotten a safe distance away, she and Aric crawled under a thick bush and watched. The warriors worked in pairs. The two coming toward Jakin grunted occasionally at each other, their words guttural and broken. "Eat," one said, but the other pushed him away. Jakin's arrow flew at the one who pushed, hitting it in the chest, but doing no harm except to enrage.

Rory saw their warts, thick, armor-like bulges that covered their monstrous bodies. They wore filthy loin cloths, held with rough ropes that barely concealed their private parts. One carried a club, caked with pieces of skin and coarse hair and the creature shook it, bellowing as he neared Jakin. The other shoved him aside and swung his mace. Jakin jumped aside, aimed his arrow at the attacker's hand and let it fly. With a roar, it dropped its mace, blood spurting from its hand. The other clubbed him out of the way and moved in for the kill. Jakin ducked behind a small tree that cracked under the force of the next blow. He had no time to fit an arrow as the enraged brute closed in on him. *Oh no, Jakin! Run!* But then, something small whirred by Jakin and he instinctively ducked. It was a knife. It lodged in the eye of his attacker, who crumpled just feet from him. Its greasy hair fell away from its face, and Rory glimpsed a brand on its forehead—a crown on the head of a dragon.

Kalvara's arrow hit between the eyes of the sharp-toothed knife thrower, who fell backward, dead before he hit the ground. Zad, wielding his ax, ducked beneath a great swipe of a mace, and returned fight with a slice that cut off the hand of the warrior. As it spun around in agony, Finn drilled an arrow between its warts, deep into its heart. Finn was good, he was really good; Rory's eyes could not see any vulnerable spots. Kalvara was backed against a tree, desperately fighting one of the hulks, jabbing at it with a dagger. With a roar of rage, Zad threw his ax, lodging it deeply in a soft spot at the base of the brute's neck. Zad, who had hated her for trying to kill Finn, had saved her life.

Without warning, a strong hand gripped Rory's foot and yanked her out from under the bush. She shoved Aric away, horrified. She kicked and screamed, but it was like fighting a grizzly. The giant held her upside down, laughing, drooling, grunting, then effortlessly flipped her over his shoulder and took off running. She screamed as loud as she could, but there was so much commotion, no one heard her. The rest of the brutes noticed, though, and turned from the fight to join them, moving quickly through the woods.

Rory pounded on her captor's warty back. "I'm not staying," she yelled, beating him with her fists. "Let me go! I want to go home." In response, the brute knocked her hard against a tree. The last thing she heard was Finn shouting her name.

Chapter 16: Dew

Dew and Catkin were exhausted from running. It had been a long while since they had seen any guards. The ceiling of the tunnel was lower than it had been, and its curve tightened as it wound its way downhill. They slowed to a cautious walk in the blackness, unable to see what was ahead. Dew finally stopped to listen. As his pounding heart settled down, he could hear the faint sound of dripping water. He led the way toward it, creeping with one hand on the wall to his right, the other extended into the inky blackness. Catkin clutched his back. The texture of the wall changed, its rough surface now riddled with holes. The dripping grew louder.

"Careful, Dew," Catkin cautioned. "Maybe the ground has holes, too, and we don't want to fall in." And, in fact, just ahead, the ground abruptly ended. Dew flailed on its edge and Cat pulled him back to safety. Shaken, they sat, clutching each other and resting, listening to the drops fall into the blackness with a soft splash.

"I wonder how much water's down there." Dew stared into the blackness until his eyes were finally able to discern a ledge that wound its way to the bottom. "I think we can climb down."

After a long, tedious descent, they reached the bottom and walked hand in hand to the pool of water, extremely thirsty and hoping it was drinkable. Dew ladled a handful into his mouth. "It's a wee bit slimy, Cat, but it slides right down me parched throat. I can't go much longer without a drink, so I'm hopin' I don't die from it." Catkin drank, as well. The blackness was not so solid there, giving way to grays. Everything was moist.

"Look at these walls. Like honeycomb."

"It's the water, Dew. It's eaten through the rock. But let's not linger; some dark life sleeps here. I can feel it."

"Lemme just take a look," Dew insisted, already climbing a short distance to explore a honeycomb crevice. He crawled into one of the holes and froze. About two feet from his head, a white snake was poised to strike. He held his breath, trying not to move. Involuntarily, he shuddered, sending a dusting of loose sandstone down the rock wall. The snake turned its head at the sound. Dew stared. It had no eyes! Deftly, he grasped a loose piece of sandstone. With a silent flick of his wrist, he sent it bouncing down the wall, away from where Catkin waited.

The snake turned instantly toward the sound and sent a spray of venom in a perfectly aimed arch that caught the pebble midair on its way down. Then, it slithered down the wall to meet it where it landed. Dew leapt noiselessly to Catkin and they squeezed behind a tiny crack in the porous rock. The blind serpent had reached its quarry and, discovering it was not edible, lifted its head, its tongue tasting the air. It opened its mouth, revealing long sharp fangs as it flicked its tongue. Then, it flattened out and slowly slithered toward the ghillies. Dew and Catkin watched through the crack. Its eyeless head turned one way, then the other as it listened for movement, its tongue tasting the air. Its jaw would open every so often and unhinge, then snap back together. They held their breath as the snake slithered near their hiding place, so close they could hear its scales scraping against the rock.

Then, they heard hissing. Another snake, smaller and pale yellow, coiled at the approach of the white one. The two serpents struck at each other, hissing and writhing, coiling and biting. The white snake shot a spray of venom directly into the yellow one's gaping mouth. It took only minutes to paralyze its victim. Then, the white snake unhinged its jaw and swallowed the yellow one. Hunger sated, it slithered off, disappearing into the vapors around the pool.

"Let's get out of here," Dew said.

The ghillies made their way around the steaming water, staying as far from its edge as possible, then turned into the next tunnel. It seemed they'd walked forever. Down, always down they went, the tunnel a giant corkscrew twisting through the mountain. Finally, they heard noise. The space opened in front of them where many torches lit a vast cave. A rank odor pervaded the space. On one side a large guarded cell held dozens of tall, emaciated, pale-skinned people. Their white hair, ragged and filthy, hung past their shoulders. One of them gripped the gate's iron bars, eyes red and furious. Others stood staring, hands over their mouths. But, most of them sat, slumped, clutching their knees, waiting. Drums pounded. Boom. Boom-boom. Boom. Boom-boom. Boom.

They crept around the edge of the open area, breathing shallow against the vile smell. It was patrolled by guards like the ones in the Queen's throne room. Inozak. Dew and Catkin crouched in terror. A line of the white-haired people was being forced forward, all male, stripped to ragged loin cloths. An enormous Inozak stood at the front, handing each man a vial of liquid to drink. One refused. He was dragged a few feet away and held down by two guards, while a third decapitated him, tossing the bloody head to the center of the room to join the skulls of previous protestors. A cloud of flies lifted as the head hit, then quickly resumed their swarming.

"Dew," Cat whispered. "Let's go; I'm going to be sick." They skirted past, hugging the dark edges, avoiding the increasing violence of those who'd drunk the potion. Amid much shoving and punching, the men were herded down a tunnel, disappearing into the gloom. Boom. Boom-boom. Boom. Boom-boom. Boom. When the drums stopped for a moment, they heard shrieks and screams coming from the depths of that tunnel. Dew's stomach twisted. What was going on?

"Hurry," Cat pleaded.

Seeing Cat's stricken face, he grabbed her hand and they leapt away, leaving the horrific scene behind. Dew could feel her trembling. "You all right?"

She was staring at the floor, one hand over her mouth, swallowing rapidly. She shook her head.

"Let's keep moving, then, if ye can," Dew said, wanting to get as far away as possible.

They kept to the darkest places and finding another tunnel, crept into it. Crude rooms had been hollowed from the rock on each side. Some held ogres, huge with child. Others held their squalling offspring. Some whelps had white hair and gray skin like the men they'd just seen drugged; others had the bulk and greenish coloring of ogres. All of them had warts.

"Cat, they're breeding those men to the ogres. And by the looks of it, forcing them to do it or die."

Skinny, sullen Trows worked the whelps, roughly examining them. "Six fingers, only, for Inozak," a large Trow ordered. These were tossed in a wagon and hauled away. The others were further sorted and moved in different directions.

The tunnel overlooked a huge, high-ceilinged cave, in which hundreds of young Inozak practiced drills and maneuvers under the direction of their hulking leaders.

"An army, Catkin. They're breeding an army."

Several tunnels branched off from the training room and they had no idea which one to take. Finally, Dew turned down one, saying, "The air in here doesn't smell so bad." They wound slowly down, down, walking carefully in utter blackness, groping for the wall and clutching each other. They lost all awareness of time; they might have walked a couple of hours, they might have walked an entire day; they had no way of judging. Finally, hungry, thirsty, and exhausted, they sat down, arms linked, backs against the wall and fell asleep.

A shrill noise scratched the air, loud enough to wake them.

"Now what?" Dew asked, his voice strained.

"Whatever it is, it's not close. Let's just stay here and rest a while longer."

Neither of them could rest, though, as the screeching grew louder. Then, another joined it, and another, until the tunnel was alive with screams and screeches and howls and shrieks. The ghillies had nowhere to run, no place to hide. There were no holes to crawl into, no crevices to squeeze behind. The tunnel walls were solid and smooth. So, they lay down single-file flat on their bellies, heads uphill, facing away from the approaching terror. Catkin buried her feet under Dew's shoulders and reached back to grip his outstretched hands.

The screeching grew louder. Then came the sound of wings. The air ruffled as something flew past. Soon, the tunnel was full of them, their cacophony of shrieks seeming to say, "Azzzzwang, Azzzzwang," as they swerved through the darkness. Dew ventured a peek. Bats! Hundreds, maybe thousands, of them. Large bats, the size of owls. But it wasn't their size that frightened him, it was their heads. They did not have bat heads; they had human skulls with living red eyes in the boney sockets. Their open mouths revealed long sharp teeth. Vampire bats, he realized with a surge of terror.

Chapter 17: The Chase

Jakin pulled Zad's knife from the dead Inozak's eye, wiped it on some thick undergrowth, and handed it to Zad. "Thanks, brother. You saved my life."

Zad clapped him on the shoulder. "Well then, I'm countin' on ye t' return the favor." He scanned the sky. "Where d'you suppose the Firebird is?"

"No way to know." Jakin adjusted his quiver. "And Rory. Have you seen her?"

Aric raced past, throwing himself into Kalvara's arms. "They took her!" He pointed. "And they nearly got me, too, but she pushed me away, so they couldn't reach me."

Finn spotted her. "Rory! Rory!" he shouted. "We're coming after you!"

Jakin whipped around and saw her hanging limply over the shoulder of one of the beasts, disappearing into the woods. They were moving fast, winding deftly through the trees, nearly out of sight.

Kalvara shook her head and said to the others. "Inozak. Draegin's army."

Jakin's heart lurched. No! Dread began to grow in him, its sinister tentacles squeezing the breath out of him. Somehow, he knew before he'd even fully figured it out. It had been Draegin that night in the woods—that terrible specter. It made sense. Morbid, predictable sense. The wolves, the dragon, the Inozak—all after Rory. Clearly Draegin wanted to kill her. Why? What huge threat could she possibly pose? Then he remembered the bracelet in his pack. I can make her love you, it'd said. Draegin wanted to use him as a pawn to get to her. Well, two can play at this game. If she loved him, he could protect her. And with that thought in mind, he decided what he'd do.

He caught a flicker of blue over Rory's head. "Look! Look there! Uriel's with her!" Hope rose and allowed him to breathe, again. "Let's go." He reached for his horse's reins.

Kalvara stopped him. "The animals cannot come. The Inozak will not follow a trail. Grab what you need from the packs, just what you can carry."

Cautiously they picked their way through the woods, fully aware that an ambush was likely. Kalvara took the lead with Aric riding on her back, peering over her shoulders. Jakin and Zad followed, Zad jogging to keep up with the pace of the group. Finn brought up the rear.

The Inozak were far ahead, moving fast, definitely faster than they were. Jakin hoped Kalvara's tracking instincts were good, and he calmed the panic he felt by looking for evidence they were on the trail: footprints, broken twigs, snapped branches. His legs ached, his arms were heavy. The morning fight had drained much of his strength. But he pushed on. For Rory. *I'm coming. I'll save you.* And he hoped she could hold on until he did. Well before the sun had reached its noon apex, the group reached the grove of black-trunked eucalyptus trees, where they'd fought the wolves the day before.

"The carcasses are gone!" Jakin was amazed.

"Food for the Trows," Kalvara said. "The entrance to their caves is over there, hidden in that heap of rocks. I want to see if they took Rory into the caves. Wait here." She handed Aric to Jakin, but the boy clearly didn't want to let go of her.

"I'm coming with you," Finn said, hurrying to catch up.

"Kalvara!" Aric screamed, reaching for her, terror on his face as she approached the cave. "No!"

Jakin wrestled with him, and as Kalvara and Finn disappeared, Aric's sobbing grew hysterical. "Bad," he gulped, "Bad in there!" Jakin stared at the cave entrance, wondering what horrors the two were facing.

A short time later, to everyone's relief, they both emerged. Aric wiggled from Jakin's arms and ran to Kalvara. "It's okay, Aric," she said, soothing him. "We are not going back. Not ever. I just thought maybe the Inozak had taken a shortcut through the caves with Rory, but no."

They turned back toward the woods, alert for clues as to the direction they should take. Aric saw the first one and pointed over Kalvara's shoulder to a few curly strands of brown hair caught in a tree. There were no tracks on the ground.

"They must be covering their tracks," Jakin said. "I wouldn't have thought them so smart."

"Don't underestimate them," Kalvara said, hurrying on.

Jakin walked close behind, looking now to the trees for signs of the Inozak's passing. More wisps of hair, broken branches, and torn leaves marked their way. They walked for hours, sure they were close on their trail, but with no sight of them. Jakin's stomach growled. Day turned to dusk, and they pushed on.

Finally, in a small clearing, they saw signs that the

Inozak had stopped. Their footprints marked the dirt in all directions where they'd walked back and forth; the squashed undergrowth indicated they may have sat, probably to eat. Their earlier carefulness to cover their tracks had obviously slackened.

Zad rubbed his beard. "Must be they figured they'd travelled far enough t'not bother coverin' up anymore."

But, as they studied the area, Finn said, "Looks like they had a fight here." He pointed out long grasses that had been trampled, and bark scraped off some of the trees.

"Blood," Jakin pointed to the base of a tree, its trunk streaked a sticky red.

Zad strode beyond the clearing. "Twas a fight, indeed," he said, "Come look at this." The group followed to see the huge girth of an Inozak laying in a heap in some underbrush, his mangled head several yards away. The headless warrior still grasped a handful of Rory's hair.

Jakin cursed. "Let's find them before they…."

Finn, eyes dark with anger, agreed. "It's getting dark. I'll take the lead now and we'll follow them as far as we can."

Fury and fear propelled them through the forest. On and on they pushed until Jakin's head pounded. No matter how hard he tried, he couldn't keep up with Finn. He fell back with Zad, trying to rally his strength.

"We'll find 'er, don't ye worry," Zad encouraged, tossing him an apple. Night was closing in when they heard faint voices. Their adrenaline spiked, and they caught up with Finn, who was peering through the trees at a narrow clearing, lit dimly by the moon.

"Keep 'er quiet," the largest Inozak commanded in a deep voice. "He'll be here soon. We don't want no more trouble."

A smaller guard hulked over Rory, who'd been tossed on the ground, her hands and feet bound with ropes, a filthy gag across her mouth. The guard glanced up to see his leader look away and with a sneer, ran his hand along the curves of her body. She struggled to move away. He leaned closer. A string of drool fell on Rory's cheek and she jerked her head away.

Jakin heard her muffled cries and started forward, but Zad held him back. "Not yet," he whispered.

Chapter 18: Zad

The air began to throb dully, like some great drum was beating in the distance. The rhythmic pounding grew louder, and even the Inozak seemed edgy. The dragon neared, its dark scales illuminated for a moment as it passed in front of the moon. It spotted the waiting warriors with their captive and roared, spouting a long spray of crimson flames. It was flanked on each side by a massive red-eyed Roc, their great curved beaks open and gruesome as they shrieked their greeting.

Jakin reached for his bow, but an instant later, he heard another shrill cry—a call to challenge—as the Firebird streaked into view behind the dragon. She skimmed just above it and drilled her long beak into the back of its head. The dragon roared with fury and spun around, catching the Firebird with the tip of its great bat-like wing, spinning her toward the ground. She recovered in time to dodge the two Rocs, who had lunged for her, talons out, beaks snapping. The dragon soared straight up, then turned and dove straight for the Firebird, a fraction of his size and weight.

"Why don't she move?" Zad whispered. "He's going to...." In that instant, the sky exploded in blue light. Six Tennins shot from the brightness, terrible in their fury. Three of them attacked the dragon, driving it away from the Firebird. The others fought the Rocs.

"Now's our chance!" Jakin exclaimed. He shot at the stunned Inozak, killing the smaller one who had touched Rory, then rushed over to her. As Finn, Kalvara, and Zad fought the others, he carried her back to the cover of the forest, cut the ropes binding her, and hugged her. Aric was there, too, telling her how glad he was to see her.

"Thanks," she muttered, unable to stop herself from trembling. Together they watched the terrible battle in the sky. Two Tennins flanked one of the Rocs, each grasping a wing and tearing it off. The shriek of agony was brief as the ruined creature plummeted to the ground. The second Roc turned to flee but a Tennin chased close behind.

Jakin stood by Rory and whispered, "So those are the mighty Tennins I've heard you all talking about. Way more fearsome than I'd imagined!" He bent to kiss her lips, but she turned her face and he brushed her cheek. He looked up when he heard a crack. The Tennin had caught the Roc and snapped its neck, sending the huge bird spiraling to the ground.

The dragon was frenzied. It twirled and pivoted, twisted and looped, dove and swerved in a gruesome dance with the Firebird, spouting fire at her. But she eluded it with speed and agility and was soon joined by all six Tennins, who gave the dragon a fight for its life. It shot straight up into the sky, its dark scales hard to see against the blackness. With an enraged roar, it whipped its snake-like neck toward them, its jaws spewing fire in a wide arc, so powerful it scorched a path on the ground far below. Jakin saw Finn shield his face and yell for Kalvara and Zad to go back into the woods. He could feel the heat even from where he stood. Finn and Kalvara joined him, but Zad stayed where he was.

"Zad," Jakin yelled. "Back here. Now." But Zad didn't move. "He's always so stubborn." Jakin kicked at the dirt. Rory tried calling Zad, but he seemed determined to watch where the view was best.

The Firebird did not hold back. She shot after the dragon, her feathers shining in the moonlight. The dragon watched her come. For a brief moment, there was silence; Jakin held his breath as the two fierce adversaries faced each other. The Firebird was tiny compared to the dragon, a single flame next to a forest fire. She streaked toward it, a flash of light so quick Jakin would have missed it had he blinked. The dragon lunged for the Firebird and missed. She was above him before he could react, diving for that soft spot on his forehead. She struck hard with her beak, driving it like a sword deep into his flesh, and the dragon's roar was confirmation she'd hit her mark. Its tail whipped up, scorpion-like, and lashed the Firebird, flinging her to the ground. Jakin watched in shock, then heard Zad scream and take off running toward the Firebird.

"Zad!" Jakin let go of Rory and chased after his brother. "Come back!" he shouted. But Zad didn't stop. Jakin hesitated, looked back at Rory and saw her terror. He was torn. He wanted to go back to her, but he needed to help his brother; Zad had saved his life. Jakin turned and shouted for him, again, then saw with relief that the Firebird had recovered from her spin and was gliding gracefully along the valley floor.

Seconds later, she was climbing upward, pumping her wings to rejoin the Tennins in their attack. One leapt atop the dragon's back, wrapped enormous arms around its head, twisting it into a grotesque and unnatural position. The other attacked with its long gleaming sword, swinging it at the enraged beast as it writhed in the air at dizzying speed. The sword connected with such power, it cut through the impervious scales on the dragon's right front leg, rending a wide gash. Hot, black blood spewed from the wound like a geyser. The dragon's roar of anguish caused the tree tops to shake.

With a burst of fury, it wrenched free of the Tennins and swooped close to the ground, bellowing its rage. Jakin watched in horror as it caught sight of Zad, still standing in the open. With a last spurt of wrath, the dragon pivoted and breathed a storm of fire on Zad. Then, it turned north, its bat-like wings beating their rhythm across the crescent moon and disappeared into the night.

"Noooooo!" Jakin took off running for his brother.

Zad was screaming long tortured shrieks, running senseless, first one way then the other, flailing his arms, batting at his head, fully aflame, a human torch.

By the time Jakin reached him, he had fallen and rolled long enough to quench the fire, but not before it took his life. Jakin knelt beside him, the grasses still lit with sparks. Zad's beard was gone. His hair was gone. Nose, eyelids, lips, gone. No trace of clothing remained. Burnt. Charred from head to foot. Unrecognizable. Smoke still rose from his blackened flesh. The smell was rank—a thick, nauseating stench, but somehow familiar. With a sickening realization, Jakin realized why. Morfyn, the giant who had killed his parents, had roasted and eaten them. He hadn't seen the horrific act from where he'd hidden, but it had smelled like this. Zad's blackened arm lay close to Jakin and he reached for it. But it was so hot, he snatched his hand back, his fingers blistered from the brief touch.

The Firebird landed in the clearing. In an instant, she was Floxx, running toward Zad, her silvery hair undulating in muted color with each stride. Six blue orbs followed her. Rory and Finn raced to their friend.

Rory begged Floxx. "Isn't there anything you can do? Save him, Floxx. Bring him back to life!"

Floxx stood silently, holding Rory, tears in her eyes. Rory waited, staring at Zad, then back at Floxx.

"Now, Floxx. Bring him back." She pleaded, but Floxx didn't move.

Jakin was barely aware of who was there, his arms clutching his stomach, tears blinding him and the smell making him sick. Running through his head, over and over, mocking him, berating him, condemning him, were Zad's words: *Well then, be sure t' return the favor.* Finn squatted and put his arm around Jakin, but Jakin pushed him away.

He'd heard Rory, the one voice he cared about. He glared at Floxx, just standing there. "You can't bring him back, can you," he said angrily. "So much for Eldurrin and all you say about him. You're powerless. Worthless." He curled over in desperate sobs. When Jakin finally looked up, the others were still there; Finn wiping his own wet face, Floxx with an arm around Rory, Kalvara a distance away with Aric sobbing in her arms. All of them waiting. Staring at his dead brother's hideous corpse. Doing nothing. Weak. Helpless. Useless.

Jakin clutched his chest so tightly, he could scarcely breathe. "We should bury him," he managed to choke, looking at no one and swiping at his face.

The air around them vibrated with the presence of the Tennins, much as it had that night by the Pool of Tennindrow, though Jakin hadn't been there to experience it. They appeared from their blue flames— six mighty warriors, strong and fierce, their wings folded behind them. Jakin saw Ingall, the man-like giant with the long sword, and Melangell with his ox horns, and Erela, the lithe fox-like Tennin. Uriel joined them, his keen wolf eyes vigilant and protective of the small group.

Uriel spoke gently, his deep voice resonating in the quiet night, "If you would allow us, Jakin, we would like to honor your brother and help you lay him to rest."

Jakin was afraid of the Tennins; they were huge and unnerving close up. He looked to Finn for help. His friend pulled him to his feet and locked him in a fierce embrace.

Uriel waited until they parted, then said, "You must leave us for a while, please. We will need some time to gather our thoughts as to how to best honor our friend."

Finn led Jakin back to the woods, past the dead Inozak, deeper into the forest where the night shadows cloaked them in fitting darkness. Floxx, Rory, and the others followed.

"Why didn't you save him, Floxx?" He overheard Aric ask. "Why did you let him die?"

Floxx reached for Aric, hugged him, then looked him in the eye. "There are some things Eldurrin allows to happen that are not in my power to change." She wiped tears from his cheek. "Life and death are both part of his plan, Aric. But neither one separates us from him; he's with us always. It was Zad's time to die. But, even so, his death breaks my heart like it does yours."

Jakin turned and glared at Floxx. He strode toward her, Finn close behind. "Breaks your heart? It rips me up. First my parents and now my brother." He squeezed his chest, choking. "Zad. He found me. He rescued me. He took me in and made me part of his family." Jakin picked up a stone and threw it into the blackness. "Zad wasn't sure about you and all the things you say about Eldurrin. He watched his own father's faith waver when you disappeared after the war. But he decided to trust you when you talked of restoring peace—the Eldur Crown and all that. And he fought for you, hoping for revenge on Draegin." He swiped at his wet cheek. "But it lives and he's dead. Whatever this plan of yours is, I'm out." And he turned and ran deeper into the dark woods, Finn following close behind.

They sat together, weeping on and off, each caught in his own memories, saying nothing. A few hours had passed, maybe more; the moon sat lower in the sky. Eventually, there were no more tears. Jakin's anger had given way to a deep, painful sadness. His throat was parched and swollen; his stomach still clenched. His voice came out as a croak until Finn passed him some water.

"Thanks," he said, crossing his legs and picking at the leaves on the ground. "I'll never forget when he found me wandering around near the dwarf caves. I was terrified of him, terrified of everyone, actually. He was so much bigger than I was, though he was just a boy, himself, yet already gruff and grumbly. I hid in a crevice between some rocks, shaking as he approached. I'd seen him pass by before and I knew he knew I was there. He talked to me gently, coaxing me out. 'C'mon, little one. I'm here t'help ye. I'll not harm ye. Look here, I have some food with me—fresh bread just baked this morning. I saved some o'mine for ye. C'mon now. Here, just reach out your hand and take some.' I was starving, so against my better judgment, I reached out and took some of the bread. It was crusty on the outside and soft in the middle."

Jakin chuckled. "Just like Zad. To this day, I've never eaten a better piece of bread. He could have grabbed my arm and yanked me out of that crevice if he'd wanted to, but he didn't. Instead, he sat down next to it, and kept handing me pieces of the bread. Then, he passed a skin of water to me and I drank the whole thing. We talked then—me still squeezed in that cleft and Zad sitting nearby. I told him about the giant, Morfyn. I told him my mother and father were gone, and I'd run and hid like they'd told me. I'd wanted to save them somehow, but I was small and terrified. Zad saw how angry I was. How lost. How scared. I talked for a long time. He just listened and agreed every now and then."

Rory stepped out of the darkness; Jakin suspected she'd been there a while, listening.

"Can we join you?" she asked shyly. "All of us?"

Jakin shrugged and patted the ground next to him continuing his story. "Eventually, after a long time, I wiggled out and stood awkwardly near Zad. He didn't stand up; maybe he was afraid I'd make a run for it if he did. So, I sat down next to him and talked some more. When I stopped, we sat a while in silence. Finally, Zad said to me, 'Well now, little fella, I've got a home not too far from here. And there's food and a place for ye to sleep. Would ye like t'come see it? Maybe stay a few days or so till ye decide what t'do?' That seemed safe enough to me; I was beginning to trust him, and I couldn't turn down the offer of food and a bed. He extended his big hairy hand and I took it and he walked me to his house where my new dwarf family was waiting. His sister, especially, took a liking to me."

Finn said, "How old was Zirena then?"

"A grown woman, maybe 20 or so, still at home. She did most of the cooking. And babied me near to death even after she married the prince."

Jakin stared off into the woods, "I remember parts of their wedding. It was only a few months after Zad had found me. The aroma of the herb-crusted roasts still stays with me. Zad carried me on his shoulders for much of the festivities, even dancing with me up there." Then he laughed, "Why even then, he loved his ale! I remember that's when I had my first sip—after a dance, he passed his mug up to me. I didn't like the bitter stuff at all and still don't."

Uriel stood in the shadows and called to the group. "We are ready. We have prepared Zad's body for burial."

Jakin was surprised at how much lighter the sky was when they emerged from the woods. But what he saw next astonished him. There in the clearing lay Zad, perfect in appearance as if he'd never been burned. He was lying on a flat wooden bier constructed from logs and tied with vines. His clothes were the ones he'd last worn, though not a scorch remained on them.

"How did you do this?" he cried, rushing over to kneel by his brother. He touched his face, running his hands lightly over his beard. He looked from Uriel to the other Tennins, waiting for some explanation.

Melangell spoke, "It is our gift to you, and our way to honor Zad. Eldurrin gave us the power to do this to his body, though the spirit of Zad is not here any longer."

Fresh tears ran down Jakin's cheeks. "Thank you," he managed to say.

Finn squatted next to Jakin, laying his hand on Zad's shoulder. "Wondrous!" he said softly. "I'd swear he was only sleeping." One by one, the others joined them beside the bier, grateful that their last glimpse of their beloved friend was of him whole. They would remember him so.

After a few moments, Jakin looked at the others and said, "Will we leave him here?" He frowned. "I don't like the idea of it; here, where none can come to pay their respects. The dwarf custom for the heroic dead is burial in the Topaz Tombs deep in the mountains near Orizin. It is a sacred place and those laid to rest there bring great honor to their families."

"Yes," Finn added. "I remember Zithreh's burial. He rests behind a window of blue topaz."

Uriel spoke. "We could bring him to Orizin. We could bring all of you. You could ride on our backs and one of us will carry the bier."

Everyone talked at once, stunned at the idea. Jakin held up his hands and looked at the group. "Yes," he said to his friends, "I would like to do that if you are all willing. It would mean a lot to me and to my family. But," he looked at Rory, "It would postpone your arrival in Byerman several more days, at least, maybe even a week."

Rory hesitated. A week! What if they missed the King? But Zad was her friend. He'd risked his life for her. How could she say no? She looked at Jakin and agreed. "Orizin."

"All right then," Floxx said, "Each of you, climb on the back of a Tennin. I will carry Aric, if you will allow me, Kalvara." And Floxx raised her arms above her head, let the shimmer of light envelop her, and changed to the Firebird.

Kalvara looked uncertainly at her, and deciding to trust her, walked over and placed Aric on the her back. "Hold on tight, now," Kalvara said sternly.

"I will! The Firebird won't let me fall off!" he said with a laugh as he wrapped his arms around her long, slender neck.

Jakin watched the others get settled. Finn climbed on Uriel, grasping his thick black fur. Erela looked at Kalvara with a smile on her foxlike face and extended her arms, inviting her to come. After a moment's hesitation, Kalvara walked over and sprang gracefully on Erela's back, taking a moment to find a place to hold on.

Jakin stood next to Rory, uncertain. "You sure you trust these Tennins?" he whispered.

"Of course. With my life. They are mighty protectors. You saw them at the Pool of Tennindrow." She suddenly realized he hadn't. "Wait. You missed it, didn't you? You missed the whole wondrous night." She shook her head in disbelief. "Where were you?"

Jakin shuddered at the memory and hoped Rory didn't notice. "I went for a walk in the woods and got lost."

"Trust them," Rory said and climbed on Ingall.

Once he saw everyone was waiting for him, Jakin walked over to Melangell, the Tennin nearest Zad, and swung himself onto his broad back. Once he was settled, Melangell reached down with his strong arms and lifted the bier, then led the way to Orizin.

Chapter 19: Tennins

They flew low over the tops of the trees as they wove their way toward Orizin, the city of dwarves. In the predawn sky, Rory could see the spread of thick forests they'd traveled through. A river shimmered in the distance, snaking into the horizon, a silver ribbon studded with the last of the starlight. Melangell led them toward it, then tracked its course upstream.

Rory had a vice grip on Ingall's shoulders as she hung on for dear life, flattened against his wide back, feeling the strength of his muscles. Tennins. So bizarre. Restorers of beauty, fearsome yet gentle, warriors and healers. A slight tip of his body and they turned, gliding, slicing the air like a kite on a breeze. She dared a peek over his head.

No fuselage. No engine, propeller, or seatbelt. Her hair blew wild, a cool and welcome relief from the heat of his body. The hilt of his sword, tucked away somehow at his side, caught the growing light each time he lifted his wings. The horrors of the night before gave way to a calm she didn't understand. She felt safe. Way up there flying on the back of a Tennin in a strange land, she felt sheltered somehow. She shook her head at the irony of it: the heart-pounding risk, yet the palpable peace, thick and real and weighty.

The Firebird swept up beside her, graceful, shimmering, beautiful, and tipped her long neck in greeting. Something inside Rory leapt at the gesture and she realized what a loyal friend the Firebird was to her. To her! Why would she bother about her? As if the Firebird had nothing else to do, she'd orchestrated her infant rescue and childhood care, waiting for the moment, the exact time to bring her back. And now she was risking her life fighting a dragon for her. What an amazing protector!

Rory thought of the knot on her bedroom ceiling where she was flying away. She'd never expected to fly like this! Chills danced on the back of her neck. She glanced at the Firebird and found her watching, as if she knew her thoughts. As if they were connected somehow.

Aric waved from the Firebird's back, his smile spread from one ear to the other. "Wahoooo!" he whooped, and Rory laughed and shouted with him. Floxx's words ran through her mind. *Life and death are both part of his plan. But neither one separates us from him; he's with us always.* What did she mean? Is Zad still alive somewhere, somehow, with Eldurrin? She looked ahead at the bier holding his perfectly restored body and thought of his hot temper, dry humor, fascination with her airplane; his kindness to Jakin, loyalty to Finn, courage in battle. To think she'd been frightened of him at first! What a friend he'd been. Does he really live on as Floxx had said? And what about Mom?

Images tangled like the strands of her hair in the wind. Mom, her fireweed crown, their wreath of hope, long stories by the fire as it snowed; Mom's tears when

Pap died, her face wet on his chest—wait for me, she'd said to him; wait for all of us. Wait where? Grief pulled at her heart and she wrapped her arms around Ingall's neck. *Mom, are you with Pap?* She caught her breath as a new thought hit her. *With Zad?* She laughed as she imagined Mom meeting him. "Rory?" he'd say, "Course I knew 'er. Met 'er in Gamloden and sat in that airplane. She said it'd fly, and I believed her." Mom would hug him and pump him for all the details.

Rory looked ahead at the Tennins winding north, following the course of the water below. On her left, the mountains rose, the tallest spikes snow-covered in the distance. On her right, the horizon glowed pink in the sunrise. She turned to look at the Firebird, again, still quietly flying at her side. She caught Rory's gaze, held it for a moment, then, with a soft croon, almost a song, she streaked ahead, catching up with Finn to linger by him awhile. Rory rested her chin on Ingall's head, and closed her eyes, feeling fat tears trickle down her cheeks.

PART TWO

Chapter 20: Lair

Dew and Catkin cowered face down in the dark, terrified of the colony of ghoulish bats streaming just above them. Piercing shrieks echoed in the tunnel, amplifying the terror. They barely breathed, terrified as they were, bracing for a deadly bite, but none came.

Finally, it quieted. Nerves tight as bowstrings, they sat up. Dew wasted no time. "C'mon, Catkin, me love. We cannot stay here." And so, they dashed through the blackness, their exhaustion forgotten, panicked there'd be another gruesome onslaught. The tunnel curved left, then right, ever downward; the air warmer, much warmer, and soon the ghillies were dripping with sweat. The tunnel eventually grew wider and lighter—light enough that they could make out their surroundings. They were entering another cave; the tunnel leading to a narrow ledge that traversed the circumference of a pitch-black hole. The source of the heat and the light soon became obvious. Far below hot lava sent occasional sprays of molten rock upward in fiery arcs. They heard a fluttering nearby and stopped. From a crack in the rocks just above their heads, a lone bat dipped toward the pit, then turned and took flight up the tunnel they had just exited.

The ghillies moved quickly around the perimeter of the gaping lava pit, hugging the walls and hoping for an exit tunnel. Their breathing came in short gasps, as they struggled against the searing heat. About a quarter of the way around the pit, Dew felt a gust of cooler air. Just ahead, was an opening. They turned into it, hopeful that it would provide a way of escape. But the tunnel was choked with fallen rock and impassable, even for the tiny ghillies.

They struggled on, their tongues swollen, throats parched. A dozen vampire bats burst from a hidden opening just a few feet ahead of them, shrieking Azzzzwang as they soared over the cavernous open gorge and into another tunnel off its perimeter. Catkin screamed and teetered on the edge, but Dew grabbed her in time, holding her tight until she calmed.

"Just a bit more, my sweet," Dew encouraged.

The air in the next branch of tunnel was also noticeably cooler and it seemed passable, so they turned into it without hesitation. Before long, they noticed they were traveling uphill.

"Maybe we're on our way out!" Catkin whispered, clinging to Dew's hand in the deep shadows. Though at first, they welcomed the relief from the heat of the lava cave, soon the ghillies were shivering.

"I think it's a bit lighter up there, Cat." Dew squeezed her hand, his teeth chattering.

They trudged uphill, turning left, then right, winding up and around in interminable circles of gloom, despairing of ever finding a way out. And then, suddenly, as they stumbled around a hairpin twist, a blast of frigid air hit them, and they were startled by light ahead. They clung to each other as their eyes adjusted, and gradually saw they had arrived at the back of an enormous cave. The far side of it opened to daylight and they could smell the snow outside. Its whiteness against the blue sky was breathtaking.

"We made it, Cat! Let's go—we're free. Let's make a run for it." They started toward the opening, but after a few steps stopped short, suddenly realizing where they were. The cave was colossal, its vast floor roughly an oblong shape; its ceiling at least a hundred feet high. Dozens of stalactites hung from its top; long, thin spikes poised above them like so many daggers.

Dew had taken all this in with a glance, but his focus was on the floor. He couldn't believe it! Silver swords and golden shields and pieces of jewel-encrusted ancient armor were strewn among piles of coins, mixed carelessly with beautiful gemstones of all colors. Crowns and bracelets, rings and necklaces were scattered about; on one side of the cave was a mountainous pile of silver cups and plates and bowls, golden forks and spoons and utensils.

Dew looked at Catkin, the gleam of gold reflecting in his eyes, "The treasures of kings, Cat!" His voice dropped to a whisper. "D'ye know what this is? A dragon's lair, sure as I'm a ghillie."

Cat squeezed his hand. "I think you're right and tis no place to be dawdling. Come on, let's make a run for it."

They took a few steps, but even as light-footed as they were, some items shifted, sending the lighter gems bouncing down the piles of treasure.

"Careful, now, Cat. What if the dragon shows up and notices things are moved."

They got to the center of the cave and stood, gawking at the lavish treasure. "Well, now." Dew scratched his head. "Mebbe's there's no reason to rush. No sign a dragon's been here recently." He picked up a small blue gem and held it up to the light. "Clear as the Dryad River!" He handed it to Cat for a look.

"So beautiful, Dew. What I'd give for just one o'these gems. Do you think a dragon would miss one little stone?"

Dew saw the wonder in her face and against his better judgment, relented. "Could be it wouldn't hurt t'look around. With all this loot, not even a dragon could keep track of it all."

And so, they lingered, marveling at the gemstones, delighting in the ancient weapons. Dew was particularly fond of a short knife, its blade just perfect as a sword for him. Its golden hilt was studded with emeralds, its leather sheath still supple; the blade, itself, light as the snow outside, slender yet sturdy. He ran his finger across its edge and drew blood. Sharp as the day it was forged. He held the knife up for Cat to see. "I know I shouldn't touch it but see how it fits me just so." He fastened it around his waist and smiled.

They slipped more than once as they jostled the loose coins and gems, but they grew accustomed to it, like walking in tree branches when it was windy. Dew picked up a gold fork and posed as a sea god, sending Catkin into a fit of laughter. She admired the jewelry and gemstones, pointing out her favorites as she tip-toed over the loose footing.

Near the wall of the cave, cloaked in dim light, a glimmer of red caught her eye. She called to

Dew, skipping over mounds of treasure to take a closer look. It was a ring, set with a large, multi-faceted blood-red stone, so clear she could see right through it. It was held aloft by a stalagmite protruding like a thick finger from the cave floor. The large golden ring was thick banded and engraved with tiny elven figures dancing under trees. In its center, the magnificent red stone scattered fiery prisms of light on the treasure around it. Enchanted, Catkin stood on her tiptoes and carefully lifted it off the spire. She turned it around and around in her hands, admiring it, entranced by its light show.

"What is it, me love?" Dew asked.

"It's spectacular!" she whispered, handing it to him for a look.

"May 'a been a Troll King's ring at one time, or a ham-handed Dwarf King, judgin' by its size," Dew said, admiring its beauty. "But, for ye, my love, 'tis a royal crown." And he set it on her head, a perfect fit, the large red gemstone centered across her forehead. Dew swept into a bow.

She twirled with delight. "And this for you, my courageous Dew," she said holding up a necklace of small gold coins she'd picked up along the way. It was strung together with a delicate piece of woven gold.

But, before she could place it around his neck, the booty-laden floor began to shake. Stalactites plunged from the ceiling to the floor, their sharp points deadly. In a fortuitous stroke of luck, a nearby mountain of cups and bowls trembled and slid, covering the ghillies completely as an injured dragon appeared at the mouth of the lair. It limped into the cave, smearing thick black blood on the treasures, and collapsed heavily, sparks bursting from its nostrils. A shiny dark streak oozed down its snout, draining from the soft spot between its eyes where Dew had punched it. Its iridescent hulk filled much of the cave, nearly squashing the ghillies, and great piles of treasure scattered under its heavy tail. Settling so it could see the cave's mouth, it tucked the tip of its tail under its jaw and with a thin stream of smoke drifting upwards from its nostrils, closed its eyes.

Dew waited until it had been quiet a long while, then dared to peek. Through a chink in his covering, he could see the left side of the dragon's head. Two scales were vibrating slightly at the back of its head where the beast's long snout joined its snakelike neck. A ray of light flickered on them as they moved. Between the scales, cleverly hidden, was a deep slit. From his close proximity Dew could see a red membrane trembling just inside the opening. An ear! Its subtle vibration likely meant the dragon was listening, even as it dozed.

He saw something else that made his heart surge, something the dragon had unearthed from wherever it had been hidden. His lucky feather! There it was, laying at the mouth of the cave atop bits of treasure, colors dancing along its barbs with each of the dragon's breaths, its stem caught tenuously under a gold cup. One great dragon snort would blow it out of the cave and it would float over the edge of the mountain, circle on the breeze, then spiral down, down, lost forever in the crevices of the rocks below. No! That mustn't happen! He must have it.

For the rest of the night and well into the next day, the dragon slept. Dew and Catkin dared not move for fear of waking it, but Dew never took his eyes off the feather. Earlier in the morning, testing the deepness of the beast's sleep, Dew had tossed a small gem toward the mouth of the cave. The dragon's yellow eyes had flown open at its quiet clink, focused exactly on the spot where the gem lay. It had raised its head and scrutinized the cave, seen the feather and snagged it with a talon, covering it with his uninjured claw. Dew's heart had sunk. Hours passed until it settled back into a light slumber. The sun sank low on the western horizon. Dew wanted to escape before dark, suspecting the dragon would awaken then, but he had no idea how to move without making noise. And how could he possibly retrieve the feather from under the dragon's foot?

In a stroke of good fortune, a flock of doves settled on the ledge outside the cave, cooing and pecking for food. The dragon's eyes popped open. Very slowly it lifted its long snout, coins stuck to the bottom of its jaw, and with a flick of its tongue, caught one of the doves, snapping it back into its open jaw. Dew nearly fainted, imagining how easily that could have been Catkin or him. The taste of food roused the dragon and as it clumsily readjusted its position, Dew and Catkin took the opportunity to move. They crept to the mouth of the cave, springing light and long as only ghillies can do, nimbly avoiding the enormous scaled tail as it swiped across their path. Dew grabbed the exposed feather with one hand and Cat with the other as they bounded into the fresh air.

They would have escaped without notice, but when they stepped out, the rays of the setting sun caught the red gem on Catkin's head, scattering ruby prisms across the snow. The dragon saw them and lunged, its snapping jaw a hair's breadth from them. But with its injured leg, the beast's balance was off, and it stumbled, scattering treasure out of the mouth of the cave. It roared, whipping its tail toward the ghillies, and its tip hit its mark as they fled, flinging them like two pebbles high in the air, and over the mountain edge where they tumbled and slid down its steep, icy side.

They landed in snow over their heads, a good distance from each other. Their luck held, though, for as they clawed their way out, Dew caught the sparkle of Catkin's red crown. He risked a shout and they scrabbled their way to each other.

"Oh, Dew, I'm so glad to be out o' that cave!" Catkin whispered, hugging him.

"As am I, me dearest love!" he whispered back, feeling the mountain tremble as the dragon raged above. "Now," he said softly, "Help me dig a place where we can hide till the mornin' light."

He used his knife to chisel a hole in the snow and they burrowed right there in a nook on the side of the mountain, the lucky feather tucked between them. Far above, the dragon roared as it took flight, spewing fire in its wrath. It circled several times, diving into the ridge where they hid, coming quite close to their location. But its fury was its foil; the angry sweep of its wings blew snow across the face of the ghillies' cave, and their presence went undetected.

The next morning Dew and Catkin emerged, slipping on the thin crust of ice that had frozen overnight. They took their time on the steep mountain, one misstep could send them careening to the rocks below. Clinging to the edges of protruding stones and branches, they made their way to a spindly spruce, its frosted branches glistening in the morning sun.

"Here we go," he said, and they bounded up its trunk, settling on a high limb, sighing as they snuggled into its needles.

"A bit damp yet, but warmer. So much warmer." Cat lifted her face to the sun. "And daylight! Beautiful daylight!"

Dew pulled a thin thread of bark from the tree and tied it to the feather, then looped it on a branch, hoping its sparkle would bring rescue. "Let's see how our luck holds, Cat; a bird may see it, and come explore. And maybe it'd be willing to fly us out o'here." She smiled at him, warming him far more than the morning sun.

Chapter 21: Tishkit

Jakin rolled over and nudged Finn as the sun peeked above the eastern mountain ridges and through the tops of the trees. "Time to go," he whispered. They rose immediately and readied themselves in silence, not wanting to disturb the rest of their sleeping friends. Together they stood at the bier, looking down at Zad's peaceful face. Sighing tremulously, Jakin set his jaw and turned toward his childhood home, Finn at his side.

No words passed between them until they cleared the forest where the sun shone brightly in an azure sky, unmindful of the grief that shadowed the hearts of the two travelers. They followed a wide rocky path cut in the side of the mountain. In the distance loomed twin snow-capped peaks, one slightly shorter than the other. "I've never come this way," Finn said, shading his eyes against the glare. "We're not going through the main entrance?"

Jakin shook his head. "I want to talk with Tishkit first, before anyone knows we're here." He pointed to the two peaks. "The Pinnacles of Haezarth. Dwarf lore has it that a dragon, Haezarth, lived there eons ago, back in the days when Thaumaturges and their dragons ruled the world. I always laughed at the story. Now, the tale is horrifying." Jakin kicked a pebble.

"I'm so sorry, Jakin. It's terribly, terribly sad. But, Zad died a hero's death. We'll see to it that his story lives; that his people sing of it for generations."

"As it should be."

The thick spine of the Caladrius mountains was divided into two distinct ridges. A narrow gorge fell between them, and thousands of feet below, the slender ribbon of the Caladruis River twisted blue from north to south. Jakin pointed ahead.

"The river starts in a small stream about a week's walk north, between the peaks of the Pinnacles. Terrible country there. I've heard that's where the giants live—Morfyn maybe, if he is still alive—in the open spaces above the tree line, feeding on most any meat, cooked or raw. They consider human flesh an unrivaled delicacy."

They walked in silence for a few minutes. "It'd be really dire," Jakin added, "Except for the Felinex. They live there, too."

"Felinex? Never heard of them."

"No surprise. They are very rare and seldom seen; large, feline creatures, clawed and fanged, though both can be retracted. They're taller than us when they stand on their hind legs and they have the ability to blend into whatever is around them, taking on the color and texture of a rock or a bush or a wall. Intelligent, perceptive, sly, and stealthy."

Finn studied him, incredulous.

"Formidable and fierce, too. Though Felinex hunt smaller game for food, they loathe giants and are the only creature known to attack them."

"They can take down a giant? Now that's impressive!"

Their path, which had been winding around the side of the desolate mountain opened up before them to reveal a hollow in its side.

"How do you know so much about them?" Finn asked.

"Zirena. She's somehow engaged one for service. I'm not privy to the details, but he watches for giants and keeps her informed." Jakin stopped. "We're here. This is one of the hidden entrances into Triaze Mountain; Orizin is deep in its belly.

"No guards?" Finn was surprised.

"Not here. Few know about this entrance; just those who live here."

Jakin entered the concave entry and studied the wall of rock on the left side. He ran his fingers carefully atop a cleverly hidden ledge. "Here it is," he said with a smile and withdrew a metal rod, cut with nubs and crevices on one end. "The key!"

Then, he pushed on a small rock that seemed no different from the others in the wall, except that it slid back, revealing a small opening into which he slid the key. As he turned the rod, a part of the rock wall slowly moved, opening wide enough to allow them to walk inside. Jakin replaced the rod on its covert shelf and the two of them entered the cave. Once inside, he stepped on a protruding stone on the cave's floor, and the wall behind them slid shut. They waited in darkness until their eyes adjusted.

As soon as he could see, Jakin pulled an oil-soaked torch from a basket on the wall, struck a flint against a rock and its light brought the beauty of the cave alive. Stalactites hung from the ceiling in various shapes and lengths, shimmering rock icicles, the torch light causing the minerals within them to sparkle. "Beautiful!" Finn whispered.

"Yes, it is. Follow me."

They wound down and around in a maze of circles and twists, Jakin never faltering, intent on where he was headed. Occasionally, they heard muted sounds coming from another tunnel, the clinking of metal pans and the mumble of morning conversations. Far away, they heard the faint sound of picks, perhaps workers in a distant mine. As they rounded a corner, an ancient dwarf approached, stooped so low his beard dragged on the floor between his feet. He looked up, startled to find the two of them in his path. But after a second, he exclaimed, "Master Jakin! Whatever are ye doing here? 'Tis nice to see you, again!"

Jakin reached out and touched the old dwarf's shoulder. "Hello, Teek! It's wonderful to see you, too! I've just now arrived; haven't even been home, yet."

"Well, son, ye're not far now! It's jest around the corner. I'm sure ye're mum is up and about. I'll be listening for her laughing when she sees ye!"

"Yes," Jakin said uncertainly, thinking that with his news, her laughter would not last long. He turned down a side tunnel, then took its left branch, then stopped after a time in front of a small blue door.

Jakin knocked. "I could just walk in," he whispered to Finn. "But I'd scare her to death."

"You'll scare her, anyway," Finn whispered back.

A scuffling noise sounded within, then a woman called out, "Comin'. Gimme a minute if ye please." Jakin took a deep breath.

The door opened to reveal a hunched dwarf woman, who would barely have reached Jakin's shoulders standing straight. Her skin was leathery and tough with wisps of curly gray hair growing from her chin. She saw his feet first and gasped. "Jakin!" she exclaimed with great joy. She twisted her face upward as far as it would go. "I'd reconize yer boots anywheres!"

"Tishkit!" he said, carefully lifting her up in his arms and hugging her. He couldn't help the tears that escaped. He set her down gently and she squinted at Finn.

"And ye brought yer friend with ye! Well now, Finn, ain't you a happy sight. I loved yer ma and yer Da and it's mighty good to see you now." She reached over and hugged Finn's stomach.

When she let him go, she peered around them. "Zad?" she questioned. Then, she saw the grief in Jakin's eyes.

"What's happened to Zad, boy? Where is 'e?"

"Gone, Tishkit. Gone to our fathers, wherever they are."

"No!" she whispered. She looked at Jakin, then at Finn, then around their backs, hoping they were playing a cruel joke on her. "My boy," she whispered. "Gone to our fathers?"

Jakin steadied her as she stumbled with the realization Zad had died, and he helped her into her home, settling her in her worn chair. She sobbed as he knelt before her, holding her hand. Finn sat at the small wooden table watching.

"He was a hero, Tish," Jakin gently ran his thumb over her wet cheeks. "'Twas a dragon 'at killed 'im." Jakin's language was already laced with his family's way of speaking.

"A dragon!" Tishkit's eyes widened. "Tell me. Tell me all of it."

And so, they did. The three of them talked for the next couple of hours, Jakin weaving the story from the time Finn met Floxx and Rory to the dragon fight. As Finn filled in pieces of the story, Jakin looked around the small home. Not much had changed in the months he'd been away. The stone floor, worn smooth over the years, needed scrubbing, the woodpile next to the hearth needed to be stocked, the cook stove held two dirty pots and pans. She needs help. Too old to take care o'things. Dried meat hung from hooks in one corner of the room near the table. A bag of salt sat on a sideboard alongside a meat cleaver and a large cutting board. No fruit. No vegetables, except a few potatoes and onions piled in a basket.

When they paused, Tishkit raised her arms and cried, "Oh my Zad! What a brave son ye were! I'm so proud of ye!" Then she dissolved into tears. "And I'll miss ye so!"

"One last part, Tishkit," Jakin continued. "He was burned really bad, but the Tennins fixed him. They flew us here, they did, on their backs, all of us, and carried Zad along. We brought him home to lay him t' rest near Zithreh in the Topaz Tombs."

"He's here!" Tishkit exclaimed and jumped from her seat, standing straighter than Jakin had seen her in many years. "Where is my boy? I want t'see him." She grabbed a basket and hurriedly filled it with meat, onions, and potatoes and handed it to Jakin to carry. "For yer friends," she said and turned toward the door.

It was well past midday when the three of them entered the forest where Zad lay, guarded by the others. They parted to make room for Tishkit and she knelt by his side, her head on his chest, her fingers buried in his thick beard. The others moved away to give her privacy. She wept for some time and no one said a word, each of them struggling with their own grief and reliving the memories both horrid and wondrous. Finally, Tishkit rose, Jakin hurrying to her side to help her across the uneven ground to join the others. They seated her on a tree stump and sat down around her.

Jakin introduced each of his friends, mentioning the part they'd played in the events that had led to this. Tishkit listened intently, nodding a wordless greeting after each introduction. When he was finished, she rose and approached each of them, saying their name and hugging each in turn—Floxx, Kalvara, Aric, Finn, Rory—with a surprisingly strong embrace.

"I thank ye for bringing 'im home," she said simply. She stood and said to Jakin. "We must take care of the burial arrangements." Then she turned to the others. "This is what we'll do. Jakin and I will go t' Zirena and Prince Tozar. They'll arrange for bearers to carry Zad into Orizin through the main entrance, which is some ways from 'ere. They'll carry 'is body down the mountain with high honor, as is custom for a slain warrior. Let's hope we can get started tomorrow or the next day. Ye will wait here, if ye please, keepin' an eye on him. And ready yourselves. Ye'll need yer strength." Then, she turned, her eyes moist, took Jakin's arm and headed slowly back up the mountain path.

Jakin arrived early the next morning, his eyes red and puffy, accompanied by a sizeable funeral party, six dwarves, solid and stout like the cast iron stoves they were famous for crafting. "Let's get started," he said, and they transferred Zad to an ornate metal bier—its sides engraved with battle scenes and studded with topaz gemstones. Despite its weight, the pall bearers hefted it onto their shoulders without obvious effort and began their march to the front entrance of Orizin. It was, as Tishkit had predicted, a ceremony of high honor.

Drummers went first, followed by the bier, then the mourners singing a dirge in a strange language.

"Tishkit isn't with you?" Finn asked Jakin.

Jakin shook his head wearily. "Too exhausted to make the trip again. She will meet us near the entrance to the city and join the procession there."

"Do you know what they are singing?" Finn asked as they walked behind the procession.

"Not word for word, no, but I do understand some of the phrases. Roughly translated, they are singing about a fallen hero, a slain warrior, a death of honor."

The sun was near its zenith when they drew near the main gate to the city. Hundreds of dwarves lined each side of the wide path, bowing formally as the procession passed by. Many joined in the song, their bass voices thrumming deep in their chests. Floxx knew the words and Jakin heard her join in, weaving a beautiful harmony.

Chapter 22: Topaz Tombs

The city gates were winched wide open for Zad's final homecoming; the stone doors massive and spectacular, embellished with ornate metal work and jeweled trim. Jakin saw the enormous common area, normally full of horses and carts, vendors and market stalls, now so crowded with dwarves they had to part to let the funeral party pass. He noticed the curious glances at those who accompanied him, but there was no unrest. He and Tishkit had told the story of Zad's death to Zirena and Prince Tozar, who had, in turn, gathered the citizens of the city early this morning to prepare them for the arrival of both the procession and the unusual guests.

The funeral party walked to the base of the raised dais where King Hazuut was seated, his Queen at his side. The drummers and singers quieted. The crowd silenced. The King stood and formally welcomed the guests to Orizin, expressing great sadness at the reason for the visit. He motioned for the pall bearers to bring the bier to the platform for all to behold their hero. Then he turned the ceremony over to Prince Tozar and Zirena.

Jakin scarcely knew Tozar. His wedding to Zirena was a distant hazy memory, and while she had come home for visits over the years, bringing her children with her, Tozar had seldom joined her. Zirena always offered the same excuse—he was engaged with kingdom business and it was difficult to get away.

Tozar bowed to Jakin's guests and extended a warm, stately welcome. He began by reading a eulogy Jakin had helped him write, commemorating Zad's battle with the dragon. The crowd gasped and booed at the story of Draegin's pursuit of Rory, cheering at Zad's courageous part in her rescue. Jakin glanced at Rory, who was both blushing and crying. *She's so beautiful, even in tears.* He forced himself to look away. As Tozar talked on, Jakin imagined how the tale would be embellished in the years to come and how Zad's stature would grow. *Dragon slayer, he'd be called. Singers would write ballads about him. Good! He deserves it! He was the stuff of legends. He saved my life—twice. But me? I failed him. Maybe if I'd shouted louder. Run for him sooner. I'm so sorry, brother, so deeply sorry.*

Zirena rose to the podium quite gracefully for a woman of her girth, her large head proudly adorned with a diminutive gold crown; her braided beard, studded with gemstones and highlighted with strands of silver and gold thread, hung long over her large bosom. Jakin noticed Rory was gaping and hid a grin.

"My dear friends, relatives, and fellow citizens of Orizin," she began, her tenor voice melodious and strong. "Thank ye for coming to honor my brother, Zadfor, son of Zithreh. No one questions 'is bravery, 'is valiant acts, 'is courage. He faced a dragon, laying down 'is life in defense of his friends. No honor is higher than that. Even so, many of ye do not know the full scope of his strengths. He was not all brawn and bravado. A gentle kindness undergirded many of his actions. Let me share a couple o' stories about him."

A hush fell over the audience. "Most of you know Jakin." She paused and pointed to him. He felt his face heat as everyone looked. "And the story of Zad finding him after his parents were killed by Morfyn." The crowd murmured at the mention of the giant's name. Zirena raised her voice to quiet them. "Zad didn't just rescue 'im, bring 'im home, and hand over 'is care to us. I distinctly remember Zad giving Jakin 'is wool cape to use as a covering when he slept, managing through the winter with a lighter weight one. His generosity extended to others. He was an accomplished hunter, and faithfully kept our family in meat. Less known is the fact he provided meat each week to hungry families. Some of you benefited from 'is kindness. Most of you have heard the story of the two-stone topaz Zad unearthed in our family mine when he was a boy—the first of many large gems to be found in that section of the mine. What is little known, however, is this: When our father, Zithreh, asked Zad what he wanted to do with 'is fortune, Zad replied that he wished to use it to buy a home for a destitute widow and 'er six children. And he did."

Jakin turned to glance at the widow Mazarelle. She had bowed her head and covered her face with her hands.

Zirena continued. "Did ye know Zad was an accomplished musician? He played the lute and often calmed my crying infant son, Ezat, strumming 'im to sleep night after night, month after month until he outgrew the night cries. Zad was the only one who could soothe 'im. He was tough and tender—a unique dwarf, both warrior and artist. He not only taught my boys to wrestle and to hunt, to throw a knife and wield an axe—he showed them how to weave gold threads into fine chain; to cut topaz with perfect facets to catch the light from any angle. My daughter, Renaz, remembers braiding 'is beard when she was a very little girl, placing colorful beads in it." Zirena stroked her own to show the effect. "He grumbled mightily, knowing it was a woman's adornment, but he didn't deny 'er the fun. Once he tried to breed snow geese for their eggs. Do you remember that, Mother?" She looked at Tishkit, whose eyes brimmed with tears. "Out on the ledge not far from our home." Zirena laughed. "He found that there are some things even he could not achieve."

The crowd was spellbound, laughing, crying, murmuring among themselves. "And so, dear friends, our hero was also a warm brother, kind uncle, caring son, and generous friend. Let's remember 'im for all these honorable qualities."

The applause thundered until the King, himself, stood to quiet it. Next came singers, then a poet. Finally, Prince Tozar commanded the doors to be opened to the great room and all were invited to a lavish feast in Zad's honor.

Zirena personally ushered Jakin and his friends to their table. Servants came immediately, bearing platters of cheeses and fruit and breads. "Enjoy whatever you want. And save room," she said, indicating the food-laden tables lining the walls. "There are many more courses to enjoy."

"May I get you something to drink?" Jakin asked Rory, gesturing to the kegs lining the far wall.

"No, thanks, I don't drink. But, I'll take some punch, please."

He touched her shoulder and smiled. "I'll be right back." When he returned, he was annoyed to find Finn had taken his seat by Rory and he was forced to sit on the other side of Finn. "Here you go," he said, reaching across to hand her the cup.

"Thanks," she said and took a sip. "Yum! This is amazing! All of this." She swept her arm in a wide arc, indicating the lavish room and the tables laden with grand displays of food. Their table held a jewel-edged three-tiered platter, glittering in the lamplight, overflowing with fruits, cheeses, and breads. Aric asked for a sweet bread and Finn was quick to oblige, taking one for himself, as well, and spreading both with butter and jam.

"But," Rory continued, holding Jakin's gaze, "I wish we were here under different circumstances."

"Of course, we all wish that. This is very hard for everyone. Nevertheless, I am pleased to have you meet Zad's family—my family—and to see where I grew up."

A servant approached, holding a silver platter of yellow blossoms. Kalvara reached for one; the petal held a dollop of something sticky in its center and was topped with a leaf. "What are these?"

"Sunbursts! Taste them! One of my sister's recipes."

"Delicious!" Kalvara said, licking the honey off her lips. "And Zad would also approve of this." She lifted her mug. "I can taste the mountains in it!"

Jakin lifted his mug to her, apprising her. He was surprised she handled both a crowd and a feast so well; she'd come a long way from the angry, suspicious person they'd caught stealing apples. He saw Aric at the next table, laughing with his nephew, Pelzar, and realized how remarkable the Eldrows were.

Servants paraded in with platters of meat on their shoulders: deer, chickens, dozens of wild ducks and geese stuffed with raisins and nuts and placed them on the buffet tables. And, finally, four servants emerged, bearing high an enormous tray. Jakin could see the tips of wings above it, and he stood. The room silenced as everyone stared.

"A Swiltingen!" someone whispered.

"It can't be!" another said. And, as the servants set the great winged beast on a table of its own, the guests burst into applause.

Zirena joined Jakin, beaming at the looks of awe on the guests' faces. She held Aric's hand. "Here ye go, dear. She's right there." Aric climbed on Kalvara's lap.

"Where did you ever get it?" Jakin asked her, incredulous.

"Just lucky, really. Our hunters came on it injured as they were trailing a herd of goats. Something big had fought with it and left it to die."

"How awful!" Rory said, leaning closer to Jakin to hear.

"Tis a shame, seeing as they are so rare," Zirena said. "But since it was dying in such agony, the hunters put it out of its misery, then hauled it back here, wings and all." A servant approached and whispered to Zirena and she apologized and left, having to see to something in the kitchen.

"I've actually never seen a Swiltingen before!" Jakin confided to Rory. "Let's go have a look." Its wings were like a butterfly's, scalloped edged and lacy, nearly as long as its body, maybe seven or eight feet; its head proportionately small for its size. The chef had left its eyes in, dull brown stones; its jaw was gaping wide, stuffed with small birds, apples, and flowers.

"It eats birds?" Rory asked.

"So I've been told. Swallows little birds whole."

"It's the size of a moose. I wouldn't want to collide with that in the air."

Jakin put a slice of Swiltingen on his plate, cut it into small pieces, and offered his guests a taste. Rory tried a bite, murmuring that it was very tasty, but the others politely declined. "Oh, you're really missing out," he said to them. "Like deer, only richer." But they preferred to fill their plates with other festive foods, then settled back at their table.

Day turned to night as the guests drank heartily and ate their fill. Stories of Zad rang from every table and numerous toasts were lifted in his honor, his friends sloshing ale liberally with each whack of their mugs. After the lamps were lit in the great room, the King stood to speak, Tozar by his side. "Fellow dwarves, friends, and family. Thank you for joining us for this day of memories as we lay our beloved brother, Zad, to rest. He will be placed in the Topaz Tombs and we trust you will pay your visits on the morrow. But, at this time, Prince Tozar will lead his family to the Tombs and there they will privately inter our beloved Zad."

Jakin spoke to his friends in hushed tones. "This is dwarf tradition. Although usually it is only the immediate family, because of the unusual circumstances, you are invited to join us."

"I wouldn't miss it," Finn said, placing his arm around Jakin's shoulder.

Kalvara lifted Aric to her hip. He laid his head sleepily on her shoulder, wrapping his small arms around her neck.

Floxx moved close to Rory and whispered, "This is quite an honor."

Rory's face was gaunt. "Walk with me, will you?"

"Certainly," Floxx replied, reaching to brush a curl from her face. "Always."

Everyone stood as the bier was taken up and the procession line formed. As one, they raised their cups in silent salute to Zad and held them there. Two torch-bearers preceded the bier followed by two drummers who set the low steady rhythm of the march. Two female singers followed, taking up a soft funeral dirge. The six pall bearers took their places in the procession, solemnly bearing Zad aloft. Then came Zirena and Tozar, followed by their four children walking two by two: Their sons, 15-year-old Azatan and 14-year-old Ezat; their 11-year-old daughter, Renaz; and their nine-year-old son, Pelzar. Behind them, Jakin with Tishkit leaning on her cane, then two more torchbearers. At a nod from the King, Finn followed with Kalvara, who switched Aric to the hip by Finn, putting a few more inches between them; then Rory arm-in-arm with Floxx. Two drummers fell in behind them, followed by two final torchbearers.

As the procession slowly left the room, Jakin heard the final public tribute. The King raised his cup and proclaimed: "Highest honor to Zad, who fought the dragon!" The crowd roared their response, "To Zad, who fought the dragon!"

It was an hour's walk through the winding tunnels of Orizin, at first wide enough for six abreast, but gradually narrowing as they descended, until the smooth rock sides were an arm's reach away. The drums set the rhythm of their slow progress and Jakin pondered, step by step, Zad's life, its simple heroism and quiet largess—it was unimaginable to think he could have survived without him, his life had made so much difference. But the memories of his death soon devoured the joy. Hideous, tragic, senseless. The nightmare replayed over and over in Jakin's mind, unbidden and impossible to stop. The gruesome images of his blackened body, the ghastly smell of charred flesh. He sighed and looked at Tishkit and saw the tears on her face. Her son. Her boy. What loss she must be feeling. She caught his eye and faltered, fatigue and grief sapping her strength, and Jakin drew her closer, supporting her as they marched.

Finally, the tunnel widened, opening into a vast room carved deep in the bowels of the mountains. The rock-hewn walls glimmered in the torchlight, hinting at rivulets of unearthed mineral and quarries of gemstone hidden behind. Hooded figures stood in the shadows along the walls, shrouded under the lit sconces of the immense mortuary. They were the Uzim, caretakers of the honored dead.

The procession halted. One of the Uzim, his black robe trailing on the stone floor, walked slowly forward to confer with Tozar. Together they went to the bier and gazed upon Zad; the Uzim nodding as Tozar whispered. After a few moments the procession continued, one Uzim at the lead, with the other members of the clan falling in behind, joining their deep voices in the funeral dirge. Their harmonies echoed in the shadowy cavern, singing of the heroic lives that had found rest here. The presence of death was palpable, raising gooseflesh on the back of Jakin's neck.

As torchlight fell on the walls, Jakin saw the dead ringing the room, entombed upright along the walls. The heroes of the ages beheld their passing, their faces preserved, eyes staring sightless and solemn through gemstone windows on their stone caskets. Gazing open-eyed through their topaz windows of yellow, purple, red, blue, or green, they remained perfectly preserved by the mysterious work of the Uzim. The Tennins had done Zad a tremendous honor by restoring his ruined body for this honorable dwarf burial.

The procession wound around a curve in a slow descent to a lower level of the Tombs. As the torches passed through the center of another cavernous, high-ceilinged room, they stopped. Tishkit and Jakin stepped forward and bowed before a tomb, followed by Tozar and Zirena. Torchbearers shed their light on the deceased encased behind a blue topaz window. Zithreh stared back at them, eyes open, looking blankly at his visitors. Jakin remembered well Zithreh's journey to this resting place; Zad had scarcely been able to hang on to his composure during his father's funeral. Tishkit wailed and the others stood back, giving her as much time as she needed. She placed her hand on the blue window shielding her beloved husband. Facets of blue light reflected on his face, a poor substitute for the light of life.

After a few minutes, they continued down the cavern, halting at the end of the wall of tombs, where an open stone casket sat on the floor, awaiting its contents. Its cover was propped against the wall in the place where it would eventually stand upright. Zad would look, unseeing, out of a yellow topaz window for the eons of time to come.

Jakin watched as the bier was set next to the open coffin. The attendants unstrapped the body and lifted Zad into his final resting place. It was lined with soft padding and covered with a rich purple cloth. Belts were discreetly buckled around his body and his head was positioned and fastened firmly, assuring he would stand tall through the ages. Then the attendants stepped aside.

One by one, led by Tishket, Zad's family filed past the casket, bringing loose gemstones for Zad's eternal days.

"May you find joy, my son, in all you do in the afterworld," Tishkit whispered, laying several large gems upon his chest.

"May you be rich and prosperous." Tozar sprinkled a handful of multicolored gemstones across Zad's body.

"May you find happiness," Zirena intoned with her handful. And each of Zad's nephews and his niece followed with final wishes and jewels to assist him in his days beyond this world's reach. When they were finished, his body glittered with gems, a bounty of wealth given as a resource against the unknown demands of life ever after.

Finally, Jakin approached with Zad's axe, which had been polished to a high shine—the weapon of a hero. It was secured next to his body, blade up where it would be visible through the topaz window.

The singers chanted a final dirge, then the Uzim moved forward to lower the casket's top and latch it securely with a series of complicated bolts and clasps. With a mighty heave, the six attendants lifted the casket to a vertical position—the gemstones tinkling softly as they tumbled to Zad's feet—and maneuvered it against the wall where it was cleverly secured on all sides.

Finn moved to Jakin's side and spoke softly. "My life-long friend. How I will miss him."

Jakin passed a sobbing Tishkit to Zirena and turned to Finn. "He was my brother. My hero. My friend. I will never forget him." And Jakin wept openly.

Rory also wept, her arms crossed tight around her middle. When Jakin approached her, she hiccupped about how sorry she was, that it was all her fault.

Jakin reached for her and held her at arm's length. "No one blames you, Rory," he said, looking intently at her. "Not me. Not any of my family. It was certainly not your fault." Then, Jakin kissed her on her forehead and turned to embrace the rest of his family.

Chapter 23: Zirena

Two more days with Tishkit was about all Jakin could take. The home was cramped with all of them there and the mood was somber, even morose. There was little food, and he'd had his fill of greasy potatoes and onions.

"Tish," he said early in the morning on the third day after he'd spoken with his friends. "We are going to visit Tozar and Zirena for a few days to see how they are doing. Will you come with us?" He saw a sparkle in her eyes for the first time in days.

"Twould be good t'see the children," she murmured.

"They make you laugh, don't they Tish?"

She smiled.

"They make us all laugh with the way they carry on," Finn said, standing up and reaching for his pack. "It's only by Eldurrin's hand they've survived each other's pranks!"

By noon they had passed unquestioned through the city's small contingent of guards and were knocking at the grand entrance to Prince Tozar's dwelling, its spacious courtyard alit with lamp light. The double doors were engraved with ancient runes and Jakin watched Floxx run her hands over the carvings, as if they were precious. He raised his eyebrows in question.

"These are very old," she murmured. "Quite ancient. Perhaps Prince Tozar can tell us how he came to have these doors."

Before Jakin could answer, the doors swung inward, slowly and soundlessly, revealing a tall creature, every bit the height of Kalvara, covered in short, silky gray hair, sinewy and graceful, clothed in the leather garb of a male servant; a great tailless cat, standing upright.

Jakin inclined his head in respect. "We are here to see my sister, Princess Zirena, if you please."

The Felinex bowed politely, his shrewd green eyes taking in the group. "Follow me," he said, his voice soft with the hint of a purr; the sharp points of his teeth visible when he spoke.

Aric whispered a barrage of questions about what kind of creature they were following. No amount of shushing from Kalvara could quiet him. They arrived at a thick inner door, which could not completely muffle the sounds of roughhousing inside. A metal doorknocker hung in its center and the Felinex gave three firm pounds. The door was flung open and nine-year-old Pelzar gaped for an instant before he threw himself into Jakin's arms. Renaz was right behind him, grabbing Finn in a hug so fierce it nearly knocked the breath from him. Zirena was quick to appear, smoothing her hair with one hand, her dress with another.

"Easy on 'em, Pelzar, Renaz; ye're strong as a couple o' bears. Let 'em go, now. That's right."

She reached out to Tishkit, pulling her into a gentle embrace. "Hello, Mother. I'm so glad ye've come." She looked over Tiskit's head and smiled at the others. "I'm glad ye've all come. We've been expecting you."

Zirena dismissed the Felinex. "Thank you," she said, and he turned on light feet and disappeared into the dimly lit hall. Jakin stared after him wondering how he could vanish so completely.

"Come, come!" Zirena said spreading her arms wide, her voice brassy and bold. "We've plenty of food and cider and," she glanced at Kalvara, "ale! Come and be welcome here." She stood aside and waved them into her home.

"You've changed everything since the last time I was here!" Jakin exclaimed, looking at all that was new. It was grand! Colorful tapestries hung from the high stone walls, heavy bronze chandeliers held thick candles, filling the room with warmth and plenty of light. The smell of herb-roasted meat made Jakin's stomach tighten. The table was familiar, though. Large and square, built with thick planks of dark wood and inlaid with an intricate mosaic of colorful quarry rock, it still sat in the center of the room, flanked on all sides with long, low-backed benches. Two dozen wide-shouldered dwarves had gathered there for many a feast, six to a bench. A couple of servants busied themselves clearing bowls from a previous meal as Zirena ushered Jakin and the others into an adjoining room where a dozen stools surrounded a low round table.

"Sit, please," Zirena said, gesturing to the stools. "Moira," she addressed a young dwarf. "Ale, cider, apples, and cheese, and be quick about it!"

Jakin's niece and nephew amused them while they ate. Renaz continually stole cheese off Pelzar's plate every time he turned his head, so innocently he didn't notice at first. But when he did, they tumbled across the floor, scarcely missing those around them, good-naturedly wrestling and punching each other. Aric laughed at each of their antics, jumping up and down, and Kalvara finally gave up trying to quiet him, realizing no one minded. Jakin was glad to see Finn eating and teasing the kids; even Rory's appetite was improved, and some color had returned to her cheeks. Coming here was a good idea.

A servant bent to speak to Zirena. She listened, then yelled over the noise. "Tozar sends his regrets, but he is not able to join us. His work is demanding, and he cannot take his leave. However, he bids you welcome. And he has sent word to our sons to come home." Jakin caught Finn's gaze and raised his eyebrows. Exactly what Tozar always said.

As if on cue, Azatan and Ezat came bursting in, hallooing greetings before they even got the door shut. They dropped their packs, set their bows against the wall, and hurried over to them, their boots thudding on the floor.

"Jakin and Finn! So glad ye've come t'visit!" They hugged them each tightly, then gently embraced their grandmother. Introductions were made amid calls for more food and drink. "Nuts, too, Moira, and hammers to crack them!" Azatan hollered after her.

"We were hunting," Ezat told the group. "Shot a buck, so they'll be steaks tonight!" Renaz, sitting on the floor near him, jabbed his leg with her elbow.

"Ow," Ezat said, rubbing it. "What'd ye do that for?"

"For not takin' me along. I'm a better shot 'an you. I could'a got us two bucks."

Azatan roared with laughter and mussed her hair. "No doubt you could 'ave, little sister! Your arrow's quick as a viper, with an aim as deadly. Next time, you come."

She hugged her knees to her chest, a slight smile playing on her lips.

"Me, too," Pelzar hollered, jumping on the couch to squeeze in next to Azatan. "I'm a good shot, too!"

"That ye are, no doubt. Maybe ye can get us a covey o' quail next time we're above. I've been wantin' some quail meat, scarce as its been."

"I can get 'em, you bet I can!" Pelzar slapped his brother's leg right in the sore spot, then reached deep into a pocket and pulled out a small leather pouch, dumping its contents in his palm. "C'mon," he called to Aric, showing him his handful of smooth rocks. "I'll show ye my slingshot." The children were through the door in an instant.

Kalvara started to follow them, but Zirena assured her they'd be fine. "Pelzar's got 'is targets set up just outside there. I'll show ye if ye like. They'll not be gone long." Though Kalvara declined the offer to see where they'd gone, Jakin saw her hands were clenched.

Ezat exchanged a sober glance with Azatan and to Jakin's surprise, bolted after the children. Azatan cleared his throat and crossed his arms over his broad chest.

Zirena fixed him with a glare. "What's goin' on?" she demanded.

His lips were a tight line between his mustache and beard. "We've heard Morfyn may be afoot."

Jakin stood. "Morfyn! Around here?"

Azatan replied, "Tis a possibility. Sit down."

Jakin sat.

"While we were trackin' some game, we met a dwarf who said he'd seen 'im a ways out, moving south, away from 'ere."

"We headed back t'be safe and to alert everyone; we were nearly home when Father's messenger told us ye were here."

Kalvara was on her feet and had flung the door open just as Aric leapt on her. "Kalvara! You should see Pelzar's sling shot! It can shoot a bird clean out of a tree. Can I have one of them, please, please Kalvara? I tried it and I can shoot it good, can't I Pelzar?"

"He's a real good aim," Pelzar said, his expression very serious as he stared way up at her. "I could make 'im one—t'wouldn't take me long at all."

Kalvara set Aric down, squatting to look into his eyes. "Would you take good care of it? And be smart with it, not shooting it at your friends?"

He held her gaze, stood up straight, and nodded soberly. "I would."

She looked at Pelzar and allowed a slight smile. "Well, then, yes, Aric could accept your gift. Thank you."

The two boys let out whoops and ran into the kitchen, causing the others to laugh despite the disturbing news about Morfyn.

Later that night, after the young ones and Tishkit were asleep, they sat at the big table talking in hushed tones about the giant.

"There's more," Azatan was saying. "The dwarf 'at told us 'e'd seen him said the giant likely killed someone. Didn't know who. But he'd crept up when the giant had gone and saw the fire pit still smokin'— and big bones scattered about."

Jakin pounded his fist into the table, startling everyone. "I'm going to kill him," he said, his gaze moving from one to the other around the table. "That monster killed my parents. I thought he was long dead, but if he's alive, I still have a chance to avenge them!"

195

It stormed all the next day. Sheets of water pelted the slopes and the granite sky slid so low it hid the tops of the pines. Inside Zirena's home, the friends visited long, feasting on the deer as well as on many of the left-over delicacies from Zad's funeral. Jakin was concerned about Rory's deadline and that each day they delayed leaving made it less likely she'd ever meet the King. She must meet him! Zad's death must not have been in vain.

They decided to take Zirena into their confidence as they had Tishkit, so she'd understand their urgency to leave, and in the late-night hours Jakin and the others shared their story with her. Curious as she was about the Firebird and her collision with the mysterious airplane, and as intrigued as she was with Kalvara and Aric; it was Rory who interested her most. "King Merek and Queen Raewyn's abducted daughter!" she said, her gravelly voice rising in disbelief. She studied the scars on Rory's face. "Unther's axes!" she muttered, "What if it's true."

She looked from Rory to Jakin, considering. "I didn't realize you had a deadline. It's only a couple of days till solstice; the King may have already left, but then, again, ye just might make it. We'll get you on your way first thing in the morning. I'll see to your supplies personally."

The next day, dawn broke in a cloudless sky. While Zirena oversaw the packing and loading of several donkeys with food, water, blankets, and gear, the group gathered to say their good-byes.

"Why are there five donkeys and six of us?" Finn asked her.

Jakin replied before she could explain. "I'm staying here." Finn started to object, but Jakin held up his hand. "I decided a few nights ago. Tishkit needs me right now. And with Morfyn ...." He let the thought die on his lips. "But I'll see you again before you know it."

Finn embraced him. "Take good care of Tishkit and bid her good-bye from me." He turned to Zirena. "This is too much," he protested, gesturing to the donkeys and all the goods. "Way too much, Zirena."

"Psssht," Zirena waved his comment away. "How else would ye manage? Tis a long walk out o' these mountains and ye will have to move fast t'get to Masirika by solstice. You'll need t' be traveling every hour of light." She turned to Rory and handed her a heavy, lumpy pouch, dipping her head in a show of respect. "Please give these to the King with our goodwill and best wishes, jewels from the mines of Prince Tozar and Princess Zirena."

Rory hesitated, saying they might never meet the King, but Finn encouraged her to take it. "All right. I'll do my best to deliver it."

"Well, then." Zirena said, abruptly ending the conversation, and went to double-check on the last of the provisions.

After Rory had stowed the pouch, Jakin asked to speak with her privately. Finn raised a questioning eyebrow but said nothing. She walked with Jakin a short distance.

"I have something for you," he said, reaching into his pocket, still wrestling with what he was about to do. Should he really give this to her? He had been so stunned when he'd actually looked at what had been dropped into his pocket that night in the woods, he'd been afraid to show anyone. Any dwarf would have known in an instant it was a treasure. He'd decided to bury it, planning to come back for it at a later time, but each time he'd tried, he'd changed his mind. He considered the specter's words. What if it did make her love him? He certainly loved her, and he could protect her better then. What would it hurt to give it a try? She would think it was from him, never suspecting where it really came from. And she wouldn't realize its tremendous value; she'd just think it another beautiful piece of dwarven jewelry.

He smiled at Rory and pulled out a braided silver bracelet, delicate and light, set with translucent white opals, each flecked with pinks, blues, greens, and yellows. "These are some of my stones." He showed her. "I, ah, mined them myself when I was a boy and, well, I asked one of the silversmiths to make this bracelet for you." He faltered. "So you don't forget me." He blushed. "Or, Zad, or any of us in Orizin."

Rory gaped at it. "It's beautiful! I mean, it's really gorgeous!" She looked at him fondly. "But, Jakin, I couldn't possibly take it! What if the King and Queen don't believe my crazy story, which they probably won't, and I go back to where I came from? I'd never see you again." She tore her eyes from the captivating piece of jewelry. "It's very generous of you, truly it is, but...."

"Rory," Jakin interrupted, his eyes tender. "Please. It would mean so much to me if you would take it now, no matter what happens in the future." He held her gaze and lowered his lips to hers, but she looked down, and he kissed her hair.

She stepped back. "You needn't worry that I'll forget you, Jakin." She gazed, again, at the bracelet, a small smile playing on her lips. "Truly, it is exquisite. Far too beautiful for me, anyway."

"Please, Rory, I'd like you to have it," he insisted. "It would be perfect for you. And I made it special."

She stared at it. "Well, it seems awfully extravagant." She studied it. The opals danced with color against the intricate silver filigree, almost hypnotic. "Really?" She looked at him. "You really want to give it away?"

"Only to you."

She reached for it, but he held it back. "Allow me, please. Hold your wrist out and let me fasten it for you." After he'd finished, he let his fingers linger on her arm for a moment.

Rory admired it, turning it slowly. Each opal was the same size as the next, perfectly matched and evenly spaced at every other twist of silver; the clasp hidden so cleverly in the silver latticework, she couldn't even see it. She blushed as she saw a small silver heart dangling between the gems. She glanced up to find Jakin standing close. "Thank you, Jakin. I will always remember you," she murmured, and kissed him on the cheek before she turned to go. That's when she saw Finn glaring at them.

Zirena returned as they rejoined the group, oblivious to what had just happened. "You will find new crossbows and arrows among your gear," she said. "Take them with our best wishes for good hunting along the way. I pray you will need them for nothing more than that."

"As do we, Zirena," Finn said, clasping her hands tightly. Good-byes were said all around and Finn turned to lead the first donkey away.

"Wait, wait!" Pelzar yelled, running toward them, breathless and sweaty, holding something in his hand.

"Aric, I made this for ye! Your slingshot!"

Aric was stunned. "I never got a gift before."

"What do you say, Aric?" Kalvara asked as she knelt to the children's height. Aric stared at the treasure in his hands, then at Pelzar. "Thanks!" he managed, then threw his arms around his damp friend, squeezing tight.

Chapter 24: Aric

Finn walked a half-step ahead of Rory as he led the way down the mountain. When she quickened her pace to catch up, he just walked faster. She didn't know what to do; she'd never seen him angry. She tucked her hand in the pocket of her cape to keep the bracelet out of sight and fell back to walk with Floxx. They travelled in silence; listening to the uneven rhythm of five sets of hooves and the occasional call of a bird. She needed Finn; this was an awful time for him to be angry. Would he come around? Didn't he know her feelings were for him only, not for Jakin at all?

Gloom settled over her and she kicked at loose stones. She missed Zad and his incessant grumbling; he'd always made her laugh on the inside, though she'd rarely let it out. His dry humor would have been salve for the hurt she now felt. She spiraled deeper. Dad and Gram. Lost, maybe forever. They'd probably moved from frantic to desperate to morose. Rosie must be crushed with grief. Would she ever get back? Certainly, she couldn't count on Floxx to take her;

Floxx was convinced she belonged here. What if it was true and she really did belong here?

And Jakin. He just wouldn't give up. She felt the bracelet on her wrist and begrudged it. Why had she accepted it? It had driven a wedge between Finn and her. She pulled her hand from her pocket under the guise of brushing her hair off her face, so she could glance at it. It really was gorgeous. How generous of Jakin to give it to her; how kind. But she had to give it back. She fumbled for the catch but couldn't find it. Finn glanced back, saw her looking at it, scowled, and picked up the pace. She shoved her hand deep in her pocket. That did it. It was coming off as soon as they stopped.

"I'm tired," Aric complained, rubbing his eyes and adjusting his seat on the donkey's swaying back. They'd been traveling steadily all day, except for a brief stop midday for a cold meal. The sun had dipped behind the mountain ridge. All of them were exhausted.

Finn called back. "We'll stop at the next spot big enough to set up camp."

"Can I hunt some birds with my slingshot when we get there?" Aric yawned.

Kalvara humored him. "I don't see why not."

The donkeys labored their way down the steep, rocky trail. It was nearly dark when they rounded a protrusion and saw they had finally reached the tree line. A thin forest opened in front of them, the scrawny tree tops swayed against the steel sky.

"We'll stop here!" Finn announced. Aric was suddenly wide awake, let out a whoop and leapt from the donkey's back before Kalvara could stop him.

"I'll stay close," he yelled and disappeared into the woods, gripping his slingshot.

They unloaded the donkeys and let them graze untethered. Finn was starting the fire when they heard Aric yelling.

"Kalvara, look!" the boy cried excitedly, "I got six of 'em!" and he raced into the clearing, his arms full of small birds. They were stunned; no one knew what to say.

Rory squatted in front of him and held out her arms. "Aric, that's so good! Such amazing hunting! Can I see what you've got?" He proudly dumped his feathery load in front of her. Two scrawny ravens, two plump doves, a large yellow and black bird, and a small red one, all with blood on their heads where Aric's rock had hit its mark.

Kalvara questioned him, trying to make sense of it. "Tell me how you got all these birds so fast?"

"I climbed a tree." He pointed. "With my slingshot. They were all around me, lots of birds. It was easy; one right after the other. I could'a shot more, but I didn't want to kill more than we'd eat, right, Kalvara?"

Kalvara cleared her throat, still staring at the birds. "Right, Aric. Only what we need to eat."

"Bring them over here," Finn said. "C'mon Aric, I'll show you how to clean them. We'll feast on them tonight!"

Rory could see Finn was ignoring her. He hadn't even asked her to help with the meal. She rummaged through the saddle bags, pulling out gear for the night, watching Kalvara and him together. They were still awkward with each other, but a friendship was building, and Rory wasn't at all sure she liked it.

As Kalvara helped with the birds, Rory overheard Finn speaking to her softly. "I was actually that good with my bow when I was his age. Must be the ancestral blood we share."

Kalvara stepped back from him, her temper flaring. "Don't cross the line, elf."

Rory hid her smile.

The next day, Aric hunted from the donkey's back as they traveled. He and Kalvara worked out a system: she held the donkey's lead and at Aric's signal, she'd stop walking, then he would shoot, leap off the donkey to retrieve the prey and hang it from the saddle. By the time they stopped for dinner, he had four birds, three rabbits, and one owl, caught by surprise sleeping in the hollow of a tree they'd passed.

Finn spent some time with the boy that evening, playing games with him. "Can you see the cluster of pinecones on the top of that tree?"

"'Course," Aric said.

"Humph," Finn said in disbelief.

"You don't believe me?"

"Well, it is twice as far as most people can see. How many pinecones are there?"

"Five large ones and two small ones behind them."

Finn stared at the cluster, counting. "Right you are, Aric. Those two in the back are really hard to see. You have eyes as keen as a Caladrius!" Aric crinkled his face and laughed, then dashed around the camp flapping his arms and shouting, "Aawwk, aawwk!" until Kalvara shushed him.

It was well past midnight when something woke Rory. She saw Aric wiggling and restless, readjusting himself close to Kalvara. Her first instinct was to wake her; she had super keen senses. Though Rory didn't hear anything; an uncanny intuition spiked her heart rate. It was too quiet. No sound at all. The dark woods usually had their noises, creaking tree tops, the scurry of night creatures, the rustle of leaves. But nothing stirred.

"Kalvara," Aric whispered. She, apparently, was awake, and as she laid her finger on his mouth, he pressed closer. A hiss split the silence, followed by a snarl, then a series of ear-splitting high-pitched yowls. A cat! And from the sound of it, a very large one not far away.

Before Rory could sit up, Finn was on his feet with his bow. A noisy thrashing followed with screams and grunts and roars, then a rhythmic thudding faded into the distance as something huge ran away. Suddenly, the night breathed, again; an owl screeched and insects resumed their buzzing.

"Was that the Felinex?" Aric asked.

"Yes, I believe it was," Finn whispered, squatting next to him. "And I think perhaps it scared off the giant Azatan told us about."

"Morfyn? Morfyn's been stalking us?" Kalvara pulled Aric closer.

In the morning, Rory was relieved as the steepness of the mountain trail lessened and gradually leveled out. As they led the donkeys through a wide, shallow brook, Aric glanced back. He gasped, then fired a rock into the shadows behind. Kalvara turned, instinctively grabbing her bow just as the giant stumbled into view, howling and holding his head.

He glared at them, bellowed an enraged challenge, and thundered toward them, his thighs as large as tree trunks. He leaned forward as he strode, his open mouth revealing pointed teeth like fangs, big enough to be seen even from their distance. He was naked except for a filthy loin cloth and a heavy necklace that thumped his chest with each step. As he drew closer, Rory was horrified to see his necklace was made of bones, human bones strung on a thick piece of rope. His wrists were encased in leather from the shanks of men's boots, one brown, one black, their mismatched buckles glinting in the sun. His hair was tied back with a long piece of dirty blue silk, perhaps a remnant of a woman's dress, its ragged edges swaying in and out of sight with the rhythm of his gait. The stones in the brook jumped from the weight of his steps.

"Run, Rory!" Finn yelled and tearing her eyes away, she turned to slog through the water. She was far too slow; Finn was at her side in an instant, carrying her to shore. By the time they had ducked behind some scrub bushes, the giant was in the brook. Kalvara was already shooting at him as Floxx knelt and motioned for Aric to climb on her back. In an instant, she transformed to Firebird and lifted off. Her shrill cry pierced the air as she flew above Morfyn. He roared as she passed over, waving his arms first in threat, then to keep his balance as he twisted to keep her in sight. She flew in tight circles above him, just out of reach, and the giant grew dizzy, lurching to stay on his feet.

Aric flung a rock, hitting him in his left eye. Morfyn howled and stumbled to his knees, one hand over his wounded eye, the other a foot deep in the water. But with fantastic strength, the brute stood up, blood running between his fingers. He grabbed a rotted tree trunk laying in the brook and lifted it as if it were no more than a branch. Crazed with anger, Morfyn blundered toward those on shore.

But seconds before he would have reached them, a sinewy gray shape leapt from a shadow in a wide arc, landed on the giant's back with an ear-splitting shriek, and knocked him back into the water. Their fight was fast and largely hidden by a great storm of splashing as they tumbled downstream. Hisses and yowls, roars and howls punctuated the tussle until it ended with a blood chilling wail. The giant limped from the water and staggered back toward the mountains. The skin on his back was shredded and gushing blood. There was no sign of the Felinex.

Kalvara, Finn, and Rory splashed downstream. By the time they got to Floxx and Aric, they had pulled the cat man to shore. One of his ears was ripped and blood soaked the fur on his face. But far worse was a long, jagged gash across his abdomen revealing a glimpse of his snaking inner parts.

Rory knelt beside him and found a weak pulse. "He saved our lives. We can't leave him here to die."

Finn closed the gaping wound in that gentle way he had with creatures, removed his tunic and wrapped the cat man in it, pulling it tight to keep him warm. They fashioned a stretcher from branches and vines and secured the unconscious Felinex to it, then pushed on to Masirika, the King's city, hoping to find help before it was too late.

As the sun was setting, they crossed the narrow rope bridge over the roiling river one at a time, finally setting foot in the country of Byerman. Just a couple more hours to the castle, Finn assured Rory, but it was nearly dark, and they had to wait until daybreak to continue. Floxx made a Tennifel poultice and applied it to the Felinex's wounds, hoping it would survive the night.

Rory's stomach clenched as she sat around the small fire. The others warmed chunks of cheese on sticks over the flames, but she had no appetite. This might well be the last night they'd be together. She had no idea what might happen after she met the king, if she even got that far. It could be good, but the chances were more likely it would be terrible. So many powers in this world wanted her dead, why would this king be any different? Against her will, she contemplated the many dark repercussions of announcing her claim to be royalty.

She glanced at Finn; he noticed and looked away. Her heart sank. Had she ruined everything by accepting the bracelet? *He's so angry I kissed Jakin. But it was only a peck on the cheek. It wasn't anything; just a thank you for the bracelet. Doesn't he know I have feelings for him and him alone? Can't he see that I'm falling in love with him?* Her hand shook as she passed a loaf of bread to Kalvara. The opal bracelet caught the reflection of fire and Finn scowled.

"Kalvara," Rory said, holding out her arm. "Can you take this off, please? I can't seem to find the clasp to undo it, myself. I don't want to wear it anymore."

She took Rory's wrist in one hand, turning the bracelet round and round, searching for the clasp. At first, Kalvara was amused, then amazed. Finally, she frowned. "Rory. I know this sounds impossible, but there doesn't seem to be a clasp."

"That can't be. It was unclasped before Jakin put it on me." Kalvara looked, again, inspecting the bracelet stone by stone, silver strand by silver strand. She pressed on the small heart, twisted it, pulled it. Then, did it again. And again. There was no way she could see to remove it.

By then, the others had moved closer. Kalvara lit a couple of torches and she and Floxx held them on either side of Rory, while Aric had a look. But, even with his exceptional vision, he could see no break in the extraordinary silver braidwork.

Finn finally crouched beside Rory and she was thrilled when he took her hand in his, slowly turning the bracelet around, studying it. "I wonder where he got these stones?"

"He said they were his own gems. That he'd mined them when he was a child. And that he'd asked one of the silversmiths to make this bracelet for me."

"His own gems?" Finn frowned. "That's unlikely. These are opals and there are no opals mined in Orizin. Only hard stones, mainly topaz, but also some rubies and diamonds."

Floxx agreed. "Opals are soft gems. They're usually found near the sea."

Rory panicked. What had Jakin done? What kind of gift was this? She wanted it off, even if they ruined it trying. "Finn," she asked, her voice trembling. "Do you have a tool you could use to cut it? Or break it?"

For the first time since they'd left Orizin, Finn smiled at her and it warmed her from the inside out. "I probably can find something that will work." He turned to rummage in the gear.

"What has Jakin given me?" Rory whispered.

Floxx frowned. "The bracelet may be under a spell of some sort," she said. "But surely Jakin didn't cast it. He probably doesn't even know."

"Then, who did?" Rory was shaking. Was she doomed to die, if not by a beast of some sort, then by a magic spell?

"It'll be all right, Rory. I'll get it off." Finn held two tools. One was about six inches long, thin and straight with a pointed tip small enough to fit between the braidwork. "Nut picker," he told her. "Found it in the sack of nuts Zirena sent." The other tool was far longer and bulkier, with sturdy scissor blades. "Harness cutter," he held it up, grinning.

"Let's try the nut picker first," Rory said, rubbing her wrist. Finn sat in front of her, placing her hand on his crossed legs. Floxx and Kalvara held the torches close and Aric scooted in to watch. Carefully, Finn fitted the tip of the picker between the strands of fine silver braid and gave a quick, gentle flick. The bracelet jerked against Rory's wrist.

"Ow!" she frowned. "That hurt."

Finn bent to see how much damage he had done, turning it around and around under the torchlight, but could find none. Not even the slightest dent in the silver.

"That's odd," he said and tried, again, concentrating fully on where he placed the point. "I'll brace it better this time," he told her as he twisted the tip into the silver threads. He carefully pushed and pulled but the braid didn't bend. He shook his head in frustration.

"I want to try something. I'll be careful." Finn pinched the bracelet away from her skin, reinserted the point into the braid work, and yanked.

Rory screamed. Finn dropped the tool and pulled her close; squeezing her so tight she could barely breathe. She buried her face in his neck; he smelled like fresh air and wood fires.

"I'm so sorry, Rory. I didn't mean to hurt you."

She melted. "I know; it's okay." Her wrist throbbed, but honestly, she'd have traded the pain for that hug any day. Maybe he had forgiven her; maybe they were okay, again. She could only hope. He slowly pulled away, holding her a few inches from his face.

"Don't worry; we'll figure out how to remove it without hurting you. For now, though, let's just ignore it's even there. Okay with you?"

"Perfect with me."

He smiled a half smile, tucked a stray curl behind her ear, then leaned down and kissed her, light and soft. Her heart leapt. Though it was over in a second, she felt it far longer; and in spite of her aching wrist, and her fear of what tomorrow might bring, she couldn't wipe the grin off her face.

Kalvara and Aric slept nearby, and Finn had finally settled down an arm's length from Rory. She had feigned sleep until she heard him whiffling, then tip-toed to the fire where Floxx was keeping watch by the Felinex.

"Any change?" she whispered.

"Not yet. I'm hoping the Tennifel does its work."

"He's an amazing creature. Not like anything I've ever seen in my world."

"You'd be surprised the creatures you haven't seen in your world!" Floxx said.

"What?"

Floxx's mouth turned up at its edges but she shook her head. "Some other time, Rory."

"Hmfff." How could Floxx drop a hint like that and refuse to say more. "Okay, fine. Can we talk about this world, then? I have a million questions. It's crazy for me here, and only you would understand how different it is from Alaska. Ghillies, tomtees, dwarves. Dragons, danger, death."

Floxx sighed. "All right. Ask away."

"Why am I the target? Why are the stakes so high? Will they stop chasing me if I am, as you say, really the stolen princess and reunited with the King and Queen? In these stories you sing, Finn is the foretold king, not me. Why isn't he being hunted?"

"That's a lot of questions, and all good ones." Floxx slid closer, so they could huddle together, cozy and private. "Let's start with Draegin. He prowls for royal heirs of all races. He understands some things about the prophecy—not everything, but certainly the reconstruction of the Eldur Crown and the ruler who will wear it. He wants it for himself or possibly for his daughter, Queen Marinna. They are consumed with eliminating any threats to their rule. He has murdered many potential heirs through the ages, far before he had an heir of his own. As far as Finn goes, Eldurrin, in his wisdom, has hidden him from Draegin's view. Finn's royal heritage is a secret known to few."

"But what about me? Eldurrin hasn't hidden me, and Draegin wants me dead." She didn't like this at all. Was she just a foil to cover Finn?

"Draegin rages with short-sighted vision, feeding on hate and jealousy, greedy to own everything, lusting for power. And when he senses a threat, he doesn't consider whether or not it is valid; his dragon nature drives him, and he will not rest until the threat is removed. I'm afraid that's how it is with you, dear."

"So, if you knew this dragon king would try to kill me, why did you bring me back? Why not just leave well enough alone?" Rory pulled away, frustrated, not understanding at all.

Floxx put an arm around her shoulder and drew her back. "Trying to kill you and actually doing it are two different things. I'm here with you, Rory, to protect you; and it's not just me, of course. The Tennins and the others with us, including Finn, are all committed to getting you back to your parents."

"Well, yeah. I see that." She poked at the coals. "But it's been so risky and the cost ridiculously high; I feel so horrible about everything that's happened." She thought about Zad. "No one else should be hurt for me. Please, Floxx, protect them, too."

They sat quietly for a while. Rory wondered about Floxx. To think she'd been sent by Eldurrin to orchestrate her rescue; protect her; nurture her, guide her. She'd had her back from the day she was born. It was all so wondrous, but the more she thought about it, the less sense it made; she just couldn't imagine why.

Floxx tightened her arm around her. "Remember those star stories?" Floxx gestured to the sky. "He had you in mind, too, you know. Not just Finn."

"Who? You mean Eldurrin?"

"Yes. He had you in mind when he set the stars in their places and put his plan into motion."

"What are you talking about?"

"The song I sang to you about the Eldur Crown. Finn is not the only one it speaks of. You are in it, too." Rory turned to her, confused. She'd listened carefully and nowhere did the song mention a princess.

Floxx began to hum the tune, then softly sang part of it. "'The ruler will find her and gently will bind her when that which was stolen is found.' Remember?"

"It's referring to Finn as ruler, and the stolen crown, right?"

"It might seem so. But there is often more than one meaning to Eldurrin's words. The refrain refers to you, Rory. He had you very much in mind. You are 'that which was stolen' and now you've been found— returned. Back here."

Rory struggled to put it together. "The ruler is Finn," she said slowly. "He was the first to find me after I'd crashed. What does it mean that he will bind me?"

"Not you. Those words speak of Finn finding me, and binding me, which he did when he bound my broken wing."

Yes, he'd done that, though she'd never attached much significance to it.

Floxx continued, intent on making it very clear. "But he had to find you—the stolen one— first, which he did. After that had happened, he found me and bound me, and so the prophecy was set into motion."

"Whoa. Wait. That's bizarre! You're saying my arrival here was orchestrated down to the second?"

"Exactly, my dear. Yours and mine both." She stood and patted Rory's head. "You watch, alright? I need a few hours' sleep." And she disappeared into the darkness.

Rory wrapped in Ardith's cloak and lay down. She doubted she'd sleep, but at least she'd rest. Her mind raced. Eldurrin had thought of her! Way back when he set the stars in the sky? That's insane! How could that possibly be? That means he knew she'd be born in this world. And he knew she'd be kidnapped and raised in Alaska. Wait. Eldurrin knows Alaska? Well, of course, he must. Her mind raced as she realized what that could mean. So, is he the One who made everything in her world, too? Why would he care about her?

She stared at the stars, thinking about the stories, about the prophecy. Who was she that she should have even a small part in a such a grand plan? She watched the three Eldur stars rise above the trees, one after the other, red, yellow, blue. To think that Eldurrin illustrated his stories with constellations—that was so incredibly awesome! Wonder filled her as she pondered how great he must be. Then she realized something more. If the prophecy about Finn was true—and she believed it was—then it must be true about her, too. Here she'd been found, yet she'd had no idea she'd ever been lost. To think she'd been moving in his plan all her life, doing ordinary things: growing up, going to school, learning to fly. And it was all a part of his great purpose.

A warmth blossomed inside her. He knew her. The One who made everything knew her. And he cared about her. Her! She was overwhelmed with emotion. She raised her arms, reaching for the stars, for him. *Thank you, Eldurrin, thank you. For loving me. For caring about me. For giving me a purpose and such hope.* A peace grew in her, powerful and inexplicable as the assurance of his love deepened. She didn't need to go home. She was home. She was exactly where Eldurrin meant her to be. On the other side of the fire, she could hear Floxx humming the ballad. She felt the song well up in her, too, and she buried her face in her cloak, humming with unfathomable joy.

Chapter 25: Masirika

They left for the city at first light, the woods thinning after a time and giving way to a few solitary homes. Floxx led the procession, assured and elegant. Finn followed, holding the front of the stretcher behind him, the furry length of the cat man draped across it; Kalvara and Rory each supported a corner of the other end. Aric followed behind them, leading the donkeys in a slow walk.

Their arrival caused quite a stir; one child playing outside was so startled she screamed and ran back into her house. Families peered from windows or stood on porches to catch a glimpse. As the crowd grew, Kalvara asked Rory if she could handle the end of the stretcher herself, and she could. So, Kalvara sat Aric on a donkey, one arm firmly around him, avoiding eye contact as they moved through the outlying town. Rory had to admire Kalvara for her loyalty and protection of the child. Aric gaped at the small, dirty homes clustered together and, oblivious to any malice or threats, waved at the guarded, staring faces. Kalvara was smart to hold on to him.

Rory spotted the castle in the distance, off to her right, its tallest tower visible over the tops of the trees. Her pulse quickened. Could that really be her home?

Had she actually been born there? She realized she'd been hoping for some subconscious recognition; something that registered inside as familiar, but, she felt nothing except fear. Were guards watching from the turrets? Would they welcome them or turn them away? The wondrous peace she'd felt the night before was nothing but a memory; chaos and confusion churned inside her now. The King will never believe her! He will chase her out. Or have her arrested. What was she thinking to believe this was a good idea? She eyed the dark turrets; did the guards have weapons?

The road changed from dirt to cobblestone and led toward the city center. Children pointed as their mothers pulled them close. Buyers stopped haggling to gawk. One merchant, working a fruit stand, dropped a basket of apples when he saw them. These people obviously had never seen Eldrows or a Felinex. But even so, couldn't they be a little more discreet?

Rory tried to keep her eyes straight ahead, catching as much as she could with her peripheral vision. Their clothing varied from rags to silks, and the poor stepped aside for the wealthy. A Tomtee family, unloading a wagon of yellow melons, stopped to watch them pass. Most of the people, though, were human. Ahead on her left, a young woman jostling a toddler on her hip had stopped at the baker's stand, the child pointing to the loaves of bread. She could smell them, fresh and yeasty, reminding her of Gram's bread, and the taste of its soft hot center soaking up her honey-butter. The mother tore a piece from the loaf for her child before she slid the rest into a woven sack slung over her shoulder. Rory's stomach growled. The woman's golden hair was twisted artfully and caught up on her head, all except the few loose strands tangled in her child's fingers. She wore a long turquoise dress fitted to her slim figure and caught at the waist with a beaded belt. She turned her head, and a silver earring dangled from one ear, so long it nearly touched her shoulder. She was certainly one of the wealthy ones. When the woman turned the other way, Rory gasped, nearly dropping the Felinex. The side of the woman's face was tattooed in turquoise swirls, speckled here and there with small gems. The design covered her cheek and ran down one side of her neck before disappearing under her clothing. This outdid any face paint her middle school classmates had come up with; maybe she wouldn't be such a freak here. Maybe no one would look twice at her scars.

The road widened as they arrived in the heart of the city, which was laid out around an impressive circular center. A spectacular stone sculpture of a horse and soldier graced the center of a round garden. The soldier carried a blue flag, a four-sided gold star set in a white circle emblazoned in its center. The sculpture was elevated on a round, rock platform about ten feet high. A stunning garden flourished on all sides; lush, vibrant greenery and proliferous beds of yellow, blue and white flowers. A wide stone road encircled the garden and many roads led from it to various sections of the city, like spokes from the center of a wheel. Banners hung at the entrances to each of the streets displaying a trade symbol. Rory understood what a few of the symbols represented: Blacksmiths, Carpenters, Bakers, Grocers, Tailors. Floxx led them half way around the circle, where a dozen uniformed riders waited.

"Halt," the commanding officer called in a loud voice. They stopped. "State your business."

They gently set the stretcher down. Finn stepped forward, bowed, and replied, "We come in peace, seeking help, if you please."

"And you have an appointment?"

"We do not, regrettably. It would not have been possible to send word ahead, even if we had known it was necessary. As you can see," he gestured toward the Felinex, "we've been attacked. By the giant, Morfyn. And this creature saved us, though he may die for his efforts if he isn't cared for immediately."

"Morfyn?" the soldier's horse moved restlessly. "Around here?"

"He was. But no longer. The Felinex sent him running."

"A Felinex!" The guard peered with interest at the creature on the stretcher. "So, they are real—not just the stuff of fables."

"Quite real, indeed," Finn replied. "And this one is dying. A creature as rare as this deserves the best possible care. We would like to take him to the royal physician."

The officer peered from the Felinex to Kalvara and Aric, then back to Finn, making up his mind. "The King must be notified of this immediately. Follow me."

The King! We haven't missed him! And we're going to the castle! The Felinix is our way in. Thank you, Eldurrin! Please, though, don't let the cat-man die!

The soldiers surrounded them, shielding them from the growing crowd. They led them under the Fish banner and down the street where skinny dogs scavenged buckets of fly-infested fish guts; the smell sickening.

Rory was relieved when they left the market behind and turned toward the castle. She could see its three towers fully now, each topped with a turret. One of the towers dominated the other two. The stone walls were a mix of brown and gray rock fitted masterfully together, flat on top and thick enough for two or three men to walk side by side. The boxy, flat-roofed sections of the castle were graced with high arched windows. She noticed a stone chapel near the castle, set among overhanging trees and manicured flower gardens; the ground behind, speckled with gravestones. That must be where royalty was buried. She wondered if she had a gravestone in there. Though the castle road was longer than she'd anticipated, eventually they reached an enormous courtyard. The soldiers dismounted even before their horses had fully stopped and surrounded them.

"Leave everything here, your mounts, your weapons and your gear, and follow me," the Commander clipped. Tall arched doors provided entrance to one of the smaller rectangular sections of the castle, flanked on each side by armed guards. While the Felinex was carried one way, they were ushered into a large, sparsely furnished room with a low-burning fire in the hearth. Even with the small blaze, the room was damp and chilly.

"Wait here," the commander growled, then turned abruptly, leaving two soldiers guarding the door inside the room and two others outside.

They pulled hard wooden chairs close to the fire. Finn's stomach growled loud enough he apologized, wrapping his arms around himself. They'd had no breakfast and what was left of their provisions was in the saddlebags outside. No one dared speak, wary of the guards at the door. Rory's heart sank. This was not much of a welcome.

After a few hours, two servants arrived; one with bread and a tureen of thick bean soup and another with a platter of fruit and cheese. Rory and the others tore into the food.

"The King must have verified our story," Finn said as he ladled more soup from the pot. He hesitated, looking sheepish and asked if anyone wanted more.

Rory was stuffed, and the others declined. He grinned and poured the rest of the soup into his bowl.

Rory dared to hope the King might grant an audience. Maybe he would have questions about the Felinex, about the nature of their journey. That would be a perfect lead-in for her. But what would she say? *Hello, Father, I'm your long-lost daughter returned from the frozen state of Alaska. You've never heard of it? Oh, right, that's because it's in another world. How did I get here? I flew in an airplane—there are none of them in your world; you have giant birds and dragons instead.* Seriously, he would never believe it. She barely believed it. Maybe she didn't even want to tell him. What if they just skipped it and said she was lost and thought he could help, but well, they'd obviously made a mistake coming here. Maybe Werner could fix her airplane and she could just fly home. Home. To Dad. To Gram. To Rosie. Where she used to belong.

Rory fiddled with her spoon and the bracelet caught her eye. It really was pretty. She turned it slowly around her wrist. Maybe she should just enjoy it, appreciate it. So what if she couldn't get it off; actually that's kind of cool in a way. She was sure Jakin could show her how to unclasp it when she saw him next. She shouldn't be so upset with him. He was a good guy. Loved his family. Would do anything to protect them. She ran a finger over one of the opals, cool and smooth, and allowed a small smile. He was so good-looking. And very brave. He'd fought just as hard as Zad did. For her. He'd always looked out for her. She wasn't being fair to him. She should warn him about Morfyn. To stay away from that monster. She felt Finn's eyes on her and slid her hand under the table. But, it was too late. He shoved his chair away and stood, turning his back on her.

Chapter 26: King Merek

The sun was nearly down when the door flew open and the Commander ordered them to follow. Rory's heart nearly burst! Follow him where? Was he taking them to the King or to prison? She gripped Floxx's arm as they went after him, needing her support, her strength, her help. From the courtyard, they entered a larger, more elaborate section of the castle. They were rushed down a long, stone hallway, past several closed doors, then turned right and climbed a set of wide polished steps, the wooden banisters gleaming. The spacious hallway was hung with enormous multicolored tapestries; the ceilings must have been 20 feet high. Rory was awed at the display of wealth. Some of the doors were open and servants and uniformed soldiers hurried by, casting surreptitious glances their way. They caught glimpses of a vast ballroom, a meeting room with a huge round table, and several smaller meeting rooms.

They approached two elaborately carved doors at the end of the hall. Rory's heart pounded as the guards opened them with a grand flourish. The Commander led them to a massive throne room where King Merek, himself, sat waiting.

Rory stood gaping, both terrified and awed. The King! Would she have a chance to talk with him? What if he just dismissed them? She tried to calm herself with a deep breath, but it didn't help much. Floxx touched her shoulder, nudging her forward with the others. Much of the floor was gray flatstone, perfectly fitted together, which formed a neutral background for its artistic center—a white marble circle about twenty feet in diameter, in which a four-pointed yellow star was inlaid. They were directed to stand in that circle, facing the throne. They stood in silence as the King consulted with the Commander.

She glanced around the room. Three white columns flanked either side of the throne, etched with deep vertical lines that drew the eye up to the capitals, which were carved into four-pointed stars. The high walls were covered with colorful tapestries, depicting peaceful scenes of trade in city and country under the protective watch of the King's troops. Enormous brass chandeliers hung from the high ceiling, fitted with a dozen thick white candles whose light danced on the cambers of the polished metal. Like good troops they were spaced in straight lines evenly across the room, ten that she could see, and she figured ten more hung behind. Three wide steps stretched across the base of the King's throne, and uniformed soldiers in gray, blue and gold stood at attention on the edges of each step.

The throne itself was surprisingly simple, white like the columns and contoured comfortably with wide arm rests. Its main adornment was a high arched back that towered above the King's head, topped with a huge golden star. An open circle studded with brilliant blue stones surrounded the star. Were those sapphires? Long, blue banners with emblems similar to the ones in the center of the city, hung from each side of the throne.

The King, himself, was deep in hushed conversation. Rory studied him. Could he possibly be her father? He wore a gray suit of clothes, topped with a long, flowing robe. The fabric was exquisite, it looked like gold-threaded silk embroidered with blue and gold handiwork on the collar. His crown was a thick gold open circle with eight peaks, each peak topped with a large blue sapphire. A glistening band of diamonds encircled the crown's base. As he bent forward to stand, she glimpsed his balding head. He was medium height and obviously loved to eat; a fact his robe did not quite hide. His keen brown eyes were etched with fatigue and something else as he observed them frankly, lingering for a few moments on each of them. He's sad, Rory realized, startled to see such grief in his eyes. He's thinking of his daughter. His dead daughter. Floxx tugged on her arm, and she knelt before him, along with the others.

"Thank you, Commander. You may go, now," the King said. Rory didn't dare look up, but she could hear the officer leave the room, closing the grand doors behind him. The King cleared his throat. "Please stand."

Rory was trembling from head to foot. She could feel the soup burning in her throat and she swallowed several times, determined not to vomit.

"I am quite curious as to the nature of your visit. It is most unusual for such a diverse group of individuals to travel together. And then facing a formidable giant's attack. How terrible! I thank Eldurrin for the strength and courage of the Felinex, who, I am pleased to tell you, is most likely to recover. What a remarkable creature! And to each of you I would like to express my greatest admiration for facing Morfyn, our dire nemesis. Not many escape alive."

Rory heard a tremor in his voice.

"It is clear you are comrades, but the nature of your mission is quite a mystery. I am most interested to hear about it. To show my appreciation for preventing the giant from entering my lands, I have arranged a dinner in your honor. Will you join me, please?"

He stood and descended the steps and led them from the throne room to a private room where a large rectangular table was set with fine silver and lit by candlelight. Troops followed them, two entering the room while the rest waited in the hallway. From seemingly out of nowhere, servants appeared, pulling back chairs for them to sit. This was completely unexpected. Dinner with the King! He wanted to hear why they'd come? Rory was numb with shock.

After they were seated, the King extended his hands. "Please forgive the brusqueness of my Commander earlier today. Your unexpected arrival in our city put us, shall we say, on high guard. But, after seeing the Felinex and investigating further, we realize you are no threat. Rather the contrary. We are in your debt for chasing off our fiercest enemy. I trust you were provided food and drink while you waited?"

"Yes," Finn said, "thank you very much; it was delicious."

"Excellent. Now tell me. What is the nature of your visit to Masirika? I will do what I can to ensure its success."

Everyone turned to look at Rory.

She cleared her throat and began. "Yes, well, your Highness. There is a lot to tell. Quite a lot."

The King waited.

"I'm not really sure where to start." Her voice cracked. She was making a mess of this. She looked away, trying to compose herself. "I just recently arrived in Gamloden a few weeks ago, though it seems much longer." She met his gaze, again. "I came from a place no one here has heard of, called Alaska."

The King frowned but said nothing.

"Apparently, I've been here before, but I don't remember it. My family in Alaska told me I'd arrived on their doorstep bloody and nearly dead when I was just a few weeks old."

The King's eyes widened, and he crossed his arms over his chest.

Rory glanced at Floxx who smiled at her, encouraging her to continue. "And now that I'm back here, I'm told I was kidnapped sixteen years ago. From this very castle. And that you, yourself, are, well, might be, my father."

The King sat very still, emotions moving across his face. Shock. Anger. Suspicion. Hope. Anger, though, is the one that won. His eyes hardened. "You make claim to be the kidnapped princess?"

She couldn't hold his gaze. She looked at her lap, fidgeting with her hands. *He hates me. I'd figured he wouldn't believe me. Who would—it's so bizarre. Floxx must be wrong. Or maybe even making it up.*

And then she thought of what it had cost Floxx. She was definitely not making it up; she'd risked too much, even fought the dragon for her. Rory remembered the night of the Tennins, the song of prophecy, the refrain. And she felt something stir inside—a strength, a certainty it was true; she was, in fact, his abducted daughter. She raised her head and looked directly at him.

"Yes, your Highness. I think I am your daughter. As do these friends with me. That is the purpose of our visit. Though I don't know how I might prove it to you."

The King exhaled. He looked at the others for confirmation.

Floxx spoke for all of them. "She speaks the truth, your Highness. I am aware there have been imposters over the years, perhaps more than even I realize, but, please, listen to our story, all of it, before you pass judgment."

The King motioned for the meal to be served. "Very well. But, it is only because so many years have passed since the last bogus claim, and because of your victory over the giant that I am willing."

Others had claimed to be her? That must have hurt him so much. No wonder he doubted. His eyes were clouded with grief. Rory'd never thought about how he must have felt when she was kidnapped. Or the queen, her birth mother, who'd lost her only child. She'd been focused only on herself. Their hearts must have been broken.

Servants arrived with the first course, setting before them small cups of creamy purple soup, sprinkled with a ground spice that smelled a little like nutmeg. The King picked his cup up and drank it in just a few swallows. She did the same. Delicate. Sweet like a pumpkin soup with a lemony bite to it.

"Wonderful!" Floxx exclaimed setting her cup down.

"Arinabog. A root that grows in abundance here. Delicious in soups and salads. Now then." The King turned his attention to Rory and grilled her with questions about Alaska, who had raised her, and how she'd gotten to Gamloden.

The main course arrived. The servant placed a huge oval gold-rimmed platter, nearly three feet long, in front of the King. "Good. Good!" He beamed at his guests. "A delicacy, to be sure," he said and nodded to the staff to serve it. Rory was horrified. The platter held a black and green striped fish, its scales oiled and slightly charred, its tail poised above a mound of colorful vegetables, its mouth wide open to showcase all six inches of its curved fangs. A small octopus seemed to struggle within its gaping jaw, several of its small tentacled arms wrapped around the fish's snout. She felt queasy.

"What is it?" Aric squealed, apparently fascinated with it. Why wasn't he afraid? The thing was nearly as big as him.

"This, my boy, is a fanged patira fish. A small one, actually. Some grow to four or even five feet. You wouldn't want to meet one in the water, now would you?"

"No, sir!" Aric said so loudly everyone laughed.

Rory did not want to eat that thing, and glanced at Finn, who much to her annoyance was trying not to laugh at her.

"I've tasted it before," he said. "You'll love it."

She narrowed her eyes at him.

Much to her surprise, though, the fish was tasty. It was mild and served with a savory butter sauce that was delicious. She was relieved to recognize the other foods on her plate: wild rice, carrots, and turnips.

The King dropped his questioning while they ate the main course but picked it up as soon as they finished. Floxx described Cue's rescue of Rory and said simply that they had both been transported to Alaska. Cue had watched over her as she grew, and when the time was right, she had brought them back to Gamloden.

"The airplane was damaged a little," she confided, laughing. "But it all ended well."

Finn recounted his discovery of them, describing his first astonishment at finding an airplane and a beautiful woman in the woods—Rory blushed deeply—and another later, when the bird with the injured wing changed into Floxx. He described the airplane, and how he'd helped rig it and flip it.

"Can it be fixed?" the King inquired.

"Probably," Rory said. "A bigger problem is fuel."

"I see."

"But, even if it could fly, I have no idea how to get back to Alaska. It's not like I could follow a map there."

The King frowned. "No." He pondered. "Yet the idea of another world—and moving between them—is not new. Old lore tells the elves left this world for another one ages ago."

Finn leaned forward. "Surely, you don't think they went to Rory's world."

"I have no idea where they went. Or even if they went. I am simply stating what the tales say."

"Well, if they went to another world, it wasn't mine," she assured them, though her mind nagged, remembering Floxx's comment. "There's no mention of elves having a part in our history." She suddenly realized something. "Except in fairy tales."

"Fairy tales?"

"Children's stories, mostly, are full of what are called fantasy creatures—make believe, pretend, not real—elves among them." She was thinking of *Rumpelstiltskin* and *The Elves and the Shoemaker*.

"Something to ponder," the King said, then redirected the conversation back to Finn, who went on to tell of his aunt and uncle, the horrible wolf attacks, our journey from Tomitarn and the bloody Inozak battles.

The King was touched as Kalvara shared her story, some of it, anyway. How she and Aric had escaped the horrors of cave captivity and survived for many months. How the Eldrow men were drugged and forced into breeding. "But, not him," she said fiercely, glancing at Aric. "Not ever. My brother placed him in my care before he was killed for refusing to comply."

The King broke the ensuing silence. "You have each overcome tremendous odds to sit here at my table. I am honored, indeed, to make your acquaintances."

Chapter 27: Crescent Moon

The time grew late as they told him about Cue's death, Rory's capture, the horrible fight with the dragon, and Zad's death and burial. None of them mentioned the prophecy, itself, or Finn's role in restoring the Eldur Crown. It just seemed too much all at once.

When Rory described the dwarves' gracious and generous send-off, the King held up his hand. He leaned forward and asked, "This was Zad's sister? Her name?"

"Princess Zirena, sir. Married to Prince Tozar."

The King's face paled. "I see."

She thought she detected another tremble in his voice. "And this brother of Zad's, the one who stayed in Orizin. I don't recall that you told me his name. A dwarf, of course." He waved his hand dismissively.

Finn answered. "His name is Jakin, your highness."

The King's eyes widened in shock.

"And, no sir, he is not a dwarf at all. He is human and about my age. Zirena kindly took him in and raised him after his parents were killed by the giant, Morfyn."

The King fell back against his seat, his lips set in a straight line, clearly agitated. The guard at the door started toward him, but the King held up his hand.

Rory suddenly remembered. "Your Highness! I almost forgot! Zirena sent you a gift with her fondest regards. It's in my pack, wherever the soldiers have put it."

"Bring their gear at once," he ordered the guard.

No one said much as the servants whisked dishes and platters away and replaced them with exquisite cookies cut in the shapes of animals and painted with pastel-colored icings. Aric, especially, was enthralled with them and he filled the uncomfortable silence chattering about their shapes and playing with them.

When their packs arrived, Rory retrieved Zirena's lumpy bundle and carried it to the King. He stared at it without moving to open it, lost in thought. Finally, he sighed, seemingly resigned to some unspoken fate, loosened the string on the cloth bag, and carefully emptied its glittering contents onto a large plate. A rolled piece of parchment protruded from the middle of the pile and the King removed it, untied it, and read its brief message. He didn't even try to hide his astonishment. He re-rolled the note and slid it into a pocket inside his robe.

The gems were beautifully cut, undoubtedly some of the choicest from Orizin's treasury. Several of the topaz stones were the size of unshelled walnuts, the rubies and diamonds as big as chestnuts. The King pushed them around with his finger, scattering prisms of color around the room, spreading the treasure across the plate, as if he was looking for something. And he found it. He picked up a tiny golden spoon, its handle no more than three inches long, and smiling in a sad sort of way, turned it over in his hand.

Rory studied him. Something bothered him terribly. Did it have to do with her? With her story? Could that possibly be her baby spoon?

After a long silence, the King asked her, "What did Princess Zirena say, exactly, when she gave this gift to you to transport?"

Rory struggled to remember. "Something like, 'Give this to the King with our best wishes, jewels from the mines of Prince Tozar and Princess Zirena.'"

"So, you told her your story?"

"I did."

"And she believed you?"

"She was guarded, only saying, 'What if it's true?'"

The King pushed the plate of jewels away and leaned back, toying with the spoon. He said nothing for several long minutes, weighing all he had been told.

Rory fretted. Why was he hesitating? Why did he still doubt? What else could she do to convince him? She wrung her hands under the table and felt the bracelet. Jakin! A giddy warmth spread through her at the thought of him. So handsome. Strong. Fearless. She wished he was here with her.

Finally, the King spoke. "It is a fantastic story, of that there is no doubt. But Zirena is a shrewd woman. And she has much at stake if your claim is, in fact, true."

He withdrew the parchment from his robe. He unrolled it and read the words aloud. *This could change everything.* He rolled it back up, his eyes locked on me. "I, too, suspect your story may be true; indeed, it seems too bizarre to have been fabricated." He paused, his tired eyes studying her face. "However, there is one piece of critical evidence missing."

Rory held her breath.

"My infant daughter was born with a birthmark on the back of her neck, just below her hairline on the left side. May I examine your neck, please?"

Oh, no! A birthmark? She was sure she didn't have one. Even if she'd had one as a baby, it might have been scratched out, covered now with scars.

Floxx walked to Rory, gesturing for her to stand up. "Let me take a look, dear," she said, turning her around. "Head down now; I'm going to move your beautiful hair out of the way."

The King joined them.

"What does the birthmark look like?" Rory asked from under a curtain of hair.

"A moon. A small crescent moon. It was white, barely visible against your pale skin."

Mom would have surely known. And she never mentioned it. Rory feared what would happen next.

Floxx's fingers were light as she moved tendrils of her hair to the side, then turned her head toward the best light, not very bright in the candle-lit room. Rory shivered when she felt the King's breath on her neck.

"There," Floxx said, tilting her head ever so slightly.

"Yes." The King's voice was husky. "Right there. Tipped on its side. Still white and not much bigger than it was when you were born."

Rory's heart raced. It's there? He remembered it from when she was a baby! It's true then. Proven beyond a doubt. She was his daughter. She really was the King's daughter! Floxx dropped her hair back in place. Rory turned to face the King.

"Karena?" He searched her eyes. "Can it possibly be you?"

Karena! Her birth name!

He cupped her face gently, brushed back her curls, touched the angry stripes on her cheek. Tears brimmed

233

in her eyes and ran down her cheeks, and he caught them with his fingers. *This is my father? Regal and proper, yet gracious, gentle, and kind. So very sad and vulnerable. And old. So much older than Dad. Dad, who taught me to fish. And hunt. And fly. Now I have another Dad? Can I love them both? Can both of them love me?*

Then the King pulled her close, huge sobs shaking his frame. What had she done to him? She thought she'd be thrilled if he believed her, elated to finally know the truth. But, she was terrified for him. What new horrors would she bring to this broken-hearted man?

Eventually, he pulled away and she asked the question that had been haunting her all evening. "Where is Mother?"

He turned to blow his nose and compose himself. "Your mother is not well, Karena, ah, Rory." He paused. "But it's very late and, well, one thing at a time. Come, sit here by me for a few minutes." He moved her chair next to his and when she was settled, gave his attention to the others. Aric had fallen asleep in Kalvara's lap, but the rest were sniffling and wiping their eyes.

The King's smile transformed his face as he reached over to take her hand. "We are all exhausted but let me share one thing with you before we part for the night. It has to do with Zirena's gift. This spoon," he held it up, "belongs to my nephew, son of my younger brother, Henri. My wife and I gave it to him. The back reads, 'Welcome little nephew. King Merek and Queen Raewyn.' His name, Jakin, and his birth date are engraved on the back of the handle below my royal seal. This same Jakin is Zirena's adopted son."

Rory gasped.

Finn stood, opened his mouth to say something, then snapped it shut.

"This is a shock, I'm sure. But let me finish." The King motioned for Finn to sit down.

"Henri was an adventurer and a valiant young leader, strong, brave, cunning, most certainly headed for a high command. We had, unfortunately, never been close. I had been involved in palace matters from boyhood, but my brother had no such royal obligations and Father indulged him in sailing voyages, mountain expeditions, ogre hunting. He excelled in every challenge; it seemed there was nothing he couldn't do. He had just returned from a skirmish with the Mermen who threatened our coastal border, his ships defeating them in a battle that lasted for weeks. While he was gone, Morfyn had made raid after raid on the farming families living in the northern outskirts of Byerman, becoming more brazen with each attack. People were terrified to work their fields." The King took a long drink of water.

"When Henri heard about Morfyn's attacks, he was infuriated, and he determined to kill the giant. He and his wife came to see us a few days after you were born, Rory, bringing Jakin, who was then a few months old. I hadn't seen them since their wedding, a few years earlier. When he told me his plans, I begged them not to go alone; I tried to persuade him to lead a contingent to kill Morfyn. But he insisted the giant would never be caught by a brigade. 'He lives far up in the mountains,' he said, 'in the craggy, desolate places near the ogres, and one or two brave souls must catch him unaware.'"

"I accused him of underestimating the giant, not thinking about the possible consequences; I pleaded with him, saying it was unconscionable to take his wife and baby with him, fairly ushering them to their deaths. He stormed out after many harsh words that I have often since regretted. They left for the mountains the next day. I never saw him, again. I was notified of his death a few years later, long after you were gone, Rory. Morfyn had killed Henri, his wife and, everyone assumed, his young son, Jakin. The giant leaves no bodies to recover."

Rory twisted the bracelet thinking of how terrified Jakin must have been.

"But Zirena, sharp as she is, put the pieces of the story together, and realizing that the child Zad had found was, in fact, Jakin, brought him to me to raise here in the castle. But, your mother had reacted very badly to your abduction and was in no condition to care for a child. I convinced Zirena to raise Jakin until your mother recovered, which she, unfortunately, never has—with the agreement that, if we had no other children, Jakin would be announced heir to my throne when he reached the age of 18."

"Jakin will be the next King?" Rory couldn't believe it.

"That's just it, Rory. Zirena was right. Your return changes everything. A daughter inherits a throne before a nephew."

She and Jakin were cousins? And she had just beat him out of the throne? And she had thought things couldn't get any worse.

"He doesn't know, does he?" Finn leaned toward the King.

"No. Apparently, Zirena has kept it a secret, as have I until this moment. But, I'm sure she'll tell him soon; she may have, already. And how he will react is anybody's guess."

The King stood, weary. "We have many other things to discuss but they must wait for morning. The guards will show you to your quarters. You are all my guests for as long as you wish to stay. If there is anything, even the smallest thing, that would make you more comfortable, please don't hesitate to ask."

Chapter 28: Draegin

Marinna paced across her throne room. Where was he? What had delayed him? It was not like him to vanish for days with no explanation. The girl—surely the wolves had finished her off; they never failed. What could have gone wrong? Had the Firebird challenged him? She was no match for him, a bird against a dragon; and yet she was wily, full of tricks and strange power, bent on their destruction, on ruining their plans. Fear gripped her; a horrible certainty that her father had been hurt. Maybe he was lying somewhere dying, out of reach with no way to call for help, no way for her to reach him; or worse, maybe the impossible had happened and he was dead. She cried out, desperate at the thought, a sob escaping; but she shook her head. No. I'll not believe it. She raised her chin, squared her shoulders. No. He lives. Invincible. Indomitable. The great Thaumaturge, whom all fear, to whom all will yield. He will triumph. And I will reign on that day.

She passed the empty ghillie cages and remembered the feather—what if it really could help? He'd seemed so convinced of its power. If only she had it now. If only he hadn't been so selfish, so greedy to keep it for himself, to hide it in his lair. It's his own fault; he should have trusted her.

She heard footsteps in the outside passage. That had to be him; no one else dared enter there. His pace, usually quick and strong, faltered. He was stumbling.

She ran to meet him. He was covered in blood, sticky and black, his face swollen, grossly distorted.

"Marinna," he moaned. "Help me."

She led him to a chair in the throne room. "Sit, Father." She saw his arm and gagged. The wound above his wrist was angry and inflamed, oozing pus, caked with filth, pierced with shards of rock. She fetched a pitcher and a basin and dribbled water over the gash. Draegin hissed. His tongue flicked, taut like a viper ready to strike. It took three pitchers of water, but once the gore had been removed, she could see the flesh had been rent right down to the red bone. She tasted bile, swallowing around the urge to vomit. She bound the wound, hoping it would staunch the bleeding, and went to work on his face, determined not to recoil, nor to be sick.

Carefully she worked, the wound deep, like someone had driven a spike into his eye. His parietal eye was perhaps blinded, there was no way to know until the swelling had subsided. His forehead, normally flat, was distended, bulbous; the swelling made him look hideous. When his head was washed and wrapped in clean bandages, she finally spoke. "Who did this?"

Rage burned in Draegin's eyes as he choked out the story. The angrier he got, the more his arm bled, soaking the bandage and dripping on the floor.

"Hush now," she said when she saw. "We can talk more later." Her voice trembled as his mortality struck her. What if he died? What if she couldn't stop the bleeding? It was so terribly infected. "I'll call for help."

"No. No help," Draegin hissed. "No one isss to know about thisss. Not the guards, no one. Do you understand?" He shook with fury.

Marinna was desperate, certain she'd lose him without help. "A bird, then, Father. I'm going to get one." And after she'd rebound his arm, she ran for one of the few Caladrius birds he had captured but not yet eaten, hoping the tale of its healing powers was true.

Chapter 29: Entranced

They met the King for breakfast in the same room as the night before. "Did you sleep well?" he asked Rory.

"I sure did! Better than in many nights!"

"And your accommodations are satisfactory?"

"My room is beautiful! Far lovelier than any I've ever seen!"

The King beamed at her. "I am glad you were comfortable. However, that is not your room, Rory."

"Oh." She blushed, not knowing what to say, flustered that she'd assumed too much. He didn't want her to live here?

"You will have a suite of rooms. Preparations will begin this week, though they will take some time to complete. They will be far grander than any of the rooms in our guest quarters."

She was shocked. "Oh," she said, again, though her embarrassment had turned to astonishment. "I don't know what to say. But thank you." He didn't seem to notice how uncomfortable she was, caught up as he was in his own thoughts.

"I imagine you will want to see them and make some choices on furniture."

Rory was quite sure she had no opinion on furniture, but she definitely did want to see them. "Yes! I would like that very much. I'd like to see the whole castle—all of us, if we may." She hesitated. She hoped he wouldn't be upset with her, but she had to ask. "But, first, please, can I meet my mother."

The King agreed, though with some reluctance. "We'll plan to visit her after breakfast." That sadness had returned to his eyes. "But we must talk first."

Breakfast was amazing! Food Rory recognized and lots of it. A gilded round platter held a teetering mound of tiny pancakes drizzled with butter and a sweet blueberry syrup; another, thick slices of ham. A tiered tray offered festive pieces of melon: cantaloupe stars, watermelon hearts, and green melon flowers set amid piles of berries. Large bowls held mounds of scrambled eggs and biscuits and she spotted a crystal crock of buttermirth jam. The servants kept their silver mugs full of tea, sweetened with milk and honey.

When they had finished, the King stood. "I haven't properly thanked you all. I want you to know you have my deepest gratitude for coming. For bringing my daughter back to me. You faced terrible dangers to get here—I had no idea of the high stakes until last night. You are brave, very brave, each of you. Kalvara, you bring your people great honor in showing your willingness to partake in this mission. As does your young, courageous Aric. And you Finn, as the leader of this valiant group, thank you; you have my deepest respect and gratitude. And Floxx, what can I possibly say? You rescued, nurtured, protected, and returned my precious child to me. A mere thank you seems so

trite and yet, I have never offered it more sincerely."
He bowed, then sat down.

"And, now Rory, about Raewyn, your mother." He
clasped his hands and brought them to his face,
absently rubbing his chin with his knuckle as he began.
"She and I did not think we would ever have a child.
And then, late in her child-bearing years, we found she
had conceived. We knew unprecedented joy in the
months preceding your birth." He smiled,
remembering. "We were caught up in exuberant
preparation for your arrival, ordering a cradle and a
matching rocking chair from our master artisan and
quilts and gowns from our seamstresses." He shook his
head, returning to the moment, and looked at her. "It
grieves me to tell you that the day I lost you, I lost my
beloved wife, as well."

What? What had happened to her mother? "But you
told me she was alive!"

"Oh, Raewyn does live, Rory, but in a world I
cannot touch." He took a deep breath and continued.
"Before dawn on the morning you were kidnapped,
your mother and I were awakened by what we thought
was you crying in your cradle. She jumped out of bed
and hurried to you. I followed, vaguely aware that
something about the cry didn't sound quite right. I
noticed that the large quilt that normally hung on the
arm of the rocking chair had been thrown over you,
covering you completely. Your mother would have
never covered your head, and I was sure I'd seen her
wrap you in a lavender blanket when she'd laid you in
your cradle the night before. If Raewyn noticed, she
didn't say anything. She threw back the quilt and lifted
you up, all in one quick motion. But it wasn't you. It
was a grotesque creature, green and horribly ugly; its
skin covered in warts; its face inhuman, its shriek
terrifying. Raewyn screamed and dropped the

monstrous whelp, so startled and horrified that she fell backward, slamming her head on the floor and losing consciousness. The guards outside our door ran into the room; one picked her up and settled her on the bed, then ran for the doctor; the other raised his bow and killed the screeching horror on the floor. The search for you began immediately, and though I very much wanted to lead it, I dared not leave my wife."

Rory's heart raced. As tragic as the story was about her mother, one thing hit her hard—they'd wanted her. They'd loved her. They'd been horrified when they'd lost her. She wasn't an abandoned orphan at all. She pressed her fist to her mouth, trying to keep the tears from coming. Floxx slid her chair close, putting her arm around her.

The King reached out and patted her hand. "Are you all right, my dear?"

"Yes. Yes, I'm good." Her voice wavered. "It's just, well, I didn't know. All my life I thought my birth parents hadn't wanted me."

The King took her hand. "Look at me, Rory." She did, and she would never forget what he said. "There hasn't been a day since that I haven't thought of you."

Something inside her broke, and she threw her arms around him. They wept for a long time right there in front of everyone, purging sixteen years of grief, misunderstanding, loss, and heartache. Father and daughter. Her father. The one she thought she'd never know. To think she'd blamed him for hating her, then hated him for abandoning her. She couldn't get over the fact he was real. And that he loved her.

They settled down and apologized to the others.

"No need," Finn said, his red-rimmed eyes giving away his own reaction.

"It's happy, isn't it Kalvara." Aric said, reaching for a star melon.

"Yes. Yes, it certainly is!"

Eventually, the King returned to his story about Raewyn. "The royal physician stayed with your mother for several days, and we nearly gave up hope she would ever regain consciousness. But after five long days, she did open her eyes."

Hope sprang in Rory but was short lived.

"She wasn't the same. She didn't recognize anyone. She couldn't, or perhaps wouldn't, talk to anyone. She wanted to be alone. She barely ate and spent most of her time sleeping. In her waking hours, she just stared, unfocused, vacant. We hoped she would improve with time. She had many visitors, all expressing their condolences over your abduction and wishing her better health. They spoke kindly to her, but she didn't respond. The doctor had no explanation for her condition. After the concussion had healed, he blamed her mental state on a severe psychological reaction to the trauma. And, unfortunately, Rory, she has never recovered."

"She hasn't spoken in sixteen years?"

"Not a word. She just stares as if she's entranced, caught in another world. She accepts me as familiar now, but I doubt she realizes I'm her husband."

Her mother had suffered the most of all! Though Rory hadn't known exactly what had happened, she'd had a wonderful life in Alaska. But her mother had never gotten over it; her life had been utterly ruined. *She won't even know me; I won't be able to tell her I've come back, I'm alive and well and she can stop grieving. That it's going to be okay now.*

Finn walked over and knelt beside her. "I'm so sorry, Rory," he said, taking her hand and holding it in both of his. The King noticed the tender gesture and glanced from his daughter to Finn but as understanding dawned, her father did not smile.

Chapter 30: Raewyn

They entered the largest tower, where the family bedrooms were. The King walked next to Rory, explaining that her mother still lived in the old nursery suite, which she had steadfastly refused to leave. It had three rooms: a bedroom, where Raewyn spent most of her time, and two adjoining rooms that had been remodeled to suit the Queen's needs. One was a small kitchen, where her attendants prepared meals for her since she would not eat those sent from the main kitchen. The other was a drawing room, meant to receive guests, though no one had visited in years. They were ushered into that room, where, opposite the double-doored entryway, a fire burned in an elaborately carved fireplace. It was flanked on each side by large windows, their wooden shutters open to let in the morning light and some fresh air.

Rory was drawn to an ornately framed painting hanging above the mantle, an oil portrait of a much younger King and Queen clothed in splendid finery, their shoulders touching. The Queen's face was turned toward the King and she looked at him with warm brown eyes and an amused smile, as if she saw a bug in his hair that the artist had left out. Her dark hair was caught up on her head, though a few brown curls escaped to frame her face. She wore a narrow gold circlet crown inset with blue sapphires and diamonds. Rory looked a lot like her. The King was gazing straight out, solemn and regal, his sturdy shoulders square, his ornate jewel-studded crown atop a full head of hair. She stood for many minutes, gazing at that portrait, struggling to maintain her composure.

The King found her there when he returned from checking on Raewyn. He put his arm around her, saying simply, "We were so happy then."

Six upholstered high-backed chairs filled the center of the room; three set in a semi-circle on each side of the fireplace with a low round table, polished to a high shine, filling the space between them. The table held a silver bowl of fresh fruit and a platter of the iced animal cookies Aric had loved so much. An oblong birch dining table flanked by six ornate wooden chairs and a matching buffet graced the left side of the room where a door led into the adjoining kitchen.

On the right side of the room, a rectangular instrument sat in a decorative wooden stand; Rory had no idea what it was until Floxx exclaimed over it, saying she hadn't seen a dulcimer in years. Taut strings ran across its front and small polished wooden hammers stood in a cup on the stand. Floxx picked up the hammers and struck the strings, playing a lovely melody. A flute sat on a nearby stool, and Aric picked it up, blowing it shrilly. He would definitely need some lessons. Not far from the instruments sat a pair of rocking chairs; a basket sat on the floor near them, filled with skeins of blue and white yarn. In the corner sat a beautiful wooden rocking horse, boasting a miniature leather saddle; its mane and tail crafted from that blue and white yarn. Aric abandoned the flute and raced to it, whooping as he galloped.

A maid-servant appeared at the door. "Your Highness, the Queen is ready."

The King had suggested they meet her in the bedroom where she was most comfortable. Then, if it seemed right, they'd bring her out to the drawing room. He took Rory's arm, hesitating at the bedroom doorway. "This is the room from which you were abducted."

Her heart nearly leapt out of her chest. This was where the nightmare had begun! She had a partial view of the room and was shocked that the baby cradle—her baby cradle—was still in front of the window. She shuddered, trying to imagine a creature capable of crawling up the vertical castle wall.

"Why is the cradle still there?" She whispered.

"Well, I actually had it removed in an effort to put the tragedy behind us, but your mother became inconsolable. When I finally figured out what was causing her the increased distress, we brought it back, and she settled right down. I've removed it a couple of other times over the years, but she notices immediately. She wants it here."

That was super weird. What had happened to her mother's mind? Raewyn sat on the far side of the window in the rocking chair, staring vacantly at the cradle. It was chilly in the room, and she was wrapped in a quilt, rocking slowly back and forth. Thin and frail, her eyes were dull and unfocused, and she did not notice their presence. Rory's heart sunk. She'd seen people like that in a nursing home in Fairbanks; broken, hopeless men and women waiting to die. Her mother's brown hair was streaked with gray and pulled into a bun at the base of her neck. She wore no crown, no jewelry at all. She was a shell of flesh with no life inside, nothing like her Alaskan mother had been, no laughter in her eyes, no love. Two mothers, both lost.

She struggled to hold back her emotions.

The King sensed it and tightened his hand around hers, then spoke softly. "Raewyn, dear, I have someone I want you to meet." She didn't respond. Did she even hear him? "Her name is Karena. Our Karena, Raewyn. Our Karena, who has at last come home."

They stood there, waiting, hoping she would respond even with a twitch, anything that might indicate she knew they were there. But, after a few moments it was clear she was locked in her prison, shutting out the pain of the trauma she'd suffered, making her numb to the entire world. Rory had no idea what to do. She desperately wanted to make some connection with her mother; she'd never forgive herself if she didn't at least try to reach her.

Rory knelt down in front of her, so their eyes were on the same level. She reached out and took her hands and began to talk. "Mother, it's me. Karena. Your baby girl, all grown up now. I'm not dead; no, I'm very much alive. I've been living far away for all these years, not knowing who I really was or that I belonged to you and the K ---, ah, Father. But I was cared for very well, raised by a wonderful family who loved me as if I was their own daughter. And, Floxx knew who I was. She brought me back. Here. Home. To you and Father."

She waited a long time for some response, but there was nothing. She studied the cradle. The gems on its edges winked in the morning light. What an incredible work of art it was, inlaid with carvings of elves and fairies and dogs. Dogs! Like somehow her fate with Cue had been set by the master carver. She massaged her mother's fingers. *What a terrible way to live. I'm sorry, so sorry you've had to suffer like this. I mean, it would have been better for you, so much better, if I hadn't ever been born.*

Aric chattered in the other room as he rode the rocking horse. Floxx was playing the dulcimer and had begun singing a captivating, tender song in that language of hers, as she often did when she drew close to Eldurrin. *Eldurrin! You're the One who made everything, who made each of us. You had me in mind ages ago and you knew what would happen to mother. You can do anything! You can make her well, again. Please!*

The minutes crept by. Rory rubbed her mother's hands, touching each fingernail, tracing the lines on her palms. She closed her eyes, remembering Floxx's words, "He had you in mind when he set the stars in their places and his plan into motion." It was so astounding, so humbling. She was in his care; he held her life as tenderly as this woman had held her. *How good you are, how powerful, how amazing that you are who you are, and that you love me.* And that same feeling she'd felt before began to grow within her. Heat but not hot. Strength. Boldness. Courage. She was sure it was Eldurrin, some kind of ability he had to move inside her; it spread through her chest, down her arms to her hands, warming her mother's. The sensation was strong, yet, she wasn't afraid. *You are good, and I trust you; I don't understand what's happening, but I won't stop you.*

Floxx's song ended and the sensation subsided. Rory lingered a few minutes in the peace that engulfed them; she would never have believed she could feel Eldurrin's presence like that, especially in the face of trauma. Finally, she squeezed her mother's hands to say good-bye, when to her astonishment, she felt her mother squeeze back! Rory waited, holding her breath, watching her mother. Father saw her expression and knelt next to her.

"What is it?" he whispered.

Mother gradually pulled her hands away. Slowly, very slowly, as if it took all her concentration, she lifted one, then the other. Then, her eyes focused. Many minutes passed as Raewyn clawed her way back to this world. Rory would never forget her look of surprise that the two of them were kneeling in front of her. Father leaned in and hugged her, gently at first, then firmer as his wife responded. Then Raewyn reached for Rory, too. Did the Queen know who they were? Did she recognize her husband? Could she guess Rory was her daughter? It didn't matter; her response was enough. They wept for the joy, for the grief, for the miracle, for the hope, for the life given back to them.

Finally, they helped Raewyn up. Rory turned her to face her husband. Father waited, holding his breath, his red-rimmed eyes tender and full of hope, looking for even the smallest sign of recognition. At first, the Queen was confused. But, as the minutes ticked by, recognition returned, and she cried out, reaching for him.

The weeping began, again, and Father, reluctant to let the moment end, held her for a very long time. Eventually, he drew back, holding her face in his hands. "Raewyn, my dear! Oh, my dearest! You've been gone such a long, long time. I'm so glad to have you back." He brushed a few loose strands of her hair away from her face.

Mother tried to answer but what came out was incoherent and raspy. "Never mind, my love," he consoled. "It's enough to have you with me."

Rory spent the better part of each day with her mother, communicating in whatever ways they could. She understood everything Rory said, answering her questions with a yes, no, or shrug. Mother loved it when Rory told stories of her life: Alaska, her parents, Gram, Cue, pointing to the carvings on the cradle and sharing her thought that maybe they had predicted her twisted destiny. Rory thought of Finn and smiled. Dogs and elves. No fairies so far, unless she counted that horrid ghillie who'd stolen her feather. She told her mother about Aric and his slingshot prowess, Finn and the night of the Tennins, the dragon killing Zad, Jakin's sweet bracelet and that she didn't understand what all the fuss was about; he'd unhook it when she saw him next. Mother soaked it all in, gaining strength each day and continually trying to speak. It took tremendous effort at first, but her stamina quickly improved, and within just a few days, she was able to utter some simple words.

One summer morning, about a week later, Rory sat with Mother and Floxx in the drawing room. Kalvara and Aric had gone with Finn to the city at the King's urging. Their clothes had been torn on the long trek here, and though they'd been mended, still looked tattered. He'd insisted they be outfitted in new clothes and boots before leaving, which, he'd hastily added, hoped would not be for several more weeks. They sat in the big chairs by the fire, she and Mother on one side, Floxx on the other, not saying much and comfortable with the silence. Floxx hummed softly. It was odd; Rory could almost feel the humming inside of her, like she stirred up the presence of Eldurrin. She was about to mention it when her mother's maid carried in a wooden chest and set it on the table in front of them.

"This is gorgeous!" Rory ran her fingers over its top, carved with figures similar to those on the cradle. "Same artist?"

"Yes!" Her mother smiled, opened it and retrieved a tarnished silver box, handing it to her.

What was in this? A baby spoon? A silver cup? Wait, maybe an infant crown. It was lined with faded blue velvet, and held only one thing, not at all what Rory was expecting: a folded piece of blood-stained lavender fabric.

"All we. Found of you." Mother pronounced each word slowly and deliberately, her eyes moistening.

Rory recognized it immediately and ran to get her lanyard. "Look, it's the same fabric! A piece of it went to Alaska with me and my mom there made this. She attached the feather I told you about to this end."

Mother turned it over and over in her hands, studying it, comparing the fabrics.

"For me to remember the special night I arrived." Rory's voice quavered.

Mother met her eyes. "Glad. You had her. She loved you. Very much."

The lump in Rory's throat made it impossible to reply.

"And you. Love her. Can you. Love us both?"

"I'm sure I can!" Rory kissed her mother's cheek.

"I never. Stopped. Loving you. I locked. that love." She pointed to her heart. "Then lost the key."

More tears. Good grief, she really could use a box of Kleenex. Mother handed her a handkerchief.

"Now," Mother said, handing back the lanyard. "What else?" She pointed to the chest.

Rory lifted out a white knitted baby blanket. "This was mine?"

"Everything. Was yours."

She admired several embroidered gowns, stiff now and yellowed, their tiny matching hats and booties faded, but still lovely. Her favorite thing, though, was a stuffed black dog with button eyes and a pink velvet tongue. Around its neck was a worn blue ribbon.

"Oh! Can I keep this? Something to remind me of Cue."

Mother smiled. "Yes."

The last item in the chest was a small blue velvet blanket.

"For your. Cradle."

"Oh, so soft!" She rubbed an edge of it on her cheek. "And its color is still so pretty, not faded at all." She held it up. A cream-colored feather fell from its folds and fluttered onto the table.

Mother freaked out when she saw it. Really bad. She recoiled like it was a snake.

Floxx snatched the blanket and threw it over the feather.

"It's okay. Just a feather. Nothing to be afraid of."

Once they had her calmed down, they asked why it had frightened her so much. Mother closed her eyes, gripping Rory's hand so much it really hurt. "I was. Sick."

They waited. It would take a while for her to get it all out.

"Visitors came." She cleared her throat and drank some water. "One pretty woman. Black hair." She hesitated. "Marinna."

"Marinna?" Floxx reached over to touch her arm. "Marinna came here?"

"Yes."

"How does the feather fit in?" Rory asked.

"Marinna had. Bird. "A Calder. A Calry."

Floxx helped her. "A Caladrius bird?"

"Yes. Bird wore a mask. Had magic. To make me well."

Mother began to cry, deep anguished sobs.

Rory took her hand. "It's all right, Mother. You're safe now. No one is going to hurt you."

She stammered, "The bird! Bad. She said to stare at bird and it would heal. Then, she took off mask. Pain. Then nothing." She covered her face.

Anger flared in Rory. "Why would Marinna do that? I don't understand."

"I think I do." Floxx frowned. "Marinna and Draegin wanted to be very sure there would be no more heirs. They'd already killed you, or so they thought. Then, they tried to kill your mother, too." She looked at the Queen. "But, you survived. You are far stronger than you imagine, Your Highness!"

Mother frowned, looking from Rory to Floxx and summoned enough strength for one more word. "Why?" she whispered. She needed to know the whole story.

Chapter 31: A Celebration

Finn eyed Kalvara as they made their way to the city in the King's covered coach. Aric jabbered on about all he saw out the window: That banner, Finn, what does it mean? What is that terrible smell; why do they wear hats like that? And on and on.

It was the first time he and Kalvara had been alone, well almost alone, and he noticed she hugged her side of the coach and faced away from him. At least she was tolerating him now, better than trying to kill him. He absently rubbed his shoulder, still a little stiff from where she'd shot him. Aric kept up his running stream of chatter, which did much to ease the tension as they left the sun-washed castle behind.

Finn felt the breeze on his face. It was so good to be outdoors! With all the excitement of the last week, he hadn't realized how cooped up he'd felt. He peered around the driver, admiring the matching gray horses, and saw the tall military statue far in the distance that marked the center of town. Somehow, its silhouette seemed thicker than he remembered.

"Aric," he said, "poke your head out and look at that statue. Anything different about it?"

"Yes! Ravens!" Aric exclaimed. "Covering the statue!"

Kalvara frowned. "Maybe we're not as safe as we think we are." She slid away from the window as Finn told the driver to avoid the center of town and take the back streets to the tailor. Though their evasive route helped, they did not totally escape notice; a few of the birds followed their circuitous route, perching in a nearby tree to wait as they dashed into the shop.

They spent much of the morning there, being measured and pinned. Kalvara, so tall and slender, was measured twice, the tailor not believing his numbers were accurate. Aric wiggled constantly through the process and the only way to keep him still was to slip his feet into Finn's tall boots.

"I'm an elf, too!" he proclaimed and Kalvara scolded him.

Finn fancied a charcoal broadcloth, lightweight yet durable; one the tailor assured him would wear well. He was fitted for long pants, a tunic, and a jacket. He also chose a long woolen hooded cloak, lined with the softest material he'd ever felt. Velvet, the tailor had told him, suggesting the red color. Finn had scoffed at the recommendation, choosing a dark blue instead. He despised the fitting process as much as Aric did, but gritted his teeth and put up with it, pleased with the King's generous gift. These clothes would last several years. And they were nicer by far than any he'd ever owned.

Kalvara found a soft green fabric that seemed sturdy, yet would flow with her quick movements, and ordered a belted, tunic style gown with a matching velvet-lined cloak for herself. For Aric, she decided on an outfit similar to Finn's, but with short pants, as well as long, and made in the same green fabric as hers.

They left the tailor shop, hearing the ravens cackle as they climbed into the coach.

At the cobbler shop, they were measured for knee-high leather boots. "Cut his a little large, please," Kalvara said when Aric's foot was traced. "He's growing fast."

Had it not been for the ravens, they would have lingered in the city, but as it was, they went directly back to the castle. Some of the birds followed, alighting on the castle walls.

The mood was somber at dinner. When he heard about the ravens, the King immediately ordered extra troops to the turrets. "Shoot the birds if you must," he said, exasperated. Then, he sighed and turned his attention to the others. "I'm afraid I have another piece of disturbing news. The Felinex is gone. Disappeared."

"I'm so disappointed," Rory said. "He saved our lives. The least we could have done was thank him."

"Perhaps we'll see him, yet again," Floxx suggested.

Finn wondered what she meant, hoping she wasn't inferring another giant attack.

After the meal, the King perused those sitting at the table, touching Raewyn's cheek and making her blush. Her improving health was more evident each day. His glance then lingered on Rory, the subtle shake of his head capturing his amazement that she was there. Finn felt a rush of feelings for her, and he hoped no one noticed the red tips of his ears. A quiet delight bubbled inside him for the King, the Queen, their daughter. That the horrible hurts they'd suffered had been healed; their nightmarish grief replaced with miraculous happiness. From the expressions in the room, he saw everyone shared admiration and joy for this reunited family.

The King's eyes were soft with gratitude as he lifted his goblet. "The time is drawing near for some of you to leave. But before you go, I would like to host a party in celebration of Rory's return and of the Queen's renewed health. A grand gala. A royal ball. We will invite all citizens of Byerman, as well as others by special request."

He looked to his wife for approval.

"A delightful idea, Merek."

When, he looked to Rory, she laughed, and Finn's heart jumped at the sound of it.

"That will be such a blast!"

"Good," the King said, immensely pleased. "It's settled. I will have my Chief Steward begin the arrangements. We will plan it for the night of the next full moon, a few weeks from now."

Excitement ran high, and the castle staff was alternately elated and dismayed at the sudden daunting workload. A few short days later, at the invitation of the Chief Steward, a line of tailors, dressmakers, bakers, cooks, musicians and other entertainers wove from the courtyard down the road, each bearing samples of the goods and services they hoped to bring to the King's ball.

Finn watched from a high, arched window as the Steward slowly made his way down the line of eager vendors, nodding every now and then as he questioned what they offered, dismissing some, and sending others to speak further with staff specialists. A group of musicians played in the distance, the strains of their songs festive. Bursts of laughter and snatches of conversation bubbled up to the window. And the aroma! Cinnamon, apples, ginger, the yeasty scent of fresh rolls and pastries made him eager to go outside.

Rory joined him. "So much going on out there!" he said, putting his arm around her. They watched the butler in charge of the wine cellar hand a cup back to the driver, nodding his approval. He gestured to him over the commotion, directing his barrel-laden wagon to the kitchen. Aric ran squealing into the room with Kalvara laughing as she tried to catch him. Finn lifted the boy to his shoulders for a better view, pointing out the confections below. "Look at that gingerbread and the sugar covered nuts over there. And, those pies! I'll bet some are apple—my favorite. Let's go down for a look!"

"Oh, more than a look," Rory laughed. "I'm after a taste!"

The Steward was relieved to see them. "Please, sample all you want. Send your favorites to the chief baker over there."

Aric ate three pieces of gingerbread, topped with a warm lemon sauce, then reached for a handful of sugared almonds. Kalvara licked her fingers, amazed with the sweet roll she'd eaten.

Finn and Rory headed for the pies. "Perfect," he said after just one bite of the apple. "Possibly the best pie I've ever eaten. Over there, my friend," he said to the pie vendor, directing him to the royal baker.

"Taste this," Rory said, holding out a pastry to him. "Elderflower cheesecake! Tangy, light, creamy, and the almond crust is unbelievable!"

The master of the wardrobe came hurrying toward Rory, Floxx at his side.

"Please, Princess, come with me now. And you, as well," he said to Kalvara, who had rejoined them. The seamstresses are waiting in the Queen's chamber to measure you for gowns."

"I don't need a gown," Kalvara said with a scowl.

"Humor me!" Rory said, taking her arm and Floxx's and heading inside.

Finn lifted Aric back on his shoulders as the ladies disappeared inside. "Let's explore a bit, shall we?" They strolled toward the music, enjoying the lilting sounds of one group in particular and wanting a closer look. They were a trio: two fiddlers and one lutenist. Their tune was lively, and Finn found himself tapping his foot.

Aric clapped above his head. "I like them, Finn!"

"I do, too. Let's recommend them." Finn directed them to the Steward.

Some distance away another group of musicians caught his attention. Quieter and more sedate, two flutists and a harpist played a haunting melody.

"What does that music make you think of, Aric?"

Aric didn't answer.

"Reminds me of that night by the Tennindrow River. Do you like it, Aric?"

But Aric still wasn't listening. Finn jostled his legs. "You all right up there?"

"Look, Finn. Let's go over there!" He pointed to two court jesters a short distance down the road, putting on a raucous show for their small audience.

"I don't know, Aric. They're not in the courtyard. We should stay close to the castle. You know, ravens and all."

"I don't see one single raven," Aric said looking around. "And I have my sling shot right here if any come around."

Finn laughed. "Well, in that case, what can it hurt?"

The jesters were acrobats pretending to fight with one another; swinging and missing, tossing each other into backward flips, one ducking as the other leapt over his head. They spun and swung drunkenly at each other, always missing, often falling and continuously amusing. The crowd cheered and applauded as they took their bows. Finn spoke to them afterwards, directing them to the courtyard. "Tell the Steward, Finn recommends you."

Aric leaned down. "Look!" He pointed to a magician further down the road, very nearly off the castle grounds. He was tall and very thin, clothed in a shimmering cape, and surrounded by a large group of admirers. His features were shadowed under a drooping headpiece, but he was looking up, his long arms swinging, his skinny wrists flicking one way, then another, like he was conducting a complicated musical sequence. And he was, only there was no music. The magician was directing two boots, suspended in mid-air above his head, to dance. "Let's go see, Finn! They're dancing in the sky!"

They were about half way there when they heard the birds behind them. Finn spun around as hundreds of the black ravens swooped through the sky toward them. He swung Aric down and ducked, covering his head with one arm, shielding the boy with the other. But the birds passed over them, heading straight for the magician, squawking a deafening cacophony. The people who had gathered to watch screamed and scattered at their approach. The magician let the boots fall to the ground, then pointed at the birds, moving his hands in a wide circle. The ravens swirled overhead as if caught in a sudden cyclone. Their squawks turned to shrieks as they were swept into a tightening spiral, a black tornadic cloud spinning so fast Finn couldn't see when the first one hit the ground. But within moments, they all lay there, hundreds of dead black lumps silenced before the last of their black feathers floated to the earth. The magician strode away, trampling over the carcasses in his path.

Chapter 32: Gifts

Rory absently pulled Jakin's bracelet around her wrist. He would love to be here for the ball. She wondered if he was coming. Wait, of course he was, with all his family! It would be so much fun. Just like in the fairy tales—a ball for princess Aurora! She laughed. That actually was one of the reasons she'd hated her name, thinking the fairy tale so dumb. But now, this was her reality.

Princess Aurora. She played with the thought. Now, who would her prince be? Jakin? She smiled as she traced the opals with her fingertips. He was certainly handsome enough! And kind. And he really did love her.

Then, Finn walked into the room and she shoved her hand into her pocket. He touched her shoulder, and she felt guilty. What was wrong with her? Why had she been imagining Jakin as her prince? She didn't love Jakin; she loved Finn. She was sure of that. They had a powerful connection; she didn't have even a fraction of it with Jakin. What was happening to her? Why would she even be thinking about Jakin? She reprimanded herself as she caught Finn's profile. *Finn is my prince. Finn. I love Finn.*

A week later, after the evening meal, Father shared news of the latest arrangements. "We have selected the choicest food and beverages, and they will be transported to the castle the morning of the ball. The Huntsmen and the Falconer have left and assure me they will return with enough meat to feed the crowd. The Tomtees have promised a bounty of fresh produce. I'm told the cooks are experimenting with sauces—rich gravies for the meats and sweet sauces for puddings and cakes.

"Sounds amazing!" Rory enthused. It would be lovely, no doubt. Elegant. Extravagant.

But, actually, she'd been thinking of Gram's kitchen. She had a craving for one of her cookies. She didn't suppose they had any chocolate chips in the royal kitchen. A flood of homesickness washed over her. She missed her. And Dad. And Rosie. Were they worried sick? Or had they resigned themselves to her disappearance? Did they think she was dead? Would they have had a funeral? She doubted it, not without finding evidence of her death. At least they wouldn't find that. *Hold on to your hope. I'll try to come back at least for a visit. If I can. Someday.*

"We have chosen three groups of musicians to play through the evening, and two groups of entertainers."

"Which entertainers did you pick?" Finn asked.

"I believe you recommended the jesters, yourself, but our biggest surprise will be a magnificent magician who got the highest accolades from all who saw him. I've never heard such enthusiastic commendations. The Chief Steward has assured me the audience will be spellbound with his prowess over the elements of nature. I think you mentioned him: the one who killed those accursed birds. For that alone, he deserves a place in the festivities."

"It was impressive. But, actually, quite frightening." Finn frowned. "I hope he doesn't scare our guests."

"Nonsense. I wouldn't think he'd need to repeat anything like that. The birds are gone now. And if he can keep the ravens at bay, and, perhaps even the powers that control them, I welcome him, whoever he is."

As dessert was served, Father asked Mother about their gowns. "Are you satisfied with them? Are you pleased? Do you need anything more?"

"They will be exquisite!" Mother assured him. "But we can't tell you any more as we want them to be a surprise!"

"I see!" He laughed. "But you will let me know if there is anything you need?" He looked pointedly at Kalvara and Rory.

"There is nothing we can imagine that you have not already graciously and abundantly provided to us," Kalvara said, and they all agreed wholeheartedly.

Rory loved her gown. Simple, yet gorgeous. She wished Rosie could see it. Wished she could be here with her. She was sure she'd love this world! Maybe she'd like Jakin and take him off her hands!

"Wonderful!" Father said, clearly pleased. "But there is something more I would like to do for each of you. I had thought to wait until the day before the ball, but with the anticipation and excitement so high, I've decided to do it tonight."

He stood and motioned to his Steward, who brought him a long, thin satchel.

"Kalvara and Aric," he said, "please, come here."

They walked to the head of the table, hand in hand, and stood before the King.

"First, I should like to say, again, how pleased I am to make your acquaintance. Your people, the Eldrows, are a gifted and magnificent race and it is, indeed, my honor to be one of the first men to know you. I am aware that you two have escaped dire conditions. Please accept my invitation to stay with us here in the castle for as long as you would like. We will take good care of young Aric, and you will both be safe here."

Kalvara smiled and bowed her head. "You are very generous, Your Majesty. It is our pleasure and a very high honor to stay with you, though I cannot promise how long."

"Excellent!" Father enthused, glancing at Rory, who was grinning ear-to-ear.

"And I have something more." He reached inside the bag and withdrew a small bow, bending to give it to Aric.

"Oh!" The boy was shocked, uncharacteristically at a loss for words.

"Let's see if you are as good with this bow as you are with your slingshot!"

Then, he handed a long bow to Kalvara. The wood was supple and gracefully shaped, its grain beautiful and polished to a gloss that caught the candlelight. She was speechless, turning it around in her hands, studying it, wonder in her eyes. "So light, yet so strong!" she murmured. It was perfectly suited to her height. She noticed some detail on its curved top and bottom limbs and took a moment to examine it. "Oh, Your Majesty!" Tears filled her eyes.

She held it so Rory could see. Tiny figures of Eldrows ran along its curve, their long hair blowing in the wind. Father must have had it made especially for her. How incredibly thoughtful.

"It's perfect, Kalvara. Just exactly perfect!"

"Do you like it?" Father asked, a little concerned at Kalvara's lengthy silence.

Kalvara bowed to him. "Like it? It's a treasure I will cherish each day, Your Majesty. It's exquisite. I've never had such a gift."

He smiled. "Good. I hear you are quite a marksman. We have an archery field behind the castle where you and Aric can practice." He patted the child on his head before they returned to their seats.

Father called Finn next. Rory was liking this night! She couldn't wait to see what he might have for Finn.

He spoke formally, as if bequeathing a great honor. "As a token of my thanks for bringing my daughter safely home, Finn, please accept this gift." And he withdrew a magnificent sword, its gem-studded hilt protruding from an oiled leather scabbard. "This sword, my friend, is from my royal treasury. Its blade is made of the strongest metal known to man, lightweight, unbreakable, honed and sharpened to a razor's edge a few days ago." He handed the ruby encrusted weapon to Finn, who stepped aside and drew it slowly out of its scabbard. The blade glistened in the candlelight as he held it aloft. Not a nick or a scratch marred its shiny surface.

"Why, this is fit for a king, Your Majesty!" He swung it slowly. "It's perfectly balanced. And absolutely beautiful. I don't know what to say." He blushed. All the way to the tips of his ears. "Thank you, your Highness. Thank you very much." He bowed to the King, then returned to his seat.

The Steward brought two smaller boxes and placed them on the table in front of Father.

"Rory. My beloved daughter." His voice cracked, but he composed himself quickly. "Please." He extended his hand beckoning her. "You are a remarkable young woman. Priceless to me. Beautiful inside and out."

She swallowed hard. Now it was her turn to blush.

"I had this made for you. It is similar to the one your mother is wearing in the painting that hangs in her drawing room." He opened one of the boxes and withdrew a narrow gold circlet, its lovely band studded with his country's signature gems: blue sapphires and diamonds. She'd never seen anything so pretty. Delicate and light, not gaudy at all. She loved it!

"It's beautiful! So very beautiful!" She threw her arms around him, hugging him fiercely.

"Let's see how it looks, shall we?" And he lifted the crown to place on her head. In that instant, she had a déjà vu moment. She was in a field of fireweed awaiting a crown of blossoms Mom had made her. She held her breath wondering what Father would say.

"For Karena, my brown-eyed beauty," he said, setting it on her dark curls, then kissing her forehead. "Light of my life," he murmured.

Shock coursed through Rory, every nerve electrified. He couldn't possibly have known what Mom had said. This was too weird. She began to panic, then she reached out with her heart to the only one who could have orchestrated this. *Eldurrin! Only you could have made this happen. Why?*

She was trembling when Floxx put her arm around her. "It's all right, dear," she said. "It's Eldurrin's way of showing you he knows where you've been. And of confirming you belong here now."

Rory drew a great breath and turned to her father. He was glancing uneasily from Floxx to her.

"What's wrong?" he asked.

"Nothing, Father, nothing at all. I love it, truly I do. It's just that what you said, well, it reminded me of something my mother in Alaska used to say to me."

"I see," he said, perplexed.

"Thank you, so much. It's very lovely and I'll wear it proudly."

"You're sure? I can have it altered. Or changed completely. I never meant to upset you."

"I'm totally sure. I love it just the way it is."

Floxx walked her back to her seat, her presence a tremendous comfort. She bridged both of Rory's worlds, she knew her like no one else did; she understood her, she loved her. Rory held tight to her, squeezing her fingers. Floxx pulled a chair close to hers and sat, never letting go of her trembling hand.

The King continued his gift giving. "And now, Raewyn, my darling, my beautiful Queen. Words cannot express how happy I am to have you back! What a treasured gift you are to me!" He walked to her chair and slid it away from the table, helping her to her feet. "I had this remade for you with a slight modification. I do hope you like it!" And he opened the second box, lifting out the crown she'd worn in the painting. He turned it to face her and she gasped in surprise. He had added an enormous round sapphire to its center, deep blue, like the sky on a cloudless day, like the waters of the Pool of Tennindrow. It was stunning. He placed it on her head atop her graying curls and kissed her.

She took her seat, beaming with pleasure, and the King looked around the table. His eyes fell on Floxx, to whom he had, as yet, given nothing. She smiled at him and tipped her head, and in that gesture told him it was perfectly all right.

Father walked over to her. "Most wonderful lady," he began, reaching for her hand. She stood. "I struggled with an appropriate gift for you. There is far more to you than I understand. I thought of giving you a weapon, but I suspect weapons are of little value to you. A jewel, I thought? A crown? What token of my deepest gratitude? As I pondered, a certain item kept coming to mind and I decided to follow my intuition.

I remembered a stone that has been in the royal treasury for many generations; my grandfather pointed to it when I was a boy, saying his grandfather had called it a "moonstone," for it is round and white. He said it had some lore to it—some enchantment— though he couldn't recall what. I have had my scholars and clerics research the origin of the stone these past days. They have discovered it was first called a "bellasol," which in our language means "beautiful sun." Though it does not have the brilliance of a cut gemstone, it does have a marvelous and astounding quality." He looked at Floxx, his eyebrow raised in question. "Do you know, by chance, what that quality is?"

Floxx smiled. "Perhaps I do, Your Majesty. May I see it?"

Father reached into his pocket and pulled out the smooth stone. It was a couple of inches in diameter, flat-backed and slightly rounded on its face. He placed it on the palm of his hand and held it out to her.

Instead of picking up the stone, Floxx tapped it with her finger. Father smiled as bright rays of light burst from the stone, casting their beams across the ceiling.

Rory gasped. That was crazy! Like clicking on a flashlight, only there was no battery and no switch. Just a rock that responded to touch!

They all talked at once.

"That's amazing!"

"What would you use it for?"

"What makes it shine?"

"Can you stop the light?"

Floxx looked at them and with a small smile, covered the stone with her hand and the light vanished.

She reached out and took it, clasping the King's hands. "Thank you!" she said, her green eyes twinkling. "It's a treasure indeed!"

Chapter 33: Reward

It's not that Finn meant to eavesdrop; it had been an accident, one he desperately wished had never happened. He and Kalvara had been invited to ride with the King before breakfast, to have a look at the fields surrounding the castle. But, the King had forgotten his riding boots. He usually left them in the stable, but he'd had no shoes to change into last time, so his boots had ended up in his sitting room, behind the door.

Finn had offered to fetch them, figuring he could do it much faster than the King. "Not a problem, sir!" he'd said as he ran off. His step was light, and he hummed as he took the stairs three at a time. In a few moments, he swung through the door of the sitting room. No one was in there, though he could hear Rory and the Queen talking in the bedroom. He reached behind the door and grabbed the boots, hurrying so as not to invade their privacy. But Rory's words stopped him short.

"I know I shouldn't love him, Mother; I mean he's my cousin and all, but I just can't help the feelings I've been having for him." Finn was too stunned to move.

"Every time I look at this gorgeous bracelet he gave me, I think of him; how kind he is to his dwarf family and how much he loved Zad; how brave he was for my sake, facing death in those horrific battles and helping rescue me when I was kidnapped. And, I don't mean to sound biased, but he's all human, Mother. Just like us. No mixed blood or special callings on his life."

Horrified, Finn realized Rory meant him. Mixed blood. Special calling. Pain spiked like lightning. *She's choosing Jakin.* He leaned against the door, feeling nauseous, struggling to shut out the rest of the conversation, but in spite of his loathing to hear more, he listened.

"Father had him in mind to rule one day, but then I showed up and now the crown passes to me. But what if Jakin loved me? And what if I loved him? I'm not saying I'm sure about it, not yet, anyway; I'm just thinking. Couldn't we rule together one day, he and I, sharing the leadership of our country?" The Queen began talking, but Finn didn't wait to hear what she said. He bolted from the room, struggling to breathe against the agony tearing his heart.

He couldn't recall much about the ride. The King had talked and pointed things out to them: Barns, sheds, gardens, animals. He vaguely remembered what had been said, and he hoped he'd responded politely, nodding and such. He was glad Kalvara had been there to carry the conversation. He'd skipped breakfast, not wanting to see Rory, and stayed in his room until he couldn't stand it any longer. He had to get outside.

Finn drilled his arrows at the target, then stalked across the field to retrieve them. *She loves Jakin.* He kicked a rock. *I've seen it in her eyes every time she touches that bracelet. And she's always fiddling with it now, turning it round and round, rubbing the stones, tracing its outline on her wrist. I thought her feelings for him wouldn't amount to anything. I was sure we had an unspoken agreement, she and I, that it was the two of us. How could I have misread her so completely?*

He'd planned to talk with her about it, about them, once they were safe; when the two of them could get away alone. He had dreamed of the moment he'd put his arms around her, tell her she was beautiful, tell her how glad he was she'd come to Gamloden, that he was so pleased to have been the first to greet her. He'd been smitten from the moment he'd seen her in the woods. But, now, it was over before it had ever really begun. *She's choosing him. She doesn't want me, my mixed heritage, or the huge challenges of my calling. She's thinking about Jakin; she won't even try to remove that bracelet now. It's like she's under a spell; her eyes get glassy at the mention of him. Even if it is dark magic, if she marries Jakin, that's the end of us.*

When he'd brought it up, though, just the one time, she'd been indignant. Love my cousin? She'd shaken her head at him like he was crazy. "We don't do that in my world," she'd said. "It can cause problems with children, and besides, it's gross." He sighed then as he remembered what else she'd said. "Finn, I only have room in my heart for one man." And she'd taken his hand.

She was bewitched; he was sure of it. And the spell was growing stronger every day. But what could he do? Even Floxx was watching and waiting. He wanted to be furious with Rory, to confront her and call her all the traitorous names he could think of. But no, it would just rip him up even more. He didn't want to hurt her further; she'd been through so much horror already. If she wanted Jakin, he would let her have him.

He slid his arrows into the quiver and heaved a big sigh. *It's time for me to leave. I'll talk with Floxx about what's next. Rory didn't come here for me, anyway, but to trigger the events of the star story. Our relationship can't possibly continue now that she's reunited with her parents. She clearly wants to stay here. But I, on the other hand, must go. It's my choice, to follow through with Eldurrin's calling and I'm going to do it. I don't know how, but I'm going to try.*

He eyed the trees behind the archery field, wishing he could get away for just a little while. He turned toward the castle, making up his mind to leave quietly after the ball. He was startled to see Kalvara and Aric approaching. He chided himself for being so preoccupied he hadn't heard them coming. The weeks at the castle had softened the tension in their relationship.

"I'd like to be out there, too," she said, nodding toward the woods.

Finn looked back at the castle where all was quiet. "I suppose we could go for a walk," he said. "I doubt we'd be missed for an hour."

Kalvara hesitated a moment, then agreed, the edges of her mouth turning up just a little. She reached for Aric's hand and the three of them ducked behind the archery targets and into the woods. The canopy of trees splattered the ground with leafy patterns. Finn took a deep breath, savoring the earthy smell of the cool forest. Aric ran ahead, crouching sometimes to watch and listen, his slingshot hanging from his pocket, his bow poised for any danger. Finn stole a quick glance at Kalvara. Her eyes were closed, her face raised to the tree tops. Clearly, she savored the solitude like he did.

She sensed him looking. "I belong here in the forest. I feel at home here."

"As do I," Finn said, suddenly glad for her company. "Must be written in our blood."

"Watch it," she said, glaring at him. "I'm starting to like you. But talking common blood is taking it too far."

Oh. So, she didn't like his mixed heritage, either. He kicked another stone.

"You all right?" she asked him. "You were very quiet on our ride earlier. And then you disappeared. Here, I actually walked out to give you this." She handed him an apple.

"Thanks!" He took a juicy bite, feeling a little better for her concern. "I'm okay. Dealing with some big decisions."

"As we all are."

They strolled, weaving through the trees, soaking in the quiet, delighting in the variety of life hidden in the woods. Aric stopped by a tree and sliding his bow over his shoulder, waved at them, then nimbly scaled its trunk.

Finn laughed. "Wait for me, Aric!" he hollered and leapt up behind him. Kalvara chose a nearby tree of her own and climbed it with the grace and agility of a cat, reaching its top before the boys. They could see each other through the leaves as they got comfortable on their branches, settling in to observe the world from the forest canopy, eyeing the castle turrets and the archers on duty. No one spoke. Finn was amazed at Aric's composure, his heightened senses, his ability to be still. He had never met a child, human or Tomtee, who'd had such stealth at his young age.

He regarded Kalvara resting against a couple of slender branches. One long leg was dangling, the other propped in front of her. Though she appeared relaxed, Finn knew her senses were on high alert. A few wisps of her long, white hair danced with the breeze. *She's quite a woman. Pretty. Smart. Terribly brave to dare escape her past horrors and courageous to fight the present ones. I wonder what made her come back that night she led us to the cave, why she took the risk? We might not have made it without her; we could have shared Zad's fate.*

As he was studying her, she straightened. Finn followed her gaze and saw dark specks on the horizon, growing larger with each second. The three of them slid to the ground and crouched in the shadows as the swarm flew over, casting a dark shadow on the archery field and up the sides of the castle. Shrieks pierced the air as the archers let loose a flurry of arrows.

"Did you see them, Finn?" Aric whispered. "Not birds this time. Bats."

"Where have you been?" Rory frowned as the three of them turned down a wide marble-floored hallway.

"Went for a walk," Finn replied, secretly pleased that she'd even noticed he was gone.

She glared at him. "A walk?"

"Oh," he stammered. "We would have invited you, but well, it was a spontaneous walk. And we didn't know where you were."

"Dancing lessons. I had to take dancing lessons for the ball."

Finn burst out laughing.

"Laugh all you want. You two are scheduled after lunch."

As the servants passed plates of fruit and cheese, Finn told the King about the bats.

"Yes, I've heard," the King said. "And there is terrible news from the north. Tragic." He stared for a moment at his plate but made no move to eat. "Morfyn has returned. He ravaged a family of three yesterday, murdering them in their fields at dusk. Then, this morning in broad daylight, he attacked a farmer driving his wagon to the city, killing both the man and his horse. Several soldiers attacked, but their arrows only enraged him further, and two lost their lives before the rest of them fled."

The King paused, his face pale. "This has to stop. The giant must be killed. I've decided to offer a reward for the giant killer, or killers; a prize for each. The victors must bring me Morfyn's head, then each may choose one thing, whatever they would like, from the royal treasury. I'll announce it this afternoon."

Chapter 34: Nephew

Zirena fretted over what to say as she walked to Tishkit's home. They will be pleased with the King's invitation, she was sure. But should she tell them first, or wait until after? This could go badly.

The Felinex appeared beside her.

"You startled me," she scolded, annoyed.

"You should not walk these passageways alone."

She ignored his warning. "What news?" she asked.

"Morfyn rages. He is blind in one eye from that fool-hearty child."

"Morfyn? Is he close?"

"Very. Keep the children inside." And the cat-man faded into the dimness.

Zirena knocked and waited. Then, a second time, louder. Finally, she heard Tishkit shuffling to the door.

"What a surprise!" Tishkit said, embracing her daughter. "Come in."

"How are ye, Mother?"

She sniffed. "Missing Zad. Always."

"Always."

"Are you hungry? I have some nice fried potatoes."

Zirena eyed the greasy, cold pan. "No, thank ye kindly, Mother." She paused, looking around. "Is Jakin here?"

"Out hunting. Left before dawn this morning. Wants meat, he said. No more potatoes and turnips."

"Hunting?" Zirena panicked. "Who's 'e with? Surely he didn't go alone."

"Aye, he did. Said he'd be back in no time."

When Zirena got home, Jakin was there, playing with her children.

She strode straight for him.

"What?" he said.

"You near scared me t'death!" she reprimanded.

He looked at her blankly.

"Hunting alone."

"Well, Tish wasn't up to it," he joked.

Zirena smacked him on the head.

"Ow! What's wrong with you!"

She stormed into the other room.

"He got a deer!" Pelzar called after her.

A couple of hours later, Zirena walked Jakin home. "I'll have the boys dress the buck and bring the meat to you tomorrow."

"You keep most of it. Tish doesn't eat much." Jakin studied her. "Are you gonna tell me what's wrong?"

"Morfyn. He's close."

Jakin smiled. "Good."

"Don't get any ideas. I don't want ye to end up like your parents. Ye can't face him alone. I know how ye feel about vindicating their deaths, but if you're set on killin' 'im, take your brothers with ye. They know how to hunt good as you."

Jakin held his tongue.

"There's more. And we need t'be alone."

Jakin raised an eyebrow. "Must be a big deal. How about in the back entry, near Tishkit's house?"

Zirena decided to first give Jakin the King's invitation to the ball.

"I'll get to see Rory, again!"

She saw his cheeks were flushed. "Well, yes. About that."

"What?"

"There's somethin' y'need t'know. Maybe I should'a told it years ago, but I didn't."

He frowned at her.

"It's about your parents."

"What? What haven't you told me about my parents?" Anger tinged his voice.

"Your father wasn't just a giant hunter."

"What are you trying to say? Just put it right out there, Zirena. Please."

"Your father was royalty. High-standing royalty."

Jakin stared at her.

"He was King Merek's brother."

He shook his head in confusion. "So, I'm related to the King, then?"

"Yes." She paused. "Ye're his nephew."

"That's impossible! King Merek's nephew? That's insane. Why, he's never said two words to me." He frowned, his face reddening. "Not funny, Zirena. Not a good joke."

Zirena fixed him with a sorrowful glare.

"You're serious. What makes you so sure? Clearly the King doesn't know; he's never treated me like kin." He paced, nervously running his fingers through his hair.

"Yes. He knows." And Zirena told him the story.

The longer she talked, the angrier Jakin got.

"Stop. Just stop. The King didn't want me? He sent me away and in all these years, he's never even wanted to meet me?"

"Jakin, ye've got it all wrong. Calm down and listen."

But Jakin turned and stormed away.

Chapter 35: Morfyn

Jakin slipped out into the night. The moon was nearly full, casting misshapen tree shadows across his path. A bow was slung over his shoulder, and he'd just sharpened the ax in his hand. He'd find Morfyn. Kill him. Cut off his head and claim his reward. Rory would love him then. He'd be a hero.

He weaved lightly through the woods, staying off the path, searching for signs of the giant. It didn't take long. He couldn't believe Morfyn had been so close. He stared at the broken limbs and crushed foliage, and proceeded cautiously, stopping to listen every few seconds.

A foul odor led him to the giant's camp, strewn with bones, and rank with rotting flesh. Flies covered a goat carcass tossed next to the pit. Bile rose in Jakin's throat. A few wisps of smoke spiraled from gray coals, but the giant was not there. He hadn't been gone long, though, and Jakin decided to wait, settling a short distance away under a thin cover of foliage within sight of the pit.

Hours passed. Jakin dozed and woke at dawn, scolding himself. You dunce. You'll be the giant's supper if you're not careful. He stood flexing his stiff limbs, and considered climbing a tree for a better view, but decided it was too cumbersome with the ax. He could leave it on the ground, but what if the giant found it? The sun reached its zenith, then began its afternoon descent. Why was this taking so long; he'd thought Morfyn would have been back hours ago. Where had he gone?

He decided to creep closer for another look. He tied a cloth over his nose and mouth to mask the nauseating stench. Hundreds of flies buzzed over piles of rotting flesh, dipping and dodging in a frenzied fight for a taste, their noise drowning out all other forest sounds. He stared, not believing his eyes. It couldn't be. He pulled the cloth tighter over his nose, but regardless, he gagged at the ghastly sight.   There on the far side of the camp, tossed carelessly under a tree, was a pile of putrid heads, at least two dozen of Morfyn's recent victims. Jakin ripped the cloth off his face and retched, wiped his mouth, then heaved, again, his stomach contracting in dry, convulsive spasms. Finally, he straightened, and with one hand clamped over his nose and mouth, stumbled back to his waiting spot.

The sky was leaden with clouds as night set in and it began to drizzle. Jakin ate the last of his dried meat and emptied his water skin, wishing he'd brought more of both; then he wrapped up in his cloak, fretting. Maybe Morfyn will be gone a long time. Maybe he's not coming back to this camp, ever. One more night, he thought as he hunkered down against the chill, then I'll go back for supplies.

Approaching footsteps woke him. He stood, aiming an arrow at the noise. The rain had stopped, but the woods still dripped. He saw the torchlight, first, then heard the voices. He lowered his bow.

"Over here!" he called, and in a few moments, Ezat and Azatan strode into view, armed with axes and coils of rope.

"Are you daft!" Azatan berated him. "Comin' out 'ere, alone. There's a whole search party out for ye. Tishkit and Zirena are out o' their minds, sure y'been eaten already."

"Might a'been better if 'e was," Ezat grumbled. "Get yer gear and let's go."

Jakin followed, sulky and annoyed. They'd walked about a half mile when they heard branches cracking.

"We got 'im!" Ezat yelled. "Over here. 'He's not hurt."

They stopped to wait for the others in the search party, but they didn't appear. The woods grew suddenly silent.

Azatan looked at Ezat. "Run!" he hissed, and they took off. But Jakin did not go with them; he crouched behind some undergrowth. This time, he had only seconds to wait.

The giant stormed into view, his enormous arms raised in challenge. Jakin stood to face him, swinging his ax as Morfyn grabbed at him, catching the giant's hand at just the right angle to sever the tip of a finger. The giant roared, rattling his bone necklace against his filthy chest. Jakin swayed at the horrifying thought that some of those bones might be his parents'. The giant squeezed his bloody hand into a fist, then swung at Jakin with it. Jakin twisted, saving his skull, but the blow caught him on his shoulder and sent him crashing through the scrub. Before he could recover, Morfyn reached him, bellowing in rage, yanked him up with his good hand and bashed him into a tree. Jakin caught the smell of his rancid breath just before he slumped.

Morfyn laughed, booming in victory, but as he bent to pick Jakin up, the giant recoiled in pain, stumbling backwards and holding his good eye. He shrieked and spun in circles, cracking trees in his haste to get away.

"Got 'im!" Pelzar whooped just as Azatan and Ezat returned.

"What in the name of Unther are ye doing out here. Ye'll be killed! Now get home!" Azatan screamed at his little brother.

"I won't," Pelzar yelled back. "He can't see. Look at 'im. I hit 'im in 'is good eye. It's our chance!" And the three of them raced after the giant.

Jakin had regained consciousness and stood to follow, clutching a tree for balance, waiting for the dizziness to pass. When it did, he grabbed his ax and wobbled after the others. He would not let them kill Morfyn without him; he would collect his hero's reward.

The giant was howling so loud, he hadn't even heard the dwarves approach. Jakin arrived to see Azatan throw his rope over Morfyn's head, ringing it on the first try. He let it fall past his neck then pulled just enough to secure it around his massive arms. Before the giant realized what had happened, Ezat had tossed his rope over his head, and in perfect synchrony, the brothers yanked. Morfyn fought, bellowing and thrashing, nearly lifting both dwarves off the ground as they struggled to hold their ropes. But Ezat and Azatan pulled with all their might, crouching low to use their weight to best advantage. The giant stumbled and fell, but just when they thought they had him, he rolled toward Ezat, trying to crush him under his weight, barreling so fast Ezat dropped his rope to jump out of the way.

As Morfyn rolled past, Jakin swung his ax at his spinning feet, hacking off several toes. His mighty legs recoiled, catching the blade of Jakin's ax and whirling it through the air. The four other dwarves from the rescue party sprinted into view and as the blinded giant rocked back and forth, howling in agony, they managed to tie his bloody feet with rope. In the meantime, Jakin crept near his huge head, took aim, and sent a perfectly timed arrow into his gaping mouth, finally silencing his screams. He'd done it! He'd killed the giant! He exulted as the dwarves cheered and slapped him on the back, then reached for their axes to cut off Morfyn's head. That was when Jakin saw his own ax buried deep in Pelzar's chest.

Chapter 33: Pelzar

Zirena and Tishkit rushed to the mountain entrance, along with several guards. Dawn was breaking, leaden and cold.

"He didn't say anything else?" Tishkit asked for the third time.

"No. Just that the giant was dead and that they were on their way home."

It wasn't long before torchlight shone through the branches. Two dwarves led the way, each gripping a handful of Morfyn's hair, swinging his head between them. They walked in silence, eyes cast down. Zirena was surprised they weren't shouting in celebration.

"Unther's axes! Lookit that, Tishkit. They really did it!"

"I can't see so well as ye," Tishkit said, gripping Zirena's arm, "But I can hear. And it don't sound like a victory party t'me."

As more of the dwarves arrived, they saw why. Ezat and another dwarf supported Jakin, who was barely able to hobble along between them.

Zirena rushed forward. "Ye daft boy!" she said, embracing him. "Ye brave, daft hero!"

Jakin said nothing, barely returning her hug. *Wonder what's wrong with 'im?* And then she felt him sobbing against her.

"What?" she pulled back, searching his face. She heard Azatan approaching, weeping out loud. In the torchlight she saw he cradled Pelzar in his arms; the child hung limp and lifeless.

"My son!" Zirena screamed and ran to them, gathering Pelzar against her bosom and sinking to the ground. "My baby," she moaned, rocking back and forth. "Pelzar. Little sweet Pelzar! Look at me. Look at me!" But Pelzar didn't respond. Zirena placed her hand on his chest, feeling for a heartbeat, but yanked it away when she felt the cold wetness that soaked his clothes. In the dark shadows of the trees, she hadn't seen the blood. She could hear Tishkit keening in the distance and began to wail with her.

Zirena stood in front of Pelzar's tomb thinking of yesterday's funeral, remembering her boy's laughter, how he'd adored his older brothers, chasing after them like a faithful pup. So brave for one so young. Gifted. Kind. *I wish I'd taken more time with 'im; spent a few more minutes answerin' a question, gone with 'im exploring, stalking deer, spying on birds. I could've cheered 'im on far more'n I did, celebrated 'is small achievements, listened more and talked less. Warned 'im of dangers 'e didn't understand.*

She reached to touch the topaz window on his small tomb. Green. His favorite color. His dark eyes, once dancing with light, stared unfocused from his innocent face. *My boy.* He grasped his precious slingshot in his hand; the victor's weapon, showcased in every hero's tomb. *I should'a never gave 'im that; young as 'e was. But I thought it was harmless. And once he 'ad it, there was no getting it back.*

She remembered what they'd said at the funeral. "He saved so many, our young hero and his sling." But, she didn't care how many. She'd trade the lives of a thousand faceless men to have her child back. She glanced down the hall of tombs, their gemstone windows dimly reflecting the Uzim's torchlight. The keepers of the tombs stood so still, she'd forgotten they were there, watching her, watching over the dead. *So many heroes. My father. My brother. My son. Gone. And for what? Where is the peace they gave their lives for? What reward for their sacrifice? What victory from Draegin's growing threat?*

And now, Rory threatened even the alliance with men she'd been counting on when Jakin came of age. She wouldn't let Rory spoil that.

Chapter 37: Reward

The crowd cheered, banners waved, trumpets blared as Jakin and the six giant-killing dwarves followed the King onto the castle portico. Jakin stared at the vast multitude gathered in the courtyard below. He hadn't expected this. He'd been told it would be a welcoming tribute, a formality, a military honor. Not a throng of hundreds cheering. He noticed the King was uneasy, though whether it was the crowd or him who was making him nervous, he couldn't tell. Why were so many people here? How did they know to come? Jakin had only spoken with a few men they'd met at an inn along the way a couple of days prior, who'd heard the rumor the giant was dead and wanted to verify it. Against Azatan's advice, he'd shown them the giant's head. They'd marveled and wanted to know all about it. Most of the dwarves had been reluctant to say much, still brooding over Pelzar's death, so he'd told the story about how he'd shot an arrow down the giant's throat. Course, they'd all been there helping. "Was that so?" the men had asked Ezat and Azatan, who'd scowled at Jakin and walked away.

Jakin glanced at the King, wondering if he even knew who he was. Of course, he must! How many human boys live with the dwarves? Their eyes met, and the King quickly looked away. *He's wondering if I know he's my Uncle. He's not sure if Zirena has told me. My uncle. Who cared so little about me that he gave me away. He hasn't spoken to me, to any of us, since we arrived. Not even a thanks for slaying the giant who killed his brother. I want to hear his weak excuse for abandoning me. I want to see him squirm. I want to claim my prize and watch him weep.*

The King stepped to the edge of the platform and held up his arms. The crowd quieted. "Hail, the giant killers!" he shouted, and the people went wild with applause. Someone in the throng started clapping and yelling something that spread quickly until it was loud and clear.

"Jakin! Jakin!" they chanted. Jakin was shocked! Azatan elbowed him but Jakin ignored it. Those men at the inn must have told everyone. *The whole crowd knows I did it; I dealt Morfyn the final blow.* He held his head high. *They are right. I am the giant killer. I set out to kill him and I did it. And I would have done it without any help at all.*

Once the crowd had settled, the King spoke, again. "Yes, Jakin, whose arrow dealt Morfyn the fatal blow. One of eight heroes, though the youngest is fallen and only seven remain. It took the courage and valor of all eight to kill the giant. To them all we owe much honor and tremendous thanks to our fearless and brave neighbors, the dwarves of Orizin. For together with Jakin, they have slain the giant, that vile predator who threatened the security of our land and theirs, who terrified our citizens and theirs, who murdered innocent victims of all races. They have freed us from the oppression of his terror!"

Wild cheering erupted, again, and the King waited tensely as the crowd continued to shout Jakin's name. Jakin found it impossible to hide his smile.

The King raised his arms to settle the crowd and bring the assembly to a close. "Now, thank you, faithful comrades and citizens of Byerman for welcoming our heroes, for honoring them openly and enthusiastically. You will have a chance to greet them in person in just two days here at the royal ball. But, for now, return to your homes in peace! Allow us to proceed with preparations for the gala and then we will celebrate together."

He signaled his troops to peacefully disperse the crowd. Then, he led the heroes inside where they were escorted by a dozen soldiers to a spacious alcove near the royal treasury. Tozar and Zirena had just arrived, having been delayed by some official business of his, and were being greeted by Queen Raewyn. Some servants poured wine, others wove among the guests, passing trays of elegantly arranged noshes.

Jakin studied the Queen as she pulled back from hugging Zirena, wondering whether the tears she wiped from her face were sincere. So, that was his aunt. She looked quite healthy to him, certainly not too ill to raise a child. She was apparently doing well with a daughter. He wondered where Rory was. He searched the room but didn't see her.

"Jakin!" Finn greeted him warmly, pulling him into an embrace. "Well done, my friend!"

As they talked, Aric ran up and Jakin held out his arms to the boy. Aric jumped into them, suddenly sobbing.

"I miss Pelzar," he said, his voice muffled on Jakin's shoulder.

"Me, too, Aric. Me, too."

"If I'd been there, he wouldn'ta died. I could've helped."

"Perhaps." He hugged him tight for a moment. "But, it's over now." Aric pulled back and Jakin confided, "He talked about you all the time, you know."

"We were friends," Aric said, as if that explained everything, and wiggled down, wiping his nose on his sleeve while Kalvara greeted Jakin.

Floxx was next and hugged him warmly. "You were very brave," she said.

But Jakin barely heard her. He was staring at Rory, who had just entered the alcove. She was stunning, more beautiful than he'd ever seen her. She wore a green silk, low-necked gown, snug in all the right places; her hair was pulled to the side and fell in loose curls over one of her bare shoulders. Her dainty crown sparkled as the light caught it, and he was thrilled to see the bracelet he'd given her on her wrist. But what excited him most was watching her look for him, turning, searching, until the moment her eyes met his.

"Jakin!" she squealed and ran to him. He caught her in his arms and swung her around, kissing her cheeks, her nose, her mouth once, twice; then pulled her into a tight embrace.

Jakin had requested to be the last to enter the treasury to choose his gift. "I would like some time with Rory, please," he'd said, and the King had reluctantly complied.

"Jakin," Rory said as they moved some distance from the others. "There's amazing news. About you. About who you are."

"I know. Zirena told me."

She caught the bitterness in his voice.

"You're upset?"

He didn't reply.

"But you're the King's nephew! Everything will be fine, now. And that makes us cousins!"

Jakin smiled thinly. "Crazy, isn't it."

Rory laughed. "Where I come from, cousins do not kiss each other. Ever."

"Well, that seems odd." He nuzzled her cheek. "But, you don't seem to mind."

"I did when I first thought about it, but now, well, I just want to be with you. That's all that matters to me."

"Good," he said and bent to kiss her, again.

Each of the dwarves took his turn in the treasury accompanied by two guards and the royal curator who was knowledgeable about the items. Azatan chose an ancient sword similar to Finn's, its hilt gilded and adorned with emeralds and diamonds. "Belonged to a King long ago," he said, when Jakin later admired it.

Ezat chose a small knife, set in a handle carved from a single block of ruby. Its red blade was sharp enough to draw blood with the lightest touch. "They don't know much about it," he said. "Called it a blood knife and recalled some lore 'at said blood knives never miss their mark. I like the feel of it. Fits good in my hand."

Zirena and Tozar had been escorted into the treasury by the King, himself, to choose Pelzar's reward. They emerged with a solid gold shield, bejeweled with precious stones: emeralds, rubies, and sapphires set above a strange coat of arms. The shield had once sealed a formal alliance between an ancient dwarf kingdom and the land of men. "An alliance we plan to strengthen," Zirena whispered to Jakin with a meaningful glance at Rory.

The other four dwarves chose gems, not weapons. They carried multi-colored opals, polished smooth, rounded on top and flattened on the bottom, each the size of a saucer. "Don't never find these in the mines," one said as he walked past Jakin and Rory.

She eyed the opals on her bracelet. "Jakin, these stones didn't come from the mines, did they."

"Ah, no, not exactly."

"Well then, where did you get them?"

"Someone gave...."

But before he could finish, the King called him to the treasury.

"Come with me," he said to Rory.

"Oh, no," she protested. "I'll wait here. You choose whatever you like."

"Please," he pleaded. "I would really like you to come. Surely your father will allow it."

The King was irritated with Jakin's request, saying it was highly unusual. He addressed the others, asking if anyone objected. When no one did, he grudgingly agreed, but insisted on accompanying them.

Jakin showed little interest in the weapons or gemstones and they were well inside the treasury before he picked anything up. It was a lady's hand mirror, its glass encircled with brilliant pink sapphires.

"The work of dwarves," he said, handing it to Rory. "Fit for a stunning princess."

"You are right about the handiwork," the curator said. "That piece is very old; the gems mined far north of Orizin, where dwarves lived long ago."

"Mined from the dragon's mountain?" Jakin asked.

"Exactly."

"Is that your choice, Jakin?" the King asked, impatience ringing in his tone.

"No, sir, I was just admiring it."

"I see. Well, you may pick anything in the treasury, whatever you want. But let's get on with it."

"I choose Rory," Jakin replied, entwining his fingers in hers.

She gasped.

The King's face reddened. "What did you say?"

"You said, sir, I could choose anything in your treasury. We would, of course, be properly married."

The King reached for Rory. "Unhand my daughter at once," he commanded, and the two guards drew their swords.

Jakin let go of her.

"Come here, Rory." The King beckoned with an outstretched hand.

Rory didn't move.

"Rory," the King said even more gently. "Come, please. Stand next to me."

But Rory stayed rooted in place, gripping the hand mirror so tight her knuckles whitened; the bracelet on that arm quivered. With her free hand, she touched the opals, winding the bangle around her wrist, round and round, over and over, again. Her face was frozen in a frown, her eyes darted from Jakin to the King and back.

"What's come over you, my dear? Surely you don't want to wed this man?"

"This man?" Jakin seethed. "This man!" he shouted. "I am your nephew, as you have known since the day I was born, though I have just been enlightened. Your nephew, whom you gave to the dwarves to raise. You abandoned me. Your own brother's son."

"Jakin, please. You don't understand. Your Aunt Raewyn was in no condit…."

"I find that hard to believe seeing her current state of health."

"Rory, tell him," the King implored. "Tell him about your mother. How sick she was."

But Rory did not speak; she stood rigid, trembling, as if gripped by an invisible force. Tears soaked her cheeks and dripped in big splotches onto her green silk gown.

Jakin was alarmed at her terror. He turned to face her. "What do you want, Rory?" he whispered. "Tell us. I won't force you."

Rory began to shake. The King reached for her but when his hand touched her shoulder, she recoiled. The sudden movement freed her voice.

"Jakin," she gasped. "I want Jakin. I will be his wife." She swayed, and as Jakin reached to steady her, she dropped the mirror, the images of those she loved shattering when it hit the floor.

Chapter 38: Betrothed

Rory sat on her bed, legs pulled against her chest, and stared into the dim room. She'd sent her maids away. Don't pull the curtains today, she'd told them. Leave them. Leave me. She needed time to think. Something was wrong with her; her mind was clouded, fuzzy; it was so hard to think. What had overpowered her yesterday? What had she done? Why did she consent? Her poor father! She'd broken his heart; watched his agony. And her sweet mother, what will she say? Would she even speak to her? Would she ever forgive her?

Rory hid her face on her knees, trying to remember, to make sense of it all. She'd been compelled; something had forced her decision. But what? She let her mind wander through the recent weeks. Finn. She remembered loving him. She remembered her heart leaping when he was close, her nerves tingling when he brushed her hand. She was sure it had been real. When did that change? How? She lifted her face, resting her chin on her knees, eyes still closed.

She'd heard Floxx yesterday in those terrible moments. She'd heard her voice. She'd been there, somehow, calling to her, reaching for her when she was trapped, clutched by whatever force that was. But,

Rory hadn't been able to hear what Floxx had said. She'd felt her warmth, but only for a second. Then the coldness moved back in, weighing her down, insisting she pick Jakin. She had plainly seen her father's pain and she'd wanted to go to him. But she couldn't move. He'd pleaded with her. A king never pleads. She'd hurt him terribly. Irrevocably. Would he ever speak to her, again?

Why was she so torn? She wasn't ready to marry anyone yet, and certainly not Jakin. Scenes flashed through her mind. The plane crash, Finn. Floxx transforming. Werner, the wolves, Finn. The star stories, the Tennins, Finn. The dragon, the dwarves. Finn. He was the one for her. She remembered choosing Finn. Telling him she cared for him. She'd imagined a life with him, joining him on his quest; discovering what her part was. She'd imagined a happily-ever-after kind of future, however that worked in this world. She was so, so glad she'd met her birth parents and she loved them very much, but she was here for more; she was convinced of that. And she had once thought it was tied up with Finn. He'd needed her. And she'd needed him. So, why had she chosen Jakin? Was it too late to change her decision?

The bracelet glimmered in her peripheral vision as she swiped at her wet cheeks. She smiled through her tears as she studied it. It was so beautiful; she never got tired of looking at it. She brushed the gorgeous color-flecked stones with her wet fingertips and suddenly felt better; she pushed her hair back and sat up. Why was she so worried? She traced the edge of an opal. Jakin loved her. He was a good man. A very good man. He would care for her always, and together they would eventually rule in her father's place. Father said she'd forfeit her right to rule if they married, but Jakin said that was ridiculous. He'd assured her they would rule together, and she believed him. She turned the bracelet around on her wrist, studying its intricate silver handiwork. She was being silly to worry about this! She tossed the covers off and got out of bed. She'd made the right choice. She would marry Jakin. She'd ask Father to announce their engagement tomorrow at the ball. Her parents would eventually see it was the right decision.

The day of the ball began well before sunrise. Rory hadn't been able to sleep but had stood by her window watching the steady stream of wagons snake through the torch-lit courtyard, stopping briefly to unload their wares before departing to pick up the next load.

Crates of breads, rolls, pastries, and fruits were hauled to the main kitchen. Rings of fat sausages and huge rounds of cheeses were hurried to the cold rooms. Flowers and greenery arrived just as the sun was rising—a whole wagonful, freshly cut from village gardens, bundled together in glistening dewy bunches to be tied into wreaths and swags or arranged in vases.

The outdoor spits were already smoking, turning pigs, deer, and sheep. The roasting meat smelled amazing; her growling stomach reminded her she hadn't eaten much in a couple of days. Four enormous pits had been lined with hot coals and topped with grates on which a bounty of ducks, geese, and chickens would be roasted throughout the day. Quiet clusters of men held cups of steaming coffee as they stood near the fires, warming themselves against the morning chill. All her worry was gone. She'd made the right decision; she was feeling strong. She wrapped her hand around her wrist, squeezing the bracelet. Somehow it was key to her peace of mind; it made her so sure of Jakin. She pressed it to her lips, thinking of his kiss.

Mother and Father will come around. Last night at dinner, she could see they'd been upset; both of them had tired circles under their eyes, but they were gracious along with the others, smiling and congratulating. Even Finn had shaken her hand and bowed, bringing back the forgotten memory of him bowing in the woods when he'd first seen her. But she shouldn't be thinking of him. Only Jakin. Tozar and Zirena were thrilled, Father had said. They'd sent an enormous bouquet of flowers that had graced the dinner table, along with a note on their gilded stationery, welcoming her to their family.

Her maids arrived with breakfast, then helped her bathe and washed her hair; no small task when all the water had to be heated and carried in. If Gram knew, she'd laugh. She and Pap had lived without running water for decades, and she'd never had maids to haul it. What would she think of Jakin? Rory remembered what Gram had said about a guy she'd fallen for when she was 15. Look at his heart, she'd said. Don't be fooled by a handsome face. Is he honest? Generous? Kind? Can you trust him with your deepest secrets? Then Gram had gotten a far-away look in her eyes, thinking of Pap. She'd smiled a little and asked her last question. Will he stick with you, loving you still when you're old, wrinkled, and stiff? Will he tie your shoes when you can't reach them? Pick berries for you? Build a fire every morning, then bring you a cup of coffee in bed? Rory wondered. Jakin loved her, she was sure of that. But she couldn't answer all the rest.

She'd sat a long time at her dressing table as her hair and makeup were done. She'd worked with Madeleine, her maid, and a local artist, to create a facial design that incorporated her scars, much like the one she'd seen on the woman who'd bought bread on the morning she'd arrived in Masirika. The artist had just left, having painted a swirling pattern on Rory's cheek and neck in pinks, creams, and tans. He had set a few small jewels into the design, just enough to sparkle when she moved. She'd wanted something subdued, not gaudy, and she was immensely pleased with how it had turned out. Her hair was caught up on her head, showcasing the full effect of the artwork. She wished Rosie could see it.

Rory could see the minstrel groups arriving. One set up outside in a field, and began playing, their musical warm-ups adding much to the growing festivities. She knew the other groups would be stationed inside. She'd strolled through the castle with mother last night after dinner, checking on the preparations. The multi-tiered ballroom chandelier had been polished and rehung with dozens of thick, long-burning candles, which would be lit late this afternoon. The wall sconces gleamed, ten on the side walls and six on the front and back walls. Swags of greenery would be draped between them this morning and tied with blue and white ribbons. The large double doors between the ballroom and the banquet hall had been opened, so guests could watch the performers from either location. The ballroom's back doors would also be opened to the cobblestone patio, twice the size of the room, itself, so those outside could also enjoy the entertainment.

The tapestries on the dining room walls had been removed, pounded, and rehung; the wall sconces in that room would also be draped with greenery, unifying the décor of the two spaces. Food tables lined the edges of the room, covered with floor-length blue and white linens, and set with royal china and silver utensils. Servants would carry platters from there to serve the guests. The round guest tables were plated and set with elaborate finery, lacking just their flower centerpieces. Rory imagined it was crazy down there right now with servants and staff racing against the sun to have everything ready by late afternoon.

She, Kalvara, and Floxx had been invited to the Queen's quarters for a private luncheon. She and Mother had planned it soon after Father had announced the ball; they'd had so much fun choosing the flutists and deciding on the menu. She'd miss spending time with her when she moved to Orizin. She was really just getting to know her and hoped she'd be able to visit often.

The others had already arrived by the time Rory got to the luncheon, fully dressed for the ball. Mother looked pale and drained. She hugged her daughter and held her at arm's length, adjusting and smoothing her gown and smiling at the design on her face. She paused for a long moment, looking deep into her eyes in silent question. Was this what she really wanted? Of course, Mother couldn't say anything out loud. What was done was done and had been officially accepted by everyone.

While it wasn't impossible to break an engagement, it was extremely difficult and would bring tremendous political tension, as well as much shame to their family. Even so, if Rory'd as much as hinted at hesitation, she was sure Father and Mother would break it, willingly accepting the disgrace, the repercussions, even an unlikely battle with Orizin. But she'd made up her mind. Jakin was a good match. He loved her, and she loved him. She mustn't let any doubts ruin today. Today, they'd celebrate. Her wedding date wasn't even set; she had plenty of time to enjoy being with her parents, living with them a while longer. And she'd cherish every second.

Floxx was her usual composed self; she didn't get rattled very often. Only once had Rory seen her angry, when the ghillie had stolen her feather. She did have an emotional side, she'd grieved for Zad, wept for joy when Mother was raised up, but she wasn't easily upset. Rory wanted to talk to her about hearing her voice in the treasury and whether she'd just imagined it, but with the others there, she couldn't. Floxx was still very much a mystery to her. A friend, yes. A protector, yes. But Rory was pretty sure she'd only skimmed the surface of who Floxx really was. She suspected Floxx understood more about her than she understood about herself. And Floxx loved her; she knew it, regardless of her mistakes. She was her ally; she'd have her back even if she was wrong in this decision. Floxx didn't say a word, just smiled when Rory caught her eye. She seemed preoccupied, distracted. She had just helped Kalvara find Aric's lost socks and had taken them to Finn, who had charge of the boy, and she'd returned quite solemn. Rory wondered why.

Kalvara was tapping her foot to the music, enamored with the giant raspberries on the table. It was true, they were the size of a normal strawberry. Rory teased her, though, that of all the fancy hors d'oeuvres and pastries, she was taken by the berries.

"Just keeping it simple," Kalvara said around a mouthful, a phrase she'd adopted from Rory.

After lunch, Kalvara and Floxx left to dress in their own rooms. Mother and Rory peeked out the window watching the wagons and carriages arrive. Most of the nobles and their wives were Father's friends, strangers to them, though Mother remembered a few. Musicians ramped up the volume, playing gaily as the festivities began. Guests were ushered into the castle; groomsmen parked their carriages and led the horses to the expanded stable areas. They caught snatches of conversation.

"To think we have a princess!"

"I would never have believed it."

"I wonder what she looks like."

"And the queen, herself, well, again. The King must be out of his mind with joy."

Rory was dying to make her grand entrance. "How much longer?"

"Soon. We have to wait until everyone is here."

Finally, the Steward arrived, dressed in formal military attire. He offered one arm to Mother and the other to Rory, then escorted them through the hall to the top of the stairs where the King was waiting.

Rory saw Floxx, Finn, Kalvara and Aric talking in the atrium below. Finn looked good in his new clothes. She'd overheard him telling Father how pleased he was with them. She wanted him to look up at her, to see approval in his glance; but he was absorbed in a conversation with Kalvara, standing a little too close to her. Rory'd been so self-absorbed lately, she hadn't noticed their friendship growing. Why should she care? She ignored the sinking feeling in her stomach as she studied them.

Kalvara looked beautiful! Two narrow braids framed her face, woven with thin silver ribbons, and hung to her waist. The rest of her hair was twisted and caught with an emerald clip at the nape of her neck. Her silver gown had a scoop neck and a soft, flowing skirt held around her waist with a silver loop belt. A gray cape hung over her shoulders, lined with dark green silk. Elegant and striking! Rory admired how she held her head high, watching as they talked, all senses on alert even here. Surely, she didn't expect problems.

Floxx was tastefully dressed in a charcoal-colored silk gown and silver satin robe, light and flowing. The sleeves on her robe were snug to her elbows, where they were clasped with silver bands, then flowed sheer and wide to her wrists. Her star sapphire necklace sat in the hollow of her neck and the white bellasol hung from a longer chain below it.

Some commotion caught Rory's attention on the far side of the room. Cheers erupted as the crowd recognized their favorite hero coming through the door.

"Jakin! Jakin!" The chanting began with a few, then grew until everyone inside and out was shouting his name.

Father clenched his jaw, color rising on his face. Rory reached for his hand, squeezing; her way of begging him not to make a scene. He squeezed back before he let go, as if to say he would not do anything rash. She turned her attention to Jakin. He walked, no, he strode—head held high as if he was already king— to the bottom of the stairs. There he stopped alongside her friends, eyes riveted on her; then bowed with flourish, spurring applause and a few bawdy comments. She blushed.

Rory glanced at her mother and straightened to match her posture. Mother remained fully composed, as if nothing at all had just happened, radiant in a gold satin gown caught at her slim waist with a thick jeweled belt. Its sheer sleeves, puffed at the shoulders, glimmered against a gold-trimmed, blue brocade vest. A maid stood ready to carry the long train of her dress down the stairs.

At the King's signal, the trumpeters announced the royal family. Silence fell as the guests turned their attention to the King. He stood at the top of the steps, arms extended to the people below.

"Welcome, friends and countrymen. This is an auspicious occasion and I am deeply grateful for the opportunity to share it with you. As most of you know, sixteen years ago tragedy befell our family and our country. My daughter, who stands here before you was an infant of just a few weeks, and was abducted one night while she slept. We had, all these years, presumed her to be dead. My wife, the lovely Queen Raewyn," he extended his hand to her, beckoning her to his side, "suffered serious health issues as a result, from which she has only recently recovered."

The crowd applauded.

"But unbeknownst to us, our daughter had been rescued and taken to another land, where she was raised by a kind and generous family, and has lived there for all these years, unaware of who she was. Recent events have brought her true identity to light, and this wonderful group of people," he gestured to Finn and the others, "made a long and dangerous journey to return her to us." The King held out his other hand for Rory.

The crowd went wild. Cheering, whistling, clapping; on and on it went. Rory felt oddly vulnerable as she waited for the clamor to subside, suddenly conscious of the cool evening air on her bare shoulders. Her ivory gown felt constricting and she wished the corset hadn't been laced so tight. It was gorgeous, Mother had assured her. She lifted a gloved hand and felt the edge of her cape, thinking she might pull it around her shoulders. She'd chosen dark blue velvet lined with gold silk, and she wanted its warmth. No, better to leave it as is, she decided, her fingers brushing the pearl and sapphire clasp Father had leant her; it had been a gift from a visiting dignitary for his own cloak, though he'd never worn it.

Father was still speaking. "Now, I would like to introduce our daughter, Princess Rory."

The cheering was loud and enthusiastic with much laughter and clapping, but as it began to subside, the King held up his arms. "There is more." The guests quieted. "Queen Raewyn and I are pleased to announce the engagement of Princess Rory to Jakin, the giant killer."

The roar of the crowd was deafening. Rory's father gripped her hand, pulling her a little closer. Clapping, whistling, shouting, stomping, even crying broke out unhindered below. Some waved their arms in celebration, strangers embraced, men pounded each other's shoulders, women wiped their eyes. A group of men lifted Jakin off the ground and held him above their heads, parading him through the throng. The cheering spread to the patio, across the archery field, and out to the courtyard.

Finally, when the uproar had quieted, the trumpets sounded a blast and the Steward boomed the official announcement. "Please welcome the royal family: King Merek, Queen Raewyn, and Princess Rory!" Then the three of them descended the wide staircase, hand-in-hand to the sound of the trumpet and the cheers of the jubilant crowd. Rory heard murmurs of approval at her appearance, and exclamations at the artwork on her face. She smiled at their reactions to her scars now. The royal family! Her family! She branded this memory in her mind, so she could cherish it forever.

The men set Jakin on his feet as she approached, and he bowed, again, and offered her his hand. Her father kissed her cheek and formally placed her hand in Jakin's and the two of them followed the King and Queen to the royal table. After the meal, the King and Queen opened the dance floor and she and Jakin joined them, followed by Finn and Kalvara. As they twirled to the music, Rory overheard Renaz, Pelzar's sister, ask Aric to dance.

"Now, that's a good thing," she whispered to Jakin, nodding at the children building young alliances.

Chapter 39: Heartbreak

King Merek swallowed a sob, unwilling to give in to his despair, desperate to keep his joyful mask in place. Rory was engaged to Jakin. Jakin, who he'd denied knowing all of his life. He watched them together, holding hands and laughing, but shared none of their joy. This was a miserable turn of events. What a mess he'd made. If only he'd tried harder with Jakin. Perhaps, he could have had a nurse raise the boy here. Or, at least, he could have established a relationship with him in Orizin. But each year that had passed made it a little easier to do nothing. He couldn't bear to watch Jakin grow, so bitter that his nephew had lived but his daughter had died. He resented his brother who had flitted off against his good advice and left his son an orphan. How could he possibly have raised Jakin while he grieved and lived in heartbreak, caring for a wife who didn't even know who he was. And now, he was caught in his own web, the victim of his own bitterness, about to lose them both.

The night before, he'd paced in the privacy of his royal suite, mourning the tragic turn of events with his wife.

"It was like something gripped her, Raewyn, some evil that wrenched her heart. She clearly struggled, but I think in the end, she gave in to it."

"Is there nothing we can do?"

"I met with our counsellors afterwards. According to law, a pledge of marriage between minors is legal when they state their intentions before two or more witnesses, as long as there is no prior betrothal or binding arrangement, and if the guardians of the male give their consent. Zirena and Tozar have consented."

"Then we have no recourse?"

"It seems not."

Raewyn hunched over in the rocking chair from which she'd been raised to health such a short time ago. "Will he take her away?" She'd choked on the words.

The King had knelt by her chair and taken her hand, his tears flowing freely. "To Orizin. They will make their home there until I die." His voice broke. He didn't know if he could bear it. He struggled to continue. "Then, they will return and Jakin will rule in my place. Rory has been told she forfeits her right to reign when she weds, though even that has failed to change her decision."

When the dancing ended, servants carried in long wooden benches, arranging them in rows in the ballroom, the dining room and on the patio. Good, the King thought. We're readying for the entertainment. Soon, this very difficult evening will be over. He watched as they rolled in the stage, about six feet high, its base draped with multi-colored fabric, and set it where the entertainers could be seen by the entire audience.

The sun was low on the horizon and guests hurried to claim their seats, anticipating the start of the show. Most of the children sat on the floor in front of the stage where they would have an unobstructed view of the grand performances. At the King's suggestion, Kalvara gave Aric permission to join them, though she insisted he sit where she could easily see him.

The Steward climbed the stage steps and stood before the crowd. Daylight was fading in the pink-streaked sky, replaced with candlelight from the two chandeliers and the wall sconces inside, and torches burning in many places outside.

The Steward raised his voice. "Our highly-esteemed countrymen, we hope you have enjoyed the ball so far."

The audience responded with applause.

"While there is yet plenty of food and drink to be enjoyed after the entertainment, we will now give our attention to our talented performers. First, we have a team of jesters, sure to delight both young and old. I am pleased to introduce to you, Hofnarr and Pudd!" The crowd welcomed them enthusiastically.

The jesters leapt on the stage before the Steward had fully descended the steps. They bowed deeply and with great exaggeration, their garish clothes trimmed with bells. One kicked the other in the rear and that began their act; one tossing the other high into the air with a kick, the other vaulting through the air in a somersault to return a punch.

The King chuckled. Not bad. Quite entertaining. The audience applauded and when it was over, demanded an encore. Hofnarr and Pudd obliged, inviting a child to join them. Aric volunteered. The King saw the unease on Kalvara's face and motioned a guard to move closer to the stage. The jesters gave Aric a large ball, instructing him to hold it tightly above his head with both hands. Before the boy realized what was happening, one of the jesters had leapt over his head, grabbing the ball from him. A game of catch ensued with Aric desperately trying to get the ball back and the two jesters clowning around with it, spinning it with one finger, bouncing it off each other's heads, and knocking each other backwards with a toss of the ball. Even Aric was laughing. When they'd finished, the audience cheered, and Aric got to keep the ball for being such a good sport. He walked back to Kalvara clutching his treasure against his small chest.

The King allowed himself a slight smile, pleased to see his guests so animated. Conversation buzzed, laughter bubbled from each table. They love this. They approve whole-heartedly of the match between Rory and Jakin and seem unconcerned for the future of their kingdom. Perhaps this will work after all. He exhaled slowly, daring to hope, but unable to convince his heart.

The Steward took the stage, again. "And now, ladies and gentlemen, it is with great pleasure that I introduce to you our final entertainer, The Shimmering Man of Magic." The crowd waited in silence so complete, the King heard the torches spitting. A few more moments passed, and the man of magic did not appear. The King shifted uncomfortably. Where was he? Then, from out of nowhere, he emerged on stage. The guests gasped, pointing. No one had seen him walk up the steps; he had just appeared, his iridescent shroud slowly taking shape in the center of the stage. He kept his hood up, his face a dark shadow within it; just the glint of his eyes showed within its folds. A hush fell over the crowd.

"Good evening, ladiesss and gentlemen," the magician said in a deep, resonant voice. "It isss my great pleasure to be here tonight. I will show you some thingsss that will make you laugh, some that will make you wonder, and othersss that will thrill you. They are all magic, a deep mysterious magic, which cannot be understood or explained. So be surprised, be delighted, as I bring you my greatest performance in celebration of the reconciled royal family."

He bowed deeply, seeming to look directly at the royal table, his gaze touching each one there, and lingering longest on Rory. The King saw his daughter shudder beneath the conjurer's stare. Jakin whispered something to her, drawing her close and wrapping his arm protectively around her. The King's nerves tingled with apprehension. Something wasn't right. He didn't like the feeling he got from this magician. He looked around for a guard and was reassured to see one still standing near the stage, attentive to all the entertainer was saying. He wondered why the Steward had chosen this magician? Then he remembered the ravens. This was the one who'd destroyed so many. His haughty nature was unnerving. The King sighed in frustration. What could he do now? Kick him off the stage? Surely not. He took comfort that this was the last entertainer. Soon, it would be over.

The magician nodded to the flutist who began to play a gentle melody. He lifted both hands in the air, his cape falling back to reveal a dark suit of clothes. As the flutist played, he moved his arms back and forth slowly to the rhythm of the music. Suddenly, to the amazement of all who watched, one of the tips of his fingers grew a flame, as if his finger was a lit candle. The crowd gasped as each of his fingers, one at a time, was lit, as if ten candles had grown from his hands. As the melody faded to its last note, the magician blew softly, just once, and the finger flames went out. The audience clapped enthusiastically!

The magician then called a man and his wife to join him, directing them to hold their hands in the air. With a wave of his hand, he set each of their fingers alight. Apparently, the fire did not burn the skin as neither volunteer gave any indication of pain. The audience held their breath, watching—30 finger flames in all, swinging through the air to the tune of the flute. Again, at the end of the song, the magician extinguished all the flames with an exaggerated puff.

That was actually quite impressive, but the King couldn't shake his angst. He looked for Floxx, wanting to discuss his feelings with her. He jolted when he saw the expression on her face; she was frowning outright, her eyes narrowed in suspicion. He wasn't the only one on edge. He moved next to her. "What kind of trickery is this?" But her answer was muffled with the noise of the guests. Children called out for a chance to have their own finger flames and the magician smiled. As the flutist played a haunting melody, he asked everyone in the audience to hold up one finger. "Hold it high in the air, pointing straight up!" he directed. Those who did as he said found to their delight they had a finger flame. Aric touched his flame lightly with another finger. He held it for Finn to touch, as well. The flame was not hot. It looked like fire, but it did not burn. It was just an illusion. With a loud, exaggerated exhale, the magician turned in a full circle, extinguishing the hundreds of flames in the rooms and on the patio. The crowd went wild.

The illusionist bowed several times to those in the various rooms. "More, more," they shouted. The conjurer held up his hands for silence and the people complied, their eyes glued to him. The flutist played a light-hearted, happy song. The illusionist lifted his hands, swinging them back and forth as if directing a large choir. Suddenly, snowflakes began to fall, slowly at first, drifting down from the ceiling inside and from the night sky outside, falling gently on the upturned faces of the delighted crowd. As the meter of the lilting tune increased, so did the intensity of the snow. Soon, it was blowing in a breeze, then driven by a wind, the cold crystals stinging the exposed flesh of the watchers. But before the crowd could react negatively, it subsided to a soft snowfall and as the last notes of the flute faded, so did the falling flakes. The audience wiped their wet faces, exclaiming loudly and clapping, craning their necks to look for the source of the precipitation. But there was none.

They resettled, spellbound, as the magician held two tall white boots high above his head. They were studded with jewels, sparkling in the candlelight. The flutist began a toe-tapping tune and the magician tossed the boots in the air, where they promptly began to dance. The audience laughed and shouted their approval! After a few minutes, the conjurer lifted a pair of lady's shoes, bejeweled like the boots, and they, too, began to dance; the two pairs circling and swirling with each other as if the quick feet of two invisible dancers moved them. The crowd began clapping to the music.

The magician tossed two more pair of shoes in the air and they took up the dance, swirling, kicking, jigging and swaying with each other. He sent two pair outside and two pair sashaying over the heads of those in each of the indoor rooms. The crowd was on their feet, dancing along with the shoes. Some hopped up on the benches to keep in step. The music reached a frenzy and the shoes kept up the pace, their fancy footwork nearly impossible in its complexity. Those dancing also moved frenetically, their abilities enhanced by some invisible power. Before they knew it, some dancers were in the air, suspended above the heads of those watching, swirling and spinning, kicking and leaping, dancing with the ease and grace of nymphs, held aloft and empowered by the conjurer's magic. And then, as the music slowed, they settled gently to the floor.

People exclaimed, some in wonder and some in fear, hugging each other tightly, astounded and afraid of the power that held such strong sway over them. The King turn to Floxx, concern in his eyes.

Floxx frowned and whispered, "Get him out."

Without hesitation, the King stood and signaled to his Steward.

Chapter 40: Bracelet

Rory watched the end of the bizarre shoe dance and pulled her cape over her shoulders. Why was it so cold in there? She was literally shaking. She leaned into Jakin, seeking his warmth, and was glad when he put his arm around her.

"That was amazing," she whispered, nuzzling into his neck. "And kind of creepy, too."

As the magician bowed, gracefully sweeping up and down to the audiences inside and out, she felt Jakin shudder.

"You okay?"

He didn't reply and when she looked up, she saw he was frowning.

Before she could ask what was wrong, the magician faced the audience and began talking. "Thank you for allowing me the privilege of entertaining you on this momentousss occasion." Good. He was finished. He was a little too weird for her.

"Before I go, I would like to do one more thing." He reached into a pocket and withdrew a wide, flat bejeweled box and held it up. With exaggerated motions, he opened it and lifted out a string of pearls. From where Rory sat she could see they were exquisite; the size of the marbles Dad had given her when she was a kid. These were lustrous and perfectly matched. The audience ooohed.

The magician extended a long arm above his head, letting the necklace dangle from one exceedingly skinny finger and turned full circle for all to admire. "Syrean Sea pearlsss. These have been in my family for generationsss. Would you agree this is a necklace fit for a Princesss?"

The audience loudly agreed.

What? For a Princess? Was he offering them to her?

The magician turned to face the royal table.

"It would be my deepest honor if you would accept these, Princesss Rory, as a token of my happinesss at both your homecoming and your betrothal."

She started to stand, but Jakin pulled her back. "Don't take them, Rory. Don't go near him." Terror showed in his eyes.

"Why not, Jakin? What's going on?"

"I can't explain right now; I just don't trust him."

But the audience took up a new chant, "Princess! Princess! Princess!" The magician stared at her for several long moments, dangling the exquisite necklace from one hand and beckoning her forward with the other.

Father was speaking to his Steward and turned to shake his head at her, telling her not to move. She looked from him to Jakin to the magician, afraid of the conjurer, but feeling inexplicably drawn to him. The crowd grew louder, more insistent.

How can I not go? All the kingdom is watching.

Princess! Princess! Princess!

"Jakin, just let me accept them. I don't ever have to wear them."

"Then, I will go with you."

As they stood, she saw all the color had drained from Jakin's face. She took his hand and it was shaking. He was horrified.

They walked to the stage and stood, looking up at the magician, but he leaned over and beckoned them up the stairs. Why couldn't he just hand them down to her? Did he have to make such a show of it? Her heart pounded, her skin prickled. Maybe Jakin's fear was well founded. Who was this wizard? What was this power he held over all of them? Out of habit, she pressed the bracelet against her side, hoping for its calming effect, but this time, it didn't help. Jakin gripped her arm as they climbed the steps. The audience went berserk, cheering for them.

The magician smiled. "There now, that wasn't so bad, wasss it?" He handed the pearls to Rory with a flourish. "They are nothing next to your beauty."

Then he looked at Jakin. "Do you remember me?"

Jakin startled but said nothing.

The magician glanced at Rory's wrist. "I see you gave her the bracelet."

A hush fell over the audience.

"I told you I could make her love you."

Rory felt as if she'd been punched in the chest; she couldn't catch her breath. Her mind raced. How did the magician know about the bracelet? Make her love Jakin? What was he talking about?

She pulled her hand away and turned to Jakin. Something was very wrong. "What does he mean, Jakin?"

"I, I have no idea."

"Ahhh, but of course you do!" The magician's laugh echoed off the stricken walls. The audience stared. Both Rory's family and Jakin's stood in outrage.

"And a betrothal! Well done, Jakin, well done."

The magician grasped Rory's arm. "May I, Princesss? Now that the bracelet hasss done itsss work, I would like it back."

"No one can remov…," she stammered.

With a touch of his finger, the bracelet fell from her wrist into his palm.

Rory recoiled in shock. The bracelet was off! She suddenly felt good, better than she had in many days. Her mind was free! She could think, again, and her thoughts came quick and sharp and focused. It had been the bracelet all along! An accursed thing, as Finn had warned. It had bewitched her into loving Jakin! She'd been its pawn, an unsuspecting victim. She was livid. Everyone was watching but she didn't care. Father and Mother were rushing toward her.

She turned to Jakin. "This sorcerer gave you this bracelet?"

He stared at the floor. He didn't even try to deny it.

"You lied to me!" Rory spun around, looking for one person. "Finn!" she cried and watched him leap over tables and chairs to get to her. And then she remembered. She was betrothed. She faced Jakin and shouted loud enough for all to hear. "I will never marry you!" She threw the pearls at him and turned to run down the steps.

The magician grabbed her arm. "You're not leaving, are you, princesss?"

Rory screamed. Jakin kicked the magician's knees in, throwing him off balance. As he stumbled backward, she yanked her arm away, and rushed down the stairs. The guards stormed the platform, seizing the sorcerer.

"You dare touch the great Thaumaturge? Your insolence will cost your livesss," he roared as they twisted his arms behind his back.

But before they could bind him, with a mere twist of his neck, the sorcerer set himself on fire. The guards jumped back, shouting, shielding themselves; those flames were no illusion. Rory could see his maniacal silhouette standing in the fire; the flames didn't seem to affect him at all.

He raised his arms in the blaze. "Come!" he shouted, looking outside. "The feast is ready!" And bursting into laughter, raucous and cruel, he turned in a circle, extinguishing all the candles and torches, then strode from the room, a walking inferno no one dared to challenge.

Rory heard a commotion and saw many outside pointing to the sky, screaming. Thousands of leathery wings scraped and grated as they swooped low over the field, the patio, through the open doors and into the ballroom, like a swollen river spilling its banks and covering everything in its path. She shielded her ears from their piercing shrieks. Bats! Fierce and huge! Her blood froze when she saw their faces; they were not bat faces, they were shrunken human skulls, their bulging eyes red. What sorcery had brought these skulls to life? What accursed power moved them? She gasped at the glint of their razor-sharp teeth. These were not bats at all; these were vampire ghouls.

Chaos erupted. People trampled each other in their haste to escape. Jakin shouted for Rory, but she and Finn were already running. Hand in hand, they squeezed through the throng at the doors, onto the patio. They were nearly to the archery field when they heard the magician shriek, his scream impossibly loud, rising in agony above the slaughter. They dared slow down to look and saw him stagger on the patio, no longer shielded by fire, his hands clutching his stomach. He lurched, catching himself on a table. Those near him hurried away, terrified. With a bloodcurdling cry, he yanked a knife from his body, and let it drop to the ground. Pressing his hands over the wound, he staggered this way and that, winding away from the castle, a dark swarm of bats shadowing him.

"Get down," Finn hissed, and they crouched on the ground. "Shhhh." They waited many long minutes for the agonized cries of the sorcerer, and the screeching of his ghouls, to fade into the distance.

When it was quiet, they made their way back to the patio, stepping over dozens slain, others crying in anguish. Those who had escaped serious injury ran from body to body, calling out names, looking for loved ones. Finn stopped to retrieve the knife, wiping black gore from it. "Ezat's blood knife!" he exclaimed, tucking it into his belt.

Inside, Kalvara held the bellasol aloft to light the dark rooms. Bodies lay everywhere, soldiers and guests alike, young and old, some face down on tables, some draped over fallen chairs or sprawled, tangled with others. Blood was everywhere, splattered as high as the chandeliers and puddled in many places on the floor. Several guards encircled a victim, but when they saw Rory, they parted. Her father lay on his back, her mother kneeling on one side of him, Floxx on the other.

Rory rushed to him, recoiling at his ravaged, bloodied neck. "No! Noooo!" His eyes were open, but they stared unfocused at the ceiling. She put her hand on his cheek and patted. "Father!" He didn't blink. She grabbed his hand, limp and heavy and offering no resistance. "Father, no. No, you can't go." She shook his shoulders. "We've only just met, we're just beginning. Please, please, don't leave me." She looked at Floxx, hope springing in her eyes. She struggled to get the words out, choking between sobs. "Heal him, Floxx. Please!"

But Floxx shook her head and wept, just as she'd done when Zad had died.

Rory pleaded hysterically with Eldurrin. *Please, don't do this. Don't take my father. Please! Heal him like you did Mother. I need him, Eldurrin. Please!* She pressed her face to his chest, clutching his bloody clothes, sobbing. She could feel Mother's hand on her back, trying to comfort her, but her soothing touch was no match for the rage and the anguish she felt.

Rory had no idea how much time had passed before she finally sat up. Floxx reached out to touch her shoulder. She looked away, numb, unable to respond. After a few minutes, she stood. Mother moved next to her. She saw that some soldiers had come with a bier and wondered how long they'd been waiting. Finn stood nearby with Kalvara and Aric and a small contingent of guards. Jakin was nowhere to be seen.

The guards moved the King onto the gurney; his head lolling from side to side, his arms hanging limp. Mother clung to her, weeping, and Floxx tried to console them both. Kalvara bowed, then all of them followed her example, paying honor to their King as he was carried out. Rory wrapped her arms around her ribs and sobbed.

Chapter 41: Viewing

Rory didn't remember much about the next few days, but somehow, they'd arranged a formal viewing in the huge open area outside the Treasury. The line of people paying their respects to the King snaked slowly past his casket. This was the same place they'd had the welcome reception for the giant killers just a week ago. Jakin had been a hero then. Now the whole kingdom knew the truth about him, how he'd tricked and manipulated both her and her father into an engagement. He was power hungry, wanting the throne when Father died. And she'd fallen for it, creepy bracelet and all. She still couldn't believe he'd been in cahoots with Draegin, himself. Had he even known it was Draegin who'd given him the bracelet? Did he have any idea it was enchanted? He'd certainly been terrified of the magician at the ball. In the quiet moments, she wondered if Jakin wished she'd died, too, then wondered if he also wished he'd died. That way he wouldn't have to face his mess, his treachery, his despicable choices and their devastating consequences.

The ballrooms were gory reminders of the slaughter and completely off-limits to visitors, though she couldn't fathom why anyone would want to go near them. Troops had been assigned to identify the dead who remained and return them to their next-of-kin, however distant they may be, for proper burials. Two or three were still unidentified, perhaps travelers from outside the city. Six soldiers and four castle staff had been killed, along with nearly a hundred guests. At least twice that number had been injured. Servants were scrubbing and cleaning and setting the rooms back in order, but she wasn't sure if she'd ever be able to walk into them again. The smell of death lingered, blood and burnt flesh; its fetid stench had clawed past her senses into her heart. Not even the urns of fragrant flowers could mask it.

The public viewing had plodded from noon to sundown for two days now, and they would continue to welcome citizens, friends, and relatives tomorrow. She and Mother stood near the raised bier at the King's head, nodding silent greetings and shaking hands with those who wished. The casket was waist high and partitioned off, and His Majesty was positioned so guests could see him through the lattice screen. Soldiers stood at attention on three sides, armed and alert, but so far, there'd been no sign of trouble. Day four would be private; a time for immediate family to say their final good-byes; they were considering holding a memorial service that evening. And on day five at noon, the casket would be lowered into the cavernous hole waiting open-mouthed in the royal graveyard.

Rory had left her father only to take care of personal things. She and her mother returned to their quarters only to sleep, though neither of them did much of it, and they were back by his side before dawn. Rory liked those quiet hours in the morning with just Mother and her. The guards were always there, of course, but they kept their distance and gave them the privacy they needed. She and the Queen sat in silence on either side of father's casket, each touching one of his hands, lost in their private thoughts. His eyes were closed, but Rory felt he could see them, and sensed he was weeping. How could this have happened? Death had snatched him away at the happiest time of his life! He'd wanted to live, to love his wife and daughter, to rule his people in peace. So kind, so generous, so wise, her father. Her King. She'd whispered to him how sorry she was for breaking his heart, for choosing slime-ball Jakin over him. For being willing to leave Masirika and live in Orizin, where she'd seldom have seen him or Mother again. She'd told him how much he meant to her, amazed that he'd been willing to listen to her Alaska story at all, and realized, again, that it was crazy miraculous she'd made a full circuit back home. She was so humbled that he'd accepted her— Rory from another world, Rory who wore jeans and flew airplanes, who'd held princesses and castles pretty much in contempt until now, who was scarred and ugly enough to be stared at. None of that had bothered him. She was his daughter and she'd come home.

He'd rejoiced over her, accepted her past, celebrated her present, and enthused about her future. He welcomed her friends and listened with an open mind as she talked about her other father and mother. Rory desperately wished she'd had more time with him; she could have learned so much. She would have treasured their days together. No. Wait. Who was she kidding? Even though she was definitely finished with Jakin, if Father had lived through the massacre, she would have eventually left with Finn. Now, though, she'd lost them both. Father was dead, Finn wouldn't stay forever, and she couldn't leave her mother, not now and maybe not ever.

The King didn't look much like himself, laying in the gold-lined box. His blue robe cast a gray pallor on his skin. The morticians had sewn up the gaping wounds on his neck and covered them with a white ermine collar. But his face was pallid and drawn, the skin on his cheekbones sunk deep into their contours; his jaw sagged. His folded hands weren't right, either; his fingers swollen, nails white.

But this morning after she'd poured out her heart to him and felt he'd heard her, something else happened. Although she couldn't explain it, she'd heard him answer her, inside her head where no one else could hear. His words were as clear as if he'd spoken them out loud. While her thoughts to him had been mostly sentiment and regret, his were all business.

Rory, my dear Rory, we were completely unprepared for this. By the time I sensed the sorcerer's danger, it was too late to act. And now, I am here where you cannot come and soon you won't be able to sense me at all. With your engagement to Jakin broken, you are the legal heir to the throne and will become Queen Aurora on your 18th birthday. Your mother will reign until then and show you how to rule with integrity and wisdom. She will need your help in stabilizing the kingdom and moving forward. Avoid hasty decisions, for once you've made them, you must live with them and their consequences. Seek counsel from those you trust and consider wise: Floxx, and your high Commanders. Consider their admonitions carefully and judge their guidance against the counsel of your own heart. Honor your mother and treat her well for as many years as she has left.

Her tears had dripped onto Father's lifeless fingers. She'd had no response; couldn't begin to sort through her thoughts. She'd nodded and hoped he saw.

Rory was so grateful for Finn. He rarely let her out of his sight. Though trying not to obviously hover, he was never more than a few feet away and in his thoughtful way, was taking good care of her. He'd arranged for some chairs to be carried in for her and mother when he'd sensed them too weary to stand.

She and the Queen dutifully spoke with many who passed through, keeping it brief and expressing their thanks for the many sincere condolences. Some, however, kept their distance, filing past the casket in disbelief, shaking their heads and considering them with pity; the recent horror still showing in their expressions. What was to become of them? How would they manage? Would they ever recover? Not just she and Mother, but each citizen of Byerman who had suffered, many having just buried their own loved ones.

But Rory couldn't think of that now. She had to focus. On breathing. One breath in, one breath out. In and out. She would not allow herself to panic. She had Mother. She had Finn. She had Floxx. She had survived. Decisions were an impossibility, a tangled web she dared not contemplate. Not yet.

"Rory." It was Finn. She hadn't seen him standing next to her. "Please come eat." Though she had no appetite, she obliged him and turned from the line of mourners to walk to a distant alcove, the one where Jakin had kissed her before they'd gone into the Treasury where he'd won her hand. She shuddered at the memory. Servants had the tables spread with fruit and cheeses, soups and fresh breads, pies and teas and honey. She managed a wedge of cheddar and some grapes, and a cup of tea for Finn's sake.

Floxx joined them, whispering to Finn, "Good job, coaxing some food into her." She rubbed Rory's shoulders briefly and at her touch, she relaxed a little. Floxx gently kneaded the muscles between her shoulder blades, speaking softly. "It's going to be okay. We are with you. We are for you. You don't have to do this alone. We will help you."

Rory wished Floxx wouldn't be so nice. It made her want to cry and she was struggling not to. She pulled away with muttered thanks and, without daring to look at either Floxx or Finn, walked back to her mother's side.

The next day was the same. Grim greetings. Well-meaning handshakes. Heartfelt condolences. Rory couldn't wait for the viewing to end. An hour before sundown, Zirena, Tozar, and their family arrived. Jakin was not with them. He's disappeared, Zirena had said when asked, her eyes cold, her words minced. She had no idea where he'd gone. Rory didn't push it; she was just glad not to have to confront him. Good riddance.

Ezat and Azatar were stiff, as well, but Renaz gave Rory a warm hug. "Everything's wrecked now," she'd whispered. "I'm so, so sorry, Rory." After the rest of the family had walked away, Renaz confided, "Jakin's afraid to come."

"I'm sure he is," Finn answered softly, overhearing. "But it is a great dishonor to shun his Uncle's funeral. If he ever hopes to make amends, he must come."

Renaz replied solemnly. "I'll tell him," she said, then turned to rejoin her family.

The dwarves paid their respects and stood awkwardly off to the side, making idle conversation with a Tomtee couple they knew. Rory had no idea what to say to them and was way too exhausted for small talk. Finn took her hand, though, and urged her to join them.

"Ezat," Finn said as they approached. "This is yours." He handed him the ruby knife.

"Ah, I thank ye, Finn! I thought I'd lost it for good and was sorely vexed about it."

"Did you throw it at the sorcerer?"

"I threw it at the fire, knowing he was in it. But I'd no idea if it hit the mark."

"It did, Ezat. Got him in the gut. Rory and I heard him shriek and saw him yank it out before he ran off into the night. You hurt him bad. Might keep him away for a while."

"We can hope. I only wish I'd thrown it sooner. Might'a saved a lot of lives." He glanced at Rory and sighed.

Zirena had been listening and perked up as realization dawned on her face. "What's this, son! Ye took a chunk outa Draegin? Why, ye're a hero, yet again!"

"I agree!" Finn said, clapping Ezat on the back.

Rory noticed Tozar didn't say anything and she thought it odd. Most fathers would be super proud of a son who'd been so brave as to attack a mighty sorcerer, especially in the midst of such terror. But Tozar was staring hard at nothing, his mouth turned down. He caught her studying him and snapped to the moment, extending a hand to his boy.

"Well done, Ezat," he said. But it was a flat, joyless congratulation and Rory thought she saw fear in Tozar's eyes.

They invited the dwarves to stay in the nicest palatial suite; it was the least they could do to honor them in the face of their public disgrace, and their bitter disappointment in Jakin's lost inheritance. It had been Floxx's idea, actually; she'd insisted they try to mend relations, and although Rory would have preferred they all disappeared from her life for a very long while, she took her father's advice and listened to Floxx.

Chapter 42: Memorial

Breakfast the next morning was served at eight in the same atrium where the viewing had been. This was the day of private grieving, set aside for family, relatives, and invited close friends. The lattice barricade had been removed and the King's casket had been repositioned against a far wall and framed on three sides with flags and flowers. Though guards were present, they were less obtrusive and stood their duty at a distance.

A couple dozen straight-back chairs sat in four rows facing the casket, back a respectable distance, leaving room to stand in front of them. The painting of the young king and queen that normally hung over the hearth in their suite was displayed on an easel next to the coffin. A harpist had already begun playing, and Rory and her mother had arranged for a flute duet to play in the afternoon. A soloist accompanied by the dulcimer would sing after dinner, followed by a memorial service—Rory's idea, customary in the world she'd come from, she'd said, and Mother had liked it. They'd asked a few individuals to speak who were willing to share stories of the King. After that, they'd send everyone home, and ready the King for his final journey tomorrow.

Rory spent most of the day writing a poem, a tribute she planned to read as she opened the memorial service. She decided to work through lunch, legitimately having trouble composing, but in truth craving the isolation of her room. She really needed a break from all the people. By late afternoon, she'd finished the poem, sobbing through many of the verses. She knew, even if it was terrible poetry, it was from her heart. Still, she hoped she didn't make a fool of herself, blubbering her way through it in front of everyone.

Madeleine came to dress her for dinner, and Rory deeply appreciated her help, feeling terribly weary. They chose a blue silk gown that Father had liked very much, and Madeleine worked a miracle with her hair. Rushing in a little late for dinner, she didn't see Jakin until she was seated between her mother and Finn. She must have felt his stare and when she looked, there he was a couple of tables away. Renaz sat on one side of him and Ezat on the other. Jakin was caught off guard when Rory met his eyes; he held her gaze briefly, then turned his head. She supposed it was right for him to come, but he made her skin crawl. Finn noted the brief exchange and took her hand under the table.

"Don't mind him," he said. "I missed you today. You all right?"

She shrugged. "Tired and anxious about tonight. I'll be relieved when this is over."

"Me, too," Mother said, keeping her voice soft. "I'm exhausted. Spent the morning making the final arrangements for tomorrow."

Rory felt a pang of guilt. "I'm so sorry, Mother. I shouldn't have left you to handle that by yourself."

Mother waved her words away. "You needed the time alone. And I wasn't by myself, not even for a moment. Military honors have a well-established order and tradition, and our Commanders knew exactly how the ceremony should be done. I just had to formally agree and make a few minor decisions. Then I joined Finn for lunch. It was a great pleasure to talk with him. He's quite the conversationalist." She smiled at him.

"Is he now?" Rory grinned, glad they liked each other.

It occurred to her Floxx was missing. She hadn't been at breakfast either and she asked if anyone had seen her.

"No," Mother said, "We haven't seen her all day."

Rory hoped her absence didn't bode ill. They were finishing dessert when she heard footsteps in the hall. They weren't expecting anyone who wasn't already here. Finn saw her concern and shook his head as if to say it was okay. She knew he could hear things that she could not. As they drew closer, she could make out the step, thump, step, thump of someone walking with a cane. Finn squeezed her hand, stood, and sprinted into the hall. Rory's heart leapt as she heard him exclaim over his uncle and aunt. Werner and Ardith had come! She couldn't believe it. How did they get here? She reached them just as they were entering the room. Floxx was smiling hugely as Rory hugged them.

"How did you ever manage to get here?" she asked Ardith.

"Tennins," she whispered. "Kind of terrifying! Oh, Rory, I'm so sorry," she said, her voice breaking. "It's terrible. Just terrible."

That lump in Rory's throat that she'd had under control threatened to burst, but Werner lightened the moment.

"Look! I'm okay!" He handed his cane to Ardith and did a little jig. "Just a matter of time and I won't need that thing at all."

Rory was elated to see them. They were like family; her family here in this world. Not just Finn's aunt and uncle, but hers, too. Floxx had known exactly what she'd needed.

Finn made the introductions. Though Jakin was stiff and held himself distant, they hugged him fondly. If they knew what had happened, they didn't let on.

Mother especially warmed to them. "Sit here with us," she insisted when they moved to the chairs for the memorial service.

Rory stood and walked to the front of the room to begin. It took all she had to hold on to her composure, but she did it for her father. She wanted him to be proud of her. She wanted to honor him. She glanced at Zirena and remembered how she had handled Zad's funeral, so proud and confident though her heart had been broken.

"Thank you for coming tonight," she began. "My father, loved as friend, family, father, husband, and King, would be very pleased you are here, as I am, to reflect on and celebrate his exceptional life, his deeds large and small, his kindnesses and his accomplishments. It's a terribly sad moment, a tragic time for us all, but while we pause to remember and honor King Merek, we will do it with a face forward, looking ahead to better times – to peace, to security, to serenity once again." She glanced at Mother, who smiled in approval, her eyes moist.

Rory swallowed against the thickness in her throat and allowed her gaze to linger on her father's body positioned so regally in his casket. "This is for you, Father," she said, then began to read her poem.

I came to you from far away
Where Kings are stiff, and often
Distant, shallow, duplicitous.

But you were nice
To me.

I trembled when you looked at me
With surreptitious glances.
I never thought you'd talk to me;
But you had time
For me.

You beckoned me to speak to you.
I mustered up the courage
And told my wild and crazy tale.
And you did not
Doubt me.

Miraculous that I'd been dead
Yet stood before you, living.
Your daughter, yes, your only child.
And you reached out
For me.

For sixteen years we'd been apart
And now since I've returned,
Faced danger, dragons, fear and terror.
And you stood strong
With me.

You welcomed me in spite of grief
And growing threats and battles.
Celebrating I was back.
You were so kind
To me.

Accepting me for who I am,
And I am far from perfect,
With grace and generosity

You spent your time
With me.

We celebrated in grand style,
My homecoming was treasured.
You lavished all that you could give
You were so good
To me.

Protection was your middle name
And you were fierce about it,
Fighting any beast or creature.
And you were brave
For me.

I wish we'd had more time for us
To get to know each other
And yet, I'll ne'er forget the love
That you poured out
On me.

She looked up when she finished and there wasn't a dry eye in the room. Even the guards were swiping discretely at their cheeks.

"Mother," she held out her hand. "Would you like to share next?" As her mother walked up, Rory took her seat between Ardith and Finn, taking comfort in their shoulders warm next to hers. Ardith patted her knee.

"Beautiful," she whispered.

"Perfect," Finn said as he slid his arm around her.

She sunk into his embrace. Safe. She relished the feeling as she turned her attention to Mother.

"As King Merek's wife, I loved and honored him, that goes without saying. But, rather than speaking of his many wonderful accomplishments, I wanted to share a bit of our love story with you. Just with you, just for this moment tonight; tomorrow we will celebrate his heroic and faithful life of service to his country."

Rory was surprised! Mother hadn't even shared this with her. Others were equally curious; she could hear those behind her shifting in their seats, leaning forward to hear better.

"I was 16 when I actually met Merek for the first time. Your age, Rory." She smiled at her. "We were already betrothed; our marriage had been arranged many years before, and though I'd seen him from a distance and knew we would eventually wed, we were not introduced until then. My family lived near the coast and Merek's father was quite the seafarer, as was his brother. My father owned a fleet of ships and managed a busy trade route. They knew each other and had negotiated the terms of our marriage when I was eight years old. Our public engagement took place by the Syrean Sea at an extravagant gala. I was not involved in the planning of the event and had no idea what to expect. I knew I was going to be royalty, a princess to start, and, eventually, the Queen of Byerman." She took a sip of water.

"As daunting as that was, I was honestly far more concerned about the man I was about to meet. What was he like? I thought he was handsome enough, but would we even care for each other? Would there be any love between us? What if he didn't even like me? What if he was cold and hard-hearted? Merek was 18, of age to take a wife, and the wedding was scheduled for the Fall. After a lavish dinner and myriad introductions, I was finally brought to him. He bowed before me and when our eyes met, I saw what I was hoping for. Tenderness. Kindness. He reached for my hand and kissed it. Gentle. And a little unsure. I fell in love with him that moment."

Rory heard Ardith sigh. The gentle side of Father. This was good. And really no surprise to anyone who knew him.

"He came to my home three times before the wedding and each time we grew closer. We'd walk along the shore, sharing stories, laughing, eventually holding hands. The chaperones gave us some privacy though they never let us out of their sight. Each time he came, he brought me a gift. He was a great gift-giver as some of you know; it always gave him much joy. First, he brought a heart-shaped locket engraved with our names. Then a string of pearls designed to weave into my hair, and finally a book."

A book? Rory hadn't ever seen it.

"I'll have to admit I was taken aback by the book. I was expecting something much more extravagant. Jewels, royal heirlooms." She winked, and everyone laughed. "But all that was to come later. In retrospect, the book was the best treasure he's ever given me."

Rory held her breath, enthralled with her mother's story.

"The pages of this book were covered with his handwriting. Merek had written me letters and poems and wonderful thoughts about our love and our marriage and our lives together. He had high hopes for a family and his yearning is clear in those pages. My years of barrenness must have greatly disappointed him, but our joy with Rory's birth overshadowed it all. You know the rest. The kidnapping, my illness, the desolate years, and finally the miraculous return of our daughter coupled with the restoration of my health. Through it all, Merek remained faithful to me, loving me, caring for me, ruling with diligence and holding onto hope for a miracle in spite of his shattered dreams. He was a man of great strength, driven by the high calling to rule his kingdom fairly, protect fiercely, guard relentlessly. And yet, underneath, he remained a man of compassion, integrity, and his seed of hope bloomed into reality when Rory returned. Remember him this way, my friends. Remember Merek the man as we celebrate Merek the King."

How special! She was so proud of her mother! Rory wondered if she still had the book and whether she could look through it.

Three of his Commanders stood and shared personal stories about the King's friendship above and beyond duty. The first told how the King had saved his daughter's life by personally rescuing her from a Trow that attempted to kidnap her. This was after Rory was gone and she wondered if he'd thought of her then. The second Commander revealed how he'd been sent many, many times to deliver food to hungry families in the city. He was ordered never to reveal who it was from, though the royal kitchens knew full well it had been the King's order. The third told how the King had saved his life in time of peace. In time of war, he emphasized, it was considered duty, but in time of peace, it was heroic. A band of thugs had ridden into Byerman that morning, terrorizing the city, vandalizing the shops, destroying the stores. The King had responded immediately, taking a few soldiers to defend his people. This Commander had been pulled from his horse and two ruffians were beating him. The King leapt off his steed, threw himself into the middle a fist fight, subdued the thugs and tied them up, delivering them to the council for justice. The King was the bravest and toughest of them all.

After the last speaker had taken his seat, Rory waited, wondering if there would be others. This was a new tradition for these people and some were struggling with the idea of standing and speaking. She was about to thank everyone for coming when Jakin marched to the front. The scowl on his face sent chills down her back. His hands were clenched, and he glared at her as he passed.

"This is nice, all the sweet things you all have shared." The guards moved in. Jakin held up his hands. "Give me a second, please." They looked at Rory and she held up a hand, so they waited.

"We all know now that King Merek was my Uncle. His brother was my father and both of my parents lost their lives fighting Morfyn when I was very young. I sent an arrow down the monster's throat just a few weeks ago, finally vindicating my parents' lives, something brave King Merek never did."

Rory balled her hand into a fist. Where was Jakin going with this? He wouldn't shame the King at his own funeral, would he? She frowned as he continued.

"You'd think I'd have a sentimental family story to share about an orphaned boy who'd been loved and cared for by his Uncle, but the King, himself, was a stranger to me. None of this love you've talked about touched me. The King abandoned me, his own nephew, to Orizin and left...."

Many gasped at the outrageously rude comments. The guards moved in, took Jakin by the arms and ushered him from the room. He didn't resist. He held his head high and walked out proud, though Rory could see tears on the edges of his eyes.

The mood was shattered. One of Father's friends stood and raised his fist, cursing Jakin and calling him a liar. Others joined in, shouting insults, angry, even after Jakin had left the room. Mother wept. Rory was seething. To dishonor the King at his memorial service was intolerable. She hoped Jakin never dared show his face in Byerman, again. But, irate as she was, she would not sink to his level. She walked to the front and waited, gathering her thoughts. Eventually, the outrage calmed and those standing took their seats.

When she had their attention, she spoke with as level a voice as she could manage. "Let's remember why we are here and who we are honoring. Jakin is clearly not in a good state of mind after the terrible things that have happened, and we will not allow him to hinder the funeral tomorrow. As for you, my family and dearest friends, thank you for coming tonight and sharing such special memories. The King has been honored in a most tender way; Mother and I will always treasure the stories you have shared. In the morning we will lay him to rest. We will see you then. Good night to you all."

Chapter 43: Honored

The trumpets jolted Rory from a restless sleep to the pain of grief. Today was the funeral. Whatever awe she'd initially had with this magical world was long forgotten. Pain was here. Death was here. Her stomach had been twisted for weeks, churning with fear, confusion, heartache. She yearned for Alaska, the smell of spruce, wood smoke, the frosty air, the silent winter forest holding its breath, the only sound her footsteps in the snow.

The trumpets blared, again. She climbed from the bed still drowsy, appalled she'd overslept on this most important day, yet terribly reluctant to face it. She'd hardly known her father and now had to say her final good-bye. She grieved that the door of their relationship had been slammed shut. Their short acquaintance had been a gift; his love a treasure she would always hold close.

She eyed the crown he'd given her. Bittersweet. A new gown was hanging near it on a hook. Black. The seamstresses had labored day and night to finish it, and it was exquisite with its pearl collar and sheer bell sleeves. But she didn't want to wear it. Not today. Not ever. She wanted him back. Her cheeks were wet when Madeleine entered the room.

"Good morning, Princess," she said, her shy eyes twinkling.

"Oh! Good morning, Madeleine." She swiped at her face as her maid hurried toward her with a robe.

Rory was tempted to linger in the solitude of her privy, but knew her mother was likely dressed and downstairs, managing the morning preparations. She needed her. Madeleine was superb at her job, and Rory was cinched in and ready in record time. In fact, her maid seemed to be rushing, quickly pinning up the last of Rory's curls with a satisfied, "There now."

She'd done a good job, and Rory looked beyond her own reflection, focusing on Madeleine for the first time. She was smiling; really beaming.

"Everything okay?" Rory was curious as to why she was so happy; she could use some joy this morning.

"Yes, everything is very good." Madeleine smiled mysteriously and adjusted the crown on Rory's head.

The breakfast room was empty when Rory arrived. Where was everyone? One of the servants laughed when she asked and pointed to the balcony. Curious, she headed that way, hearing a lot of commotion as she got closer. Laughter. Joy. What in the world was going on? Mother, Floxx, Ardith, Werner, Finn, Kalvara and Aric were all there. Mother was pointing with one hand and wiping her eyes with the other.

"I can't believe it!"

"It's absolutely stunning!"

"A fitting tribute."

Kalvara had Aric on her hip, and he saw Rory first. "Look!" he pointed, grinning from ear to ear. "A little castle for the King!"

She broke into a flat-out run, her satin skirt shushing like cross-country skis over the snow. Finn held his arms out for her. "You won't believe it!" he laughed. He was totally right.

In the graveyard, covering the interment plot, stood a castle in miniature, about 15 feet tall and twice as wide. Two bejeweled doors stood open in front, reminiscent of the ones at the entrance to Orizin. One side of the room was dark, and she assumed covered the hole in the earth that would soon swallow Father, but she could see a floor on the other side, the room lit with many candles.

Mother, laughing and crying at the same time, put her arm around her daughter's waist. "We've been waiting for you. Let's go see it."

It was grander close up. The stone turrets that sparkled in the sunlight were flecked with gold. The windows were edged in sapphires and topaz. These gems were not from around here. Where did this all come from? Who built it? How?

Rory stood rooted a short distance from the entrance, gaping. Finn stood with her, gripping her hand. The others went inside, and she could hear them exclaiming.

"Must have been the Tennins," Finn said. "Floxx bid their help to bring Werner and Ardith here."

"Yes, there's no other explanation."

A blue orb peeked from behind one of the turrets and floated down to them. In seconds, Uriel stood before them. He bowed. "Are you pleased?" he said, his voice much like Cue's deep growl.

"Pleased? It's completely, unimaginably gorgeous!" Rory threw her arms around him, encircling a third of his hairy girth. "Thank you. It's magnificent!" Her voice choked with emotion. "But, why?" She looked from him to the exquisite mausoleum.

"Eldurrin wished to honor your father," Uriel rumbled. "We have watched him live an exemplary life, making his difficult decisions every day.

Choosing to forgive and not begrudge, to love and not hate, to give generously, to rule fairly, to fight valiantly. But most importantly, your father loved Eldurrin. He was thrilled to meet Floxx and understood quickly who she was and that Eldurrin had sent her to bring you back to him. The realization that he, himself, played a small part in the unfolding prophecy was the greatest honor of his life."

Rory fought to hold her emotions at bay. She squeezed Finn's hand and he squeezed back, helping her maintain her composure.

"Rory," Uriel rumbled. "Your return was partly a result of your father's faithfulness. Although he thought you were likely dead, he never let you go. He loved you. He yearned for you. Against all reason, he pleaded with Eldurrin for you."

She had no words. Her father really had loved her. He'd never given up hope. And when she'd finally returned, he'd showered her with love.

"Thank you," she whispered, and taking Finn's hand walked through the open doors. Beautiful marble floors reflected the candlelight, and she caught a glimpse of picture windows she wanted to see, but the room was crowded. She and Finn turned toward the side that held the grave. They approached the rectangular hole and saw that narrow steps had been cut in the dirt on either side, footholds allowing a graceful bearing of the casket to its resting place. The troops could easily carry the King down. And then they would cover him up forever.

An oblong marble slate was laying on the floor near the grave, cut to cover it. The slate was inlaid with precious jewels, engraved in elegant script, and the seal of the Kingdom had been inset beneath the three-line inscription she and Mother had written. But one last line had been added.

Merek, the King
Honorable, valiant, noble, faithful
Beloved ruler, husband, father
Favored by Eldurrin

Finn squeezed Rory's shoulder. She pressed her fist hard against her mouth, willing herself not to sob. The astounding skill of a Tennin, engraving marble with a fingertip! If their abilities were so wondrous here, she couldn't imagine what they were like there, where her father was, with Eldurrin, with the rest of the Tennins. Was Zad there? Perhaps they would meet at last.

They walked to the candlelit room, over to the stained-glass windows. She was delighted to find each one depicted a scene from her father's life. The Tennins had thought of such wonderful ways to honor him! Mother and Kalvara were standing in front of one, a magnificent composite of Father and Mother's early years together, the central picture a colorful rendition of their wedding by the sea. Smaller scenes were blocked in separate frames around it, creating a border for the large wedding mural. How was it they could remember all that detail?

Mother was exclaiming, "And there's the book I was telling you about!" She pointed to one of the small pictures. Rory glanced at it but was distracted by another window. The large center glass showed the King holding an infant; the Queen by his side. They were standing on a balcony, perhaps the one they'd just left, and there were hundreds of people around them cheering, arms in the air. It was her. She was the baby. Her father and mother were presenting their child, the heir of the kingdom, celebrating her birth.

Mother came to stand beside her. "How well I remember that day," she said softly. "We had never been happier. I'd been reluctant to take you outside in the chilly air, but your father convinced me that if we bundled you up and kept you warm, no harm would come to you." She cleared her throat. "Not that day anyway. Friends came to visit. Citizens sent gifts. Harm was a week away and if we'd known, we would have fled the country."

"How could we have known, Mother? How could any of this tangled mess have been foreseen?"

The Queen sighed. "And yet, none of it was a mistake. Nothing happened by accident. Eldurrin's hand was in it all, guiding us through both the horrible and the wonderful. He didn't stop it; he allowed it. I don't understand why, but I know it's true. It has to be – I mean, look at this!" She gestured at the spectacular sepulcher. "Eldurrin loved your father. Not one day of his life went unnoticed."

Floxx joined them. "And he loves you and Rory as well. He will show you what to do going forward; I am sure of it. And I will stay and help you if you would allow me the privilege."

Mother threaded her arm through Floxx's. "We would be most appreciative of your guidance and counsel. Thank you, my friend."

Rory swallowed hard. If she focused on Eldurrin; held on to the love he clearly had for her father, for her, for all of them, if she could just keep her thoughts on that, she might be able to stay composed and make it through the day. She didn't understand why, and couldn't think about it right then, but she had visual proof in this incredible mausoleum that maybe, just maybe, there was a plan far bigger than she could imagine. That was enough for her to hold on to.

It was crazy, but Rory couldn't recall much about her father's interment service. They had deferred to custom, wanting him to have all that was considered high honor, and Mother had handled all the arranging. Many hundreds of citizens packed the castle grounds as six of his highest-ranking guards bore his casket to the magnificent mausoleum amid the throng of mourners. Drums set the rhythm of the funeral march and trumpets heralded his arrival at the bejeweled door.

She and her mother walked immediately behind the casket, everyone else kept some distance. Father's chief commander stood on a platform above the crowd and gave a brief eulogy in which the crowd had a scripted response. She couldn't remember what he'd said. She did, however, hear a lot of whispering and squeals over the Tennins' astounding creation.

For her, the sting of death was already diminishing. She would miss her father, no doubt, but the rip in her soul was mending. She was hollow, yes, and aching, but she was engulfed in awe, wrapped in peace. Somehow, she knew he lived, and was convinced she'd see him, again. The mausoleum was visible proof that her father held high favor with Eldurrin, the same Eldurrin who loved her, the same one Floxx said she knew so well.

How amazing that Eldurrin could care so much for one individual. She had a deep, settled peace that she mattered, too, way more than she realized. He'd given her a part in his song, his story, his plan for restoring the damaged, war-torn world. He was watching her make decisions. Listening to her heart, understanding her motivations. He knew her, maybe better than she knew herself. It was bizarre! The warmth she'd felt before in his presence began to spread through her. She reached out to him with her heart telling him she loved him. And he answered back, like he'd done before. *I love you, too, Rory. Trust me. Listen for my voice and I will lead you.*

Mother squeezed her hand as they watched Father's casket disappear down the steps to its resting place. It was just the two of them and the guards for a few moments. They'd left the crowd in the big room where flowers were being passed out to the guests. She and Mother each held a stem of Tennifel, compliments of Floxx who had found it somewhere on her journey. After the bier was in place, they were escorted down the steps to say their final farewells.

Mother took Rory's hand and said aloud, "Eldurrin." She paused, and his presence felt palpable. "You have done us a great honor in building this resting place for the King, my husband, whom I loved. You have given us back Rory, the daughter we'd thought we'd lost forever, and yet, through all the years, you cared for her, and prepared her for this time. You have given us many good things, friends and family, wealth, and power. We thank you and ask that you will guide us as we carry on that we may bring honor to the King's name and to yours."

Rory watched her mother as she spoke to Eldurrin, eyes closed, holding her Tennifel next to her heart, amazed that she could offer such a wonderful prayer, say such an eloquent good-bye. When Mother opened her eyes, she smiled at her daughter. It was her turn.

Taking a deep breath, Rory struggled to speak through a swollen throat. "Eldurrin, please take good care of Father. Tell him how much I loved him and how sorry I am this has happened." Her voice broke. Mother took her hand. When she was able, Rory continued, "Introduce him to Zad, and to my Alaskan mother, so they can all get to know each other. And please, please, show me what to do now."

Mother lay her bloom across the center of the casket with a whispered I love you, then stood back.

Rory placed her flower across Mother's and said softly, "I'll never forget you, Father."

They were escorted to the main level and the guards blocked off the steps behind them. The mourners would file through the room and drop their flowers onto the grave from above; eventually blanketing the King in colorful blooms. Outside, Rory and her mother waited on a bench in a side garden. A meal was set for guests, heaping platters of fruits, cheeses, breads, and cakes. Father would be pleased if he could see it. In the few moments they had before the guests would join them, they sat close; letting the tears spill unchecked, and speaking in whispers about the peace they felt.

Chapter 44: Portal

The next morning when Rory arrived at breakfast, Werner was deep in conversation with Ezat and Azatan, huddled over something she couldn't see. They glanced up as she approached and broke into broad smiles.

"Rory, look!" Werner held out a book, printed and bound in the United States—the Pilot's Operating Handbook for the Cessna 172. She couldn't believe it.

"Zad had it," Azatan explained. "We found it among his things and wondered if you'd want it back."

She riffled the pages, then handed it to him. "The book should stay with the airplane."

"It's in Werner's barn."

"I know."

"I've managed to get the propeller off," Werner said. "And I think we can make a new one, using the damaged one as a pattern."

"He's told us all about it!" Ezat's eyes twinkled. "We want to see it fly!"

"You really think you could make a prop?" Rory asked Werner.

"I'd give it a good try. We've lots of wood and a scale to weigh it to be sure it's close to the original." He tipped his head toward the dwarves. "These boys here are quality craftsmen."

"With wood?" She was surprised. They were miners, working with stone and gems.

"We are also builders," Azatan confirmed, and she remembered the handmade tables and chairs in their home.

"And they could help me prepare the field to give you room to fly the airplane off the ground."

Rory was stunned. What if she could fly here? She thought of the steep mountains, of the flight to Orizin on the backs of the Tennins, and how in just a few hours they'd covered the miles it had taken them weeks to walk. The possibility of flying opened this world up wide. And then a thought thundered so loud she startled. Maybe, just maybe, she could fly back to Alaska! Her heart surged.

"Okay. Yes." She couldn't manage anything more.

"They will come back to the farm with Ardith and me. We'll borrow some horses, and Floxx has offered to escort us. Give us some time, a few months, Rory, after things are settled down here, then come for a test flight."

By this time, Mother had joined them. "Wouldn't that be wonderful?" She patted her daughter's shoulder.

Later in the morning, Rory walked into Father's magnificent tomb hoping for some time alone to think about things. Floxx was there.

"You've talked with Werner? You're going back with them?"

"Yes, it's perfect; Ezat and Azatan will be a great help to him in many ways. And I think they can figure out how to repair the airplane."

"I could fly it back here. I could land right on the road to the castle."

"You could. I'll try to stay out of your way this time!" Floxx teased, and they both laughed.

Then Rory got serious. "Floxx? What about Alaska? Do you think I could ever go back? Fly back?"

Floxx hesitated. "Would you want to stay there?"

"I don't know. Maybe. I'd have to see."

Floxx considered this for a long moment, and Rory grew uncomfortable with the silence before her friend finally came to a decision. "A portal. You need a portal."

Rory's heart leapt. There was a portal? Why hadn't Floxx said so before? She could go home! She could see Dad and Gram and Rosie!

Floxx reached behind her thin neck and unclasped the gorgeous sapphire necklace she always wore.

"Here," she said simply, and fastened it on Rory.

"Oh, Floxx, no. You keep your beautiful necklace."

"The necklace is a portal, Rory."

She couldn't believe it. This was seriously amazing. "How does it work?"

"You touch it and you think of where you want to go. You envision the place, the people, the time."

So simple. Rory started to touch it, but Floxx caught her hand. "Wait, Rory. Just listen. There's no practice required, and I don't want you vanishing. Think about what you might want to do here before you go. Your mother will need your help. Finn is here for you. Kalvara and Aric. Ask Eldurrin. Follow what he tells you. You can go anytime. But you probably should let them know you are going."

"How does it work? Is time the same there as here?"

"You move from one to the other like moving from shadow to sunlight. You will return to the person or the place you envision. And you can come back here the same way. You could return to this moment and it's likely no one would know you had ever left."

"So, I could go back to a time just before our collision and Gram and Dad would never have missed me?"

"That's right. Just be careful not to do anything in either world that would affect the other."

Oh my. She needed to think about this.

The Queen smiled as she signed the agreement. Rory was so proud of her. Mother had risen to her royal responsibility and was ruling well and would remain in charge until she came of age in about a year when she turned 18. In the three months since they'd buried the King, Mother had proven herself a very capable diplomat, forging trade agreements with both the dwarves and the rulers of Syrea, strengthening peaceful relations.

Zirena and Prince Tozar had been a little reluctant to sign agreements with them, still harboring anger over Jakin's loss of the throne and by extension, any power they might have gained with his rulership. However, they saw great advantage in keeping their kingdom as an ally, especially for trade purposes. The citizens of Byerman were their largest group of customers, loving the gems from Orizin and having the wherewithal to purchase them.

With the giant's death and the dragon's terrible wound, they had rest from threatening enemies and could focus on restoring order in the castle and peace in the country. Jakin had disappeared; no one knew where, and Rory, for one, didn't care. Ezat and Azatan had safely arrived with Werner and Ardith at their farm. Floxx had returned to them and was providing wisdom and guidance on a daily basis.

Finn and Kalvara had stayed to ensure the transition to power was as smooth as possible, providing help and support as needed, which lately, hadn't been very often. They'd spent more and more time together, and sometimes Rory would overhear them laughing about some story from long ago. Two strains of elven blood; two heritages; but common ancestors from ancient days. She'd watched them move from enmity to tolerance, from coolness to friendship. She hoped it stopped there but sensed they could be perfect for each other. It became clearer each day that she and Finn had different destinies. She cared for him deeply, loved him still and perhaps always would. She'd entertained dreams of spending her life with him, helping him fulfill the prophecy, restoring the crown, then taking his place as the Eldur King. But as the months went on, it was clear her place was in Byerman, ruling with Mother, listening to counsel as they made hard decisions. She was to be Queen.

They had a dusting of snow in late fall and Rory yearned for Alaska. For Dad and Gram. The snowfall stirred up feelings in Finn, as well. She saw him returning from the woods where he and Kalvara often went together, though he was alone that morning. She walked out to see him.

"Hey," she said smiling.

"Rory." He wore a small, sad smile. "I was hoping to see you. I'm glad you could get out of the castle for a while."

"Yeah. Feels good to get away even for a short time."

"You've done well. Both you and your mother. You will rule well. I'm proud of you." But his eyes held no joy. She knew what was coming and dreaded it.

"Rory," he said, again, touching her cheek. "You are the dearest of friends and I care for you deeply."

She tried to keep the tears from coming, but they came anyway.

"Kalvara and Aric and I are leaving soon. I'd thought about just going and avoiding this difficult good-bye, but I felt you deserved an explanation."

She shut her eyes against the inevitable. He touched her eyelids and she opened them. She had to face this. She wanted to be angry. To accuse him of not caring, of leaving her in a mess, but she knew it wasn't true. He cared, and he'd stayed by her side many months to prove it.

"You have a wonderful calling and a great duty to fulfill as Queen of Byerman."

"Yes."

"And I have a wonderful calling and a great duty to fulfill the prophecy. You remember the Tennins and the night at the Pool?"

"I will never forget it."

"It's time for me to go. To search for the jewels and the pieces of the crown, and once I've gathered them, to find someone—only Eldurrin knows who—to reconstruct it in the ancient ways."

"You will do it, Finn. I know you will."

He smiled and touched her lips with his fingers, then leaned in and kissed her lightly before he turned and disappeared into the woods.

Her heart broke. She stared for a long time at the empty path, the trace of snow on the tree branches, willing him to return, not believing he'd left for good. What about his stuff? His clothes? Weapons? She found out later he'd already taken them; they'd been in the woods, waiting with Kalvara and Aric. Elves. They traveled light. He had, it seemed, come back just to say good-bye to her.

In the days that followed, she grieved and sought guidance from Eldurrin. She wanted to go home to

Alaska, to see Gram and Dad. She could envision herself in the airplane on her way to Fairbanks. She could remember the moment when Cue had seen the sheep on the mountain. She thought about Gram's grocery list, which was long lost, but she remembered most of the things on it. She could travel back to that moment, a few minutes before the Firebird had collided with her, then fly to Fairbanks, get the groceries and fly home as if nothing unusual had ever happened. They'd never know she'd been missing, never have to grieve over her, thinking she was dead. She wouldn't break their hearts. Mother was ruling well. Rory was sure she could get along just fine without her. Besides, she could return to this moment and it'd be like she'd never been gone.

"Rory, no, please don't make such a sudden decision." Mother sobbed, gripping both of her shoulders, her tear-streaked face inches away. "What if something goes wrong? What if you can't get back?"

Rory had laid out her thoughts as logically as she could. Father was gone. Finn and Kalvara were gone. Peace ruled. Mother could handle the kingdom with no problem, especially if Floxx would stay awhile. She hadn't counted on her mother's reaction and it caught her off guard. Was she being rash? Had she hurt her terribly? She looked at Floxx, desperate for help.

"Rory, I understand what you are saying. But your mother has a point. It is very sudden."

"But I have been thinking about it for weeks; I've just not said anything."

"Perhaps we could find a middle ground. Give her time to adjust."

"How?"

"Can you stay one more week, dear?" Mother pleaded. "A week. To cherish the time together. To be sure you have a way to come back?"

Floxx agreed. "You can go back to that Fairbanks flight and another week won't make any difference at all to your Dad and your Gram. They'll never know."

"Okay." She was kind of disappointed with the delay but could see their point. She hugged her mother. "I'm so sorry I upset you. I love you so much and would never want you to think I don't. So, yes, another week together is a good idea."

It went fast, that week, and she was glad they had it. She and her mother talked every day, reminiscing and sharing stories of her father. Mother gave her the book, full of father's poems and love letters to her. She gave her an infant gown, too, and the scrap of her lavender baby blanket, and insisted she take Father's pearl and sapphire clasp.

"That way, they'll believe you," Mother said. "You've got treasures to prove your story."

Floxx gave Rory the bellasol. "For those dark winter days in Alaska!" She smiled. "Think of me whenever you touch it and it lights up the night."

They grilled Floxx on other possible ways of traversing between the two worlds. The star sapphire was one way, a Firebird feather, another, and holding on to Floxx, herself, a third. So, even if the worst happened, and the necklace was somehow lost, Floxx could come get her just like she'd done before.

One week later with her backpack full, Rory hugged her mother for the last time.

"You be safe, dear," Raewyn said, crying openly.

"I will," Rory promised.

Floxx hugged her. "Neither Eldurrin nor I will ever leave you, you know. This world or that."

If Rory doubted anything, it wasn't their love.

"I will talk with you there; listen for me."

"Always," Rory promised.

Floxx took Rory's hand and wrapped it around the star sapphire, then stepped back. "The airplane, Rory. It's trimmed and flying at 110 knots. Stay away from the collision area and head for Fairbanks."

Rory hadn't even gotten a good-bye out of her mouth when she heard the engine purring. Next second, she was banking away from the point of impact. She was back! Home! The trees were bare, and the snow-capped mountains rimmed the horizon. Alaska! But then she realized Cue wasn't in his seat. She remembered Floxx's warning not to do anything in either world that might affect the other. Death was final in both worlds. But, wait till she told Gram and Dad how he'd died.

Rory dialed their family frequency hoping she wasn't too far away from home for Dad to hear. She made their standard radio call. "Cessna 745AK to company. Do you pick me up?"

Dad's voice came booming. "Rory! You are loud and clear! How's the flight going? Anything wrong?"

She could hear his concern. "No problems, Dad. I just wanted to hear your voice. I'll call you when I get to Fairbanks, okay, and I'll be back well before the weather moves in. Promise."

"Roger that, Rory. I'll stay close to this radio until you're safely home."

About the Author

Kathleen King and her husband, Dwayne, are
missionaries with Kingdom Air Corps, a non-profit
organization in Alaska that trains pilots to operate in
the remotest areas of the world.
She was a technical writer for the Aircraft Owners
and Pilots Association (AOPA) for 30 years. She was
an adjunct professor teaching writing classes at
Shippensburg University for 10 years.
She holds a Master of Fine Arts in Creative Writing
and a Master of Business Administration.

This is the first of three young adult, fantasy fiction
books in the Firebird series.
Please consider leaving a review of this book at
Amazon.com.

Read more about the author and her upcoming books
by visiting her website, www.kathleen-king.com.

Made in the
USA
Columbia, SC